HUNTRESS

More Anthologies from
ST. MARTIN'S PAPERBACKS

FAERIES GONE WILD
MaryJanice Davidson
Lois Greiman
Michele Hauf
Leandra Logan

DEAD AFTER DARK
Sherrilyn Kenyon
J.R. Ward
Susan Squires
Dianna Love

NO REST FOR THE WITCHES
MaryJanice Davidson
Cheyenne McCray
Christine Warren
Lori Handeland

LOVE AT FIRST BITE
Sherrilyn Kenyon
L.A. Banks
Susan Squires
Ronda Thompson

HUNTRESS

Christine Warren

Marjorie M. Liu

Caitlin Kittredge

Jenna Maclaine

St. Martin's Paperbacks

This is a work of fiction. All of the characters, organizations, and events portrayed in this novel are either products of the author's imagination or are used fictitiously.

HUNTRESS

"Devil's Bargain" copyright © 2009 by Christine Warren.
"The Robber Bride" copyright © 2009 by Marjorie M. Liu.
"Down in the Ground Where the Dead Men Go" copyright © 2009 by Caitlin Kittredge.
"Sin Slayer" copyright © 2009 by Jenna Maclaine.

For information address St. Martin's Press, 175 Fifth Avenue, New York, NY 10010.

ISBN: 0-312-94382-2
EAN: 978-0-312-94382-0

Printed in the United States of America

St. Martin's Paperbacks edition / July 2009

St. Martin's Paperbacks are published by St. Martin's Press, 175 Fifth Avenue, New York, NY 10010.

10 9 8 7 6 5 4 3 2 1

CONTENTS

DEVIL'S BARGAIN

Christine Warren

For Jojo. Because she threatens me.

ONE

Sitting at the right foot of the devil could give a girl a complex about her pedicure. At least, that's what Lilli Corbin had to assume when she walked into the designated meeting place and surveyed the tableau laid out before her. The small strip-mall nail salon had five nail stations ranged along the right wall and an equal number of pedicure chairs opposite. While three of the pedicure chairs were currently occupied, only two of the customers in them appeared to be availing themselves of the services of the frighteningly efficient nail technicians. The third lounged in the high, faux leather chair as if it were a carved and gilded throne.

Rounding the front desk, Lilli leaned back against the black laminate surface and crossed her arms over her chest. "Busy night, Sam?"

Neither of the female patrons glanced up from their toes or the workers bent over them, but the man between them moved his mouth in a smile as dark as envy.

"Lillith," Sam purred. "I'm so glad you could make it. I was afraid your schedule might place too heavy a burden upon you."

His voice was as smooth as velvet, sweet as honey, warm as affection. And as deceptive as his fair, angelic features.

Lilli gritted her teeth and ignored the instinctive tug in the pit of her stomach. She couldn't stop herself from responding to him—no living woman, and very few men, could—but she could use her knowledge of him to nip that response in the bud. When she got home, she could try to shower off the memory of it.

"I suppose I could say something about how I've always got time for old friends," she said, "but you're not my friend, and we both know why I made it a point to rearrange my schedule for this."

His smile never wavered. "You would consider it a matter of honor, of course."

"That, and after this one, I'm done. I'll be off the hook for good. That's way too good to pass up."

"You're certain you wouldn't like to sign a longer-term contract?"

Lilli leveled a sardonic stare at the devil. "Thanks, but I'm afraid I'm using my soul at the moment."

"Hmm, pity."

She left the bait alone. She'd already had almost twenty-four hours to revel in the idea of finally fulfilling her bargain with Samael and being free of his influence; there was no way in Hell she would risk that freedom now. Not when she could already taste it.

Seven long years ago, Lilli had made a deal with the devil: in return for his permission to enter his portion of the underworld and bring out a fugitive she'd been hired to apprehend, she agreed to do him three unspecified favors in the future. He could not ask her to kill anyone, nor to maim, torture, or deliberately injure or scar anyone. He couldn't ask for a task beyond her abilities, and he couldn't bind her soul in any way, shape, or form. He also could not demand or require any sexual favors from her, nor ask her to procure them on his behalf. Beyond that, Lilli agreed to grant Samael her assistance three times between the date the bargain was struck and the date of her physical death, without the option of refusal.

She'd regretted it immediately, of course, but at the time she'd had very little choice. The fugitive she'd been after had been a particularly nasty one, but then, when weren't they? When you specialized in the identification, tracking, and apprehension of visitants (as the polite world liked to call the kind of preternatural things she dealt with, in spite of their inconveniently native origins), you learned that "nasty" could be a disturbingly relative term.

In the end, Lilli had caught up to the visitant—a goblin that time, one who had decided to branch out from the usual mischief-making to more fatal activities—and turned him over to the proper authorities. Without Samael's help, the goblin's killing spree would have been ten times worse, and Lilli would have had ten times the number of souls on her conscience, so she supposed the bargain she'd struck had been worth it. It had saved lives, and so far it had cost only one week's duty as a personal bodyguard during a council of devils, and a thirty-six-hour imp hunt that had left her with nothing worse than a small scar on her left ankle and a four-day headache.

Judging by the glint in Samael's eyes today, "so far" were likely going to be the key words in that particular thought.

Lilli knew better than to look directly into those eyes, though. She focused on a spot just between the devil's toffee-colored eyebrows and decided it was in her best interest to move this little interview along.

"I'm a busy girl, Sam," she said, her tone even and business-like. "Why don't you just cut to the chase and let me know what you need from me this time?"

"Now don't be hasty, my dear." Samael accepted the hand towel a technician handed him with absent grace. "You'll make me think you're overeager to end our association."

"That's because I am."

"I'm hurt." He pressed carefully buffed fingertips to his chest. "But hardly surprised. You always were a stubborn little thing, so determined to draw a line in the sand between you and me."

Lilli reflected that she'd actually have preferred a line in the reinforced concrete, but she kept the thought to herself. If he really was going to request his third favor tonight, she didn't want to jeopardize her chances at freedom.

"Personally," the devil continued, "I've always thought we had more than a few things in common. Our determination, our focus . . . the sense of pride each of us takes in our work." His sharp obsidian eyes sliced toward her, hooked deep into her face. "Our ancestry."

Lilli flinched beneath her mask of indifference. She knew better than to let Samael see a reaction. Exploiting weaknesses was his bread and butter, and she had no desire to satisfy his hunger.

It shouldn't surprise her that the devil would bring up her heritage, or even really that he'd been able to dig up the truth she normally kept hidden. Few people outside of the underworld felt comfortable face-to-face with the daughter of a devil, even if her mother had been a completely average human. Being half Hell-blooded was enough to make most distrust her on principle, and she couldn't blame them. If she were human, she'd probably distrust someone like her, too. It would be hard not to, considering her line of work. Bounty hunters routinely dealt with the dregs of humanity, but since Lilli specialized in hunting visitants, she saw the dregs of that population as well. She wouldn't trust a devil farther than she could throw him, and a devil's spawn only an inch farther than that.

On bad days, she even wondered if she could trust herself.

"It's not like we're cousins, Sam," she said, forcing her dark thoughts back into the mental closet they'd escaped from. "We're in no danger of meeting up at the next family reunion." She had no desire to think about the rest of his comments, or to contemplate things they might have in common. If she did, she'd end up collecting a bounty on her own head. "You might have guessed as much if you'd thought about the fact that the only way you can get me in the same room with you is to call in one of the favors I owe you."

The devil's eyes narrowed. "You sought me out first, Lillith Corbin. Remember that. I would have remained in blissful ignorance of your existence if you hadn't sought me out."

Lillith saw a spark of genuine anger in his eyes and fought the urge to shift her weight to the balls of her feet. Fight or flight. Either way his mood shifted, she wanted to be ready; but in the meantime, maybe focusing him back on the business at hand would diffuse the situation long enough for her to walk out with her intestines *and* her dignity intact.

That was her definition of a win.

"And here I am, seeking you out again," she said, "only this time I heard that you wanted to see me. Any truth to the rumors?"

Samael's fingers tapped out a wave on the arm of his chair. His black eyes studied her from beneath narrowed lids. Lilli could feel the air pressure increase as he weighed whether or not to let her disrespectful demeanor go for now. She knew perfectly well she should have curbed her tongue, but that was a skill she'd never managed to master. The only excuse she could muster was that her mouth was just as sharp around those she did respect as those she didn't. It wasn't like she was playing favorites.

Maybe she'd have that engraved on her memorial.

"A possession of mine has gone missing," he answered abruptly. "You will determine where it is and retrieve it for me."

That didn't sound so bad, which immediately made Lilli suspicious.

"What kind of possession? I collect bounty on bodies, not souls, remember."

"Yes, you are quite the puritan, aren't you?" He swiveled in his chair and snapped his fingers. Immediately, the basin at the foot filled with water that begin to froth and churn even though the motor for the built-in jets remained silent. Samael slid his feet in and leaned back. "You needn't worry, however. This is merely a book—a folio, actually. Early medieval, I believe. Vellum, illuminated, and bound in leather. It looks something like this."

A wave of his hand and Lilli found herself blinking at an image of a large volume hovering in the air near her head. It looked old, the leather scuffed and cracked in places, worn smooth and slick in others. The image revolved slowly, showing her the thick spine, the uneven, hand-cut edges of the thick, vellum sheets. When the cover turned back, she could see the ancient, golden color of the animal skin pages, the still vivid red and blue inks of the illustrations, the faded black of the careful, stylized script. She could just imagine the robe-clad scribe, bent over the pages, carefully copying line after line of text in the light of the unfiltered sun and smoky tallow candles. She could almost smell the smoke.

Shaking her head, she looked away from Samael's spell and lifted an eyebrow. "What kind of book is it?"

The devil's brow mirrored hers. "Does that matter? It's not ensorcelled to imprison a human soul, if that's what your suspicious nature wants to know."

It was.

"What about other kinds of souls?"

Samael made an impatient sound. "It's not ensorcelled at all. Not cursed, not bespelled, not warded. For all I know, it's not even charmed. It's just a book."

"Then why do you care about getting it back?"

His black eyes fixed on her, and Lilli had to struggle not to meet that gaze. She focused hard on an angelic golden curl of hair that tumbled over his temple and curled an inch above his cheekbone. Her life would have been easier if she could have looked into his eyes and read the truth of his statements for herself, but even if she had possessed that kind of gift (which wasn't one generally passed on to offspring by generals in the armies of Hell), Lilli knew better than to attempt to use it on Samael. She already knew what she would see if she looked into his eyes—seduction, pain, pleasure, death. Lucifer, his master. The great abyss of evil of which Samael was only a small, pretty part.

She swallowed hard, counted the strands that made up the golden curl, and waited.

"It was mine," he said, anger and avarice tangling in the rough silk of his voice. "I keep what is mine, and I do not allow it to leave me. No one steals from me."

Chains, hot and black and heavy, rattled in the back of Lilli's mind. She pushed the sound away and closed her nostrils to the smell of brimstone. Suddenly, only one more question mattered to her, so she asked it without artifice.

"And if I get it back for you, our bargain will be fulfilled?"

"Once the book is in my hands, you'll never have to see me again, dear Lillith." A smile slithered across his face. "Unless, of course, you discover you miss me."

Lilli caught the snort before it escaped. Fat chance. She'd miss a cancerous tumor before she'd miss this dysfunctional little relationship of theirs. The glimpse of freedom he dangled before her tempted her like nothing she'd ever seen, and he promised all she'd have to do was return his book to him.

Just a book.

It was too easy, a voice inside her whispered. Much too easy, and too uncomplicated. Why would he be willing to use his last favor on so trivial a task? And for something as mundane as a book? No matter how old or rare, could there possibly be any book valuable enough to matter to Samael this much? But did she really care? After all, if she did this, her bargain would be fulfilled. She'd be free of the devil and the weighty stain their association left on her conscience. Could she afford to overlook that opportunity?

Was she overthinking this?

"Fine," she said, pushing aside the doubts and straightening away from the counter. "I'll get your book back. And when it's done, I'll expect to see our contract dissolved. Burning it works for me."

His smile taunted her. "You know how I feel about fire, sweetheart. It always turns me on."

Lilli grimaced against the wave of nausea that rolled in her stomach and turned toward the exit. "I'll contact you tomorrow for the details on when and where the book was last seen and who else might be interested in it. You'll have it as soon as I can get my hands on it."

"Excellent." His voice followed her as she pushed open the door and gulped the fresh, un-devil-tainted air. "You have three days. Always a pleasure doing business with you, Lillith."

He tossed something at her, and she caught it reflexively even before his words managed to sink in.

Lilli stopped dead, her feet seeming to sink into the pavement as if it had turned to quicksand. She shrieked out the words before her brain could catch up with her mouth. *"Three days?!"*

Eyes wide, she spun around and pushed hard at the nail salon's etched glass door, determined to let Samael know what she thought of that ridiculous deadline. The only problem was that the door refused to budge. Probably because it no longer existed.

In the place of the nail salon's entrance, Lilli found her-

self facing a solid brick wall with a rather crude and physically implausible suggestion scrawled across it in bright
blue spray paint. The door, the salon, and the devil were
nowhere to be seen. She cursed a blue streak.

In her hand, the thing he'd thrown at her seemed to throb
mockingly.

Lilli looked down. She'd caught it when the devil had
thrown it, more out of reflex than intent. God knew she
didn't like to take gifts from Hell-spawn like that, but when
she studied the small pewter pendant suspended from a thin,
silver chain, she knew this was most definitely *not* a gift. It
was a hangman's noose.

Formed in exquisite detail was a miniature hourglass.
The pewter casing had been etched to look like scales on
every surface, but the clear glass inside was pristine and perfect, showcasing every single grain of crimson sand that fell
from one chamber to the other.

A line from her favorite movie musical popped into her
mind, and Lilli guessed her expression probably mirrored
the one she'd seen a dozen times on Marlon Brando's as she
slipped the chain around her neck and let the clock start
running.

"Daddy," she quoted on a groan, "I just got cider in my
ear."

TWO

Aaron Bullard's hands shook as he turned from the photo in the text on his left, removed his glasses, and polished the lenses on the tail of his rumpled shirt. They continued to shake as he shoved his already mussed brown hair away from his forehead and replaced the rectangular frames before his wide, bewildered, muddy-green eyes. They didn't even stop when he stared down at the delicate ancient volume spread out on the desk before him.

Could it possibly be true?

For a minute he wondered frantically if he'd just been working too long, as usual, poring over lists and catalogs and books for an hour or four too many. He couldn't possibly have just made the discovery of his obscure and geeky career in the basement of his Uncle Alistair's dilapidated old house.

But he had.

His secret hope and worst nightmare had just been simultaneously confirmed—the leather-bound tome he'd found secreted behind a collection of inconsequential eighteenth-century herbals on the bottom shelf of his late uncle's occult library was indeed the world's only surviving copy of Valterum's *Praedicti Arcanum*.

Arcane Prophecies. The legendary playbook for the end of the world. The script that told how the devils of the underworld would start a war that would bring humanity to its knees and enslave the mortal population into eternal torment.

Wow, didn't that sound like fun.

Blowing out a breath, Aaron rubbed his hand over his face, scrunched his eyes closed, and mumbled another curse, but when he looked back at the table, nothing had changed. He really had found the *Prophecies*, and Uncle Alistair had had it all along.

Christ.

Aaron tried to remember if his uncle had ever mentioned anything. He didn't think so. After all, Aaron had been obsessed with the text for almost fifteen years; surely he'd remember if Alistair had ever said anything about owning it. He'd have leapt on the chance to examine it like a terrier on a barn rat. Provided, of course, that he'd believed the story.

Alistair Gerrald Eratosthenes Carruthers had been a remarkable storyteller. As a child, Aaron had begged his mother's eccentric older brother to tell him stories every time the man had come to visit. He'd thrilled to the tales of Alistair's occult experiments, his magical discoveries, and his adventures as a demonologist and defender of mankind. Of course, at the time, Aaron had been about seven, tops. By the time he hit the ripe old age of ten, his parents had taken him aside and explained to him in words a child could understand that his beloved Uncle Alistair was a total crackpot.

Oh, the man had been a renowned occultist, a gifted sorcerer, and a devoted researcher in the field of demonology, but he'd also possessed a wide streak of dramatics. He'd often become so caught up in his own stories that he forgot which parts of them had actually—*technically*—happened. An embellishment here or there was completely understandable, but in the most exciting of Alistair's stories, the embellishments tended to obscure the facts of the matter. In fact, in the best tales, there was very little fact at all. Once Aaron understood all this, he had treated those stories very differently. He had still asked Alistair to tell them when they were stuck inside because of rain or snow or childhood groundings, but at some point, he had stopped really listening to much of what came out of his uncle's mouth. Could that be how he'd missed something like this?

Well, he had no intention of missing anything now. Aaron leaned forward, reached for the corner of a fragile, vellum page, and cursed under his breath. In his excitement, he'd nearly forgotten all the years of his training and touched the manuscript with his bare hands. Some curator of rare books and manuscripts he was acting like. A wave of his hand and a tweak of his will and white cotton gloves appeared on his fingers.

He'd heard of the *Prophecies,* of course; he couldn't think of a single witch, wizard, sorcerer, demonologist, or occult historian who hadn't. Written by a ninth-century magician living somewhere in what was now Germany, the codex was reported to contain a record of prophecies that had been spoken ages before by a greatly respected oracle of the ancient world. Most experts had long assumed it had been lost or destroyed centuries ago, though rumors of it popping up in esoteric collections or middle eastern caves did crop up occasionally, only to be almost immediately disproved. Aaron himself had written an undergraduate thesis on this very book during his days in the Yale history department. Never, not in his wildest dreams, had he ever expected to see it, to touch it. To own it.

The knowledge hit him like a shot of single malt, heating his belly with excitement that spread faster than the glow of a good scotch. Uncle Alistair had left Aaron not only his house and his modest life savings, but also his extensive and eclectic collection of occult items. From the skull of Ezekiel of Bramley (a well-known magician, anatomist, and unfortunately poor alchemist who had been killed when the iron demon he'd summoned with the intention of transmuting it into gold had burst into flame and ignited the cottage around them), to the brass dog bowl owned by Pope Eugene III and supposedly blessed by St. Bernard himself, Aaron had inherited it all. Including the library.

Including the *Prophecies*.

God, he couldn't wait to read them.

He swallowed a sudden mouthful of saliva and turned to the first page of the codex to stare in wonder at the sight before him. The first quarter of the page was filled by an intricate drawing of a serpent, huge and thick and crowned on each of three massive heads by a pair of wickedly sharp horns and sets of razor sharp teeth. The detail in the illustration almost made him see the gleam of venom on each curved fang and smell the taint of blood and death in each gaping mouth. The serpent's red-and-black body coiled around an enormous capital letter *C*, twining in and out of the open curve. Dark smudges of black appeared to spread from its body to stain the vivid blue of the letter. In the background, lush greenery sprang up from bloody soil, but rather than looking alive and fertile, the vegetation managed to embrace and oppress the viewer as if drawing him into the page and suffocating him in moist, humid decomposition.

As his eyes moved across the page, they caught the first few Latin words, and he could almost hear them echoing in his mind in a deep, rumbling, oily voice. The imagined sound of it made him feel somehow compelled and tainted all at once. It hissed in his ear, until he could feel something inside him shrink back in horror . . .

Caveo rex malefic—

Blinking, Aaron drew back from the page and shook his

head to clear it. Sheesh. He really had been working too hard. The words were just words, the picture just color and lines on tightly stretched and conditioned sheepskin. If he could read sinister intent into any of that, he clearly needed a break—a few hours of sleep, maybe a shower, and a cup or seven of coffee.

He pushed back from the desk, a huge, tall affair he imagined his uncle had gotten from either a British headmaster's office or the Jolly Green Giant. It offered more space than any one person could possibly need, but the lack of drawers on both sides indicated that it wasn't meant to seat two. Which was a good thing, Aaron decided, since currently every square inch of it was piled with books and papers and mostly empty mugs of the coffee he'd just decided he needed.

"Good idea," he muttered to himself and headed up the stairs into the kitchen of the old Queen Anne–style mansion. He would put on a new pot of coffee, stretch his legs for a minute, let his eyes focus on something other than dense reference texts and oddly compelling illuminations. Maybe he'd even check the answering machine or bring the newspaper in from the front porch, just to make sure the rest of the world was still out there. When he was working, he tended to lose track.

Reaching the top of the stairs, he turned the lights on with a flick of his will, but lit the ancient gas stove and assembled the makings for coffee by hand. There was no rhyme or reason to his use of magic for mundane tasks. He used it when he remembered, or maybe more when he *didn't* remember, but he didn't neglect to use it for any particular reason. He filled the kettle with water and the French press with coffee grounds manually because he liked the ritual of it, but if he'd been in a hurry, he might just as easily have conjured a full mug of brewed coffee with magic. Neither method broke or obeyed any rules; he'd always figured the

Elders who made and administered the Laws of Magic had bigger things to worry about than whether or not people with power chose to tie their shoelaces by hand or by wand.

Aaron raised his hands high over his head and linked his fingers together, gloves disappearing as he pressed his palms toward the ceiling. While he waited for the water to boil, he stretched cramped and tired muscles until he felt his vertebrae realign themselves with a series of satisfying cracking sounds.

God, that felt good. He let his arms swing back to his sides and reached for the kettle just as the spout began to whistle. The scent that rose from the mingling of water and coffee nearly made him weep with gratitude. Just the fumes infused him with a renewed burst of energy. In a few swallows, he figured he'd be ready to head back downstairs and translate some pages. As he recalled, the last time the *Prophecies* had been compared to actual events for accuracy had been just after the martyrdom of Joan of Arc. It would be fascinating to see if anything since 1431 had happened the way the oracle had predicted—

Thump.

Aaron froze, mug just inches from his lips. What the hell had made that noise? He had heard a noise, hadn't he?

Scrape.

That had definitely been a noise. And it had come from the basement.

Shit.

Probably the cat, he told himself. The ancient and portly tabby, who had lived with Uncle Alistair for as long as Aaron could remember, didn't get around with much grace anymore. Last night while Aaron had been relaxing in the living room and watching a movie, it had attempted the jump from the coffee table to the sofa, and landed on his shoe with an indignant yowl. He hadn't noticed it downstairs when he'd been working earlier, but it did tend to trail around wherever he was, as if it missed human company. Most likely it had tried to climb the stairs and tripped over its own belly.

Setting the coffee aside, Aaron began to ease back toward the basement door. The noise had almost certainly been the cat, but it never hurt to make sure.

He really hoped it wouldn't hurt.

A burglar would have to be insane to break into this house, he told himself. The only thing that kept it from looking like it had been condemned back in the fifties were the lights he turned on to keep from tripping over the threadbare rugs as he walked from room to room. The lot around it was overgrown; the house's paint was peeling, its shutters falling, its porch steps rotting. And the battered pickup truck outside that he'd used to haul away the armoire Alistair had left to his sister shouldn't have raised any hopes. Anyone who thought there was something worth stealing in this dump would have been sadly mistaken.

It had to be the cat.

Aaron eased down the stairs, sticking close to the edges where the joists still held strong and were less likely to creak. At first, the walls at the top of the stairs blocked his view of the space below, and he could see little but the pool of golden light cast by the lamp above the desk that he'd left burning when he went upstairs. Then, as he reached the seventh step, the room opened up to his right and he could see what had made the noise.

He blinked, froze, blinked again, and felt the breath in his lungs seize up like setting cement. In front of the floor-to-ceiling bookcase that lined the back wall of the cellar stood a woman, dressed all in black, with long hair so thick and black he took it at first for some sort of hood worn as part of a disguise. More than the hair told him she was a woman. The position she was in helped, especially where her otherwise loose trousers stretched taut and cozy over a round, heart-shaped ass that should never have been allowed on a burglar. Her indented waist and the sleek curve of her side gave him another clue beneath the snug, long-sleeved knit top she wore. All in all, the picture she presented made him wonder if she wore that body as the chief tool, or weapon, in her arsenal, because if so, he imagined she had to be the most successful criminal since the invention of crime.

Oblivious to his presence, she scanned the shelves with silent efficiency and the focused air of someone looking for something particular. When she got to the lower shelves, she shifted into a crouch, which simultaneously stretched her trousers even tighter across that mouth-watering bottom and caused the curtain of her hair to shift and the strands to part, revealing to him the curve of her jaw and the sleek, pale shell of her ear. The delicate lines seemed suddenly almost as erotic as her ass, and Aaron realized that if he didn't draw breath again soon, he'd announce his presence to her by passing out from lack of oxygen and tumbling into a blue-tinged pile of stupid on the floor at her feet.

The air he sucked in nearly choked him when she stood and turned toward his desk, giving him his first look at her face. Not to mention the front of her body, which sported sweetly rounded breasts accentuated by a gleaming pendant that dangled between them on a thin silver chain. He figured he might have been more distracted by that body if he hadn't immediately noticed that it was decorated with pockets and straps of leather that seemed to contain a whole host of weapons even more lethal than her figure, including a gun, a compact nightstick, three small throwing daggers, and a pair of knives that appeared at least as long as his forearms.

She also had a pair of wide, thickly lashed eyes the disconcerting copper color of flame.

Even as he watched, something must have alerted her to

his presence, because she stiffened almost imperceptibly a moment before the gaze from those unsettling eyes fixed on him and went as clear and hard as amber.

"Well, shit," he thought he heard her mutter, but then it got very hard to concentrate due to the matte black and lethally sharp dagger she sent hurtling toward his chest.

THREE

Lilli cursed her luck, Samael, devil's bargains, medieval manuscripts, and interfering homeowners all at once, and all without opening her mouth. She should have known it couldn't possibly be as easy as it had sounded. Even with the hourglass she wore cheerfully marking the time, it had taken her barely more than a day and a half to determine who had Samael's missing book and where it was likely being kept, almost as if the thief hadn't even bothered to cover his tracks. Another twelve hours and she'd been able to find out enough about the guy to decide that, even with the ridiculous timeline Samael had given her, she would be able to pull off this job in her sleep. Then, if that hadn't tipped her off, her sources had told her the thief had died almost a month ago, just days after he must have taken the book to begin with. It played like some sort of cosmic coincidence.

She didn't believe in coincidence.

She also didn't believe in walking into any situation blind, which was why she'd lived to the ripe old age of twenty-eight still breathing and still in possession of all her limbs. Lilli had done her research on Alistair Carruthers. The man had been born into a very old magical family, but one whose family tree had stopped sprouting much new growth. He had only one sibling, a significantly younger sister, and his father and grandfather had both been only children. As far as Lilli had been able to tell, he had no aunts, uncles, cousins, or other relatives to speak of. He didn't even have any children, having never married and apparently having been so devoted to his work and hobbies that she hadn't even been able to find much in the way of a dating history. He'd lived alone and apparently died alone, and judging by the appearance of the house he'd died in, Lilli had assumed no one had very much cared.

She'd been expecting to find an empty house that no one would mind her breaking into, much less making off with one small book and none of the family silver (okay, a big book, but she wasn't even going to look for the electronics). She hadn't expected a tall, lean, rumpled-looking man wearing faded jeans that were worn at the seams, a Ramones t-shirt, a battered flannel button-down, and black-rimmed eyeglasses that made him look like a nerd and a face from a *GQ* cover at the same time.

She also hadn't expected him to try to sneak up on her from the main floor of the house. That was why she threw the knife at him, she guessed. It was reflex. Most of the time, the things sneaking up on her didn't have her best interests at heart, so she could be forgiven for trying to stop theirs.

The man on the stairs, though, he didn't look very forgiving. He looked intent, then startled, then angry as he raised his own hand just as her fingers released their grip on the knife. With the flat of his palm, he slapped at the air in front of him, and her knife screeched to a halt, quivering as if it had impacted on wood and buried itself to the hilt. Only it hadn't hit anything. It hovered in mid-air for a second, then dropped to the floor with a clatter. Clearly, Alistair Carruthers hadn't been the only sorcerer to live in this house. Instinctively, she reached for a second blade, and the man on the stairs threw himself toward her with a growl completely at odds with his computer geek appearance.

The impact didn't feel very geeky, either. It felt solid and heavy and knocked her ass-over-elbows onto the very hard and dusty concrete floor. Who would have guessed that all that solid muscle lurked under such worn and rumpled cloth?

Lilli didn't pause to ponder the incongruity. Instead, she let the momentum of the impact and the fall send her into a roll that should have let her reverse their positions and put the sorcerer on the bottom with her knees planted on his elbows. Somehow, it didn't happen that way.

The man reacted faster than a light switch, leaning into the roll until it became a sort of crocodilian death spin that sent them all the way across the floor until the immovable object known as the cellar wall brought them to an abrupt stop. Lilli squirmed to keep herself from being pinned between the man and the concrete. She sent an elbow toward his face, swearing when he jerked back so that the blow that should have shattered his cheekbone bounced off the edge of his jaw instead.

He countered with hands that moved faster than they had any right to. They reached for her wrists, and she took advantage of the distance his recoil from her attack had put between their torsos, twisting her upper body and planting her hands flat on the floor.

Lilli braced herself and executed a straining push-up against the weight of his body pinning her legs. She couldn't get her hips more than a couple of inches off the ground, but that was all she needed. Grunting with strain, she lowered her head and pushed her hips back into his chest, using the leverage to drag her legs free. As soon as she felt the cool air on her calves, she swung her lower body around and flipped herself to her feet, wincing when the pendant swung up and smacked her between the eyes. Her movement shoved the man off balance, and he lurched backward with a curse to land on his butt a few feet away.

Adrenaline propelled her forward. She had her misericorde drawn and the edged blade pressed to his throat before she stopped to think, but not before he spoke a hoarse, curt word. A second later her hand seemed to slip involuntarily, sending the long knife clattering to the floor.

Jerking back, Lilli balanced herself on her haunches and cast a wary glance from her adversary to the knife and back again. Her blade had been warded, so for him to disarm her would have taken some serious mojo. It also would have required that he cast his defensive spell not on her weapon, but on the hand that held it. She'd remember that trick in the future, and she'd sure as hell be buying herself a pair of warded gloves just as soon as she got out of here. In the meantime, she needed to keep from getting her ass kicked.

Quickness counted in this kind of situation, and it looked like Lilli had that advantage over her opponent. She executed a quick pirouette on one heel, sweeping the other leg out in front of her and knocking the man's legs out from under him just as he tried to scramble to his feet. He hit the concrete with a grunt. Shifting forward, Lilli planted her palms on the floor and vaulted herself back onto her feet. She intended to throw herself right back into the fray, but something stopped her.

Across the space that separated them, Lilli met the man's grim, hazel gaze, then watched it shift to his left. She followed his sightline and felt a surge of excitement when she saw what he was looking at. On top of the disordered desk across from the bottom of the stairs lay a huge leather-bound manuscript of certain antiquity. Lilli recognized it instantly from the images Samael had shown her. She'd been right; the *Praedicti* codex was in this house and almost in her grasp. She could practically taste her freedom. Between her breasts, the pendant seemed to pulse with anticipation.

Renewed determination flowed into Lilli. Jerking her attention back to the last obstacle in her path, she launched herself into an attack. Two lunging steps built her momentum so that when the man in front of her finally gained his feet, one of hers instantly whipped around and plowed straight into his stomach.

That was the idea, anyway. To her surprise, he reacted with unexpected speed, sweeping his arm down to knock her ankle up and away from its target. A quick balance adjustment allowed her to keep her feet, but it cost her a couple of steps backward. Raising her hands into a defensive posture, she danced forward until she came within arm's length of him and punched the heel of her hand up toward his nose.

Again, he moved quickly. He slid to the side and turned his head in time with her blow so that the impact softened and glanced off his cheekbone instead of sending shards of bone and cartilage up into his sinus cavities. Before Lilli could follow through with the other hand, the man in front of her stepped back and began to mutter something under his breath.

ShitshitshitSHIT!

Again with the magic. Lilli did not intend to stand around and let someone cast spells on her, no matter what job she was here to do and no matter how much his glasses made her contemplate what it would be like to try to fog over the lenses. Quickly, she looked from the magician to the manuscript and calculated a few angles in her head.

Here goes nothing, she thought as she lowered her head and took a deep breath.

Several things happened in the next moment: the sorcerer in front of her raised his right hand and aimed his open palm at Lilli's chest; Lilli bent her knees, gathered her strength, and threw herself into a flying somersault in the direction of the desk; and the open manuscript of the *Prae-dicti Arcanum* seemed to rustle its pages with a restless air of discontent.

"What the hell?" she heard the man—now behind her—roar as she landed hard where a wheeled desk chair had been sitting, sending the seat spinning and the entire chair rolling crazily into the far wall.

Not bothering to look around, Lilli made a grab for the book and gave a breathless cry of frustration when a body slammed into her back and pinned her to the surface of the short filing cabinet beside the desk. She tried to scramble forward, her fingers stretching toward the book, but a large, masculine hand attached to an arm with much greater reach shot past hers and shoved the manuscript off the other side of the desk. She cursed as she heard it thud to the ground.

Ironically, so did the man on top of her.

"I. Need. That. Book!" she grunted and shot her elbow back into her attacker's ribcage.

She heard the dull thunk of the impact and his hoarse shout of pain, but the bastard didn't move. That pissed her off. Gritting her teeth, Lilli pushed her hands into the top of the cabinet and tried to gauge her amount of wiggle room. With his hips pinning hers and his abdomen pressing down on her lower back, she didn't have much.

Still, a girl always had options. Letting him take her weight, Lilli lifted her feet off the floor, spread her legs, and hooked her feet around the backs of her opponent's knees. At the same time, she arched backward, raised her hands off the cabinet, reached back, and boxed his ears firmly.

The man behind her roared in pain, surprise jerking him backward. Unfortunately, with Lilli's feet hooked around his knees, he couldn't step back. He lost his balance and toppled onto his ass, curses ripe enough to peel paint coloring the air around him. Lilli tried to untangle her legs from his before he hit the ground, but gravity moved faster than she did. She landed on top of him and rolled off immediately.

Tucking her knees under her body, she attempted to hurry to her feet, her hands reaching automatically for her second misericorde when the magician's fingers shot out and shackled her left wrist, pinning it to the floor. His other hand pressed against the center of her chest while the tip of her sharp, narrow blade pressed hard against his, directly above his heart.

Stalemate.

"You might be able to stick that knife in my heart before I can stop you," he panted, his breathing as hard and rough as hers, "but I'm not sure you want to bet on it."

Lilli hesitated. Was speed really the question here? She had no desire to kill this man for the sake of a damned book, even less when she thought about who had sent her after the book in the first place. She had taken this job as a way to free herself from Samael once and for all; if she killed for him, he'd own a piece of her for eternity.

Still, that didn't mean she couldn't bluff.

"I like to gamble," she said, deliberately stripping her voice of all emotion, making it hard and cold and deadly. "People tell me I have the devil's own luck."

"Go for it then. If you think you can beat me to the punch, why don't you demonstrate?"

Lilli frowned. "You want me to kill you?"

"I already said I'm not sure you can."

His voice sounded taunting, but his eyes were deep and serious. There was something in them that tugged at her. Lilli had been a hunter for years; she'd been in situations once or twice where she'd had to kill something, so she'd seen what eyes looked like when the light went out of them. She didn't want to see his eyes that way.

"What are you waiting for?" he demanded. "If you think you're that fast, prove it. Try to kill me."

Cursing, she turned aside her blade so that the flat of it

pressed against the man's faded black t-shirt. From behind the desk nearby, she almost thought she heard a rumble of discontent.

"You first," she snapped, jerking her wrist free of his surprised grip.

Slowly, cautiously, the man took his hand away from his threatening position over her heart and pushed himself into a sitting position. "How about you answer a few questions for me before I make up my mind?"

"Name, rank, and serial number?"

He shook his head. "Maybe later. But first, why don't you tell me what you want with the *Praedicti Arcanum*?"

FOUR

Aaron watched the woman's face as he pushed to his feet and took careful note of the emotions expressed there.

"Personally?" she asked. "Not a damned thing."

She didn't appear to be lying, but that didn't make sense. "I saw you make a grab for it, and I assume that's why you're here. Are you a professional thief?"

"At the moment, what I am is damned sore." The woman rose—her five feet and six inches looking much more impressively feminine when they weren't concentrating on breaking his bones—and slapped her hands against her flanks, sending a cloud of dust flying from the seat of her pants. "You might not look like a linebacker, but you pack a hell of a punch when you've got gravity on your side."

Aaron fought back a surge of pride at that. He'd never been a terribly physical guy, and he'd been afraid that he was the only one who felt like he'd just failed to outrun the bulls in Pamplona.

"Don't try to change the subject," he said. "Are you some kind of professional burglar, or is breaking and entering a hobby of yours?"

She appeared to consider that for a minute before she answered. "No, more of an occupational hazard."

"In what occupation?" he demanded, attempting to mask his confusion with impatience. "What exactly is it that you do?"

"I'm an authorized Appearance Enforcement Agent."

"A what?"

She sighed as if she'd expected the question and yet had been hoping not to hear it. "I'm a bounty hunter."

"A bounty hunter?" he repeated incredulously. When in God's name had he entered a surreal parallel universe? "I'm obviously missing something. How about we start again? I'm Aaron Bullard, and this is my uncle's house. Who the hell are you and why did you break in and try to steal the *Praedicti Arcanum*?"

"Lilli Corbin." She gestured to the knife she'd dropped in their earlier struggle and raised an eyebrow. "Do you mind if I pick that up?"

"That depends on what you're planning to do with it."

"Just put it away. I promise. The blade is warded, and I'd hate to lose it."

Aaron couldn't say he felt completely reassured, but he nodded his permission and only twitched a little when she picked up the misericorde. Sliding it into the sheath along her leg, she even went so far as to resnap the hilt guard. How much more could a guy ask?

"Now what about question number two?" he prompted when she seemed content to keep quiet.

Lilli frowned. "What?"

"You never answered my second question," he said, folding his arms over his chest and fixing her with his fiercest stare. "Why did you break in and try to steal the *Praedicti Arcanum*?"

Damn, he had a good memory.

Lilli took a good look at the man in front of her and weighed her options. In her experience, people often reacted negatively to hearing you were working for a Prince of Hell, and she really had no desire to tussle with this guy again. He might look like a bit of a wimp, but he was surprisingly wiry. And intriguingly hard. She'd hate to tell him the truth and then have to knock him upside the head and steal the book while he was unconscious. Not to mention that, given the demonstrations he'd offered earlier, she thought she'd do well not to underestimate his magical abilities. A power blast to the head would not improve her mood for the remainder of the evening.

On the other hand, she was disinclined to lie. Telling the truth made her life easier, so Lilli always tried to stick to it where possible. It kept her from forgetting which lie she'd told earlier, and given the sort of company she tended to keep when she was on a job, a secret part of her had always assumed she had less wiggle room than the next guy when it came to keeping a pure soul. She also just flat-out revolted at the idea of lying for Samael, which was what this would feel like since he'd been the one who sent her here in the first place.

Maybe, this time, omission was the better part of valor.

Actually, the last thing she wanted was for there to *be* a next time. Her new mantra was "Get it over with!" She might even work it into a tattoo, one that featured an hourglass that seemed to run faster the closer she got to her goal.

Time to lay the tarot cards on the table.

"I was hired to retrieve the book by a client who claims that it was stolen from him."

Aaron barked out a laugh. "You're trying to tell me that you think Uncle Alistair was a thief? Lady, I don't know who your 'client' is, but you need to go back and explain to him that my uncle wasn't the type to cheat on his taxes, let alone steal from someone. You've come to the wrong place."

Lilli watched his face as he spoke. He clearly believed what he said. In fact, his expression so clearly telegraphed his thoughts, she had a fleeting hope that he never acquired a taste for gambling. He'd suck at poker.

"Actually, I don't think I have," she said steadily. "I'm not a take-his-word-for-it kind of girl. I did a little research before I came out here, and from what I hear, Alistair Carruthers was asking some pretty detailed questions in the last couple of weeks before he died. The kind that wouldn't just tell him what the manuscript was and where to find it, but the kind that could help him decide what to do with it if he happened to have it in his possession."

Aaron shrugged, but a crease had appeared between his brows. It gave him an intent and worried sort of look. "So what? Asking questions about something has nothing to do with owning it. I can ask questions about the Book of Kells, but I think Trinity College and the Irish government would have something to say if I claimed to have it in my basement."

Hm, he had books on his mind, did he? Maybe that was a sign. "Oh, and did you visit Dublin just a few days before they noticed the book was missing?"

He stilled. He hadn't been moving, but stillness suddenly gripped him like a fist, tightening before her eyes. "What are you talking about?"

Lilli hesitated only a second before she laid it all out. No guts, no glory. "My client claims that he has evidence that Alistair Carruthers was on his property a few weeks before his death. He would have had ample opportunity to find and take the codex and to conceal it before my client got around to noticing its absence."

"If that's true, then it's likely any number of people would have also had access and opportunity in that same time frame. How does your 'client' intend to prove that my uncle was the one who actually stole it?"

"Um, I'm not sure he's really worried about offering proof . . ."

"Well, he should be. Unless he's prepared to produce a bill of sale or some other documentation of his claim of ownership, I doubt there's a court in existence that would support a claim of theft and order the artifact be returned to him."

She snorted. "Record keeping is not my client's forte. Mr. Bullard, while I didn't see a bill of sale, my research turned up no evidence proving your uncle's ownership, either; so I have no reason to dispute S—, um, my client's claim."

"Well, I do. I know my uncle, and I know he was not a thief. I've seen the man give back a penny of change to a store clerk if it was a penny too much. His family has lived in this town since it was founded. Heck, *his family* founded it. Honor and honesty were everything to him. But he was supposed to have broken into your mysterious client's house and made off with an item as valuable and unique as the *Praedicti*? I have no reason to doubt that my uncle came by his ownership of the text in a completely innocent and above-board manner."

She narrowed her eyes at him. "Are you some kind of lawyer?"

"No, a curator. Why?"

"No reason." Lilli shifted and sighed. "Look, this obviously isn't getting us real far. I came here to get the book. I was hoping I could do that quickly and discreetly, but we both know that didn't happen. Now, we could turn this into a legal battle and pit you against my client and let you two duke it out to see who can prove they really own the thing, but I doubt anyone would want to do that. My client wants the manuscript. I have a feeling he's willing to do a lot to get it. Why don't you tell me how much you want to sell it back to him? I'll run the number by him and see what we can do."

"I don't think I feel comfortable with that. Not when I know so little about your client. You haven't even told me his name. He could be completely the wrong sort of person to allow to take control of the *Praedicti*."

"There's a right sort of person?"

"Absolutely." When she opened her mouth below a rather offended glare, he bowled right over her. "You've already admitted that I know more about the codex than you do. Given the context of this conversation, I'm going to take it to mean that you also fail to understand what exactly the *Praedicti* is capable of."

"It's a book. I pretty much figured it was capable of lying there and being read."

"And that's it?"

She scowled. "I already made sure that it wasn't cursed or enchanted in any way. And it's obviously not a spellbook. So what else could it do? Prophecies don't cause future events, they just speculate on what they might be."

"In general, yes, that would be the definition of predictions; but the predictions in this book aren't general. They are highly specific and are divided into two groups: the first set predicts events like the spread of the plague across Europe, the Norman Conquest, even the execution of Joan of Arc."

"Right. I don't see how that's the sort of thing that becomes dangerous in the wrong hands."

He ignored her. "The second set predicts the course and outcome of a great apocalypse brought about by the unleashing of the fury of Hell upon the mundane world."

"The Revelation of St. John does the same thing," she pointed out impatiently.

"Yes, but St. John doesn't preface his vision with a recipe for how to accomplish that unleashing."

Lilli froze, felt herself go cold. "The *Praedicti* does?"

"Add a sprinkle of brimstone and bake at three-fifty until golden brown."

She closed her eyes and groaned.

"Well, shit."

FIVE

The coffee had gone cold while Aaron and Lilli tried to kill each other, but it didn't take long to boil the kettle and fix another pot. Pouring a cup for each of them, Aaron set Lilli's in front of her and then slid into his own chair across the kitchen table.

"Thanks."

"I suggest starting at the beginning."

"That would take way too long. There's just too much."

"Sum up."

She took a drink, lingered over it, obviously stalling. "A few years ago, I was doing a job that involved tracking down a particularly bloodthirsty goblin."

"I thought you said you were a bounty hunter."

"I am. I specialize in non-human tracking, capture, and rendition."

"Non-human?" Aaron repeated. "You mean visitants."

She made a face. "I've always hated that term. Doesn't it imply that they're visiting from somewhere else? Because I can guarantee that most of what I go after is completely homegrown."

"I think it has to do with their ability to visit to or from those planes that humans normally can't."

Her shoulders shifted in a shrug. "Anyway, yeah. I go after the nasties. Mostly I contract out with the police, the courts, bail bondsmen. When a non-human doesn't show up for court or when the police lack the expertise to handle a supernatural creature, I step in and get them or return them to custody."

Aaron nodded for her to continue.

"A few years ago, one of the things I was after—a goblin—thought he would be able to give me the slip if he beat a path into Hell."

That made sense to Aaron. Hell was the nickname given to the parallel plane of existence inhabited and controlled by nine devil princes, immortal beings of great power and no discernible redeeming qualities. Devils lived to accumulate wealth and power, and one of the ways they did so involved the enslavement of unsuspecting humans and visitants alike. Aaron had never paid the plane a personal visit, and he intended to continue to stay very far away. If he'd been following someone who had ducked into Hell to evade him, he'd have waved goodbye and headed out for ice cream.

"Not a bad move."

She shot him a very level glance. "I don't give up on a case," Lilli informed him steadily. "If I agree to bring something in, I bring it in. I don't care where I have to go to make it happen." She paused. "Well, okay, I care, but I don't let it stop me. I went in after the goblin."

Aaron shook his head. Already he could tell this story would not end happily.

"I decided to do it the smart way, though," she told him. "Instead of just following the trail and stepping on a bunch of pointy tails, I found out which part of the pit he'd gone to and I decided to ask the prince of the area for his permission to wander around his land. And then I decided to go for broke and ask if he would be willing to ensure me safe passage until I found the goblin and left."

"With brass balls like that, I'm surprised you don't rattle when you walk."

Lilli snorted. "It had less to do with balls than with a sincere desire not to have to fight my way into and out of the principality. So anyway, the prince agreed, provided I paid for the favor."

"How?"

"I agreed to do him three favors in return," Lilli explained her agreement with Samael, including all the restrictions she'd insisted on. "This—getting the book back for him— was supposed to be the last favor. I almost had it."

He could hear the wistful tone in her voice and felt a stirring of sympathy. She might have broken into the house and attempted to steal part of his inheritance from his uncle, but frankly he couldn't swear he wouldn't have done the same if their positions were reversed. He figured he'd be willing to do whatever it took to get a devil off his back, too.

"I understand the bargain," he said, "but how did you get into Hell to begin with? I always thought that humans had to either be summoned there or escorted by a demon or devil to get onto the plane in the first place."

Lilli shrugged. Her gaze held steady on his, but he could see a flare of defiance in her unusually colored eyes. "Humans do, but I'm only half human. My father was a devil."

He experienced the shock just as if he'd built up a bunch of static electricity and then grounded with a jolt. "You're a demi?"

Her mouth tightened. "If you want to use the term. Personally, I'm not wild about it. Labels aren't really my thing."

Aaron could sense her discomfort with the subject, but he couldn't stifle his curiosity. He'd never met a demi-human before. They were incredibly rare, mostly because few humans chose to associate with Hell-folk, let alone mate with them. Of course, according to the stories, choice often had very little to do with it. Often the children of human-devil matings owed more to rape than to romance. He longed to ask her about her parents, about her history, but his conscience managed to step in and rein him back.

"That must be where you got your eyes," he said finally and a little weakly. "They were the first thing I noticed about you. Well, after I noticed you were in my house when you weren't supposed to be, and you were armed like a Navy SEAL."

"Yeah, the eyes are hellish. Some people get freaked out by them, but I've always considered myself lucky not to have inherited horns or something even worse. I knew a kid when I was growing up who had the complexion of a three-day-old corpse—kind of a greenish, purplish gray. He went to the tanning salon every damned day, but no matter what he did, he couldn't change his skin tone. Made weird eyes seem like not much to worry about."

Aaron shook his head. "I don't think they're weird. I think they're beautiful."

Lilli stilled and raised her eyes to his, her gaze searching his expression for the truth. "You do?"

He nodded. "I do."

"Oh."

She swallowed, and he watched the muscles in her throat work until the urge to lean forward and trace the movement with his tongue nearly overwhelmed him. He swayed forward, caught himself, jerked back. He cleared his throat.

"So, uh, like I was saying," he coughed, struggling for calm, "I, uh, I think what we should do next—"

He never got to finish his sentence, ridiculous though it would have been. Not when Lilli rose slightly from her chair, leaned forward, and laid her soft, warm, expressive mouth over his and stole his breath in a kiss.

The world froze. Time may have stood still, the universe may have stopped expanding, he couldn't be sure. All Aaron could be sure of was that sinking into Lilli's kiss felt like coming home. He may as well have been the people of Israel, wandering the desert for forty years, and now finally entering the promised land. She tasted of coffee and strength and a subtle tang of smoke that wrapped him up in an ever-tightening ball of fascination.

Moving without thought, he rose from his seat, careful not to lose the contact with her mouth. He would rather have lost his mind, which seemed like a distinct possibility. Two shuffling steps brought him around the corner of the table toward her and more importantly allowed him to get his hands on her. He slid them around her waist, his fingers flexing on the soft, muscled warmth of her. She felt as resilient as youth and as tempting as experience. When she answered his touch with a soft sigh that filled his mouth with her flavor, he felt his body tighten and his knees go weak. She laid her hands over his, then slid her palms up his arms, kneading as she seized the opportunity to explore him.

Aaron deepened the kiss, pouring into it the mysterious, inescapable intensity that had seized him. He slid his arms around her back and explored the slim length of her spine even as his tongue explored the slick, inviting cavern of her mouth. He could feel the superb conditioning of her muscles, the hard, faintly intimidating capability of them to move, attack, defend, absorb, and carry her through places as dangerous as Hell and still guide her back to safety. But he also felt the blatant flare of her hips, the incredible, luscious femininity of the bottom he cupped in his hands and kneaded with frank appreciation.

Lilli moaned and pressed herself against him, her arms twining around his neck, slim, clever fingers burrowing into the shaggy fall of hair at his collar. He felt the scrape of her fingernails across his scalp and his head reeled, his entire body tightening and quivering as electricity jolted through him. He tugged her closer, his hands on her bottom, pressing her hips against the hardness of his erection. Instead of backing away, she rubbed against him like a cat in heat, all elastic muscle and shameless sensuality.

Christ, he couldn't ever remember being this aroused. Not from a first kiss, that was for sure. One taste of her, and he was ready to lay her back across the table, drag those no-nonsense BDU pants down around her ankles, and sink into her up to his damned fool neck. He guessed this was what people called "chemistry." Morons. Aaron had never in his life felt a more powerful magic.

Magic, he thought hazily as he skimmed one hand up her side to close it around the soft swell of her breast, was the only possible explanation for this madness.

But at least he wasn't alone in his insanity. Lilli continued to press and rub against him as her mouth ate at his. It was like she was trying to climb inside him, which made perfect sense to Aaron; the only thing he could think of right now was getting inside of her.

Shifting, he pressed her half a step backward until her ass—and his very appreciative left hand—bumped against the edge of the kitchen table. He had urgent, heated, erection-swelling thoughts about whether the ancient piece of furniture would hold up to what he planned to do to her, but by then it was too late to care. Tightening his grip on her bottom, he boosted her up a few inches and nearly swallowed both their tongues when she parted her legs and wrapped them around his hips, pushing the hot, damp softness of herself against the monster in his pants. He could almost picture coming just like that, like a teenager dry humping on his parents' sofa.

Aaron struggled for control, found the last few threads that remained, and gathered them up in a tight fist. If he didn't get ahold of himself, he was going to last about fifteen seconds, most of which would be spent muttering apologies for his technique of shoving it in and then shaking like an earthquake while the force of this mad chemical magic overwhelmed him.

He reached for the hem of her shirt only to find that she'd beat him to it. Their kiss broke just long enough for the fabric to whisk over her head and go sailing in the direction of the refrigerator. The strange little hourglass pendant she wore dropped back to her chest with a thump, the red sand inside seeming almost to flash with inner light at the movement. Then he laid his hands on her bare skin and jewelry was the last thing on his mind.

Her skin felt like warm cream, soft and smooth and voluptuously silken beneath his fingers. At the moment, he could see a flush of pink adorning the pale expanse of it, and he wanted nothing so much as a taste . . .

She reached behind her and flicked open her bra clasp.

Make that a huge, greedy mouthful.

Brushing the scrap of dark fabric out of the way, Aaron cupped a soft mound in his hand and lifted it to his mouth. Bending low, he took the rosy tip between his lips and drew her inside himself, groaning in pleasure at the sweet, warm, dusky taste of her. His tongue played over the hardened nipple, teeth lightly scraping the sides until he felt her quiver under his hands.

"Aaron," she breathed.

He released her nipple with a soft pop and dragged his lips across her chest to the other peak. He felt her fingers tighten in his hair and hoped he'd still have some by the time they were finished. Of course, shaved heads were in, he reflected, and baldness seemed like a small price to pay for something so astoundingly perfect.

Rearing back, Aaron reached for the fastening on her jeans, watching as her eyes fluttered open and blinked hazily up at him.

"Wha—?"

He leaned forward, pressed a hard, hungry kiss to her mouth and drew down her zipper. "Sh."

Something hot passed between them, but it wasn't until Lilli muttered something against his lips and began to press her hands into his shoulders that he realized it wasn't their mutual attraction.

Tearing himself from the kiss, Aaron reared back and frowned down at his own chest where a black singe mark now stood out against the top of the white O in the name of the band on his shirt. "What the hell?"

Lilli wasn't paying attention, but Aaron could hardly blame her, not when he saw the patch of livid red skin above her breastbone and the brightly glowing pendant that seemed to be causing it.

"Damn him," she hissed, reaching for the chain with both hands and yanking it off rather than fumbling with the clasp. "He didn't just want me keeping track of the time, the bastard; he wanted to keep track of me."

"Ah, Lillith," a voice purred from the shadows in the hall door, "you always were such a clever girl. You get that from your father. It's just such a shame you won't be able to pass it on to a child of your own one day."

Aaron turned and instinctively placed himself between Lilli and the intruder. That earned him a smack on the shoulder blade hard enough to make him wince, but he didn't step aside.

"Who are you?" he demanded, even though he had a sneaking suspicion he already knew the answer. Behind him, he heard the shifting of cloth as Lilli tugged her shirt back on. Good. Now at least neither of them would be naked when they were slaughtered by a devil prince.

"Didn't you tell your new friend?" the figure asked, finally stepping forward into the light from the chandelier above the table. "Lillith, darling, I'm hurt that you wouldn't think to mention me."

With every step the devil took, Aaron felt more intensely the sensation of things crawling on his skin. He knew better than to look. Devils and demons often gave humans who glimpsed them the feeling of being somehow contaminated, either by insects or vermin or even acidic liquids. It was purely psychological.

At least, that's what Aaron hoped.

"Sam," she bit out, her voice sounding as grim as the face he glimpsed when she stepped out from behind him and squared off against the intruder. "Checking up on me already? I thought I had until dawn to run your little errand."

The devil shrugged and propped one shoulder against the refrigerator in a negligent pose that did nothing to disguise the malevolent power he embodied. "Technically, I suppose you do, but you appear to be a little distracted. I was afraid you might have forgotten why I sent you here."

"Not likely."

"Really?" His black, blank gaze shifted from Lilli and Aaron to the bra she had discarded on the floor beside the table and not bothered to put back on in her haste to redress herself. "Funny. I thought you looked quite absorbed." His gaze shifted to Aaron, focused, glittered dangerously. "Maybe if I gave your beau a few lessons in seduction you'd have better luck next time."

Aaron's skin gave up crawling and felt as if it were trying to leave the room at a dead run. He would have very much liked to follow it. Straight into a boiling hot shower. The idea of Samael, Prince of Hell, Lord of Deception, and Master of Depravity, teaching him anything about women held even less appeal for him than apprenticing at the hands of de Sade. He didn't think immersing himself in a vat of full-strength bleach until his skin melted off would be enough to remove that kind of filth.

God, he thought suddenly, how the hell would he ever get this kitchen to feel clean again?

Now that he thought about it, Aaron couldn't understand how the devil had even gotten into the house to begin with. Uncle Alistair had the place warded from attic to building site. Aaron remembered teasing him years ago about his paranoia. After all, Alistair was just researching the darker forces, he wasn't offering to show them a good time. All the wards and charms and spells and blessings that encircled the house and gardens had seemed like overkill. Now, he couldn't have been more grateful for them.

Fixing his eye on Samael, Aaron studied the devil closely, looking for a clue as to how he'd gotten past the guards. He didn't appear to be harmed in any way, and he knew several of those wards were strong enough to burn a body to a crisp if they were tripped. He might have suspected that the devil had used magic of his own, but that would have been impossible. No creature could take down a ward specifically designed to keep his kind out. That was what made them effective. So how had he gotten inside?

Aaron craned his head and tried to look around the demon. That was when he noticed it. Despite the uneven light in the kitchen, Samael cast no shadow. The floor and refrigerator behind him remained blank and well-lit, which would have been impossible if the devil were actually in the room. He wasn't; the figure Aaron and Lilli were seeing was a projection, a kind of magical hologram that looked and sounded exactly like the real thing, but had actually been created to be used as a sort of live-action attendee at a supernatural conference call. He could speak to them, and his presence could still cause them the same physical symptoms as if he were in the room, but the projection was essentially powerless. It could not touch them, and more importantly, it could not use magic against them.

Aaron let himself relax. Just a little.

"Unfortunately, your luck doesn't seem to be holding out so well, does it?" Samael continued. He smiled, and Aaron marveled that a face so beautiful could be so chilling at the same time. "Of course, you are doing better than your dear uncle, but considering he's dead, I don't suppose that takes all that much effort."

His chuckle made Aaron's blood run cold. Something tickled at the back of his mind, something he'd heard about the *Praedicti*, or something he'd maybe even included in his thesis. Something about the coming of an apocalypse . . .

Lilli just continued to glare at her client.

"I think we're doing just fine without your help," she snarled.

What had it been? Aaron wondered frantically. Images flitted through his mind—a burning tower, the crack of whip, long lines of rattling chains. Was that why Samael wanted to get his hands on the codex? Did he think it would help him to bring about a war between humanity and the powers of Hell?

"If that were true, he'd already have fucked you, wouldn't he, my dear? But then, I've always found that those who try too hard to resist temptation have the hardest time giving in to it. Or rather, the softest, to be frank."

Something about an offering. Not raised up to the Gods, but lowered into the abyss.

No, not offerings, Aaron realized, feeling himself stiffen. Sacrifices. Three deaths were required to bring about the war foretold in the *Praedicti*. The one who possessed the book had to sacrifice three people and use their life force to crack the seals that divided the planes of Hell from the ones of mortal reality.

Aaron uttered a word so foul he hadn't even realized he knew it. Throwing up his hands, he stepped forward and sent a stream of rage-fueled energy straight at the projection of Samael.

"*Vade!*" he shouted and watched as the figure of the devil straightened and snarled something in a language Aaron was glad he couldn't understand. Then, with an ear-popping pressure vacuum and a whiff of brimstone, the projection winked out, leaving him alone in his uncle's kitchen with Lilli.

"What the hell just happened?" she demanded, looking from the refrigerator to Aaron and scowling. "How did you make him leave?"

"It wasn't really him," Aaron explained, but he didn't wait for more questions. He turned on his heel and headed straight back down the stairs and carefully retrieved the *Praedicti* from where it had fallen during their earlier struggle. He heard Lilli following hot on his heels, still spouting out questions about Samael and Aaron's banishment spell, but he didn't stop to explain. He just flipped carefully through the pages until he found the prediction he was looking for. Quickly, he skimmed the text, located the correct passage and read the Latin with a growing sense of mingled rage and dread.

"You need to forget about upstairs," he said, cutting Lilli off mid-rant and pointing to the words he'd just read. "We've got much bigger things to worry about at the moment."

"Like what?"

"Like the world as we know it is about to end, and it looks like Samael will be leading the parade that brings a new and literal meaning to the phrase 'Hell on earth.'"

SIX

"Um, ex-queeze me?"

Lilli felt a bit like she'd just taken a home run swing straight to the stomach. She wondered vaguely if she looked like it as well, since she was having a hard time keeping from bending over as she struggled to get back the breath that had been knocked out of her.

Aaron gave her a sympathetic look and gestured toward the page he'd just read on the left side of the book. "This is one of the most famous prophecies in the *Praedicti*. Scholars have been debating it for centuries. Some of them link it to the same sort of events depicted in the Revelation of St. John of Patmos, but there have always been a few dissenters who thought that this pointed to an entirely different war between good and evil."

Lilli took a good look at the ancient manuscript for the first time. Before, it had always been just a means to an end for her, but now she could actually appreciate the beautiful illustrations, the colors still vivid and vibrant, even after centuries had passed. Even the pages it was printed on were beautiful, more striking than the finest luxury paper she'd ever seen, still thin and delicate, yet somehow conveying the strength of all those years of survival.

"My Latin is a little rusty," she said, bending closer and struggling to make out the antiquated script, "and I'll never get used to *u*'s that look like *v*'s, but this looks like it's talking about exactly the same thing as the Bible—armies of good and evil meeting in a final battle for domination of the world."

"Okay, so there are similarities," he said impatiently, and she couldn't help but raise an eyebrow at his dismissive understatement. "What's important is that in this version, there's no antichrist and no certain victory for the forces of good. According to whomever wrote this text, if this book falls into the hands of a leader on the side of evil, three human sacrifices could be used to break the seals that separate the planes of Hell from ours, and thereby unleash every kind of devil or demon that has ever plagued mankind, and every one who hasn't. The population of the earth right now is around six billion, right? Well, there are experts out there who estimate that the legions of Hell encompass at least five times that number, all of whom have powers humans can't even dream of, and the kind of bloodlust that makes Adolf Hitler look like a Girl Scout! And the only way to avert it for once and for all is to do the impossible—to get a righteous child of Hell to spill the blood of both human and devil. Why do they even offer that as an out? It's completely ridiculous!"

Lilli heard every word Aaron was saying, and it wasn't that he didn't make a good point; it was just that when she finished reading the prophecy he was pointing out—which was much shorter than she'd imagined, really—her eyes skipped naturally to the next page, which contained a striking illumination of a medieval knight locked in battle with a huge, serpentine dragon against the backdrop of a lush garden. In the picture, the knight brandished a long, silver sword and wore only a tunic of chainmail over his regular clothes. The dragon, by contrast, appeared to be covered with thick, heavy scales that glistened almost like steel in the light of the afternoon sun.

The illustrator had made sure to indicate that this battle had not just begun, but had raged on for hours, perhaps even days. The knight's garments were torn and stained. Debris consisting of splintered wooden shields and broken scales littered the ground at their feet, and several less stalwart knights lay dead in a heap beneath a castle wall. Once again, the theme here was good against evil, but this time, the illustration seemed to imply that good might very well win out in the end. The knight's expression was grim and set, while the dragon's head bobbed low, its red eyes narrowed in pain or exhaustion as blood seeped from a wound in its side. The death blow would come soon.

Around the edges of the illustration—above, below, and running down each side—were four brief paragraphs of text that appeared to discuss three different prophecies. They almost resembled the quatrains of Michel de Nostradamus: succinct, poetic, and emphatically honest. It was the one on the left side of the page that caught Lilli's attention. Even with her shaky declensions, she recognized it as a verse and translated in her head as best she could:

A valiant knight, the page acquired
   with love and brilliant mind,
Shall slight a prince both dark and fair and fat
   with kith and kine.
A battle fought, a battle won, a price by both agreed
A knight is fall'n, a prince is fled, the magic's in the seed.

Lilli frowned, then repeated the lines over in her head. Typical poetic rambling, she told herself. Most likely it meant nothing. Prophets loved to make their visions as vague as possible so that they could be interpreted to fit any given situation or outcome.

Something about this, though, niggled at the back of her mind. She read it again.

Valiant knight.

She looked back at the apocalyptic page, then back at the verse that intrigued her.

Prince both dark and fair.

As if in the distance, she could hear Aaron still talking and knew he was trying to get her attention, but she had felt an idea, still amorphous and shaky, grab hold of her and tug her insistently back to the page with the knight and dragon illustration. She quickly skimmed through the other three verses and discovered with a jolt that each of them shared a common theme—a battle between two single adversaries, one dark and one light, who would settle between them a greater dispute between their peoples. The dark warrior would have superior numbers, superior funding, and greater overall power, but the bright warrior would be able to win the battle by paying a kind of forfeit that would not only avert the coming war but would somehow undermine the loser's ability to rise up again.

Lilli felt a sudden rush of understanding. Excited, she turned to look back at Aaron and hushed him with an impatient gesture.

"I think you're wrong," she said, almost laughing when Aaron recoiled as if she'd just told him she thought he was Jack the Ripper.

"I beg your pardon?"

Then she really did laugh. He sounded so indignant.

"I think you're wrong," she repeated, "and I'll tell you why. I'm sure Samael would very much like to bring about the apocalypse if for no other reason than to curry favor with Lucifer. He's always looking for a way to suck up to the head honcho, but that's not what I think he's after at the moment. Sam doesn't need the book to bring about the apocalypse. If he wants to do it, all he needs is to perform the right actions in the right order and, voila! Instant Armageddon." She shook her head and pointed to the verses on the next page. "I think this is why he wanted the book back. Specifically, I think this is why he wanted the book away from you."

She waited while Aaron skimmed through the verses, then looked up and shook his head. "I don't get it. Why would Samael care about these prophecies? They have nothing to do with the apocalypse page. I don't even think they were written by the same oracle. They're in a completely different style, almost nursery-rhyme-ish."

"I know, but just think about the main characters in all of them—a dark prince and a valiant knight?"

"So?"

Lilli rolled her eyes. "I think they're referring to Samael and you."

"What?"

" 'Dark prince' is pretty self-explanatory, don't you think? I mean, come on, that one is practically handed to us. It took me a minute to think through the 'valiant knight, brilliant mind, acquires a page' thing—that's a little more esoteric—but it has to be you. You said your uncle left you the house and the contents, right? Including a whole lot of pages. Books full of them. Including this one. Because you were his favorite. He loved you."

"But—"

Warming to her topic, Lilli didn't let him finish. "And the brilliant mind thing is a given. I'd bet you a year's income you've got an entire bowl of alphabet soup after your name. You probably got perfect scores on your SATs."

"I still don't see what that has to do with anything. Why would Samael care about four badly written rhymes about an interpersonal conflict between the two of us when he could be instigating a rebellion that would lead to the destruction or enslavement of the entire human race?"

Sheesh. For a smart guy, Lilli realized, Aaron could be really thick. "Because if one of these 'badly written rhymes' comes true first," she explained patiently, "Samael wouldn't be able to start a rebellion. He'd be finished, at least for the foreseeable future. And you, my friend, are the one who's going to bring him down."

SEVEN

Three and a half hours later, Aaron found himself standing around his uncle's basement and feeling like an idiot while Lilli drew a huge circle on the floor with a thick stick of white chalk. Dawn was still more than an hour away, which according to Lilli meant that Samael and his hologram would leave them alone a while longer. He would pop back up once Lilli's time ran out for retrieving the book for him, but he wouldn't want to be caught in this realm for very long with the sun approaching. His powers were already weak on earth, and the sun would only drain him further, so he would wait until the last possible minute before he showed his face outside of Hell. When he did, the wards would keep him outside the house, unless someone invited him in.

That should give Lilli just about enough time to answer one more question for Aaron.

"Tell me again why this idea is not completely ridiculous and suicidal," he urged, leaning against a bookcase with his arms folded defensively in front of him. He was trying not to stare at her ass while she crouched down to draw her circle, but frankly, it was an extremely fine ass, and he could still remember the way it had felt cupped in his hands up-stairs.

Aaron swore and shifted. The erection he'd sported then had finally subsided and he really didn't think now was an appropriate time for its return. Unfortunately, the fire that fed it seemed disinclined to go out as long as Lilli was anywhere within a fifty-foot radius of him. It was becoming damned inconvenient.

"I already told you, I'm sure this is going to work," she said, setting aside her chalk while there was still about a twelve-inch gap at the base of the circle. "The prophecy says so. You're going to kick Samael's ass, the apocalypse will be averted, and then we can call live happily ever after and you'll know you're the one who made that possible. Think of the sense of satisfaction that will give you."

"I'm too busy thinking of the sense of pain I'll feel when Samael decapitates me with his bare hands and uses my head for an impromptu game of Hacky Sack."

Lilli shot him a quelling look as she began to place white and black candles around the perimeter of the ten-foot-wide circle. "Your pessimism is not going to be helpful."

Aaron threw up his hands. "You know what would be helpful here? Automatic weapons. Before today, I was always an advocate of strong gun control laws. No one needs a machine gun to defend themselves unless they're being invaded by the Turkish army, I told myself. But you know what? I've changed my mind. Give me an Uzi; give me an AK-47. Hell, give me a Gatling gun. I don't care. Just give me something that will allow me to pump the maximum amount of lead into Samael's body in the minimum amount of time. That's all I care about. Just call me Charlton Heston with a death wish."

"Oh, relax. You know as well as I do that bullets are like mosquito bites to a devil as powerful as Samael. A gun wouldn't do you as much good as a letter opener with a good steel blade. An iron fire poker would work even better."

"Really? I'll just run upstairs and get one, then."

She stood and put her hand on his arm. "Aaron, it will be

fine." Her fire-colored eyes, the ones he now knew came from a true devil of a father, glowed up into his, warming him. "I'll be right there with you. And I believe in this prophecy. You have nothing to worry about, because you're going to beat him. I promise."

Aaron felt the predictable tightening of his body the instant she touched him, but this time he felt something else, too. Something just as strong, but softer somehow. Something new, like a kernel waiting for the right time to flower.

He uncrossed his arms and lifted one hand to her cheek. Cupping her face in his palm, he lowered his head and brushed his lips over hers. When this was all over, he promised himself, they were going to finish what they'd started on the table in the kitchen. He didn't care if Lucifer himself interrupted.

"Okay," he said softly, lifting his head. "I still think that deliberately summoning Samael in the flesh is the dumbest thing that any human being has ever attempted in the entire history of human stupidity, but if you think this is what we have to do, why don't you run me through it?"

Lilli smiled, and despite all her reassurances, Aaron thought he detected a hint of nerves. "Sure."

She stepped back and gestured briskly toward the area she had set up in the center of the open area of the floor. The white chalk stood out starkly against the dark gray of the cement floor, and fourteen stout black and white candles, seven of each, ringed the outer perimeter of the space. In the middle of the circle, she'd laid down the soft fleece lap blanket his uncle had always kept folded neatly over the back of the desk chair.

"We're going to cast a basic circle of protection first," she explained. "I'm sure you know how to do those, so I won't bore you with details."

Aaron shook his head. "I'm far from an expert. I've done

one or two, of course, but not since I was still studying with my father. I'm more of a magus than a summoner. I generally leave circles to the people who know how to use them. I just work in the open and rely on my personal words to keep away the baddies."

"Oh, right. I see. Well, um, it's really pretty simple. You can just watch me and follow along." She cleared her throat, her glance sliding away from his and toward the center of the circle. "We'll need to raise a pretty intense level of energy, though, Samael isn't a garden variety demon or a low-level devil, so it's going to take more than a quick chant to get the job done. Then once he's in the circle," she continued hurriedly, "I'll ask him what the price is for his agreement not to break the seals to Hell."

"See, this is where things start to break down for me," he said. "I know what you read in the *Praedicti,* but what could either of us be able to offer than would make a Prince of Hell give up the quest for world domination? That's like asking how much a bird would want in exchange for giving up its song."

Lilli nodded, her mouth settling into grim lines. "He's going to ask for a soul. At least one of ours, maybe both."

"And you think that's a fair exchange?" He tried not to sound as appalled as he felt, but wasn't sure he succeeded.

"Of course not. We're going to negotiate."

"I thought there was supposed to be a battle."

"A battle of wills."

Aaron knew his skepticism was showing. "I'm not quite sure prophecies are really as elastic as you seem to think they are. When they talk about battles, they usually want battles, complete with injuries and the potential for death and/or putrescence."

"Don't worry. If it does come down to an actual fight, just remember two things. Number one: even in the flesh, Samael's powers are limited in this realm—severely limited as long as he stays inside the circle—so whatever you do, don't open the circle. Keep everyone inside and he'll be at most equivalent to an elder master magus."

"Oh, right. No problem, then. Do you have any idea how many elder master magi there have been in recorded history? Three! Three out of all time! But sure, piece of cake. I can take him with one hand tied behind my back."

"And number two," she continued, her mouth curving into a smile that both infuriated and tempted him, "remember that you have a secret weapon."

"What?"

"Me."

EIGHT

Lilli glued her smile in place like a Kabuki mask. She could feel her cheeks threatening to quiver from the strain, but she ignored them. She had no intention of giving in to her own fears, especially not when Aaron obviously had so many of his own. To be honest, she had no idea whether or not her plan was going to work, but she didn't see any choice but to give it a try. Their current choices consisted of dying now, together, in an attempt to save the world from Samael's apocalyptic war, or dying in a few weeks or months along with every other human being who resisted his dominion. She'd rather die on her own terms.

She thought Aaron would feel the same, but thankfully he wouldn't have to make that choice. If a sacrifice had to be made to keep Aaron alive and avert the apocalypse, Lilli would make it herself. But before it came to that, she had a plan that would make the next few moments ones she would always remember, whether or not they ended up being her last.

"Are you ready to get started?" she asked, her voice already gone husky with anticipation. She held her hand out toward him and saw him hesitate for an instant before he took it and clasped it warmly in his own.

"Ready," he smiled.

"Then come into my parlor." She chuckled as she stepped into the mostly completed circle and tugged him in behind her. She gestured toward the blanket spread on the chilly floor. "Have a seat while I finish this up. It'll only take a minute."

Once he had folded his long legs beneath him and settled himself on the floor, Lilli turned away and picked up a book of matches, a small bowl of salt, and the chalk she'd used to draw the outline of the incomplete circle. First, she moved around the circle and lit all of the white candles. When she got back to her starting point, she repeated the process with the black ones. The tiny flames didn't look like much, but when they were all lit, their collective warmth began to raise the temperature in the circle by a couple of degrees. She knew they'd be glad for that in a little while.

Lilli pushed back a tickle of nerves and knelt down to close the gap in the drawing, making sure the line was thick and solid with no blank spaces. Then she set aside the chalk, returned to her feet, and began to sprinkle salt along the edge, making her third trip all the way around the circle. She might not be a magician, but even she could feel the way a wall of energy seemed to form around the perimeter of the space, stretching into a dome above their heads. When she glanced back at Aaron, she could see him staring at it with a hint of a smile on his face.

He must have sensed her eyes on him and glanced back at her. "Nice work," he said. "That shade of blue is a good color for you."

Lilli looked back at her handiwork, but she could see nothing, just the light of the candles rendering the room beyond them shadowy and indistinct. Still, it was nice to get the vote of confidence.

She completed her binding of the circle by spreading the salt back to her starting point. Setting aside the tools she'd used, she dusted the chalk off her hands and took a seat on the blanket facing Aaron.

"Okay, so that was the easy part," she said with a wry smile. "From here on out, things might start to get tricky."

"Devils and demons and apocalypse, oh my?" he grinned back. "Bring 'em on."

She laughed. "Down, big boy. You'll get a chance, but first I want to go over just a couple of things."

He took her hands and held them between their bodies. "Shoot."

Lilli took a deep breath, blew it out long and slow. Then she looked directly into his eyes and said, "I want you to know that I'm sorry for getting you into this."

"What? Why? What are you talking about? You didn't get me into anything."

"Yes, I did. If I hadn't broken into your house and tried to steal the *Praedicti,* you might not be caught up in all of this."

"That's a stupid thing to think," Aaron said, squeezing her hands gently. "I got caught up in this, so to speak, the minute my uncle left me his house and the contents. He's the one who got me involved with the *Praedicti*, not you."

"I know, but I'm the only reason Samael is paying any attention to you. If I'd done the job right or left as soon as I heard you come down those stairs tonight, he never would have known you were alive."

"Um, hello, but aren't you the person who told me that he's been trying to get back a book that basically warns him about me in four different ways?"

"Actually, I've been thinking about it, and I think it's just as likely that the prophecy was talking about your uncle as about you," she said, which was at least half true. She did think there was an equal chance for Alistair and Aaron to be the knights; she just thought there might be another knight in there entirely whom they hadn't talked about yet. "Especially since he's dead. Fallen, as it were."

"Then what we're about to do now is make the prince flee, huh?"

"That's the plan."

"And tell me again how you're planning to manage that."

Lilli made a face. "I'm going to offer to give him exactly what he wants. If he'll agree not to start the rebellion, we'll give him back the book. I think the four small prince verses are the real reason he wanted it in the first place. If he had those, he'd be in a much stronger position to know where his enemies were likely to attack."

"He didn't see us coming."

"No, because your uncle had the book. Samael had no way of referring to the prophecy ahead of time. I think that may be why your uncle was killed. Samael was responsible, and he did it to get the book back. But since your uncle wasn't a stupid man, he made arrangements to keep Samael from finding it—namely concealing it on the wrong shelf and ensuring that you were put in place to take charge of his effects after his death."

"You really don't believe in coincidence, do you?"

"Not when Samael is involved, I don't."

"Then I'm glad I get the chance to face him again," Aaron said, and his hazel eyes hardened behind his scholarly glasses. "Are you sure we can't make this a more traditional sort of battle?"

"I don't think that would be a good idea."

The thought of it made Lilli's stomach clench. Even she had no intention of trying to best Samael in a physical contest. She'd been telling the truth that he would be less powerful here in his physical form than if they had confronted him on his own plane, but he could still squash either one of them like a bug with the same effort it would take to blow his nose.

"Let's just stick to the original plan. We'll summon him, we'll offer him a deal, we'll send him back where he belongs. Agreed?"

"Agreed."

"Good." Lilli let herself relax and rose to her knees to inch forward until she could slide into his lap and wrap her legs around him. "That means it's time for the fun part."

His hands rose instinctively to steady her and secure her close to him. "You didn't tell me there was going to be a fun part," he said, his voice low and a little hoarse when she dipped her head and dragged her lips along the side of his neck.

"Oh, absolutely. Don't you think we deserve a fun part?" She rocked slowly against him and felt his instant, gratifying response.

"Sure I do." Her teeth closed lightly on his ear and made him shudder. "I just, ah, thought we might save it until after we finished here. You know, give ourselves a sort of reward."

"Why wait?" Lilli felt his fingers tighten on her hips and pressed closer, dragging her breasts across the warm plane of his chest. "Did you know that aside from a blood sacrifice, the most effective way to raise energy for a magical purpose is through sex?"

She slid her hands under the open edges of his flannel shirt and pushed it off, dragging it down his arms and dropping it to the floor. When those curious fingers brushed against his belly as they sought the hem of his t-shirt, he groaned softly.

"I'd . . . heard about that." Aaron lifted his arms to allow her to pull off his tee and leave him bare-chested on the claret-colored blanket. She could hear his voice deepening, see the gooseflesh on his skin, which she knew had nothing to do with the ambient temperature.

"But like I said," he continued, "I'm not a summoner. Magi tend to, ah, work alone."

Lilli let her mouth curve into a grin. Crossing her arms over her chest, she drew her own shirt up and over her head, revealing nothing but bare skin underneath. When Samael had interrupted them earlier, she'd been in too much of a hurry to cover herself up to wrestle with her bra. Now she relished the convenience of one less layer.

Almost as much as she relished the way her breasts seemed to draw his gaze like magnets. His gaze and his elegant, long-fingered hands.

Lilli leaned into his touch and lowered her head until her breath brushed across his mouth like a caress. "Oh, but it's so much more fun with a partner," she whispered. "Don't you think?"

NINE

Think? At the moment, Aaron considered himself lucky that he could still breathe, and if Lilli shifted a little further to the right, all bets were off on that, too.

Groaning, he angled his head and took her mouth in a kiss he could feel all the way down to his toes. Or maybe she took his mouth. It didn't really matter. What mattered was that they sank into each other as easily as the ocean, riding a wave of mutual desire that threatened to swamp him at any moment. He didn't think he could ever get enough of her taste, of the sweet, smoky tang that was Lillith Corbin. He drank it in like water and never seemed to quench his thirst.

She returned the kiss just as avidly, whimpering as she struggled to get closer. Her arms twined about his neck, tangling him in an embrace he could cheerfully have called home for the rest of eternity. She had no need to hold him to her, since the last thing he wanted was to get away, but maybe, like him, her head was swimming and she had to hold on to him to keep from losing her balance.

Come to think of it, he realized, they would both be a lot safer if they were a little closer to the floor.

Easing himself back, Aaron carefully lowered himself to

the soft fleece blanket beneath them, reluctantly removing one hand from her breast so that he could help her stretch across him like the sky. He felt her purr of pleasure against his lips and sent both hands back to wandering, briefly cupping and cuddling her breasts before sliding along her smooth, curving sides to knead the mounds of her amazing ass.

The feel of fabric beneath his hands irritated him and he suddenly, violently, wanted them both to be naked. He supposed he could have done things the old-fashioned way and fumbled with buttons and zippers, tugging and rearranging cloth to reveal the hidden prize beneath. There were times when he loved that process, relished its slowness, but this was not one of them.

With a wave and a thought, their clothes melted away and his mouth caught her gasp of shock when she felt the hot press of his erection between her legs. Aaron echoed the sentiment and froze for a moment, battling against the primitive urge to grip her hips, position her opening, and plunge deep inside her tight little channel. A minute ago being cradled between her legs had felt so sweet and almost innocent, like they were a couple of teenagers necking in the back of a car. But now he could feel the slick heat of her wetness coating his shaft, and innocence was the last thing on his mind.

He felt Lilli stiffen and pull back from him, bracing her hands on the floor and levering her upper body off of his so that she could look down at his flushed and desire-hardened face. He couldn't stop his fingers from clamping down on her like vises to keep her from escaping him, but he tried to school his features into something that would at least not scare her away.

She watched him for a long moment, her flame-colored eyes so filled with heat that he swore he could feel it against his skin. Then her reddened, swollen lips curved into a smile as old as Eve and she freed one hand to reach for his glasses.

"Let's just set these out of the way, shall we? We wouldn't want anything to happen to them," she said, tugging the frames from his face, carefully folding the arms over each other, and stretching to put them beside the salt dish at the far edge of the circle. Then she leaned back into him and dragged her teeth along the edge of his jaw in a way that made his eyes roll back into his head. "If you have any trouble seeing something, I want you to feel free to lean in real close."

With a desperate laugh, Aaron gripped her tightly and flipped to reverse their positions. When he had her pinned beneath him, he reached back to grip her knees and lift them high along his rib cage.

"Close, hm?" he growled, reaching between them to grasp his erection and position the head against her weeping entrance. "Let me get a little bit closer and you can let me know if it's too much."

She laughed up at him, her face gorgeous and mysterious and expectant in the wavering light of the candles. Perspiration glistened on her skin as she spread her arms wide in welcome and tightened her legs against his sides. He could feel her body thrumming with expectation, wondered if she could possibly want this as much as he did.

"Come on then," she urged, beckoning him forward. "I promise to let you know if it becomes too much."

Taking her at her word, Aaron fixed her gaze on his, drew a breath and thrust hard inside her.

Lilli bent beneath him like a bow, a look of exultation dawning on her features, her eyes going dark and hazy with pleasure.

"Too much?" he panted, bracing his hands on the blanket on either side of her and struggling not to pound into her over and over like a barbarian intent on plunder. But he wanted to plunder. God, he wanted it more than he wanted his next breath.

She shook her head, her dark hair spilling in tangled waves around her. It framed her face like an ebony halo, and Aaron wanted to tangle his fingers in it and use it to hold her still while he sated himself within her.

"More," she gasped, her voice so low and choked that he had to lean close to hear her. "Please. More."

He was happy to oblige.

With a grunt, he shifted and seated himself more deeply inside her. Her breath rushed out in a sound of urgent pleasure that acted like spurs to his flanks. Bracing his knees against the floor, he grasped her hips and lifted them off the ground. He pulled her with him as he leaned back until he held her lower body almost in his lap, making his penetration almost terrifyingly deep within her.

Lilli offered not a sound of protest. The only sounds tumbling from her lips were moans and cries and whimpers of pleasure. When he began a deep, steady thrusting rhythm, she moved with him, letting her legs fall to the side, her feet bracing against the floor to give her even greater leverage to meet his thrusts. Her upper body arched off the blanket, her head thrown back. To Aaron, she looked like a pale, perfect altar, soft and sacred. He could have worshipped her forever.

She clearly had other ideas.

He had settled into a rhythm designed to give them each the maximum amount of pleasure without the risk of ending things too soon. He wanted to savor the tight warmth of her wrapped around him, the feel of her body beneath his hands, the sight of her blind and quivering with pleasure. He wanted to take hours, days, weeks, to enjoy her, and he might have come close if she hadn't slowly and deliberately tightened her muscles around him like a fist so that every thrust felt like a direct assault on his most sensitive nerve endings.

God, she was going to kill him.

He could have cared less.

Determined to torture her as thoroughly as she tortured him, Aaron leaned forward again, changing the angle of his penetration until the length of his shaft rubbed against her swollen clitoris on every hard stroke. Within seconds, he had her writhing. A minute after that he heard her breath strangle in her chest and felt her orgasm swallow her like a giant black hole, leaving nothing behind but waves of pulsing pleasure.

Her face in that moment became the most breathtaking thing Aaron had ever seen. Her eyes stared up at him, unfocused and unseeing, the pupils almost swallowing the rings of copper fire that surrounded them. Her mouth fell open on a silent cry of awe. She looked as if she beheld the face of eternity and the beauty of it reflected itself in her expression.

Aaron felt his heart clench and knew himself to be lost. Love at first sight? He wondered, but only for a moment, because in the next instant the pleasure dragged him under, leaving him limp and dazed and thoroughly in love in the center of a magical circle.

TEN

Dear God, Lilli thought as she lay still and breathless beneath Aaron's equally limp form. How could this have happened? How could she have fallen in love with a man she'd known for less than a single day? Less than a single night! This wasn't supposed to be possible. It had been bad enough when she'd known that if things didn't go well with Samael, she would never get a chance to find out what might be between them.

Now she knew, and it was so much worse.

"Lilli?"

She lifted a hand as far as the back of his head, which took about all the strength she could muster, and sifted her fingers through his damp, shaggy hair. "Mmm?"

"I don't suppose you'd like to grab a cup of coffee with me sometime. Maybe have dinner?"

In spite of the gloom that threatened to overwhelm her, Lilli felt herself smiling at his goofy charm. "Are you asking me on a date?"

She felt him nod against her chest and press a kiss to the breast that cushioned his head. "I hope you don't think it's too pushy of me, but I think you're really attractive and easy to talk to and I'd love to have the chance to get to know you better. What do you think?"

Lilli tilted her head down and kissed his cheek, then rubbed her own against the sandpaper stubble she found there. "I think that you should ask me that question again in the morning."

Planting his elbows on the floor, Aaron levered his shoulders off of her torso and grinned down at her. "It's a deal."

When he leaned down to kiss her, Lilli answered him eagerly, savoring one last taste of him before he rolled to the side and let out a long, low whistle.

"Was that for me?" she joked, pushing herself into a sitting position and looking around for her discarded clothes.

"The sentiment is the same, but no." He pointed toward the ceiling. "It was for that."

Lilli followed his gesture up, but all she could see was a collection of shadows above them. The light from the candles blinded her to the rest of the room. "For what? I don't see anything."

Aaron laughed. "Wow, you really are energy blind. That is the biggest, thickest cloud of hot pink energy I have ever seen in my entire life. It's got to be the size of a Volkswagen. You must at least be able to feel it."

Grateful to discover that Aaron's disappearing act with their clothes had been more like a teleportation act, Lilli shrugged and dragged on her dusty BDUs. "Sort of, I guess. I couldn't tell you where it was or name the color or size or anything, but I can tell that the air in here feels . . . thicker somehow." She pulled her shirt back over her head, covering up the gooseflesh that had risen on both of her arms. "I know there's more energy in here than there was before, which was at least part of the point. Let's hope it's enough."

Aaron caught her by the wrist when she began to turn away and held her still. "You do realize that raising energy wasn't the only reason we did that, don't you? It wouldn't matter to me if the apocalypse had already started. If I didn't want you, we wouldn't have had sex just now."

"I know." Lilli offered him a weak smile and wished he wouldn't press. This was going to be hard enough for her as it was. If he kept being so sweet and affectionate, she might not be able to manage it at all. "I'm sorry. I'm getting a little wound up here. That was just nerves talking. I'm reeeeally anxious to get this whole thing over with."

He watched her for an instant longer before his expression relaxed into the easy grin of a satisfied man. "I suppose I should just be glad you didn't say that fifteen minutes ago," he quipped and reached for his glasses before levering himself to his feet.

While Aaron dressed, Lilli moved the blanket, reclaimed her tools, and moved to the southern side of the circle. With the chalk in hand, she knelt and drew a second smaller circle within the confines of the first. The smaller circle was about two and a half feet in diameter and at least a foot from the outer edge of the larger one. It looked big enough for an adult to stand in, but not large enough to allow any steps to be taken. When she was satisfied with the outline, she took a deep breath and used the chalk to draw a complex, sinuous figure in the center, making the sigil large enough to fill most of the blank space. Then she reflexively wiped her hands on her trousers as if even drawing those particular lines and left her somehow dirty.

She bound the circle efficiently with the salt, glad she had poured herself enough to do the job. In the end, only a few grains were left in the little bowl. Setting it aside, she rose and turned to face Aaron.

He had finished dressing while she worked and stood watching her with an intent and focused expression.

"What?" she asked, suddenly self-conscious.

He shook his head. "Nothing. You just do that so seamlessly for a woman who claims not to do magic."

Lilli shrugged. "I don't claim I can't do a few useful spells; I just know better than to call myself a magic user. That would be like only knowing how to make one edible dish and calling myself a chef."

"I think you underestimate yourself. I mean, your father was a devil, so it would make sense that you would have inherited some kind of ability from him."

"The only thing I inherited from my father is my eyes." She hadn't meant the words to come out quite so forcefully, but once they did, she couldn't take them back. "I'm sorry again. I'm just . . . I don't like to talk about my father. Mostly, I don't like to think about him. I really have no idea who he was. He was some sort of hellish soldier who picked my mom up in a nightclub somewhere, talked his way into her pants, and then disappeared."

Unlike the Princes of Hell, minor devils and demons had much greater access to the human plane, many of them able to move freely between the two worlds. Too bad for Lilli.

"I don't remember my mother ever talking about him after she told me the story on my ninth birthday, and frankly that was fine with me," she said. "He's not important to me. He never was. What is important is convincing Samael to exchange the *Praedicti* for his vow not to harm you or start any world-ending wars."

Aaron didn't look convinced, but he let it drop. "All right. We'll leave it alone for now. Does that mean it's show-time?"

"Places, everybody," she confirmed, pushing aside all thoughts of her past and focusing on the future she had left. "The show is about to begin."

ELEVEN

Aaron didn't realize he was holding his breath until he saw the column of energy Lilli had wedged inside the small chalk-defined space begin to spin like a tornado, forming a vortex of power that bounced off the edges of the summoning circle like a possessed, misshapen pinball. Beside him, he could feel Lilli's tension and he wanted to reach out to take her hand in reassurance, but she had warned him not to touch her. If Samael saw the connection between them, she had explained, he would view it as a weakness to exploit. It could give him power over them, and they couldn't afford to give him any advantages.

It took a force of will to keep his hands at his sides, but he managed it. At least he didn't have to worry about trying not to look at her. The sight inside the small circle was so compelling, he didn't think he could have turned away if he'd tried. As he watched, the tornado of energy seemed to bulge in places, as if something trapped inside of it struggled to get out. Before their eyes—or at least before Aaron's—it began to expand, stretching and widening until it filled nearly the entire circle. Then, as fast as it had grown, it contracted, shrinking into a tiny pinprick of light before seeming to explode with a sort of subsonic boom that Aaron didn't so much hear as feel. A hot, bitter wind, it stank of blood and sulfur, and when it passed, Samael stood in the center of the circle, his angelically beautiful face drawn tight and pinched in its intensity.

"I taste lust," he hissed, his soulless gaze locking on Lilli. "I can even smell it. It clings to this place like sewer gas. Have you finally decided to take me up on my offer, pet? Are you going to let me taste that sweet, human flesh of yours?" His expression shifted, smoothing into lines of sly seduction. "I could make it good for you. Mind you, I probably won't, but I'll make you beg me for it anyway."

Aaron knew Lilli suppressed a shudder at that, because he had to do the same. If he'd thought that Samael's presence had made his skin crawl before, this time it was infinitely worse. He had to clench his hands into fists to keep from scratching at the millions of tiny things his nerves told him were swarming over him.

"Not if the future of humanity depended on it," Lilli retorted, and Aaron felt a surge of pride at the steady timbre of her voice. He could sense her disgust as well as her fear, but not even Samael would guess it to hear her speak. "I'd rather see the world go up in flames than let you lay one filthy little hand on me, Sam. That I will swear on the bones of all the saints."

Samael sneered. "You shouldn't make promises you might not be able to keep, little girl. One day I might just make you eat those words."

"But not today." Reaching down, Lilli picked up the manuscript she had placed inside the circle earlier and cradled the heavy volume in her arms. "Now, about why I brought you here tonight."

Aaron saw the devil's eyes fix on the codex and sharpen.

"You found it." A spark of avarice gleamed in Samael's countenance. He quickly hid it behind an expression of mocking disappointment. "Too bad you brought it to me too late.

The deadline passed almost ten minutes ago, Lillith, my love. I'm afraid this means that our agreement is nullified."

"You're welcome to shove your agreement anywhere you'd like. All I want to know is, do you still want the book?"

The devil made a show of indecision. "I'm not sure. I'd hate to gain a reputation as someone who is willing to overlook shoddy performance . . . On the other hand, my extensive private library is a bit of a weakness of mine, I'll admit. Oh, decisions, decisions."

"Before you make up your mind, you might want to hear my price."

"As I already told you, Lillith, dear, I'm afraid I can't consider your final favor repaid after you failed to meet the terms I set out."

"I'm not interested in the favor." She looked grim to Aaron, grim and a little sad. "I'm ready to strike a new bargain. I'll return the book to you if you give your word that you'll make no further attempt to unleash the apocalypse."

Samael threw his head back and laughed. To Aaron, the sound was like a thousand cries of pain all unleashed at once. The devil laughed long and hard. When he finally calmed enough to speak, his voice still quivered with amusement.

"And why on earth do you imagine I'd be willing to strike such a lopsided bargain, my pet?" he asked, and the eyes he fixed on Lilli held something much sharper than laughter. Something more like hatred. "While it's true that having the book in my possession would make everything much, much simpler, it certainly isn't necessary for my plans. This war has been the fondest wish of Hell since the beginning of time. Once I bring it about, every inhabitant of the Nine Hells will owe me allegiance, from the lowest demon to the haughtiest prince. My dear, there aren't enough magical texts in existence to make me abandon my plans, but if you would like to pledge your soul to me now, I would consider keeping your torment brief after my victory."

Aaron heard the hubris that laced every one of the devil prince's words and knew that Samael could already see himself as the newest overlord of Hell. The devil had, oddly enough, been telling the truth; he had too much at stake to accept Lilli's bargain. Seeing that knowledge reflected in her eyes, he felt a surge of anger fill him. Their plan had failed, but while Samael remained in the summoning circle, they were safe from him. The only power he had to hurt them resided in his words. Still, Aaron couldn't help but wish he could blacken the bastard's eye without breaking the protective barrier between them.

"Oh, don't look so disappointed," the devil purred, all of his attention still focused on Lilli. "Just because the book doesn't meet my price doesn't mean that I don't have one. I suppose there is one thing you could do for me that would make me consider postponing my plans for war."

"And what would that be?"

Even before the devil answered, Aaron knew they had walked into a trap. The hair on the back of his neck stood up and the crawling sensation on his skin abruptly changed to the feeling of thousands of angry fire ants all stinging him at once.

The devil smiled a smile that made Aaron's soul cringe and gestured in his direction. "Kill the magus. His family has never brought me anything but trouble. I thought I'd taken care of the last of them when I killed his uncle, but clearly I was mistaken. Correct my oversight and I'll not only halt my work on that little pet project of mine, I'll mark the last favor you owe me paid in full.

"What do you say?"

TWELVE

There it was.

Lilli heard the devil's words through a of fog of pain and fought hard not to let him see their effect on her. Ever since she had laid eyes on that page of four prophecies, she had feared it would come to this. It was the only explanation she could think of that justified Samael sending her after the book. Like he'd said, he hadn't needed it to foment the apocalypse; the only reason he could have needed the book back in his hands was to keep it out of Aaron's.

Aaron—and his uncle, too, Lilli suspected—had looked at the problem from the wrong angle. Each of them had believed that the most powerful prophecy in the book was the one with the greatest potential impact on humanity, but Lilli knew Samael and she knew that he would always view the world through the lens of his own selfishness. To Samael, the question wasn't how would a prophecy affect the world, it was how would a prophecy affect *him*. In the devil's mind, the only prophecy that mattered was the one that spelled out his own downfall.

Samael had never cared about the apocalypse, at least not in the way Aaron and his uncle had assumed. Sure, he wanted to go to war with humanity and wreak havoc and destruction on the mortal plane just as much as any devil, but Lilli would be willing to bet the plans he had supposedly set in motion were a long way from completion. She would bet that he was more than willing to be patient. All that had mattered to Samael had been getting the book back before Aaron realized that the prophecies on the dragon page placed the devil's downfall squarely in his hands.

It was the same reason why the devil had murdered Alistair—because the prophecies said that someone from Aaron's family would be the one to destroy Samael's power. Aaron was a smart man. As long as the codex remained in his hands, Lilli knew that chances were he would put two and two together and decide to take care of the devil once and for all.

But all of those worries would disappear, Lilli knew, if Aaron were dead.

And Samael wanted her to kill him.

"He must have been a pretty good lay," the devil drawled, yanking her attention back to him, "otherwise it wouldn't be such a hard decision. You can kill him, or I can lay waste to all of mankind." He held his hands up like scales and pretended to balance them. "Hm, yes, I can see where that would be a tough call."

Lilli turned her head and looked at Aaron. He was frowning, his brow furrowed, but the hazel eyes watching her were steady and unafraid.

"You do realize he's up to something, don't you?" he asked. "He's trying to trick you. My uncle could count as the first sacrifice. If he gets you to kill me, that's number two. One more and he's won. Game over. The prophecy is fulfilled in one fell swoop, the world is ended, and oops, bad time to be human, I guess."

That's when it hit her, the most ridiculous bits of prophecy suddenly illuminated by an unintentional turn of phrase.

She felt like laughing and crying and knew that either would give her away and ruin her chances of saving the only things that mattered to her.

"Lilli." Aaron's insistent voice dragged her attention back to him. "You know I'm right. You can't trust him. He's the Lord of Deception. You don't think they gave him that title because he's got a talent for acting, do you?"

"I'm not lying about this," Samael pressed. "Kill him and there will be no apocalypse. Is that the kind of offer you're really willing to pass up?"

Lilli shook her head, unable to completely suppress her smile or her tears. She guessed her eyes were glistening as she drew her misericorde from its sheath and held it aloft, the blade catching the light of the candles and sending it bouncing around the circle.

Aaron reached out his hand toward her, his eyes full, not of fear, but of concern. "Lilli, you have to ignore him. You know he's not being honest. If you were to kill me, what's to stop him from reneging on his promise? Who would be able to hold him to it?"

Samael glared at Aaron. "I do not take having my honor impugned lightly, magus," he growled. "I would watch my tongue if I were you."

"You're a devil," Aaron snapped. "The only honor you have is the kind that suits you in any given moment. Lilli is too smart to fall for your lies."

His faith in her made Lilli struggle even harder not to cry. She gripped the hilt of her knife in suddenly damp fingers and stepped forward to press her fingers to his lips.

"Sh," she urged, replacing her touch with the brush of her lips, then repeating the gesture helplessly. "It's okay. You don't have to worry about me."

"Oh, spare me the touching display." Samael's voice grew louder, angrier, but Lilli ignored it. She was not about to let him intrude on the last moment she would ever have with Aaron. She didn't care what the devil had to say. "Get it over with already. You've fucked him; now *kill him!*"

Aaron gripped her upper arms, not as if he were trying to restrain her, but as if he needed to touch her, to feel her beneath his hands again. His palms rubbed at her skin as if to warm and soothe.

"Ignore him," he repeated. "He has nothing to say that you need to hear."

She nodded. She wished she could tell him something that would reassure him, but her throat had closed up against the welling tears, and speech was impossible. Instead, she stepped even closer, until every rise and fall of his chest brought the fabric of his shirt into contact with hers. She wrapped her free hand around his neck and pulled him close, pressing her forehead against his shoulder until her tears soaked through the fabric of both his shirts.

His arms went around her and he cuddled her against him, ignoring the cold steel of the knife she held poised between them as he soothed her with words and touches. "Sh, it's okay, sweetheart. It's okay. You don't need to cry." He slid a finger under her chin and tilted her face up until their eyes met. He smiled down into hers. "Don't cry, Lilli. Everything is going to be fine. I know you're not going to kill me."

Swallowing hard, Lilli licked her lips and managed one final smile before she brushed her lips against his mouth. With skin pressed against skin, she savored the last taste of him and drew him in until his breath become her breath.

"Lilli," he repeated, "I know you're not going to kill me."

"You're right," she whispered brokenly just before she turned the knife and drove it high between her own ribs and deep into her heart.

Aaron felt her body sag against him and tightened his arms automatically. He couldn't manage to wrap his mind around what she had done. While the devil urged her to kill him to save the world, she had chosen to kill herself and condemned him instead to a lifetime without her. He had never guessed she could be so cruel.

In the very instant the knife struck home, the devil behind them let out a howl of fury and threw himself against the side of the circle that imprisoned him, but Lilli's magic held strong. Samael gathered himself for another attack, but before he could launch it, Aaron watched in disbelief as the frantic movement of energy that had presaged his arrival began again in reverse, moving from explosive brightness to a pinprick of light and back to the swirling vortex of energy the magus had witnessed before. This time, however, the energy seemed to suck Samael in, sweeping him up into the funnel cloud and carrying him away until not even the echo of his raging cries of protest lingered inside the summoning circle.

Aaron could have cared less if the circle had suddenly filled with dancing monkeys. Lilli had sacrificed herself for him and now she hung pale and lifeless in his arms. He felt as if the world itself had ceased to spin.

Numb with shock and disbelief, Aaron shifted his grip on the woman he'd first met only hours before and brought her into his lap as he sank to the cement floor. A thin trickle of blood seeped out from around the dagger blade and spilled into his hand, staining his skin an obscene liquid crimson. He felt it cooling rapidly in the open air and thought vaguely that here was the proof of the futility of blood sacrifice. Blood was only precious as long as it flowed inside the body of someone you cared about. Otherwise, it had about as much intrinsic value as tap water.

The first stab of grief hit him with the force of a freight train. If he'd still been standing, he knew his knees would have buckled beneath him. As it was, he doubled over in agony, feeling as if he'd just taken a mule kick right to the kidneys. His heart and stomach clenched in unison and the only thought in his head was that after thirty-five years, he had finally found the woman he loved, and now he would be expected to live the rest of his life without her. He didn't believe it was possible.

What he was thinking in that moment, he didn't know. He acted purely on instinct, which was likely what did it, because if he'd stopped to think, he'd have decided that what he attempted was impossible. Not even the most powerful sorcerer on Earth could bring life back to the dead. Death was the one finality in the universe, and spells that reanimated flesh could never restore the soul that had existed in the living being. So when Aaron placed his palm over the still-bleeding heart of the woman he loved and poured every ounce of energy he had and every ounce of the energy they had raised together into that tiny, cold muscle, he knew somewhere in the back of his mind that his magic was bound to prove useless.

Bending toward her, Aaron rested his forehead against Lilli's silken hair and tried to remember how to breathe. More than his heart felt broken. He felt as if everything inside him had fractured, leaving a million tiny, jagged pieces behind, allowing the tears to seep out from between them.

The first of them fell on her hair and glistened against the dark, shiny strands. Another followed close behind, then another and another until he was weeping for the first time in his adult life.

Maybe the experience confused him so much that when he felt the first tiny movement, he wrote it off as something he had done. He had shifted or jostled her somehow and that was why it felt almost like her fingers had twitched against his leg.

But then he felt a second twitch, and fear and hope began to war inside him.

"Lilli?" he ventured, and his voice was hoarse and soft with grief and doubt.

The soft moan that answered him was the sweetest sound he'd ever heard.

Well, maybe the second sweetest, after the sound of her distinctly cranky voice saying, "Christ, do you think you can pull the knife out for me before it gets welded in place?"

THIRTEEN

Lilli felt as if she'd not only been stabbed in the heart by a lethally sharp assassin's knife—which Aaron quickly removed, praise be—but as if said assassin had then hog-tied her, strapped her down in the middle of the African savannah, and allowed herds of zebra, musk ox, and elephants to stampede across her body. Repeatedly. Too bad she knew she had only herself to blame.

"Lilli!" Aaron's voice held a wealth of emotion, but it overflowed with hope and excitement as he shook her like a pair of dice and called her name repeatedly. "Lilli! You're alive? You're alive! Are you all right? Are you okay? What happened? God, baby, you scared me to death!"

Clenching her teeth mostly kept them from rattling around inside her head, but she would have preferred not to have to put in the effort. "If you don't stop shaking me," she hissed through clenched teeth, "I am going to start having serious doubts about this relationship."

Immediately, the shaking ceased and Aaron's arms wrapped around her, cradling her against his chest while he rained kisses down upon her face.

"God, Lilli, I thought you were dead," he groaned, his body shaking as he said the words. "I thought I'd lost you.

Come on, sweetheart, open your eyes and look at me. Let me see you in there, baby, please. I thought you were dead."

Lilli sighed and took a minute to gather her strength before she could manage to drag her eyelids up and fix her gaze on his. "I'm pretty sure I was, but don't worry about it. I'm feeling better now."

She saw his fear and nearly felt overwhelmed, but then the fear faded and was replaced by relief and joy that left her truly humbled. If she had planned to entertain any doubts about whether he felt as strongly about her as she did about him, they disappeared immediately in the light of those emotions. No one in her life had ever looked at her like that, as if the world would no longer exist if she left it. It kind of frightened her to think she could be that important to someone, but then she realized that was how important Aaron felt to her, and the fear melted under an onslaught of tenderness.

"What happened?" he demanded, shifting her in his lap so that she could meet his gaze without craning her neck. His hands moved over her almost compulsively, as if he needed to touch her to reassure himself that he wasn't imagining her with him. "I saw you stab yourself. I saw you die. What happened?" He paused and glared down at her, his eyes narrowing. "No, wait. Scratch that. First you're going to tell me why you did it, then we can discuss what happened. Lilli, you killed yourself! What the hell were you thinking?"

Lilli sighed. "It hit me when you were trying to convince me not to listen to Samael. You said something about the prophecy being fulfilled in one fell swoop and I realized that it was possible. Not to fulfill the apocalypse prophecy, but to thwart it and to fulfill the valiant knight prophecy all at the same time."

"Explain."

She shifted, feeling strength slowly beginning to return

to her body. At this rate, she might just be able to get up and walk up the stairs to the kitchen by Christmas.

"When I read the valiant knight prophecy, I got hung up on the idea that you were the knight," she explained. "It seemed to make so much sense that it would be talking about you and your family, especially given your uncle's role in all this. I had no reason to look at it any other way. But then Samael kept urging me to kill you and I knew I couldn't do that. Not only could I never bring myself to hurt you, but there was a small part of me that feared you might be right and he was trying to turn you into the second sacrifice for the apocalypse. And that's when you brought up the fell swoop."

Lilli paused for breath and sighed with relief when she realized that the pain in her side had lessened to a dull throb as the wound knit itself back together. She didn't have to look at it to know that was what was happening; she could feel it. Plus, she knew she'd be dying again if a wound that serious stayed open.

"It was like a bolt of inspiration," she continued. "All at once, I remembered what you said about the way to avert the apocalypse being for a righteous demon to spill human and devil blood in one blow and I realized that I was the only person in this situation who could do that. My blood is both human and devil, because of my parents, and while I'm not going to claim to be a saint or anything, I thought there was a pretty good chance that I could qualify as a 'righteous child of Hell.' I mean, I try not to hurt anyone who doesn't deserve it."

Aaron squeezed her gently. "Oh, so I deserved to have my heart broken, did I?"

Lilli stilled and watched him intently. "Did I break your heart?"

He nodded. "But you're doing a pretty good job of putting it back together now, so I suppose I'll be able to forgive you."

She felt happiness warm her like an internal sun and let him see it in her beaming grin. "I appreciate that." There was a short pause while she tried to remember what she'd been saying. "Oh, yeah. Anyway, when I realized that I could fulfill all the requirements for averting the apocalypse, I started to think that maybe the valiant knight in the dragon prophecy wasn't you after all. Maybe it was me."

Aaron looked stunned for a moment, then his expression turned thoughtful as he mulled that over. "You have a brilliant mind?"

"No, you do. And I got the book from you, in between falling ass-over-elbows in love with you. I think you just have to look at the words from a different perspective."

"I think you should forget my question. Your mind is *definitely* brilliant."

Lilli grinned. "So then it just seemed to make sense. If I paid the appropriate price, I might die, but Samael would be banished. And even if I was wrong about the valiant knight prophecy, my sacrifice could still prevent the apocalypse. It seemed worth it to me."

"Well, next time ask me before you decide on that kind of thing." His voice was fierce as he issued the order. "You might have thought it was worth it, but it was a hell of a lot higher than the price I was willing to pay. I'm crazy-assed in love with you, no matter how long we've known each other. That means that the idea of living the rest of my life without you, believing that you killed yourself to avoid having to kill me, is *not* on the list of noble gestures that I can afford."

Lifting her hand, Lilli laid her palm against his cheek and smiled. "I think I'm in love with you, too," she murmured. "In fact, I'm pretty sure I must be, since I think that's what fulfilled the final part of the knight prophecy."

"What do you mean?"

" 'The magic's in the seed,' " she quoted, grinning.

He scowled, then sighed and gave her a raised eyebrow of inquiry.

She repeated the entire line. " 'A knight is fall'n, a prince is fled, the magic's in the seed.' The fallen knight was me, clearly, having just stabbed myself and quite literally fallen, I assume. The fleeing prince was Samael. The payment of the price meant that he was banished back to Hell, at least temporarily. And the magic . . ."

Lilli broke off to feather a kiss across Aaron's lips, smiling when he returned the gesture with interest. It took several breathless minutes before she managed to tear her mouth away from his and another couple to catch her breath.

"The magic," she repeated, her voice husky with tenderness, "was what brought me back to you and healed my wound."

She watched as Aaron verified that for himself. He shoved her shirt up under her arms until he could see the round pink mark where Lilli's misericorde had punctured her fair skin. It was the only remaining sign of her injury.

"You know, my uncle once told me that love was the greatest magic in all the world." Finally relaxing, Aaron cuddled Lilli close and asked about the final aspect of the prophecy. "But where was the seed?"

"Right here." Lilli pressed her palm against his chest, right above his heart, feeling its strong steady beat beneath her fingers.

"And here." Taking his hand in hers, she mirrored the gesture and laid his palm over her own steadily beating heart.

"The magic was in the seed of the brand new feelings we have for each other." She grinned. "It was pretty nice of the prophet to word it that way, actually. If he'd said we had to be fully, deeply in love, things might have gotten hairy. After all, we barely know each other."

In the dim light of the candles and the first faint traces of dawn that peeked into the basement from the open door at the top of the stairs, Lilli and Aaron gazed into each other's eyes and knew that the seed they shared had already sent up a beautiful, leafy bloom. The prophets could say whatever they wanted; in the end, it was love that called the shots.

"Right, that reminds me," Aaron said, reaching up to tuck a stray lock of hair back behind her ear. "I know we've only known each other a few hours now, but what would you say if I asked you to go out with me? I know a place nearby that makes really killer waffles. We could head over there and have some breakfast. My treat. How does that sound?"

Lilli laughed and threw her arms around his neck, hugging him with a burst of returning strength. "I'd say that sounds like one hell of a bargain!"

THE
ROBBER BRIDE

Marjorie M. Liu

ONE

Maggie was too young to remember life before the Big Death, but she had a brain for books, access to books, a great deal of uninterrupted time on her hands with which to *enjoy* those books—and so had, over the years, pieced together a history of the world that she knew was, in part, fiction—but that, like most good lies, rang true. Not that anyone else was privy to her secret history: Maggie knew better than to draw attention to her eccentricities. It was enough that she ran the junkyard for Olo Enclave, and lived alone, and was twenty years old without a husband or prospect.

She had been on her own for years. Her junkyard lay on the outskirts of Olo, which bordered what had been, and still was, the Ohio River. It was settlement number six on the government grid—six out of several thousand, scattered across the former United States—located smack-dab in the new territory of Inohkyten, an acronym of the states thrown together after the Big Death: Indiana, Ohio, Kentucky, and Tennessee. Other territories had their own odd collective names, but when folks in Olo talked about the rest of the country, they just called those places what they had become:

South, North, East, or West, with the Rockies, the Dakotas, and Alaska thrown in, all on their own.

It was spring when the motorcycle man came looking for Maggie. Blue sky morning, with the dew glittering like diamond drops on the tips of the green grass, and the cardinals and magpies lilting full-throated on the naked branches of the oaks and maples, which threatened any day now to burst bud-first with leaves. Maggie, in the old barn workshop, had a clear view of the meadow. Junkyard business stayed on the other side of the building, but when Maggie worked the foundry and tinkered with her machines, she liked a bit of the world in front of her: the *old* world, the world she figured had almost reclaimed itself less than two decades past; a world that undoubtedly would swallow humanity, again.

That very morning, Maggie was experimenting with clay flowerpots, which she had found years ago while scavenging for scrap in the burned-out garage of a home less than ten miles south. Up until now she had used the pots—in vain—to grow miniature roses and small pepper plants. But as no seed she touched ever seemed to reach the sprout stage, there was no loss in finding other ways to take advantage of the unique shape and material of a flowerpot—such as turning it into a furnace for smelting brass.

So far, success. Just some brick to stand the pot upon, a long copper pipe fitted through the hole in the bottom—at the end of which Maggie tied the balloon of an old turkey baster to make the draught—and voilà (a word that she had appropriated from the tattered pages of her dictionary, and that seemed to fit her mood, most days). Charcoal was burning, the heat was intense, and the scrap of brass pipe she had tossed inside was quite obviously melting.

I am, she thought cheerfully, *a clever girl.*

Outside, the gate bell jingled. Maggie thought about not answering—brass was much more interesting than flesh and blood—but out here, folks would come inside anyway and start poking around until they found her. She never liked that much. Her grandfather hadn't, either. Territory was a precious thing, especially now. And word of mouth carried far. You had to keep reminding people of what was yours, until the knowing went so deep that it twined and twisted into the fabric of a place. Until it became part of your identity. Something no person could ever steal.

The bell rang again. Maggie maneuvered an old steel lid on top of the flowerpot foundry, caging the raging heat, and walked quickly through the barn. She shed her gloves, goggles, and a heavy leather apron along the way, running her fingers through her short-cropped hair, and picked up one of the old sledgehammers hanging neatly against the wall. She slung the tool over her shoulder, and ambled out of the barn into the yard.

A man stood just inside the gate, fingering the string of steel bells hanging from the barbed wire wound around the old wooden rails. Maggie stopped in her tracks when she saw him, and not simply because he was a stranger. He was big and lean, dressed in black dusty leather that matched his eyes and long hair. He wore no shirt beneath his open jacket, and his skin was impossibly pale. *Colder than ice,* she thought. Cold as the winter sun, or the river at dawn. His presence cut her senses, and for one moment Maggie knew him, in the same way that she had known her grandfather was dead before ever seeing his body: with certainty, and dread, and vast terrible loneliness.

The man looked at her sideways, tilting his head just so, away from the bells; an odd, graceful movement that affected only his head, so that the rest of him remained perfectly still. He had a piercing gaze, sharper than anyone Maggie had ever met; sharp like a hook in her gut, drawing her toward him. She wanted to take a step, more than anything, almost as much as breathing. But she was good at holding her breath, and did so now as she forced herself to stay rooted in one spot, sweat trickling between her shoulder blades and down her breasts. Her eyes burned from holding his gaze. She felt naked. But after a moment, the strange compulsion to walk toward the stranger eased, and she allowed herself to breathe again.

The man frowned. "You are the fixer?"

"You have something broken?" Maggie asked, surprised at how calm her voice sounded. Her hand felt broken, fiercely aching from squeezing the handle of the sledgehammer.

His frown deepened. "On the road, yes."

Maggie hesitated. "Show me."

He had to think about it, which only made her more uncomfortable. She imagined her sledgehammer swinging toward his perfect face; her heels dug in and she was ready, ready, ready for anything. Maggie had not yet found cause to kill a man, but she had scared away several of them since her grandfather's death. She had a feeling that this one would not take a fright all that easily.

But work was work, and when strangers showed up on her doorstep needing a fixing, it never seemed right to tell them to go away. The nearest Enclave was over a day's walk to the south, across the river. This was the only junkyard in the region to service all those folks looking for spare and rare parts—and she could not, in good conscience, tell anyone desperate enough to make the journey to mosey the hell off her spread.

So Maggie waited, clear-eyed and tense, until the man finally backed away, around the gate. She followed at a safe distance, walking down the short, overgrown drive toward the cracked paved road. Watching him carefully. Finding it hard to determine his age. He had flawless skin, as though he had never spent a day beneath the sun, and he was effortlessly graceful—footsteps light as air. He did not move like the men from Olo or other Enclaves, whose feet seemed to be part of the earth; and as solid. Watching him made her afraid, but she spied a glint of silver through the young oaks, and then passed around the bend and saw the machine that the man had brought to be fixed.

It was a motorcycle. Maggie had never seen one in real life; only in bits and pieces, wreckage, bent scrap; and in pictures from magazines. Like comparing paintings to fossils. But this was real. Onyx, obsidian, made of night; metal polished and shining like some reckless mirage of the past. For the second time since the man's arrival, Maggie stopped breathing. She would never breathe again, if it would keep the machine genuine, and whole.

"Oh, my," she said, unable to look away—knees locked, heart racing. Aware, dimly, that she deserved what she got if the stranger decided to take advantage of her distraction with a good wallop over her head.

He remained near the motorcycle, though, regarding her with a thoughtfulness that continued to unnerve. Sunlight splashed against his hair and clothing, but only served to make him seem more like a shadow.

"It is a small problem," he said, his voice a slow rumble; a rubbing purr against the air. "A torn tire, and nothing more. But I am . . . far from my tools."

Far from home, she imagined he would say instead. *Far from everything known.*

"You need a replacement," she replied, finally looking past the dazzle of chrome to find the ripped tread, so badly torn that there was little doubt he had lost most of the tire while moving at some considerable speed. "I have something."

"And is it right?" asked the man. "Will you serve me well?"

An odd question—or perhaps just odd phrasing—but it irritated Maggie, and before she could stop herself, she replied tartly, "If you plan on paying."

A cold smile touched his mouth, and though the road was bright, the sky blue, and the morning sun shining, the light seemed to dim around him for just a moment; and the spring chill worsened with a snarl of wind.

He reached inside his jacket and then held out his hand. Small flecks of color sparkled against his gloved palm: rubies, emeralds, diamonds. Gemstones. Or plastic. No way to know for certain, though Maggie couldn't imagine anyone parting with the real thing. Not for a tire.

Maggie did not touch the jewels, afraid that doing so would constitute a sealed bargain. She studied them from a distance, marveling at their glitter, but finally shook her head.

"I have no use for them," she told the man.

"Then, what?" he asked dangerously. "What do you want?"

"My life," she said, without thinking—and froze in embarrassment, and fear. But the words slipped off her tongue, and could not be taken back. Part of her wanted to say them again, louder. *My life. Do not take my life.*

Maggie thought he might. She thought he would be able to, if he wanted, no matter how fast she moved, or how hard she fought. He had a way about him.

A cold gleam filled his eyes. "I heard of you. Miles away, I heard of you. The woman who fixes machines. But you are more than that, I think."

"Am I?" asked Maggie carefully. "Where did you come from, that you heard such things?"

But the man did not answer her. He hid away the gems inside his leather coat, and inclined his head so that his long hair fell around his pale face, sharpening and hiding his features until he resembled a fox more than a man—nothing but a pointed chin, high cheekbones, and eyes that glinted golden. Maggie found herself unable to look away from his eyes, and though he studied nothing but her face, she felt as if he was all over her, touching her body in places she did not want to be touched.

"Your life," he said. "I believe that will be an interesting trade."

And then he moved—blindingly quick—and kissed her mouth. Maggie could not fight him. He was too strong. His lips were cold as ice—so cold, dunking her face into a raging winter river might have felt warmer—and in one dizzying moment it seemed as if all the air in her lungs was sucked away, and she was drowning. She screamed, but heard her voice only in her head. She tasted blood.

The man let go. Maggie fell, hitting the road with a grunt, sledgehammer clattering. She stayed on the ground, sprawled on her side, unable to move or lift her head. Paralyzed, drained into boneless exhaustion, trapped; and when warmth oozed unexpectedly through her lower stomach, followed by a stroke of blinding pleasure, she still could not react beyond a startled, sharp inhalation.

Her vision blurred, back-scuffed boots edged close to her face, and a pale hand touched the pavement. Hair brushed her burning cheek.

"Rest," he whispered.

Maggie growled, furious, struggling to move. Her pinky twitched, but that was all, and a terrible feeling of helplessness cut through her anger. Fear filled her, growing until she could barely remember her own name. He had poisoned her, Maggie thought, heart hammering. Poison on his lips. Poison *somewhere*.

The man walked away without a backward glance, and was gone a long time: until the sun rose to midday, and she glimpsed turkey vultures winging high overhead. He returned lugging a tire and some of her tools. Everything exactly as she would have chosen.

He worked quickly to fix his motorcycle, ignoring her efforts to move, and only when he was done, and she was propped up on her elbows, sweating and nauseous, did he look down at her from astride his machine. Shadow rider, shadow steed.

He tossed her lug wrench into the grass beside her. "You have your life. For now. But you waste it in this place, little one. You waste more than you realize."

Maggie gave him the most hateful stare she could muster, which only made him smile.

"Kit with claws," he murmured. "We will see if we cannot make you a lioness."

And then he did something with his feet and hands—kicked and twisted—and the motorcycle roared to life with a wild, deafening, thunderous growl; a glorious, wicked sound that fell through Maggie's bones into her blood, and burned her heart with envy. A black cloud erupted from a chrome pipe, and the man threw back his head, laughing. Maggie's fingers dug into the cracked pavement, reaching for the sledgehammer.

"I am Irdu," he told her, baring his white teeth, which suddenly appeared quite sharp. "Remember that."

His tires squealed with magnificent power, engine roaring, and then he was gone—the growls of the motorcycle drowning Maggie's own sounds of frustration. And yet she watched that machine fly down the road—watched it for as long as she could—and even when it disappeared, its sleek metal body felt more real than the man; like freedom and thunder, and all the perfect beauty that humankind had once held at its fingertips, and taken for granted, and lost in blood.

But where did he get the gasoline? Maggie wondered suddenly.

She was still lying there, thinking about that, when the Junk Woman found her.

TWO

The Junk Woman was *the* oldest woman Maggie had ever known—well ripened, well done, and well wrinkled at the ancient age of seventy-three. She was a "crusty broad" (her words) who had once, long ago, driven a massive sixteen-wheeler across the country, hauling freight for a corporation that made toilet paper and diapers. She had been in Mexico during the first outbreak of the hanta-bola pox— gone into the hills to find herself (and maybe some gold treasure her daddy had told her about)—and by the time she'd come out, the world had changed.

Maggie heard the mules first, the steady clip-clop of their hooves on the old road; and then the jangle of loose metal and bells, and the creak of the axles beneath the wagon. A loud voice sang out about darlings and Clementines, and then the melody shifted into a hearty braying rendition of "A Hundred Bottles of Beer on the Wall," which Maggie was convinced should have stayed dead with the other 70 percent of humanity.

But a thrill of relief passed through her, wild and heady, and she managed to finally sit up as the wagon came into view. Her head hurt, and she spit into the grass, trying to rid her mouth of the taste of blood and ash, and dirty ice. She fumbled for the sledgehammer and the lug wrench, and ignored the tattered remains of the torn motorcycle tire, which the man had tossed aside with no reverence whatsoever.

A horn squawked—a fat sound, repeated in three short bursts—followed by a hoarse, "Hay*looo*, Maggie!"

Maggie raised her hand, waving weakly as the old woman stood up in the wagon, reins held tight in her brown leathery hands. She wore patched denim overalls, and a puffy black coat made of synthetic cloth that was leaking its stuffing at the elbows. A green knit cap covered her head, and two long white braids framed a fine-boned face that might have been pretty once, but had been hardened by sun and wind, and death. Silver glinted against her throat; a bundle of shark's teeth, capped in the precious metal and dangling from a thick chain.

Maggie's gaze skimmed over the flatbed wagon with its large rubber wheels, and salvaged junk glinting through holes in the bolted tarp. Unable to help herself, even now, from wondering what treasures might be hidden beneath. *Crazy,* her granddaddy would have said, and Maggie would have agreed. She forced a lopsided smile as the Junk Woman reined in the team of mules, popped the wagon brake, and hopped down off the rig and came running.

"Hell," muttered the old woman, stopping short to shield her eyes and stare. "Tell me the motherfucker who did this to you is missing his nuts."

"Not quite," said Maggie dryly. "Nice to see you, Trace."

She grunted, and slapped her hand around Maggie's wrist, hauling backward. It took a couple tries, but the younger woman finally rocked upward onto her feet, swaying unsteadily.

Trace slung her sinewy arm around Maggie's waist. "You hurt? Broken?"

"Just my pride," she replied, comforted by the solid, strong warmth of familiar arms. "I thought there were weeks left before you'd come back up this way."

Again, the old woman grunted. She could hold an entire conversation without saying a word, just by the tilt of her eyebrows and the small soft sounds her throat produced.

Words are worthless for everything that matters, she had once told Maggie. *But a little bit of silence can say it all.* And what Maggie was hearing now in Trace's silence was nothing short of *uneasiness*.

The old woman eyed the sledgehammer, and the other scattered tools. "Let me get you to the house. I'll come back for those."

Maggie almost protested, but she shut her mouth when Trace shot her a sharp look, focusing instead on her footing, as she carefully walked up the drive to the junkyard gate. The short distance made her breathless, and she swallowed hard against the bad taste in her mouth. When she was eight, her granddaddy had traded big for a case of old-time Coca-Cola, and for more than a year the two of them had stretched out that fizzy sugar water. Maggie wished she had some now.

She wanted to sit down in the dirt, maybe close her eyes and rest a spell, but once they were on the other side of the gate, bells chiming along the barbed wire, Trace said, "Tell me."

"There was a motorcycle," Maggie replied.

Trace blinked, turning slowly to stare, her expression curiously empty. After waiting in vain for the old woman to say something—anything—Maggie went on from start to finish, fighting to keep the tremble in her knees from spreading to her voice.

She left out the kiss, though. She did not share the man's name, either—or what he had said to her. It was too embarrassing, and more than she wanted to say out loud.

In the end, Trace did little more than grunt, her gaze downcast and thoughtful as she fingered the shark teeth hanging around her neck.

"Well?" asked Maggie, leaning her elbows against the rails of the fence. "Don't you have anything to say?"

"You're lucky to be alive," replied the old woman. "And if you see that man again, don't go lusting after his motorcycle 'fore you bust his brains in with that hammer of yours."

Maggie shook her head. "You should have seen that machine."

Trace rolled her eyes. "Seen 'em plenty, 'fore you were born. Rode 'em once or twice. Just a way of getting around, Maggie Greene. Nothing worth losing your life over. And," she added, "leave it to you to care more about metal than about losing your life to a dangerous man."

"I am what I am," Maggie replied, which was something her granddaddy had been fond of saying.

And that's all I am, he would have added.

Trace frowned, tugging one of her thick white braids. Her dark eyes glinted, as though sparked with sunlight. "Long dark hair, you say? Lily white skin, like a corpse?"

"Cold like one, too," Maggie said, before she could stop herself.

Trace's gaze snapped up. "Didn't say he touched you."

Heat warmed Maggie's face. "Briefly. It's how I got . . . knocked down."

Anger flittered through the old woman's gaze. "And he came here . . . looking just for you."

"Yes," Maggie said uneasily, and pushed herself away from the fence. "Come on, I'm fine. And if he comes back, I'll be ready."

Trace yanked her braid even harder, her other hand tightening around the shark teeth. Maggie tried not to squirm under her sharp gaze, which suddenly felt more intimidating than any strange motorcycle man.

"We'll see," the old woman said ominously, and raked her gaze down Maggie's body. "You've lost weight. Promised your granddaddy I would make sure you stayed strong, and here you are, wasting away."

Maggie blinked, struggling with the change of subject. "You gained some, looks like."

Trace grunted. "Found a gentleman down South. Old Mississippi, if you can imagine it on that antique map of yours. He lives near the coast, in Arbo Enclave. Fat, sassy man who makes the meanest, *hottest* gumbo I *ever* found." She paused. "I think you should come with me, next trip down. You'd like him. And you'd like it *there*."

Maggie looked down at her boots. "I wish you'd stop asking me to leave home."

"Gah." Trace waved her hand, turning in a slow circle to survey the junkyard. "Young people need to see a bit of the world. You, Maggie, you see it all up here, with your books." She tapped her head with one long brown finger. "But words aren't living."

"I'm happy," she protested.

"You're a hard girl to bring down," Trace agreed. "But think about it. You come with me, it's not permanent. Just a season, on the road."

It was a familiar speech, but there was an urgency in her voice that was different, and that made the hairs on Maggie's arms rise.

"Trace," she said carefully, "forgetting, for a moment, what just happened . . . is there something else wrong you're not telling?"

The old woman's expression turned grave and quiet. Maggie stood very still, watching her. The last time she had seen this look had been months after her grandfather's funeral, when Trace had returned from her road trip and discovered that her friend was dead.

"Things are changing," she finally said quietly. "I can

taste it. Life was bad after the Big Death, but folks with common sense stepped in and life smoothed out into something I never expected. Peaceful, Maggie. We got peace in place of death."

"You're saying that's no longer the case?"

Trace gave her a sharp worried look. "I'm saying I've heard rumors, strange ones, and I don't know—"

She never finished. A bundle of black feathers tumbled from the sky, landing roughly on her shoulder. Maggie jumped backward, alarmed, but Trace, aside from a slight flinch and the raising of her eyebrows, seemed none too surprised by the creature suddenly perched on her.

Maggie stared. "You have a crow on your shoulder."

The bird tilted its head, meeting her gaze. Trace shrugged—carefully. "He found me near one of the old city forests, not long 'fore I entered Tennessee. I think he was lonely."

Maggie made a small, non-committal sound—because that was what one did when old women said that crows were lonely. Although, there *was* something about the bird that seemed odd—and not just because it had attached itself to a human, out of the blue. She stepped closer, peering at the crow, and felt herself examined in turn, sharply. Maybe *too* sharply. She felt dizzy, her vision blurring. Again, blurring.

"Maggie," Trace said, touching her shoulder. "Maggie, girl. What's wrong?"

"Nothing," she mumbled, blinking hard. Her dizziness faded. So did her blurred eyesight, though the morning sunlight suddenly seemed too bright, glaring against the old junk and metal heaped around the yard. Everything hurt to look at: the gutted rusting cars, the iron rails, oil drums filled with the detritus of decades past, toasters, hair dryers, television sets, and cell phones. The useful components had already been removed, and what remained suddenly looked less like poetry to Maggie (poetry being the myths that people created) and more like trash.

It unsettled Maggie to feel that way; and it saddened her, too. She liked fiddling with relics from the past. She liked making up stories about objects that had been treasured not so long ago. It made her feel closer to her parents, long dead from the hanta-bola pox. Made her feel close to her grand-daddy, too, who had happened to be looking after her when her folks got caught up in the city outbreaks. He had been gone now for five years, taken by the influenza.

"Come on," Trace said gently. "You head in. I'll take care of my babies, but after that, I've got a surprise for you."

Maggie said nothing, just started walking through the junkyard to the old farmhouse. She looked back once, watching Trace stride down the drive to the road, and saw the crow perched now on the gate, staring back at Maggie. It had a peculiar gaze. She felt assessed and judged all in the same moment, and it made her skin crawl—but in a different way than it felt with the motorcycle man. She was not afraid of the crow. His presence seemed to tickle memories in her brain. Like dreams, forgotten.

Secret histories, whispered a small voice in her mind.

Maggie went into the house and shut the door.

Her grandfather had been a junk man, but only because he had trouble throwing things away. Maggie had a similar problem, but she drew the line at dirty toothbrushes, used floss, underwear past its prime (though nowadays, with cloth at a premium, you would have had to go without it, if you got too picky), and other items that tended to accumulate mold or germs, or were just plain unsightly to behold. Her grandfather, bless him, had not been so discerning, and af-ter he died, it had taken Maggie three years to clean out the house. The problem was twofold: Some things, no matter how disgusting, had sentimental value; and as for the things that could be tossed, there was no good place to put them, so they had to be burned, buried, or stored elsewhere.

The kitchen was clean, though. So was her bedroom. And now there was a much wider path that led through the house to the stairs, and even to the musty couch in the living room, which was only half-covered in books and old newspapers, and glossy magazines with pictures of places, things, and people that Maggie would never have believed or imagined had she not seen them for herself, on the page.

She fixed breakfast for Trace. Eggs were something she had plenty of—animals thrived under her care, unlike plants—and she had made a small business for herself on the side creating odd little toys for children, as well as fixing machinery, whenever she could. Enough to trade for butter and meat, and for some much-needed gardening help from several local teens whom Maggie had taught to read.

She went into the cellar to cut some ham for them both—a special treat—and by the time she returned to the kitchen, Trace was already there, boots off, washing her hands under the pump in the sink. Maggie was grateful that the crow had remained outside.

The old woman was quiet while she ate, and Maggie could not help but notice how her gaze roved from the door to the windows, and flicked back to her, again and again, as though—like the damn bird—she was taking her measure.

"What?" Maggie finally asked, sorely tempted to lick her plate.

Trace looked down at her own plate, pushed her thumb against a small shred of egg her fork could not pick up, and placed it in her mouth.

"Rumors. Rumors about men." Uneasiness filled the old woman's eyes. "A gang of men who travel from Enclave to Enclave, stealing women, sometimes men. Just a handful, here and there."

"They take only people?"

"What food they can carry—but the living seem to take

priority. And 'fore you ask, I don't know where they go with 'em, if they go far at all."

Maggie had read stories about this kind of thing in her books, and in magazines, too—stories about wars where lives were worth more in slavery and in death than in freedom. "You think the man who came here this morning is one of them?"

Trace watched her carefully, tugging the shark teeth hanging around her neck. "Been told they ride motorcycles. Old-time muscle machines. A friend of a friend saw 'em from a distance, out west 'round Oklahoma. He knows what a motorcycle looks like."

And now so did Maggie. Chills rushed through her. She could certainly believe that Irdu might be a kidnapper, and a thief. Though he had not, in the end, hurt her. Or stolen her belongings. He had kept his word, in a rough manner.

"It doesn't make sense," Maggie said. "I've been trying to figure it ever since he left. Motorcycles take fuel. Only the government has access to that, and most solar cells aren't good enough to power a vehicle. Not so that it moves faster than a horse or bicycle, anyway."

"You trust what you saw, and I trust what I was told," replied the old woman solemnly. " 'Sides, you're forgetting something. There *is* gasoline available. Lots of it."

"No," Maggie replied automatically. But as Trace's meaning became clear, the very thing that Maggie had been trying not to consider reared its ugly, horrifying head. "You're crazy."

"It's been long enough."

"There are still bones there."

"Viruses don't live in bones," Trace replied. "I don't think."

Maggie suddenly felt ill. "The government would have opened up the cities if it was safe."

"There's barely a government at all. And after almost twenty years of farting around and letting the forests grow in, and the infrastructure crumble, it would be easier, and cheaper, for 'em to start over somewhere else." Trace leaned forward, drumming her knuckles on the table. "There's gas there, Maggie. Gas in the old cities. Who knows what else?"

Maggie hardly heard the old woman. She had been only a child, but she had lost her parents to the hanta-bola pox, and most everyone knew what *that* was like: to lose someone, maybe everyone, and not in a good, clean way, but in the virus way, which had been spread by breathing and by touch—the virus penetrating into cells, removing skin with neat efficiency, coring people like apples until they flushed their guts and blood. No cure. No time. Death occurred in two days. And almost everyone had started dying at once.

Murder, survivors said. *Terrorists.*

But the scale of the crime still baffled, and haunted. Not just America had suffered, but everyone *everywhere*. Maggie still had old newspapers from those days, before they quit printing. Europe, Asia, South America, Africa—no one had been spared. And for folks who had survived, there was still famine and lawlessness, and other diseases, to contend with.

The idea that men had returned to the city forests, slipping through the lockdown barricades to make homes among the dead—possibly catching the disease, only to spread it, again—was horrifying.

The idea that one of those men had *kissed* her . . .

"No one's doing anything?" she asked, wondering how much time she had before her breakfast reappeared upon the floor.

"No one is *admitting* anything," replied Trace. "Duck their heads like turtles in a shell. Just you wait. It'll happen here, too. No one wants to be responsible for causing a panic."

"We should warn someone anyway."

"No." Trace shook her head, fingering her necklace. "Folks don't believe the bad news until it hits 'em. And once it does, they'll be looking to spread blame."

"Doesn't matter," Maggie protested. "What's right—"

"What's right isn't the same as what's real," interrupted the old woman tersely. "Even if you warn 'em, it'll change *nothing*."

Maggie didn't say anything else but gritted her teeth and began to clear the table. Trace caught her wrist. "I just want you to be prepared, that's all. But I guess you are now."

The young woman nodded carefully, ill with unease. "More than one motorcycle, you said?"

"Listen for thunder and lions growling." Trace smiled grimly. "You hear that on a clear day—any day—you head for the hills."

But that, Maggie later discovered, was easier said than done.

THREE

The crow hung around for two weeks after Trace left. The old woman had a timetable, a set route of junkyards and Enclaves that needed someone who could haul away all those undesirable fixings that no one knew what to do with. *Fools,* Maggie's grandfather had once said. A thing, even an old rundown thing, always had a purpose to it. And if a person waited long enough, they would eventually find out what that was.

If the *crow* had a purpose, he refused to share it with Maggie. Instead, she found herself working long hours in the workshop with that bird perched on chairs and shelves, or the edge of her cold flowerpot furnace, watching her, watching the meadow, watching the things she put together. She'd been bothered at first—a lot—but by the end of the first week, she had gotten used to the bird's company, and by the end of the second, she had to admit that she would miss his sharp little face if he ever decided to take off and find more interesting company.

And she needed a friend now.

It was another clear blue morning when she packed her nylon backpack and headed into town. She rode her new bicycle—Trace's surprise, hauled all the way up from Mississippi. It was a clever little thing the color of a robin's egg, which generated its own electricity every time she pedaled. Not a motorcycle, but almost as fine, and Maggie could kick down the stands attached to its tires and ride it in place inside her workshop to charge her old reclaimed batteries. She had done so every morning and evening to make enough juice to hook up her granddaddy's music box with its silver mirrored discs. She couldn't play many songs, not for long, but it was something special to sit and savor voices that had not been heard for almost twenty years: Gladys Knight, Glen Campbell, Sting, and Vince Gill. She had never heard anything so pretty.

Maggie this morning had toys to trade: puppets made of metal and leather scrap, with wire strings attached to the arms and legs; and whirly-gig fans built from carefully cut fragments of tin sheeting that whistled like ghosts in the wind. She could feel them poking her spine as she rode her bicycle, but it was a good discomfort. She had *made* something; little somethings that might not be food or clothing but that would still be important to someone, somewhere.

The crow came with her into town. He flew above her head, chasing the breeze, silent as her own shadow while she pedaled down the old paved road and over the rolling hills still naked from winter. She passed farms, and was barked at in a friendly manner by both sheep dogs and small children, as she tried to enjoy the early sunlight and the scent of spring.

She tried, too, not to think about Trace alone on the long road, where men might be prowling. And she tried not to think about the motorcycle man and his frightening eyes and dangerous touch. But that was impossible.

Out on her bicycle, alone, all she could think of was that encounter. Night had become insufferable; her dreams, full of thunder and chrome, and faces, pale and wild as lightning, that passed through her mind: men, smiling; men, heads thrown back to pray to the night; men, with mouths filled only with darkness.

You waste more than you realize, Maggie would hear whispered in the shadows, and then she'd bury her head under the covers, trying not to listen as other voices murmured—voices she had drummed away as a child, and hidden deep. She had forgotten what it was like to hear things that others could not—nonsensical sounds, incomprehensible chattering, soft as the wind and the new buds of leaves bursting from the branches of the trees.

She had known when her parents died. Screamed and screamed, clawing at herself. Her granddaddy had been forced to tie her down. Trace had been there, too—the old woman sitting with her, two days straight. Maggie remembered, when she let herself. She could still feel the aching pull of her parents slipping away—and Trace, holding her back, keeping her from joining them.

She remembered what it felt like to die, and not be dead, and how Trace had breathed for her, breathed heat into her mouth, into her body, and made things better.

Or maybe that was her imagination. Holding both truths and lies, like the history she had spun for the world—a secret malleable thing, much of it fantasy—where humankind had traveled once in cars and planes, while in millennia past, flown upon the backs of dragons like storybooks claimed. Or the sphinx, somewhere in the world now stone, moving its slow thighs, in the words of Yeats, gazing upon the world with pitiless eyes.

Sunlight burned. By the time Maggie reached the old highway, she was not the only one on the road. Bicycles were everywhere, along with horse-drawn wagons and small buggies. She recognized all the faces. Folks were bundled up in patched pants and old ragged coats, or hand-knit sweaters fraying at the edges. Refugees had been assigned to different Enclaves by the government, or come to Olo on their own and been accepted by the town council. Maggie re-membered playing with the new children her age, some of whom had not been able to speak English at the time.

Having familiar people around soothed Maggie's nerves, just a little—though the closer she got to town, the more her heart ached and her belly hurt.

Dread, she named it. The same kind that she had felt climbing the stairs to her granddaddy's bedroom, listening to his silence—after a week of constant coughing and fever—even after she had called his name, and knowing, *knowing,* what she would find. Knowing, and going to him anyway.

Just as she was going to town today.

Farmland began making way for clusters of homes, and Maggie heard a lone fiddle playing a mournful tune some-where out of sight. Ahead, the crow landed on the road in front of her, and began cawing, urgently. He had never made a sound, not one that she had heard, but his voice was stri-dent, and he hopped up and down, his wings flapping and his feathers ruffled until he was almost twice his normal size. Maggie stared into his glittering eyes, and her vision blurred so badly that she almost turned her bike over.

One of the men riding nearby aimed for the crow and tried to run it down—Otis Farlowe, his bicycle basket brim-ming with potatoes. The bird squawked impatiently and flew out of the way.

"I remember when my dad used to shoot those things," grumbled the middle-aged farmer, slowing his bike to ride alongside Maggie. "Now we got no bullets to waste."

She nodded, tight-lipped, and glanced up at the sky to search for the crow. He was nowhere in sight.

The road curved around a residential street filled with homes that had been white twenty years ago, but now were gray and battered; though the yards were neat, with not a thing out of place, and the children playing outside looked bright-eyed and freshly scrubbed. She tried to smile at them, but her stomach felt sick. All she could do was stare at the pavement directly ahead of her front tire, and stay upright.

Because of that, it took Maggie a moment to realize Otis had been talking to her.

"I'm sorry," she said, "what was that?"

Otis smiled, tugging down the brim of his ancient cap. "Head in the clouds, Maggie. World is gonna pass you by."

And then he pointed up the road. "I was saying that something seems to be going on in town."

Maggie looked. Main Street was in the distance, a narrow strip of brick buildings and wood-slate awnings covering sidewalks loaded with wares. This time of year, after a long winter, the pickings were limited to nonperishables traded from other Enclaves; or potatoes, cabbages, and jars of preserved fruits and vegetables. Most of the shops in town belonged to the Amish, who had done well during the outbreak—and done even better, afterwards. Partially because they knew how to survive without the old modern fixings, but mostly because they helped each other out.

Maggie could see many of them now, the women clothed in simple dresses and black shawls, while the men stood about in their work clothes: dark trousers, and dark blue and purple shirts, sleeves rolled up to their elbows. Wide-brimmed hats covered their heads. They, and others, stood at the side of the road, watching a man who watched them, in turn.

Just one man, sitting on a motorcycle.

Maggie stopped pedaling, stopped steering, stopped breathing. All she could see was that man. For a moment she thought it was Irdu, but then she saw that a blue flame had been painted against the side of the motorcycle, which made her look more closely at the man. His hair was also long and dark, but he wore faded black jeans instead of leather, and he had a dark feather knotted into a thin braid that hung past his thin face. Other feathers fluttered against his back, forming a long, draping cape, black as ink. Silver flashed at his throat. He wore no shirt, and his skin was so blindingly white, he would have appeared sickly had his body not rippled with lean, hard muscles. His dark eyes, his slow-burning gaze, roved over the crowd—and found Maggie in moments.

The man smiled faintly. Maggie's heart lurched. Very far away, a crow cawed—a stark, bitter sound, cold and lonely— and the man looked away to stare with a sharp glance, into the sky. Maggie clung to the crow's voice, to his angry despair, and found the strength to pedal her bicycle off the street, down a narrow lane between two old homes. No one paid attention. Everyone watched the man as though compelled—as if he was the only thing in the world that existed. She felt it, too, but as with Irdu, she held her breath and stayed steady, strong.

The moment she was behind one of the buildings, with the man out of sight, Maggie slumped against the handlebars and gulped for air. Wings fluttered. She glanced up in time to see the crow swoop close, and managed not to flinch as it landed on her shoulder. The bird was heavier than she had expected, but comfortingly warm, and it stroked her hair with its beak for one brief moment, as if it, too, needed soothing.

"Mister Crow," she whispered, forgetting for a moment that the bird was just a bird. "What just happened?"

The crow made a clicking sound, deep in its throat, and hopped from her shoulder to the ground. Maggie climbed off her bicycle, holding on to the handlebars for balance. Her knees were weak, but she forced herself to inch closer to the street, listening as a single voice floated, soft and insistent. The crow pecked at her ankle, and then snatched at the frayed hem of her old patched jeans, tugging backward. Maggie ignored him. She knew for a fact there was more than one of those men—just how many was the problem.

Maggie peered around the corner of the building. Edward Stoll, Amish patriarch and owner of Stoll's General Store, was scratching his long grey beard as he watched the man on the motorcycle. "Stranger, you've been sitting there for some time now with nary a word. Think you might share your thoughts with the rest of us? We won't bite," he added, smiling faintly, though Maggie heard the tremor of concern in his voice.

He was not the only one who seemed unsettled. Otis stood nearby, his large arms folded over his chest, frowning. Other men, too, were gathered in clusters, trying to look strong, but coming up short against the robber man, who, in his stillness and silence, radiated a terrible natural menace that was, in its own way, utterly alluring. Maggie still felt the pull, and saw that the other women in the crowd did as well. Young and old, all of them staring in fear, but the kind of fear that kept the pulse fluttering high and sweet, with a breathlessness indistinguishable from wonder.

The crow slammed his beak into Maggie's ankle, drawing blood. She flinched, giving him a dirty look, but the pain helped her focus. She looked at the people gathered, more and more arriving by the minute, because it was morning and this was where business got done. Word would have gotten around by now. Not much happened in Olo. Not many strangers arrived, riding machines that should have been impossible to fuel. Everyone would come see. Everyone *was* coming.

In the distance, she heard a rumble; low, like thunder, and so deep and sonorous, she felt the sound in her blood.

Not a scout, she realized. *Bait.*

Maggie choked, frozen, and the roars ripped louder, wild and raw with throbbing heat. Folks started turning, looking around with frowns and whispers, and she fought for her voice, for movement, for anything but the paralysis sinking in her bones.

Move, screamed the voice in her mind. *Move now.*

The crow fluttered up to her shoulder, placed his beak inside her ear, and shrieked. Maggie cried out, knocking him away, but she found herself able to move, and screamed, *"Run!"*

No one did. Men and women she had known her entire life stared at her like she was crazy. Maggie stumbled into the street, grabbing Otis's arm. She swung the farmer around, searching his eyes, aware of the motorcycle man sitting straighter, staring holes into the back of her head.

"Please," she begged him, "Otis—"

Behind her, the motorcycle kicked to life: a magnificent, mechanical snarl that cut through Maggie like an ax. She flinched around that sound—that beautiful sound—and glanced over her shoulder. She saw all of him in a flash—denim and muscle and steel, feathers fluttering wildly—and watched in terrified wonder as the motorcycle's tires squealed, burning rubber, lunging toward her.

Men and women scattered. Otis grabbed Maggie's arm, trying to push her aside, but her legs locked as the motorcycle accelerated—and she finally saw what had been flashing in the sunlight around the man's neck.

Shark teeth, capped in silver, hanging from a chain.

Maggie's vision narrowed. Blood roared in her ears. A dark blur fell from the sky like a hammer, slamming into the side of the man's head. He fell sideways and the motorcycle skidded, trapping him beneath. The crow began screeching, beating his wings with furious energy against the air.

She started to run—running was all she wanted to do—but lurched to a stop after several steps, teetering and looking over her shoulder at the trapped man, who was shoving viciously at the motorcycle that had fallen on his leg. Maggie ran back to him, bent low to the ground. His head was turned away from her, and the sounds of her shoes on the pavement were drowned out by cries and shouts.

He turned to look at her just as she reached him, and she saw his eyes were the same as Irdu's: black, and filled with glints of gold. He snarled at her, but the crow swooped, shrieking, and under a flurry of black feathers, she reached down and snatched the necklace off his neck. The man's hand flashed. His fingers snagged her wrist, his grip so tight, it felt as though he was crushing bone. A strange lassitude flooded her—a split-second desire to lie down and give up—but Maggie focused, and reached into her back pocket for a switchblade.

She stabbed his arm—hesitating for one brief second before sinking the knife into his flesh. Wincing, even as the blade went deep and grated off bone. The man made no sound, but instead writhed, baring his teeth—sharp white teeth.

His fingers loosened and she slipped free, falling on her backside. The switchblade remained in his arm, and the crow flew at her, cawing wildly. Beyond the bird, the man continued to stare, his gaze burning through her with power. But not the same power as Irdu's. Weaker, different, like the heat of sunlight in winter and in summer.

"Stay," hissed the man, wrenching the switchblade from his bleeding arm. "Stay."

Maggie did not stay. She scrabbled to her feet, turned, and ran. Shark teeth dug into her palm. She barely saw the faces that stared at her, or heard their voices calling out. She wanted to tell them to run, but her throat choked, and she could not stop. Her legs refused to slow.

She raced back to her bicycle, leaped onto the seat, and began pedaling hard. No direction at first; just steering across lawns and narrow streets, heading in a straight line out of town. Somewhere near, engines roared, and a bitter acrid scent filled the air. Burning gasoline, she thought, and suddenly glimpsed leather-clad men between the houses, all of them headed toward the center of town.

They were already nearby, she thought grimly. *And you knew. You knew they might be coming and warned no one.*

Behind her, screams filled the air, but all she could see were shark teeth, dangling and glittering. Trace's good luck charm. She never took it off. Maggie tossed the necklace over her head to keep it safe. It was heavier than she expected, the chain cold. She rubbed her palm against her stinging eyes, and pedaled harder.

The crow flew overhead. At the edge of town she rode through the old graveyard, heading straight from the walking trails into a farmer's bordering land. Maggie threw her bike over the fence, followed awkwardly, and started pushing. Halfway across the pasture she heard the ripping roar of motorcycles, and dropped down into the scrubby grass. She could see the road from where she crouched, and glimpsed chrome flashing.

Maggie flattened herself even more, but not enough to keep her from watching as thirteen motorcycles rumbled out of town. At least five of the men held women in front of them, dresses and shawls fluttering. They only seemed conscious: none were struggling, just sitting upright, eyes open and staring blindly. The man who had worn Trace's necklace was easy to find—he was the only one without a shirt—and the feathery cape flowed behind him like wings. Blood flowed down his pale arm.

Irdu led the pack. Maggie was certain of it. He turned his head to look in her direction, and she knew his face, even from a distance. She recognized his motorcycle, the only one that was unadorned.

She watched the men until they rode out of sight, and when they were gone, the growls of their motorcycles fading, she rolled on her back and stared at a sky that was not quite as blue and a sun not as warm, and wiped her eyes and nose, trying not to cry.

The crow landed beside her, making small throaty noises.

Maggie rolled on her side, staring into his dark eyes, and clutched the jangling shark teeth in one hand, and then pressed them against her flushed cheek.

"What do you know?" she asked him, certain now that he was no ordinary crow versed well enough in myths and fairy-tales of magic that she could believe in odd things. In a world where most everyone had died, it seemed to her that *odd* was the new normal, and that normal was in the eyes of the be-holder . . . as the old saying went.

The crow, of course, said nothing. But words were in there, crow words, ticking around his brain. Maggie knew it. She could almost hear them, and stroked his chest with the back of her trembling hand. "A necklace doesn't mean much. She might be alive."

Or not. But the *might be* was stronger. So was Trace. She had survived the Big Death and the chaos that followed, and was still sharp and whole and healthy. Robber men and their motorcycles were nothing. *Nothing.*

And if she told herself that long enough, she thought she just might believe it.

Maggie did not go back to town. She could not bear it. She traveled cross-country toward home, pushing her bicycle among cattle and horses, and through idle fields waiting for their spring plowing. She walked through the forest, hauling her bicycle up and down the barren hills, and though she sweated and her muscles ached, she did not notice. All she could think of was the old woman. The shark teeth re-mained cold against her skin.

It took her all day to return home. Sunlight was almost gone. The air still smelled acrid and there were wheel marks in the dirt of the yard. Maggie leaned her bicycle inside the barn, surveying her workshop: half-finished toys and other items she tinkered with, her tools, decades of junk stacked and neatly organized. Her sledgehammer was the only thing out of place. She found it on the bench. A message had been written into the handle, in a thick black ink that Maggie had not seen in years.

A test of truth. Find us, if you can. You know why.

Maggie closed her eyes, pressing her brow against the cold, hard steel. She took the sledgehammer with her into the house and laid it on the table; then cooked a big meal. She fried up all the ham and boiled eggs. She made corn bread. She ate only a little and wrapped the rest, along with some clothes and a blanket.

Maggie strapped on her tool belt, and slid the sledgehammer into place. She went outside and set her chickens loose.

And then, carefully, Maggie locked her house, loaded her things onto her bicycle, and rode under the cover of darkness away from the junkyard. She headed north, because that was where Trace had gone, and the direction that Irdu had been leading his men. Fistfuls of stars glittered, rivers of stars, and the night was cool and quiet.

Maggie listened for thunder.

FOUR

For the first two days, Maggie rode only at night, resting during the day off the road, inside the forest. She had been surprised twice by the motorcycle men, in broad daylight, and though she was quite certain that traveling at night provided little, if any, protection at all, it made her feel better. She could see well in the dark, and the crow rode upon her shoulder as she pedaled silently down the long road, listening to the tread of her tires, the wind, and the thrush of branches beneath the glittering stars.

She met no other travelers at night, though she passed the skeletons of old towns, fallen into rubble. If folks lived there, they did so quietly—and Maggie did not linger. Enclaves might be full of busybodies and gossip, and folks who rubbed you the wrong way, but there was something to be said for familiar faces and community, and knowing you had a place in the world.

Fixer, Maggie reminded herself, trying to bolster her courage. *You fix things. You'll fix this.*

"I don't suppose *you* have a plan?" Maggie asked the crow.

Not one you want to hear, she imagined his reply, masculine but soft.

And because Maggie was more than willing to indulge her imagination, she replied, "Try me."

The crow fluttered his wings, giving her a sharp look, but she attributed it to a deep crack in the pavement that made the bicycle bump up and down. After steering around clumps of weeds, and a lonely hubcap that Maggie very much wanted to salvage, she imagined a quiet male voice whisper, *You must trick them. You must be them.*

"I'm not anything like them," Maggie protested.

But the crow remained silent, even when she reached up and poked him gently in the chest. He merely rocked a bit on her shoulder, and then rubbed his head against her ear.

It was near dawn when Maggie stopped to rest, venturing far off the road into the woods. She did not want to get off her bicycle. She was ready now, because of the crow, to go on the road during the day. A little faith, some trust, an idea that he would warn her if danger was close; all these things that should have been impossible she accepted, if with some trepidation—and desperation.

I just need to know, Maggie kept telling herself, feeling her stomach sore with hunger and fear. *Alive or dead, I need to know for certain what happened to Trace.*

But her body refused her. She could not go another mile without sleep.

The redbud trees were blooming so thick in the undergrowth that in the predawn light, they seemed less like trees and more like a vast pink mist, delicate and rosy. Maggie brushed her fingers against the soft clumps of blooms and left her bicycle leaning against one of the stout little trees, then she unfolded her blanket and spread it over the dead leaves.

She unbuckled her tool belt, and pulled the sledgehammer free, laying it on the blanket beside her. She ran her fingers over the message, and then through her hair, rubbing her scalp, searching for unusual bumps. It was too cool yet for ticks, probably, but if she stayed out in these woods much longer it would be a problem. She had cut her hair short for that reason, and because it was hard to keep long hair clean and out of the way.

Maggie ate her last boiled egg, and shared small chunks of cornbread with the crow, giving him the very last piece in her handkerchief. The crow tilted his head, picked up the cornbread, and dropped it back into her hand.

Maggie sighed, stroked his little head, and split the piece in half. She ate one chunk of it, and this time, he pecked away at the other.

"You're not normal," she said to him, as he ate. "I get that. But why stick with me?"

The crow did not stop tearing at the cornbread, though inside her head Maggie heard a soft voice whisper, *You are not so normal either.*

Obviously, thought Maggie, scowling—stretching out on her blanket and trying to roll herself up into a warm ball. She adjusted the shark teeth necklace so it did not poke her skin. "And?"

This is a new world. He stopped pecking at crumbs and gave her a long look that was uncanny and keen. *A world where girls may speak to birds, and where birds might be more than feather and bone.*

"I'm imagining this," she told him, eyes drifting shut. "I'm indulging voices in my head because I'm lonely."

The world has become a lonelier place, he replied, hopping close. *Some of us miss the humans.*

"And some prey on them," Maggie mumbled, half-asleep, not quite certain what was coming out of her mouth.

She hardly felt the crow touch her cheek, and was barely awake enough to appreciate the surprising softness of his beak as it rested near her lips.

There are some who prey on us all, he whispered, and that was all Maggie heard before drifting deep into sleep.

* * *

Maggie heard voices in her dreams, a swift endless chatter from the shadows. Soothing voices, familiar, and she drifted upon words and sighs, eavesdropping in her sleep though she could not understand a thing that was said. She woke slowly, and the warm thrush of voices continued unabated, chirring and sweet. A faint breeze stirred against her face. She opened her eyes, just a little, and found the redbud blooms rising off wizened branches to flit like fireflies, but with flowers instead of light. Maggie watched them, thinking she must still be dreaming, and smiled at the wee symphony of movement.

Perhaps that was too much awareness. Flying flowers faltered. Maggie's vision became blurred, and she rubbed her eyes. When she could see again, the dance had ended, and the world had resumed its natural order: still, quiet, and ordinary.

She lay unmoving for quite some time, staring at those branches and the redbud blooms—taking note, too, of the blue sky overhead and the glint of sunlight through the trees. She did not think she had slept long, perhaps only to mid-morning. Maggie rubbed her face. Her nose felt cold. She untangled herself from her blanket, stretching out the crick in her neck. Two nights now, sleeping under the sky in the cold spring air. Not ideal. She jumped in place, rubbing her arms, trying to get her blood moving. She searched the trees for the crow.

She did not see him.

Dismay set in, and then concern. Maggie struggled not to feel either; or worse, not to feel fear. The crow was just that—a bird—and if he chose to fly about, doing what came naturally, that was his business. It did not mean he had abandoned her. At least, she hoped not.

Maggie stumbled around the redbud trees, searching for a good spot to use as a latrine, and heard water splashing.

She froze, head tilted, and then heard the sound again, faintly. She followed, pretending she was a ghost, silent as she picked her way over dead leaves, ducking under redbud branches. Petals floated down upon her shoulders and head.

She found a creek nearby, flowing around the base of a small hill. Oaks and maples twisted their roots through the water, which rushed quietly over large glistening rocks. Downstream, where the current quieted, there crouched a naked man. He was ankle deep, bent low as he furtively spilled handfuls of water over his lean, muscled back. His dark hair, cut short and ragged, hung wet and rough around his face, which she could see little of except for the profile of a strong jaw. His skin was golden brown, his hands large and elegant, moving with particular grace.

Maggie stared, rooted to one spot. Suffering from a compulsion, not unlike the one she had experienced with Irdu, to draw near, to see more, to be close for no reason, other than that it seemed right. Only, this was her own particular desire, and not something forced into her mind, as she suspected Irdu and his men had done, to her and others. She remembered how docile those women had been, as they were carried away on the motorcycles. No woman in Olo was that meek, Amish or otherwise.

Maggie took a step, and the man flinched, looking over his shoulder at her. She glimpsed a raging, burning gaze, wild and dark, and she felt a physical jolt, like a good shake. The man burst from the water, snatching up a dark robe from the dead leaves on the shore.

He ran. Maggie stared, voice choking in her throat. She wanted to tell him to wait, but it was no good. He was too fast. The robe he clutched to his chest trailed around him, fluttering. It was made of black feathers, she realized— long, shining, and sleek.

She thought about that for a moment, breathless, and then turned slowly and walked back to her bicycle, staring at nothing in particular as she stumbled through the redbuds, replaying that scene over and over in her mind. She searched those eyes. Considering the possibilities.

By the time she started pedaling down the old road, the crow was high overhead, little more than a speck of shadow.

Maggie reached Dubois Enclave late that afternoon. The border was marked with a single government-posted sign, jammed into the side of the road. It still looked new: bright green, with neat white letters. Olo's sign was only five years old, and every now and then one of the Amish families sent their children out to weed around the wood post, and in the summer, to tend the petunias planted at its base. Dubois did not seem to care as much. Dead leaves and tall grass were its only decoration; but then, it was hardly spring.

She followed the road as it curved and twisted upward, into the hills. Her thighs burned, as did her lungs. The shark teeth were cold against her flushed skin.

The crow swept low over her head, into the trees, their branches bursting with new buds of green leaves. The air was cool and smelled like rain, and the sunlight flowing through the clouds was silver. No vultures in the sky. It had been years since Maggie had traveled outside Olo, but she had never been this far north to Dubois. She passed dirt tracks that faded into the forest, and somewhere in the distance she heard dogs barking. Maggie saw no signs of people, though she felt watched—and startled a small herd of deer grazing at the side of the road.

The barricade took her by surprise. She came upon it while pedaling up the curving road. A ravine was on her left, and a steep hill of jutting limestone on her right. She had to brake fast, front wheels wobbling, and she slammed her boots into the pavement to keep from tipping.

Fallen trees blocked the road, a very deliberate wall of logs and branches, so freshly cut she could smell the sap and sweetness of new wood. Two men and one woman sat on the logs, holding axes, old hunting bows, and rifles that Maggie thought were probably not loaded (though she was unwilling to bet her life on that). All three were dressed in old pants and thick jackets, glimpses of synthetic cloth still visible between hand-stitched patches of fur, leather, and government-issued cotton.

No one spoke as she drew near, no warnings, not one greeting—nothing but cold scrutiny and silence. Approaching them, Maggie felt a bit like a robber herself: dangerous, an outlaw. She watched their hands tighten around the weapons, and the shadows deepening in their eyes.

"I'm looking for someone," Maggie called out, dismounting slowly from her bicycle. "Trace, the Junk Woman. I know she comes through here sometimes. I'm worried she might have been hurt. By men on the road."

"Men on the road," echoed the woman, who was as brown and wrinkled as stiff leather, though her fingers were supple enough to hold the ax handle. "Motorcycle men, though God only knows how those machines still run. Yes. We've had dealings with them."

"And Trace," added another fellow, who had a different look about him, with his coarse black hair and eyes—Asian, maybe, or Native Indian. "She was here little over a week ago, stayed for a bit, and left. She was fine then."

Fine. Alive. Maggie struggled with herself. "Do you know if she went north?"

"Up to Martins. Said there was a detour she had to make, but that she would take some letters for us."

Martins was another three days' journey from here—never mind any detours. Maggie had a bad feeling that Trace had not arrived at her destination. She tapped her thigh, thinking about the message written on the handle of her sledge-hammer, the necklace hanging heavy beneath her shirt, and felt those people scrutinizing her with an intensity that made her uneasy. Best not to linger, she thought. Strangers were unwelcome now.

"I don't suppose I could trade for food?" asked Maggie. "I won't bother you for more than that."

The woman gave her a skeptical look. "Trade? You've got nothing I can see, except maybe your tools and the rig you're riding."

Maggie took off her backpack and crouched. Carefully, a little afraid they would be bent or broken, she removed the small puppets and whirly-gig fans that she had intended to trade in Olo. Much to her relief, all the small toys were intact, and she dangled the puppets and made them dance; and blew on the whirly-gig until its fans spun and whistled like ghosts. The men and woman were not easy to make smile, but they did finally, nudging each other with grim amusement.

The Asian fellow relaxed his hold on the compound bow, leaning it against his leg. "Just food, you want?"

"That's all I need. And I can only afford to part with one of these." In case there were other Enclaves she needed to trade with, Maggie thought.

The woman tore her gaze from the puppet to Maggie. "I know you now. You're the Fixer from Olo."

She might as well have called Maggie a bad name. The men gave their companion a startled look, and then turned their sharp focus on Maggie. The little progress she had made in relaxing them disappeared. Distrust settled again in their eyes, and anger.

"Is there a problem with that?" Maggie asked slowly.

"One of the robber men mentioned you," said the woman, eyes narrowed, but with thoughtfulness, and not the same suspicion as the men. "You, specifically. He made a point of telling us that you might pass through here. He said . . . you were good at fixing things."

"Like motorcycles," added the other man; a freckled,

tousled redhead who had been silent until now, and who had not stopped staring at Maggie since her arrival. "Is that what you did for them? Did you *help* those men?"

"No," Maggie replied sharply, giving him a hard look. "But one of them . . . knocked me out. Took what he needed."

"But not you," said the woman. "He didn't take *you*."

"He took enough." Maggie stared dead into the woman's eyes, daring her to interpret that as she wished. "Am I going to have trouble here?"

"No," began the Asian man, but he stopped as the woman's frown deepened, and she chewed the inside of her hollow cheek.

"I knew your grandfather," she said finally. "I came to Olo once so he could fix my plow. I remember you. Little spit of a thing, not more than five or six. You told me my future that day."

"I doubt that," Maggie replied, though a chill rolled over her arms. She bent to pack up her toys, and the woman crouched, touching her wrist.

"You said," she whispered, "that I would have no children of my own, but that I would take in new blood. You said to watch for the green man, because he would try to hurt my family."

Maggie went very still, memories rushing—memories that she had not known she possessed. She recalled a hot dusty day sitting in the shade of the barn, playing with a little wooden horse her granddaddy had carved for her. A long shadow had joined her, a woman in jeans and boots, with a long knife strapped to her waist. The woman had asked her a question about the toy, and her voice had melted into the shadows, sparking images; dreams, waking in Maggie's head.

She remembered that, and more, and it made her breathless, and ill. "Hello, Ellen."

The older woman rocked gently on her heels, rubbing her

jaw. "Not long after I met you, some kids came in on the last of the refugee buses. I was forced to take them, even though I had no interest. But we got along. I loved them. And then a man came to town, one of those traveling types—a teacher, he said—and oh, what a fine green coat he had! But I remembered what you said. I kept an eye on him. And when I found him one morning with my little Eddie . . ."

The woman stopped, and looked down at the puppets. "You saved the boy. Other children, too." She fingered one of the toys, tweaking a small metal arm. "I'll trade you for this one."

Maggie stared, stricken. But the deal was done. Ellen offered a jar of pear preserves, a chunk of dried beef, a loaf of bread, and cheese. Maggie accepted without argument, and the men—after a brief hesitation—helped drag her bicycle over the barrier of fallen logs. Neither one looked her in the eye. Maggie did not want to be around them, either. She did not trust herself—not her memories, nothing. She wondered what else she had made herself forget.

Ellen did not invite Maggie into town. She left her to fetch the goods, riding away on a lean fast bicycle. Maggie waited uncomfortably with the two men, who sat with equal discomfort a short distance away, on top of the barrier. The crow perched in a tree above them, but she did not think they noticed.

"So, you're psychic," said the Asian man finally, looking sideways at her from his survey of the empty quiet road.

"No," Maggie replied.

The redheaded man muttered, "Your town was hit, right? People taken? Not a good psychic if you didn't see that."

"I'm not psychic," she said, wondering if she would have to use the sledgehammer, after all; or make a run for it. But neither man moved, or looked at her, and after a short time the Asian fellow slowly, haltingly, shared a tale of men and motorcycles. Dubois, it seemed, had lost four women and two young men. Some had families. Nothing had slowed the kidnappers; not rocks, not baseball bats, not knives. They had not played bait and snatch, but simply roared in on thunder and taken what was in front of them.

Maggie frowned. "Did you try to follow your people? To see where they were taken?"

"We tried," said the redheaded man hesitantly, a flush staining his cheeks. "They were too fast. We had others to think about, in case there was a second attack."

You gave your people up for dead, she thought, but hardly blamed them. Death had become common. It was survival that mattered. Maggie knew she was nuts to look for Trace. She knew, too, that she was cold-hearted for hardly thinking of anyone else who had been kidnapped—forgetting them, even. But she could not help everyone; couldn't even help herself.

Silence, after that. The men did not even ask about Olo, which under other circumstances would have been odd. News from other places was rare. They watched the road and Maggie, and Maggie watched her feet and the crow. She was almost sick with tension by the time Ellen returned with the food.

Maggie turned down offers of a free bed, though her body ached for something soft to rest on and a hot meal. But the shark teeth were cold against her skin, and above her head the crow fluttered his wings. She packed up her toys and loaded her bicycle with food. She waved good-bye to the men, who acknowledged her only with a nod, and pushed her bicycle a short distance down the road, while Ellen walked by her side.

"Are any old city forests nearby?" asked Maggie, knowing full well the answer, but wanting to gauge the woman's reaction.

The response was as Maggie expected. Even after twenty years, Ellen flinched, distaste and fear flickering in her eyes.

She was old enough to remember the bad times, and Maggie was suddenly glad she had been too little, too well protected in the distant countryside, to do more than learn from afar that her parents had died.

"Several days east of here, along the old freeway, if you're on foot," replied Ellen, a warning tone in her voice. "But I wouldn't really know."

Maggie nodded, and swung her leg over the bicycle. Ellen grabbed her arm. "Those men had another message. It was also meant for you."

Maggie's gut twisted painfully. "I'm surprised you're letting me walk out of here, as much as I was mentioned."

"I'll get flak for it. But you'll be gone, and folks trust me."

Maggie shook her head. "What was it?"

Ellen hesitated, grim. "Don't give up. That's what he told us to pass on to you. *Don't give up if you want to find your teeth.*"

A bad taste rose inside Maggie's throat, and she swallowed the urge to spit on the road. *Son of a bitch,* her granddaddy would have said, and Maggie found herself mouthing the same words. *Son of a bitch.*

Ellen had not yet released her arm, and her fingers tightened. "You, girl. Do you know what you're doing?"

"What I have to," she said coldly.

"And can you still see the future?"

Of course not, Maggie almost replied, but in that moment her vision blurred, and images raced through her mind; a torrent of shadows shrouding petals, feathers, and chrome. She blinked once and saw Ellen sprawled facedown in snow. A brace of frozen rabbits hung from her belt. Her skin was blue. She was not moving.

The vision broke. Maggie blinked again, rubbing her burning eyes. When she looked at Ellen, the woman was too bright, the entire world shining, and she had to squint just to see.

"Girl," said Ellen.

Maggie looked down at her hands, searching for words. "If it snows . . . don't go out alone. Don't check your lines. Stay home. Stay home if it snows, Ellen, even if you're hungry."

Ellen's hand fell away. Maggie forced herself to look at the woman, and found her gaze hard and flinty. But Ellen tightened her mouth and nodded once, like she understood.

Maggie said good-bye and pedaled away.

FIVE

Near evening it began to rain, winds kicking up with wild strength. The crow had led Maggie to an abandoned farmhouse, sagging on its foundation some distance off the road.

"You're sure no one's in there?" she asked the bird, wiping rain from her face, hesitant to venture inside. Most of the window glass was gone, and an oak tree was growing through the porch.

Trust me, the crow replied, perched on the edge of her bicycle's basket. *We're beyond humans now.*

Maggie was still cautious, though. She kept one hand on the sledgehammer. Inside was dark, and a cursory examination revealed little that was useful. Most everything except the floorboards had been taken away, and she supposed that eventually those would go, too. Maggie would not have waited this long to harvest them. There was linoleum in the kitchen that would be worth a good trade, and the insulation behind the walls could be used in another home. The Formica countertops were still in place, but the cabinet doors had been taken. An old clock hung on the wall, tilted at an angle.

The crow sat with Maggie during dinner as she curled up on her blanket, eating with her fingers and tossing him bits of bread and pear. She was in the dining room, just outside the kitchen. The wallpaper was peeling. Her tool belt lay beside her head, but she had pulled the sledgehammer free. She did not read the message on the handle, though it was impossible not to notice. The words, so large and black, seemed to crawl like spider legs in the corner of her vision. When she lay down, resting her head in her arms, she turned away from the tool and faced the crow. He remained at the edge of her blanket, and stroked her hair with his beak.

"Why are you different?" she asked him softly, as the rain began drumming harder against the roof, and the winds howled. Shark teeth had spilled out from beneath the collar of her shirt, and the floor was cold beneath her blanket. When her fingertips brushed against the dark, scratched wood, she heard children laughing, and smelled sweet cake, freshly baked and warm.

I am me, replied the crow gently. *Just as you are you. We were born this way.*

"My parents were normal," Maggie said. "I think."

The crow flipped his wings. *There would be no shame in it if they were not.*

"And the men with their motorcycles?" Maggie peered into his dark glittering eyes. "What about them?"

He ducked his head, busying himself with an invisible crumb. She touched his wing and pushed gently. He hardly budged. Sturdy little bird. Maggie thought about the man in the creek—lean, brown, effortlessly wild—and stopped stroking the crow's sleek back.

She imagined that he sighed, gently. *They are not men. They are something older. Their kind existed before the humans died, existed while humans were in their infancy, but in secret. Always, in secret.*

Maggie thought of Irdu's cold kiss, and shivered. "What do they do with those people they take?"

They hurt them, said the crow.

She closed her eyes. "One was wearing Trace's necklace. You think she's dead?"

I think she is strong. I think there is time.

"He was also wearing feathers."

The crow made a small throaty sound. She opened her eyes and found him staring at her, so intensely and with such sharp intelligence that she gave up thinking of him as a bird. Never again. He was only pretending, she thought. Wearing a mask.

Maggie mumbled, "Why are you *really* helping me?"

Lightning flickered outside, and thunder rumbled. The crow flinched, and hunched so deeply, his head almost disappeared within his ruffled feathers.

Someone was stolen from me, he whispered. *Very long ago.*

Maggie did not know what to say. Her hand inched close, but she did not touch him. She just waited, and closed her eyes. The crow, after a moment, pressed the side of his sleek, warm head against her fingers.

She was not certain who was comforting whom.

Silence was heavy. Maggie tried to relax, but her thoughts stumbled over Ellen, and then Trace. She thought of her granddaddy, too. Big strong man, always pale, with large freckled hands and silver hair that sometimes in the sunlight revealed glimpses of red. Carver Greene. Maggie had some of his red in her hair, passed down through her daddy—who had been a football star before the Big Death. "Professional ball-thrower" sounded kind of odd to her.

She tried to remember interacting with her mother, but that, as usual, was impossible. Maggie had pictures, but nothing else. She had been small, though very elegant and keenly dressed in suits and heels, which no one in their right mind would wear now, at least not in the Enclaves.

Her family. She had never questioned those bonds, and still did not. But she was different from other people—just a bit—and she wondered where that came from. Granddaddy had been eccentric, she thought, but not . . . odd. Not strange—as in telling the future, or hearing voices.

Maggie knew nothing about her parents, though. Or what they had known about her.

There's more you're not telling yourself, came the unbidden thought. *More you can do. More you can become.*

Maggie hoped not. She wanted nothing of it. Just her quiet normal life—fixing things, making toys for children. Playing with the relics of the past, and turning them into something new.

She was still thinking about that as she drifted off to sleep and began to dream, gently, at first. She stood in her workshop, staring out the barn door into the meadow where the morning light trickled, sledgehammer in hand, and the foundry fires burning. But the gate bells jangled, and dread filled her heart. Maggie, in her dream, turned—and found herself plunged into darkness.

Irdu floated like a single claw, surrounded by men, and she tumbled through shadows hiding pale faces, and bottomless mouths that swallowed her whole. She could not fight their hunger—not even to run and hide—and in her dream she squeezed shut her eyes. As if not looking at them would save her.

But it did not. Instead of seeing the men, Maggie saw herself—and her face was a mirror of their hunger, pale and haunted, and merciless. She scratched at her cheeks, and her nails were claws; and when she screamed, her voice merely groaned, an aching sound like the shifting grind of mountain stone.

Behind her, Trace floated free of the darkness. She was younger, her brown skin as flawless as dark cream; only, her eyes were as black as ink, inhuman and cold, and her mouth was full of long white teeth.

Things change, she whispered throatily. *We can change. We can forget what we were meant to be.*

I am not this, Maggie told her.

You don't know what you are, Trace replied, and reached inside her mouth. She began to pull out her teeth. One by one. Sharp and white. Like a shark's.

Maggie stared, horrified. Until, suddenly, another presence entered her dream—someone solid and real—and strong arms slid around her waist, pulling her close against a broad, warm chest. Trace faded into the shadows, as did Maggie's monstrous reflection.

Do not be afraid, whispered a familiar voice. *Maggie, I am here.*

Here, where? she murmured in despair, accepting him as though he had always been with her—her crow, who was now a man. *What am I? What am I doing?*

Hunting, he rumbled. *Hunting hearts.*

Maggie sagged within the circle of his arms. *I don't know what that means.*

His warm mouth brushed against her ear, and those arms turned her around until she placed her hands against a hard chest that was searing to touch and shockingly naked. She had never touched a man—not like this, even in a dream—and the sensation sent a jolt from her heart into her stomach.

He kissed her cheek, and then her mouth, gently. "Never mind," he said, his voice no longer echoing through her mind. "Maggie, rest. Go back to sleep."

"I *am* asleep," she mumbled, wanting more of his mouth.

"Yes, of course," replied the man, after kissing her again, more deeply. Maggie's hand slid around his chest to his back, tracing the hard line of his spine; and down, down even more, as she discovered he was truly naked, everywhere. She pressed closer, grinding her hips against the hard pulse of his body, and realized dimly that she was not standing, but resting on her side. The man made a slightly strangled sound, and kissed Maggie so hard that she sighed with pleasure.

And then he disappeared, abruptly, and she found herself holding nothing but air. Awake, she listened to the rain drum against the old tin roof, her body still aching and her mouth still tender from kisses that had been only in her dreams.

Or maybe they were not dreams. Maggie dragged in a deep ragged breath, curling around herself. She tried to remember those arms holding her, especially when thunder rumbled and lightning flashed outside the window, but it was the man's voice that lingered instead. Warm, steady, and reassuring. Familiar now as her own.

Mister Crow, she thought, sensing something behind her. She twisted, glancing over her shoulder, and found the bird perched on the edge of her blanket. Not quite looking at her. Tense. Feathers ruffled. She stared at him, remembering that man in the creek who had run from her. The man in her dream. Heat filled her cheeks.

"It's okay," Maggie said weakly, just to break the ridiculous silence. She rolled into a little ball, and felt the crow settle against her back. He was a small, warm lump. An hour ago he would not have been noticeable, but now his presence burned.

"I lied," she told him, after several minutes of discomfort. "It's not okay. I'm going insane."

We both are, replied the crow. Maggie hugged the blanket more tightly to her chin. It was still dark inside the house, but the rain had stopped, though not the thunder. It continued to prowl, a rolling, restless sound that throbbed through the night with an ever-deepening growl.

Maggie sat up, listening hard, skin prickling. The crow fluttered his wings and, after one short bounding hop, flew through the dining room to one of the open windows. He perched on the sill. Maggie ran to the window after him and saw lights flashing along the road—a long line of them, one after the other.

She hurriedly packed her things, but by the time she raced outside, the motorcycles had passed from sight. Maggie could hear them, though, growling beneath the thunder. She dragged her bicycle from the farmhouse and started riding hard, chasing them through the lingering fumes of their engine fuel. Faint light touched the eastern horizon, and stars peeked from behind fast-moving clouds.

In the distance, at the crest of a hill, she caught the glow of headlights and watched as the motorcycles turned off the road, following a ramp that joined the long cement loop of the old interstate. Maggie's heart sank. She knew where they were going. She had known since leaving home where this journey would end—in one of the dead cities.

They might not have Trace. And if they did take her, she's probably dead. There's no need to do this.

Go home, she told herself wearily.

But those thoughts were like ash in her mind: dead and bitter and burned out. Her only instinct that felt right, and real, was the worst one.

The crow swooped in and landed on Maggie's shoulder, his wings buffeting her head. She did not duck away or flinch, but kept watching those headlights move farther away from her.

"Mister Crow," she said quietly. "I'm about to do something stupid."

The crow said nothing. She started pedaling again, and followed the men.

There were always stories, always. Most everyone had something to say about the Big Death, but only a handful in Olo could talk about escaping the cities. Kids, and some adults, still paid attention with bated breath, but Maggie had stopped listening. She was no stranger to violence, but there was a wildness that crept into the eyes of the men and women who had survived those early evacuations that scared her. What was in their eyes, what went unspoken, was the real story. The rest was filler.

As she rode her bicycle along the interstate, Maggie saw the evidence of other stories, twenty years dead. There was only empty road the first ten miles, cracked and pitted with shrubbery. Then a concrete barricade, shoved aside, presumably by the motorcycle men, who had disappeared ahead of her, hours earlier. Her tires rolled over abandoned guns, rusted by two decades of rain and sun.

Beyond that, nothing but cars; more cars than she had ever seen, parked bumper to bumper. Small holes riddled the hoods of the vehicles nearest the barricade—bullet holes, she guessed—and for a moment all she could see were men in green uniforms and gas masks, standing on ladders behind the tall concrete walls, aiming their weapons and shouting—shouting at a roaring, desperate mob of men and women rushing from their cars, trampling one another.

A loud shriek filled her ears. Maggie winced, then rubbed her head and her eyes. She found the crow perched on top of the blanket inside her bicycle basket. His black feathers were ruffled.

Be careful, he said, tilting his head to stare at her. *Your mind is sensitive. And this is an unpleasant place.*

"I'm fine," she muttered, her eyes still burning, and then leaned over to gag as another image pushed flush through her head: a little boy, left alone in a backseat, sobbing helplessly while outside, men and women screamed, cut down by bullets. His face was red and dirty, his fear agonizing. Maggie pushed her palms into her eyes, groaning.

Maggie, whispered the crow, more urgently. *Shut it out.*

She shook her head, unable to speak, as the boy disappeared and was replaced by an elderly woman, sprawled in the grass outside her car, clutching her heart. A small dark dog licked her face. No one helped her. No one looked. The simple despair of being alone—that poor woman, dying and alone; that little boy, afraid and alone—sickened Maggie in ways that bullets and disease did not. She could *feel* their fear and misery, and not just theirs, but everyone's who had died in this place, on this road—hopelessness so thick in the air that every breath felt like murder in her heart.

Maggie heard her name said again, distantly, and then warm hands took hold of her shoulders. She was so startled, so distracted by that unexpected touch, that all the pain flooding her senses receded just enough for her to gain control over herself.

She began to twist around, and those hands tightened. Warm breath touched her ear, and her heart raced.

"Maggie," said her crow, no longer just a little bird. "Maggie, breathe."

It was impossible to breathe with him touching her, but she could not say that. Instead she nodded, bowing her head—those memories of the past threatening to devour her again. Tears burned her eyes.

His hands tightened, and his warm mouth grazed the back of her neck, shooting chills and heat through her body. "Leave it alone, Maggie. Just let it go. You do not have to see what is there."

"I can't help it," she muttered through gritted teeth.

"You can," he said firmly, and his hands trailed closer to her neck until his thumbs skimmed the base of her scalp. His fingers squeezed gently, again and again, and the slow, easy strength of his hands kneading her shoulders sent such soothing heat through her that those ghostly feelings of despair faded away.

She reached back and touched his right hand, warm and smooth with muscle. His movements stilled as she persisted and wormed her fingers through his, knotting their hands together.

"Maggie," he whispered, and before she could ask him a single question—like, What kind of *oddness,* exactly, was he?—he leaned forward, slid his large hand under her jaw, and turned her head. Then he kissed her.

It was a slow, deep kiss. Maggie forgot everything but him, so wrapped up in the deliciousness of his mouth, she could not even open her eyes to look at his face. She tried, but everything was too heavy, and all she could do was to breathe and stay upright. She wanted to be back in that farmhouse with him, or home; anywhere but here.

He broke away from her, making a small, frustrated sound. Maggie tried to turn with him, wanting to see his face, but all she glimpsed was a flash of shining black feathers, and then nothing. He was gone, and in his place flew a crow, wings beating furiously, ascending into the cloud-scattered sky.

Maggie stared after him. Burned up, seared to the bone. But there was no man here now, just a bird, and she looked away, embarrassed and aching, sensing she was more than a bit insane.

Think of Trace. Keep moving, she told herself, and began pedaling down the interstate. She passed miles of rotting cars, as far as the eye could see, all pointed in the same westbound direction. Both sides of the interstate were occupied, six lanes of traffic. It was a graveyard. She saw bodies in those vehicles, behind dirty tinted glass; desiccated remains, skeletons held together with only the thinnest, driest vestiges of flesh. She had no doubt what had killed them, and saw—as if time-traveling—flash images of men and women sitting behind their wheels, trying to stay conscious as blood trickled from their nostrils and ears, and pain crippled their joints.

She blinked hard, sickened, and glanced through the

windshields. She saw those people again, but dead for two decades now: sagging, locked inside metal coffins that Maggie doubted would ever be opened—not until folks forgot about the Big Death and stopped being afraid. Maybe never. The hanta-bola pox had disappeared, perhaps, but the miasma remained. She could taste, in these endless rows of cars, the bitter tangle of desperation that had led nowhere. Luggage still sagged atop the rusted roofs. She saw plastic toys in the road, unable to disintegrate. All those belongings: grave markers.

The crow swooped in close, over her head. *Maggie, look.*

Maggie stood on the pedals, staring at the horizon. The road curved, but not enough for the hills to obscure the wall of trees that cut across the cold distant line of the interstate. Beyond the forest, or within it, glittering towers rose toward the sky: steel and glass shining with shears of sunlight. She held her breath, coasting until her bike almost slowed to a stop, and then sat back on the seat and pedaled hard before she remembered that there . . . that there was death, and blood and loneliness, and men on motorcycles who hurt people. That was the forest, the city forest, and deep within monsters awaited.

The interstate had been eaten by the forest. The road ended at the tree line, without evidence that it had ever existed. There was pavement, where Maggie stood with her bicycle, and then nothing but dead leaves and thick curling roots that supported massive trees, as though the concrete had been more nourishing than the soil; or the trees had grown from magic seeds embedded in stone. There were still cars in the forest, parked on the interstate that had been. Maggie could see faint outlines of them, like ghosts, but the trees had grown through and around the vehicles, crumpling steel. Naked branches were budding with green spring, and redbud blossoms floated in the undergrowth.

Maggie had heard about the forests that had grown wild around the cities, but she never imagined what one of them would look like. The trees had a reputation that preceded them, told by the government men who rattled into town once or twice a year on their large gas-powered trucks, hauling clothwares and steelwares, and bringing news from three different coasts.

No more cities, the men had said years ago. *The trees have swallowed all the dead cities.*

But no one, as far as Maggie knew, had devoted much energy or thought into finding out *why*. Better things to do, after all. Like, survive. As far as most people were concerned, nature reclaiming places of so much horror, even with impossible speed, seemed preferable to the alternative: that the cities be accessible, and remembered. No one wanted to remember anything from the Big Death.

The crow landed on the road and pecked at a dried leaf. Maggie glanced down at him. "This growth looks older than twenty years. Are all the cities like this?"

All that I have flown over, he replied. *And there have been many.*

"Doesn't make sense," she muttered. "Did the hanta-bola pox cause this? Did it . . . infect plants?"

The crow jumped into the air and flew to the low-hanging branch of a squat, fat oak that looked as though it had grown in that spot for more than a hundred years. *It was an unnatural disease. Even among my kind, we do not understand the how or why of it. But we do think it caused . . . this. There is no other explanation, and the disease was localized in the cities, even though it spread elsewhere.*

"Were you alive then? Did you witness the Big Death?"

I lost family to it, he said, which surprised her. *We were not immune, though we suffered less since we lived apart from humans.*

Maggie forced herself to breathe. "Anything else?"

You could still turn back.

She stared at him and thought about Trace. She touched the shark teeth hanging cold around her neck, and her other hand traced the head of the sledgehammer dragging on her waist. Messages floated through her mind; Irdu's voice behind them all.

A test of truth. Don't give up if you want to find your teeth.

I've got plenty of bite, she told him silently, and said, "I don't see an easy way in. Not for motorcycles."

The crow launched himself off the oak branch and flew around Maggie toward her right. He landed more than thirty feet away on the ground, and hopped lightly ahead of her. She pushed her bicycle over and saw a narrow trail leading into the woods, and a long streak of lines as though tires had rolled through the leaves.

Maggie hesitated, exposed to sunlight and miles of endless concrete, cars, and corpses at her back. The crow dove from the tree to the handlebars of her bicycle. He perched there, wings flared, staring into her eyes with familiar intensity.

Fear knotted up her throat. "Well, you don't have to come along, if you don't want."

The crow said nothing, simply settling his wings against his back. Maggie brushed his chest with her knuckles and whispered, "I'm scared. I don't know what I'm doing."

Trace, she told herself. *If it were you, she would never turn back. Even if she thought you might be dead.*

Heart thundering, Maggie rolled her bike forward, using her feet to push herself along. The crow rode on the handlebars. When she was inches from the edge of the forest, she stopped again, staring into the lengthening shadows and the endless supple variations of the trees. Sweat rolled down her back.

"You and me," she said to the crow; and then, feeling a bit pathetic, added: "Don't leave me, right?"

The crow leaned toward her, and when she held out her hand, he rubbed his beak against her fingers. Warmth tingled. Maggie smiled grimly. Not alone. She was crazy, but she was not alone.

The golden light of sunset warmed her back. Maggie pedaled slowly into the forest, imagining robbers, and the dead; and other stolen hearts. *Hunting hearts,* she thought. She was hunting. A hunter.

An hour later, Maggie found another barricade.

SIX

The barricade was lost in the woods. Maggie followed vainly the tracks and scuffs of motorcycle tires, and was finally forced to dismount and walk her bicycle. The forest swallowed everything within it, but as dusk spread into silver, the world seemed to sharpen, as though night allowed a deeper vision than day.

Or perhaps her eyes were changing. She had noticed that. Shadows hid nothing from her anymore. Every day since leaving her junkyard in Olo, she had found herself able to do more, feel more, hear more. And all of it was familiar. She had been able to do these things before, she realized, but had made herself forget. Maggie simply could not understand why.

She walked along the barricade, and found it almost exactly like the one on the interstate: tall, thick, and made of concrete. Sharp, rusted barbed wire coiled on top, and bullet holes had fractured the smooth, dark surface, along with the fading remnants of painted messages that were too obscured by vines for her to read.

A piece of the barricade had been pulled aside and was bordered by the trunk of a towering maple tree. Maggie imagined voices whispering in the shadows of the undergrowth, but that did not frighten her. She had heard those ageless murmurs back home, in her dreams; in the other forest beyond the city, beneath the redbuds. She felt as though she had heard them always.

Maggie lingered outside the barrier, staring through the break into another world. She saw more road and rusted cars, along with distant buildings half-eaten by trees. A ghost land, empty and quiet, the silence rimming her skin with ice.

She took a deep breath. This was the city.

Maggie pushed her bicycle through the gap in the barricade. She had imagined she might feel differently on the other side, but the air tasted the same, and the darkness was no deeper in the underbrush. The crow flew ahead. Maggie followed, and after several minutes of quick travel, found that many roads split from this one, tributaries and concrete veins. The interstate suddenly seemed elevated above the ground, and she peered over the edge of a bent steel railing. More forest spread out below her, shrouding the outlines of rows of decaying box homes. All she could see were rooftops and the hint of dark windows through the branches.

Her heart hurt, as she looked at those abandoned homes. Their emptiness made her feel small, and the silence hurt her ears, frightening in its finality.

Maggie followed the road and found another barricade, and another, as she passed deeper into the forest. She walked for a long time. Color was bleached from the world. All she saw were etched buildings, gray and black; monoliths, hunched and molding with disuse.

And the bones. She finally saw the bones, everywhere: in the road, off the road, on the front steps of buildings, and on sidewalks. Tangled, sprawling skeletons begging free of moss and brown leaves. Countless men and women who had simply dropped dead, on top of one another.

Maggie did not want to contemplate what it had been

like when flesh still covered those bones and people had
lain there, passing away in their own blood, their own slough-
ing skin. Her own parents might have died like this, exposed and helpless, watching each other fade, listening to
the screams of a dying city.

She could hear those screams, echoing through her brain.
She shut her eyes, pressing her knuckles to her brow. Maggie forced a deep breath, and then another. Trying not to
see, she fumbled for the shark teeth, gripping them tightly,
and it was suddenly easier to focus.

Be strong, she told herself fiercely, but it was difficult.
She had thought she was strong all these years, but her
strength had been built upon routine, and the familiar. Her
junkyard. Her tools. The occasional stranger to mix things
up. A false sense that this world was normal, no matter how
much she had imagined otherwise from her books and day-
dreams.

Dead leaves crackled behind her. Maggie spun around,
heart pounding, and glimpsed a coyote peering at her from
behind the remains of a large truck. She met its gaze, startled.

The crow swept low, cawing loudly. His wings buffeted
the animal's head, and the coyote flinched but did not attack, or retreat. It just gave the crow a long look, and then
flicked its gaze back to Maggie. Until, quite abruptly, it
turned and loped away into the forest shadows.

"A friend of yours?" Maggie asked the crow, who settled
on a branch above her head.

The crow flipped his wings, a gesture that looked distinctly like a shrug. *He was too curious.*

Maggie raised her brow. "That's no crime. I'm curious
about you."

She heard a small harrumphing sound in her mind, and
for the first time in a long while felt like smiling. But she
thought of the old woman, and touched the heavy necklace.

"Do you know if Trace is close? Could you find her? And those men?"

Before now, it had not occurred to her that she could ask him to do such a thing. He had been a bird. He had been a creature she did not understand; perhaps a man, perhaps not. She still did not understand him, but she felt freer to ask small favors.

The crow tilted his head, looking away down the road, which was white with bones. *I can do that.*

But there was uncertainty in his voice. Maggie said, "Is there something wrong with that?"

He hesitated, still not looking at her. *I will have to leave you alone.*

Maggie looked down at her hands, which were scarred from steelwork and hard with muscle. Slender hands but strong.

Be strong, she told herself again, and sighed. "I've been alone a long time. I can take care of myself."

You know this is different, he said softly, finally settling his gaze on her. *You know you are more than food to those men who hunt.*

No one had ever said anything about food, but Maggie understood what he meant. She had interested Irdu. He had seen something in her that was different. She knew it was the only reason he had not taken her life. She thought he might very well change his mind about that, the next time they met.

"I need to know," she said.

Then follow me, he replied heavily, and flew from the branch. Maggie hurried after him, her skin crawling as bones crunched beneath her boots and tires. It was impossible not to step on the remains. She wondered if the bones still held traces of the hanta-bola pox. Maybe she was breathing in the disease, becoming infected, her cells already breaking down.

The crow led her down a narrow path crowded with cars parked closely together in tight, neat rows. Oak trees had grown between and through the vehicles, roots curling around the remains of rubber tires. Ahead of them she saw a vast low-lying building, the dirty glass windows revealing nothing. Vines obscured large blue letters embedded in brick. Maggie could not read them.

The crow swept down to the leafy ground, hopping to a slow stop. *In there. Wait for me.*

Maggie gave the building a dubious look. "What is that place?"

A relic, he said, and hopped closer, peering into her eyes. *If there should be trouble—*

"Don't," Maggie interrupted, crouching in front of him. "Won't do much good, will it?"

The crow lowered his head. She briefly stroked his chest with the back of her fingers, touching him tenderly, her heart in her throat. He quivered, and she whispered, "What are you, Mister Crow?"

He said nothing, and pressed the side of his sleek head against her hand. For a moment, Maggie's vision blurred, and she felt his life pulsing white hot, as though she could taste each beat of his heart, and the blood coursing through his veins. It was not her imagination, but instead felt as real as the leaves underfoot and the trees wrapped tight around the city.

It was also a curiously intimate sensation, one she did not pull away from. She studied her emotions with rare detachment, questioning why she felt the way she did, with a creature—sometimes a man—she barely knew. She had no answer to give herself. Only that it felt right, and safe.

Maggie placed her palm on the cool ground and glanced up at the sky. Stars dazzled beyond the tree branches. She was surprised to see them. Her eyesight had improved so much, she had forgotten it was night.

She turned briefly to look at the building behind her, heard a flapping sound, and felt cool air move across her neck and face.

When she glanced over her shoulder, Maggie found him gone.

The doors to the building were unlocked. Maggie ventured inside with some uneasiness, as she usually did most abandoned structures. Twenty years was a long time, and closed spaces could be dangerous if animals had taken up residence, or if other people were hiding, or had beaten her to the job. A good scavenge was never that safe. There was too much at stake. She wondered, even now, if all her junkyard belongings were still in place. She trusted most folk in Olo to do right by her, but there were a handful capable of small acts of theft.

It was very dark inside, but Maggie's eyes adjusted almost immediately, and she found herself staring at an interior far larger than any she had ever seen. Long aisles spread away from her, and the ceilings were high. She stood beside a line of large mesh baskets, packed tightly together, one inside the other.

So still. So quiet. A dead silence. Maggie imagined she was the first person in twenty years to enter this place, and her skin prickled with chills. She clutched the shark teeth in one hand, while the other grazed the sledgehammer hanging from her tool belt. Slowly, she walked, and passed clothing hanging from racks—more clothing than she had ever seen, and of tremendous variation. Twenty years had left some things ragged, and dust and cobwebs lay heavy, but Maggie could see enough. She took in rows and shelves of jeans and coats and sweaters, and then socks and underwear. Trading just this much would keep her busy for years.

That would have been enough, but there was more. She passed aisles full of makeup, which she recognized from ads in the old magazines that her grandfather had kept, but she ignored the powders and lipsticks for the great variety of medicines displayed nearby. Most of them, she figured, were too old to do any good, but the diversity amazed her nonetheless. She marveled at what had been lost. The government issued aspirin and a narrow range of antibiotics, but most people had taken to relying on herbalists for treatment. Death took care of the rest.

Maggie wandered through aisles full of toys—stuffed animals partially devoured by mice, staring dolls encased in plastic, small cars for plastic men; as well as hoops and balls, and bats. She found bicycles and gardening supplies. She discovered sections devoted to blankets, curtains, and pillows, pots and pans, and thick glass bowls. She stumbled upon countless tools she wished she could carry out with her, still gleaming and new inside dusty boxes.

You are a greedy woman, she told herself, staring nearly with lust at all the useful things she could scavenge and trade, and use back at her workshop. Until she remembered that this was the city forest, and no one would touch a thing that came from this place. No one would touch her if they ever learned she had been here, assuming she made it back to Olo or any other Enclave. Some lies were bigger than others.

She found guns at the back of the store. Of all the varied things she had seen thus far, these looked the most picked over. Still, there were rifles and smaller weapons locked behind glass; and, more important, bullets—boxes and boxes of them. Enough to cause an uproar in trading, and to keep her fed for a long time. And draw all kinds of unwanted attention. Bullets were as rare as hen's teeth—as rare as gasoline. The government controlled both, and shared neither.

Something rustled close by. Maggie turned, staring into the shadows. It had been perfectly quiet until now.

Two aisles down, in the opposite direction, someone

hooted softly. It was not an animal. Not a bird. Not her crow. The voice was masculine, though, and full of quiet laughter.

Her first instinct was to run, and she almost did, but she gritted her teeth and tried to focus past her hammering heart. Guns everywhere, but not a single one she could use. Even assuming that not much dust had penetrated the glass cases, she could not risk using any of those weapons without cleaning them first. Twenty years was too long to take a chance, even if desperate. Bullets could jam, or go off inside the gun.

Maggie pulled her sledgehammer free and hefted it in her hands. Farther away, she heard a soft humming melody, and in another direction, closer, a heavy crash made her jump.

Surrounded. She was surrounded.

"Did you truly think you could come to this city without us feeling your presence?" called a soft familiar voice behind her. Maggie turned, and found Irdu leaning against a rack filled with long, thin metal rods, clubbed at one end. He watched her, his black hair spilling down the left side of his pale, sharp face. His eyes glittered.

"We know our own," he whispered. A chill rode down her spine, and with it, a terrible dread. She could not breathe, and when a pale hand grabbed her arm from behind, lights flickered in her vision. Her fingers closed numbly around her sledgehammer.

Maggie did not think. She twisted in that hard grip, swinging with all her might. Solid iron connected with a very human face, and all she saw in that split second was black hair flying. Bone smashed as the entire side of the man's head caved in. Blood sprayed from his nose and mouth, spattering her cheeks and clothing.

He let go. Maggie ran but did not get far before men moved in, graceful and low to the ground, like wolves. Hands snared her legs. She swung wildly, striking good, clean blows. No one let go, though, and she fought desperately for control over the sledgehammer as someone much stronger began prying it from her hand. She bit and clawed, searching blindly for his eyes.

Someone yanked her hair, jerking her head so hard her neck made a cracking sound. A fist connected with her face.

Everything went dark.

SEVEN

Pain found Maggie first, even in sleep. She dreamed of it as steel needles pricking her skin, sewing wires in her flesh: her ankles and wrists, and the sides of her face. She dreamed she'd been tied to a steel bar, as giant hands yanked her strings and made her dance. Alone, except for a steel crow, frozen on a floating branch—staring, because his eyes were all he had left of his flesh.

She woke up. Disoriented, head throbbing, so thirsty her tongue stuck to the roof of her mouth. She saw a pale ceiling above her, trimmed in dark wood. Shades of golden light flickered unevenly; small candles burning beside her on the carpeted floor. She smelled something sweet.

Maggie turned her head sideways and found herself staring at long aisles of shelved books. It was a remarkable, unexpected sight. She had many books, more than almost anyone in Olo, except for old man Reeves, who lived near town and ran his own personal library. But these numbers were countless, overwhelming; and though Maggie had been told of bookstores, she had not imagined their existence. Not like this.

She was untied. Carefully she rolled on her side, trying not to wince as she pushed herself into a sitting position.

Her head began throbbing again, making her nauseous, but she forced herself to focus, and stood. Her tool belt was gone, as was her sledgehammer. She tried working up enough spit to moisten her dry mouth, but all she succeeded in doing was making herself sick.

Maggie turned her head slowly. She was not alone. Irdu stood beside a table covered in neatly arranged piles of dusty books. One of her steel puppets dangled from his pale hands. He manipulated the strings with care—little arms twitching, feet dancing through the air. Candlelight seemed to give the toy a spectral power, as though it might come to life.

"Amazing," he said quietly, "how some things never change. The world dies, and yet we still find room in our hearts for wonder."

"Children deserve that much," Maggie rasped painfully, unsure what to do, except to engage him; and worse, feeling stupid about it. "Do you have any of children of your own?"

"Rarely," he said, which was an odd answer. He tore his gaze from the puppet and finally looked at her. "It is just as rare to find the children of others."

Maggie let those words sink in, watching his cold gaze study her face as though he expected some reaction; as if his words had been calculated to get one.

She tried to show nothing, and instead pulled the heavy necklace out from underneath her shirt. The shark teeth were cold against her palm, but holding them made her feel stronger. She dangled the necklace in front of him, watching the teeth catch the candlelight. "Where's the old woman who wore this?"

Irdu's face darkened with surprise, and then distaste. "My brother should have destroyed that thing."

"You used it to bring me here."

"No," he said, tossing the puppet at her feet. "I did not." Irdu turned and walked away, down another aisle.

Maggie hesitated, staring at the puppet collapsed in a heap, and then followed. "What do you mean by that? Your . . . brother . . . was wearing this necklace."

Irdu turned, so suddenly and with such speed that she could not stop herself from running into him. He slammed her up against a bookcase, his cold hands sliding up her throat, into her hair. His gaze burned through her.

"That is no simple necklace," he whispered. "That is a repudiation. An abomination. You would do well not to admire its previous owner."

"She—" Maggie began, but Irdu covered her mouth with his, kissing her hard. His mouth was as cold as she remembered, and as draining, but this time something rose up within her—a spark of heat—and without thinking, she rocked forward, exhaling sharply.

Irdu broke away, stumbling backward. He touched his mouth as though stung, and stared at her with narrowed eyes.

"Good," he finally said, but his expression was not in agreement. He turned again, more slowly, as though unsteady, and began walking down the bookstore aisles. When his back was to her, Maggie touched her own mouth. Her lips tingled, but not with pleasure, and deep down in her stomach, hunger rumbled—a different kind of hunger, vast and yawning.

She followed him, fingers trailing against the soft spines of dusty books. Maybe twenty years was not so long after all, she thought, noticing how well the books had stayed preserved, despite cobwebs and time. So many stories. So many secrets and histories, wrapped up in fantasy. Such lovely lies.

Candles dotted the tops of the shelves, burning like small stars. Irdu led Maggie to a small area with tile floors, filled with tables and chairs. Even more candles covered the tables—more than she had seen in a long time—and mugs lined small shelves in the wall, as if placed there for decoration. A large glass case sat on a long counter filled with odd-looking machines. Inside the case were jars of preserves, dried meat, cheese, and bread. Some of the food looked as though it had come from her belongings.

Five men lounged around that small area, fewer than she remembered seeing on the road. Several were reading books by candlelight, feet propped up on chairs. Others were playing chess. All of them seemed relaxed, but there was a coiled quality in their long, lean bodies that was careless, cold, and lethal. Most wore black, chrome details glinting in the glow cast by the candlelight.

The men were so much alike, it was difficult to tell them apart. They shared the same long dark hair and aquiline noses, pale skin, and sharp cheeks. Brothers or cousins, perhaps. Only one man was distinctly different, and he wore a cape of black feathers around his neck. Maggie had a feeling about where those feathers had come from.

One side of his head was a mess. His cheek and jaw had smashed so far inward, she wondered how he lived—let alone stayed conscious. Blood covered his entire face, and his hair had matted into tangled clumps. But he was sitting up, staring at her, and holding one of her whirly-gigs and blowing on it, blades spinning gently. All those men stared at her, until she felt like the focus of one giant eye—the men, a single entity, not individuals; a force, hungry and strange.

She stood before them, trying to act bold and brave, and glanced at Irdu. His eyes were as black as the inside of a cave located ten miles under; unfathomably, inescapably dark, without light or even the smallest inner glow. Dead eyes. Cold.

"Welcome to our home," he said quietly. "One of many, for we are rootless, and old as the wind."

"Where are the people you took?" Maggie asked. "The

women from Olo, the folk from Dubois? Have you hurt them?"

Irdu's expression did not change, but the other men looked at one another, and faint, knowing smiles touched their mouths. Chess pieces clicked, and several books were put facedown. She could not see what those men were reading, but the spines were thick and creased, and their fingers were gentle upon the covers.

An odd sight. Maggie could still see them in her dreams, their heads thrown back, darkness spilling from their mouths—and somehow she managed not to flinch in revulsion when Irdu dragged his fingers up her arm, and brushed the underside of her breast with his palm. His face grew colder, and harder, until it was barely human.

He was not human, Maggie thought. None of them were.

"I will show you where those people are," he whispered, and snapped his fingers. One of his men rose gracefully from his chair and strode behind the counter to a closed door. Keys jangled. He entered, and Maggie heard a faint tired voice.

A young woman stumbled out. She was not from Olo. She was dressed in a dirty wrinkled skirt and an unbuttoned blouse that exposed her breasts. Her hair was tangled, her face gaunt and smeared with gray dust marks. Maggie searched her face for fear, but there was none—just a languid quality to her expression that was not terrified or hungry, but full of weary pleasure. The woman seemed unbothered by her partial nudity. When she saw Irdu, a spark entered her eyes—a dull spark—and she gave him a tired, mindless smile.

"Pet," he said to her, "bend over the table."

"Yes," she whispered, still smiling, and Maggie watched in horror as she bent over one of the few tables not laden with candles, her hands stretching out to grip the rim. Irdu undid his trousers and pulled free his penis, which was large and already erect.

Nausea rose up in Maggie's throat. She took a step—unsure what to do, only that she had to do *something*—but strong fingers gripped her arm. It was the man who wore the black feather cape. He smelled like blood, and gave her a brief, merciless shake that rattled her teeth. His head seemed a little less caved-in, as though his bones were knitting together. Those feathers reminded her too much of her crow—her crow, whom she suddenly missed desperately—and Maggie tried to knee him in the groin.

He spun her around with a quiet snarl and forced her to watch Irdu, who pulled up the woman's skirts and placed his palms on her naked rear. He did not look down at her exposed body. Just at Maggie.

"Watch and learn," he said, and drove himself forward.

The woman cried out, but not in pain. Pleasure filled her face, mindless satisfaction, and the sounds of her gratification only grew louder, and more piercing, as the robber thrust harder and faster, never once taking his gaze off Maggie.

Maggie watched him, too, and for the first time in her life, she felt hate—burning through her like fire.

She saw something else, too, as the woman's shrieks grew louder and more urgent—as she writhed against the robber and grabbed her breasts with one squeezing hand. Maggie saw a pulse of light surround the woman. Golden, precious light. And as the woman stiffened against Irdu, her voice breaking with pleasure, he threw back his head, opened his mouth, and breathed in the light surrounding the woman. He sucked it down like smoke.

The young woman collapsed forward, gasping for air. Irdu also gasped, but for a different reason: He was still breathing in flickers of the woman's light.

Until no more. The light disappeared. The woman looked

no different, showed no lessening of her pleasure, but Maggie knew, in her gut, that she was staring at a dead person. Something vital had been stolen from the woman. She would die, and soon.

Irdu stood back. His glistening penis was still erect, and he stroked it as he stared at Maggie. She fought not to tremble, to show nothing of her terrible rage and fear, but her voice still shook when she asked, "What *are* you?"

"We are those who came before," said Irdu, moving close to Maggie as he continued to stroke himself; roughly, with increasing intensity. "We, who were worshipped once, and sacrificed to with flesh and honor." He stood directly in front of Maggie, holding her gaze as his hand pumped up and down. She could barely hold it in to not be sick.

"It was easier before," he said almost idly. "There were so many humans who could fall unnoticed. But now we must hunt in plain sight, and it is difficult to sustain us. We have so many hungers."

And then his hand stopped moving and he said, "Touch me."

"No," Maggie whispered.

The robber reached out to finger the shark teeth hanging from her neck. "I thought you would come because we had forged a connection. Because I awoke what was sleeping inside you. And now I know you came because of *her*." His hand squeezed hard around his penis. "Touch me, and I'll tell you what happened."

The idea of touching him made Maggie want to scream. And if she did as he asked, she was afraid of what he would want next. He could have anything. He could force her to do anything, outnumbered as she was.

"No," she said.

"No," he echoed.

"And if you make me—" began Maggie, but he held up his hand.

At first she thought he was merely telling her to be quiet. He tilted his head, his gaze sharpening as he stared past her. She heard footfall, something dragging, and terrible dread curled through her heart. Irdu's mouth broke into an awful smile, and he bared his teeth—as sharp, white, and long as those hanging from her neck.

Which Maggie suddenly sensed had not come from a shark.

The fingers holding her arm loosened. She turned, slowly, and saw men walking toward them from across an expansive lobby filled with tables laden down with books, and shelves, and large windows that she had not previously noticed. Someone had propped skulls on the edge of a long wooden counter, grinning human bones staring endlessly at the books.

Seven men were striding across the floor, their long hair flowing like water around their cold sharp faces. Their eyes glittered with flecks of gold. The eighth man in their midst, whom Maggie did not see until they were almost on top of her, was being dragged. He was naked and lean, his skin covered in shallow crisscrossed cuts as though a net had bitten into him. His dark hair fell over his eyes. One of the men dragging him by the arm also held a cloak of feathers, much like the one being worn by the bloody heap who had been holding her.

Maggie stared, heart hammering in her throat, a scream building. She swallowed it down and remained utterly still and silent as the men tossed their captive at her feet. She looked at the familiar line of a strong hard jaw, and felt something snap inside her, just a little. She touched the teeth hanging around her neck and they burned cold against her palm. Her own teeth ached.

"A skinwalker," whispered Irdu, walking up behind her. "Distant cousins. Sly creatures, but easy to catch if you know how. We see them rarely."

"He was just outside," said one of the men softly. "Watching for her."

"Curious friend you have." Irdu reached out, and took the black feather cape from the man who had been dragging her human crow. The feathers gleamed and seemed to Maggie to pulse with light and power. "Ekir. Put them both away."

The injured man—Ekir—grabbed Maggie's arm, and then reached down and twined his fingers through the crow's hair. He yanked hard, pulling backward, and she watched the crow man's eyes flutter open, dim with pain. She had never seen his human eyes, not up close, but they were wild and dark as night, and thunderous.

He saw Maggie first, and the faintest hint of a smile touched his mouth. It broke her heart. A small, pained sound escaped from her, and it was like a slap across his face. Awareness, memory, flooded his eyes. He looked up and sideways at Ekir, and his expression hardened quick as death, staring like death: implacable and grim.

He lunged upward toward Ekir, as did Maggie, digging her fingers into the crushed bone of his cold sharp face. Ekir arched his spine, breath rattling in his throat, but he did not release her, and his boot smashed into the crow's head.

The sight made her wild. She fought harder, but strong arms wrenched Maggie backward, cold lips pressing against her ear. Words whispered, but she could not hear them past the roar and thunder of her pounding heart. Her vision blurred. All she could see suddenly were her dreams: men with their heads thrown back and darkness spilling from their mouths. Shark teeth burned against her skin. Her blood burned in her veins.

You could stop this, she imagined Trace saying. *Listen.*

But Maggie did not. She could not. And only when she and the crow were thrown inside a small room packed with corpses did she finally remember how to breathe.

EIGHT

Everyone was dead, or near death. Less than a week gone from their homes, Maggie thought, and their lives had been drained dry. The woman who had just been taken on the table lay in a heap by the door, barely breathing. Maggie tried to wake her, but nothing worked. She was asleep, her pulse so slow, Maggie could hardly feel it. Her face looked peaceful, though. Just as peaceful and still as the faces of the other seven women crammed inside the room. The two men from Dubois were dead, too. Blankets covered the floor, and the remains of food and some clothing. The air smelled dirty, but not rotten. Almost as if the bodies had been preserved.

Maggie did not linger over the women from Olo. She knew them. She knew their names, and tried to remember some of the Amish prayers she had heard growing up. Most of them were spoken in German, but one or two had been translated. She could recall only a smattering of words, but she did her best to say something kind over their still bodies. Her heart ached the entire time; with fury and grief. Life was too precious now to waste like this. Life had always been too precious.

"Maggie," whispered her crow, struggling to rise from where he had been thrown down on the floor.

She crossed to him quickly, and crouched. "Don't move," she said, her hands hovering over his shoulders, afraid to touch him. "Something might be broken."

"Only my head," he muttered, and peered sideways at her. "You?"

"Alive," Maggie said, but her voice croaked on the word. She sat down even closer, and finally let herself touch him. Her fingers threaded gently through his dark fine hair, searching for an injury—or just an excuse to be near him. Her heart felt so lonely she thought it might break. Brittle and tired, and full of grief.

His hand caught hers, and he pressed his mouth to her palm. Maggie closed her eyes, shuddering. "You have a name?"

"Mister Crow," he murmured. "My favorite, I think."

"Mister Crow," she replied softly. "What else?"

He hesitated. "Samuel."

She sighed, and allowed herself to be drawn down, all the way to the floor. She curled on her side, facing her crow—looking only at him, trying to pretend they were not so near death, or faced with their own deaths. He was naked, but she did not care. It was a clean nudity, compared to what she had just seen. Downright wholesome, even.

"I was foolish," he said. "I came back too late. I saw you being taken, and I followed. I should have known they would feel me close."

"They," she said.

"Demons," he said softly. "Incubi, or vampires. A bit of both, I suppose. Depending on what they are hungry for. Energy or blood."

Maggie was quiet for a long moment, turning those words over in her head. She was familiar with both, having read them in her books—sometime, long ago. Vampires, full of teeth and cunning, with an allure that seemed to make people tumble over themselves like fools; enthralled, in lust, ready to give their lives for nothing but a kiss. There were so many stories like that, so many in such varied forms, Maggie had come to half-believe that those creatures existed. How could they not, when so many had dreamed of them? How, indeed?

Incubi was a word less known, but she knew it had to do with sex, and power.

Either way, death. Either way, truth.

"I don't know how this is possible," she said. "The Big Death, the forests around the cities. You. Those men. What does it all mean?"

He shrugged helplessly. "Must there be a meaning? The world is a different place now. This happens. Civilizations rise and fall, and are erased in time. The essence of everything that was, twenty years ago, will be forgotten the moment the last survivor dies. Those born now, even you, know nothing of the living past. You'll make your own—a new world on the top of the old."

"Alongside magic? Consumed by it?"

Samuel closed his eyes. "Not all of us prey on humans."

Maggie curled up tight around herself. She had hid under her covers from monsters, as a child. Monsters in her dreams. Monsters she could see while awake, inside her head. She remembered now. She had made herself forget that, too. Whatever else might be inside her head, she understood why forgetting was better. Life was hard enough without searching shadows for the unreal. There had been enough death.

Home, she thought, aching. She could have been home, in her own bed, among the safe and familiar. Ignorant. Blissfully so. Content to live and die in Olo as nothing but a fixer, a salvager, a toy-maker. A dreamer, watching the changing seasons through the great doors of her barn.

For one brief second Maggie wanted that again so badly, she wished she had never seen those shark teeth hanging around Ekir's neck. Never laid eyes on the necklace at all. She wouldn't have known Trace was in trouble.

She would not be in trouble.

Coward, Maggie told herself, ashamed.

Strong fingers wiped her cheeks, which were wet with tears. Samuel whispered, "I should have told you everything."

Maggie rubbed her nose. "Why didn't you?"

"It was ugly," he said simply. "And I wanted to spare you that. Even if it was reckless of me."

"You were scared to show me your face."

He hesitated. "You are not looking at me now."

It was true, she realized. While lying so close, she had stared at his chest, his throat, past his ear—but not at his face, or his eyes. She did not know why. And yet, when she began to raise her gaze to his, fear gripped her.

"Let me meet you halfway," he whispered, and scooted lower, his muscles flexing in the shadows, until there—in front of her—was his face. Lean and rawboned, with dark, wild eyes searching hers. Maggie stared back, drinking him in, her heart beating unsteadily.

"You're a bird," she breathed.

"And a man," he replied with sadness. "Your friend, too."

Maggie closed her eyes, but only for a moment. She missed his face, and had to look at him again simply to keep from feeling sick. But that was impossible. Bodies everywhere, and pretending that was not the case could last only so long.

"We've got to get out of here," she mumbled, and pushed herself up on her elbow, struggling to stand. Lying down felt suddenly too much like giving up.

Maggie scrabbled to her feet, swaying. Samuel stood far more gracefully, his hands outstretched to steady her. Her fingertips grazed his, ever so lightly, and she felt the pulse of his life shimmering for one hot instant: lovely golden wings beating inside his heart. She could taste them.

"Those feathers that . . . thing . . . wears," she began to say, and then stopped.

"Those feathers belonged to her," he said. "Her skin. Steal

our skin, and you steal our ability to become . . . something
else. You steal our power. The demon did that to her. And
then . . . used her up. Used her like these people have been
used. I . . . found her. Afterwards. I think, maybe, I lost my
mind when that happened. I no longer wanted to be a man.
Ever again."

Samuel's elegant dusky hands twined light as air around
hers. Maggie wanted him to tell her why he had chosen to
become a man, for her—and if that was the reason he had
hidden from her for so long, in shadows and dreams—but
he answered none of those things. Not with his voice. He
continued to hold her hands, and then he leaned in, very
carefully, to kiss her cheek. It was not chaste, or distant.
Simple, maybe, but that brief touch of his lips filled her with
more longing, and heat, than a million of Irdu's forced inti-
macies.

"I wish I could have known you earlier," she confessed,
almost afraid of saying that much.

He hesitated. "There is something I did not tell you."

The quiet urgency in his voice made her straighten, staring. But before he could explain, she heard scuffing sounds
outside, and the door was pushed open. Men came inside, a
blur of sharp lines and dark hair, and hands were rough,
cold as ice, as they took hold of them both.

She did not fight them, and neither did Samuel. Instead
he gave her a terrible, knowing look that made her heart
ache. Whatever was going to happen next, he had already
gone through it once before, on the periphery. He had lost
someone he loved to these men. And now he was going to
lose himself in turn—all for helping Maggie. It made her
sick. Furious.

Irdu waited outside the room. Maggie felt all the men
watching her, as if she was as much a curiosity to them as
they were to her—not normal, an oddity.

You are a fixer, she reminded herself fiercely, pretending she stood inside her barn, tools at hand. *You help people. You make things better.*

She told herself that, again and again, digging in her heels. Hands dropped away until no one touched her. The men—*vampires, incubi, demons*—did not make a sound.

Robber King, she named Irdu, savoring the weight of the shark teeth hanging around her neck. His gaze flicked down to it, and disgust briefly filled his eyes; difficult to see through the curtain of hair partially obscuring his face.

"You have no way to leave us," he said coldly. "And I think I am tired now of trying to woo you with kindness. I tried to give you time. I tried to set you on a path that would wake you to us, with care. A greater courtesy than has been shown others, I promise. But that is *done.* You *will* serve me. You *will* become us, even if I must force the waking of your blood."

"I have no idea what that means," Maggie replied, trying not to tremble. "But I'm not your pet. I asked for my life once, remember? I bargained for my life, and you agreed."

"You'll have your life," he said coldly. "A better life. One not subject to human weaknesses."

"I *am* human," she shot back. "I like my weaknesses."

Anger flashed through Irdu's eyes. "You still have no idea what you are. After all this, you *still* fight yourself."

He snapped his fingers, and Maggie watched in horror as Samuel was dragged to one of the tables and slammed upon it face first. Ekir stood close, caressing Samuel's cloak of feathers with a faint grim smile on his face, which seemed to Maggie as much of a violation of the man as any other gesture, this touch more intimate. Samuel snarled at Ekir, fighting the hands holding him down.

Irdu stepped close to Maggie, his body so cold she could feel him near her like a sheet of winter ice. "Another bargain. Give yourself to me—willingly, now—and I will set him free, with his skin intact."

"No," rasped Samuel, and Ekir slammed his fist into the man's face.

Maggie flinched, her hands flying to grip the teeth hanging around her neck, which were cold, but with a reassuring bite that steadied her. She met her friend's dark, wild gaze, and every moment—each one—spent with him as bird or man flashed through her mind in one split second of pure rock-solid clarity.

"Leave him alone," she said softly, and despair crept into Samuel's gaze.

"You agree then," Irdu replied, and for such a dangerous man, Maggie thought, there was a great deal of greed in his eyes. A weakness, she told herself, such a human weakness.

"Kiss me," Maggie told him. Irdu hesitated only a moment—as though sensing the possibility of danger. But it was not enough to stop him. He leaned in and clamped his mouth over hers; a rough touch, and violent. Maggie braced herself and kissed back.

She knew nothing but instinct, although she had been fighting that, and herself. She closed her eyes, reaching deep inside, and felt a great fury and hunger rise strong and hot within her belly. Irdu pressed closer. Maggie grabbed his head between her hands and held him to her, her lips sucking on his, stealing his breath—stealing him.

It happened so naturally she hardly knew what she was doing until Irdu stiffened, his eyes flying open. He tried to pull away, but strength flooded her body—as though all those years of steelwork had turned her into steel—and she opened her eyes, locking gazes with him, savoring his fear. Using it to stoke the hunger burning inside her belly.

Fixer, she told him silently. *I am going to fix you.*

Maggie inhaled him like smoke, filling her lungs, and still he remained frozen, eyelids fluttering. She could feel his life pulsing like a black flame, and she sucked hard, pleasure growing heavy between her legs as she pulled sharp, loosening the demon—*vampire, incubus, be mine*—from his moorings. Irdu's life slid through his mouth into Maggie's own; he tasted like bone, baked dry and hot; and the tail of his spirit slithered down her throat, making her fit to burst—which she did, pleasure rocking through her body. She gasped, and shoved him away.

Irdu collapsed. Maggie did as well, falling hard on her knees. She felt sick to her stomach, sick at heart, but there was something else in her, too; a rising scream of power that was silent and awful and heavy against her skin. Her heart hammered with such strength, she thought she could pull the vital organ from her body and it would still keep pumping.

She looked up, her vision blurred, but saw enough pale faces staring at her to know she was in deep trouble. Irdu was dead. She knew it. Killing had been easy, like a disease.

But I can't fight them all, she thought, with both defiance and despair.

No one touched her, though. Samuel was still pressed to the table, but he was watching her as well, grim satisfaction in his eyes.

Behind the men, Maggie heard the loud squeak of hinges. A door, opening and closing. Boots scuffed the floor. The men turned, staring, and a quiver rode through them as though they shared the same nerve endings. Maggie watched as they stood back in slow retreat, heads bowed, revealing a dark-skinned woman with white braids and a knit green cap tugged low over her ears. Her eyes glinted, and she looked from the men to Samuel, and then to Maggie.

"Well," said Trace, smiling coldly, "isn't this a pretty party?"

NINE

It was like being bludgeoned in the head, Maggie thought. Seeing Trace felt like a physical blow, and the young woman stared for one long moment, blood roaring in her ears. The sickening crunch of taking another life—even a life that had threatened her own—faded in comparison to seeing Trace.

The men released Samuel. He slipped off the table, dropping quickly to Maggie's side. She clutched his hand, leaning heavily against his shoulder as he helped her stand. She could not stop looking at Trace. The old woman looked good and healthy, with a light raging through her eyes that could have been anger or pleasure.

Ekir strode to Trace but did not attack her. He clutched the cape of feathers, and the old woman reached out and took it from him. He let her, and when she held out her hand and pointed to the cape he already wore, his expression darkened, but he did as she asked. Yielding to Trace as though he feared her.

"She won," said the old woman. "Just as I promised. Just as we *bargained*. She beat your leader at his game, and so she owns you now. She *owns* you."

"She knows nothing of us, or herself," Ekir rumbled, the

side of his face not quite as caved in, though his eye was still hidden—or perhaps just smashed beyond recognition. "She could never lead us."

Trace grunted. "Crow. The demon questions your lady."

Samuel rose to his feet and in two steps snatched one of Maggie's forgotten whirly-gigs off a nearby table. Ekir began to turn, but Samuel was too fast—so fast, Maggie wondered if he had let himself be captured. Nothing but a blur, and then blood spurted and she saw that he had shoved one of the tin blades into Ekir's remaining good eye.

The wounded man staggered, blind, against the table, grunting with pain. Trace kicked at the back of his knees, and he went down hard. She grabbed his hair, yanked back his head, and kissed him hard.

Not just a kiss, Maggie realized in horror. She was sucking him dry, stealing his life, just as Irdu's spirit had been stolen, consumed.

Trace was not human.

And neither, Maggie realized, was she.

The other men backed away toward the doors. Something came over her. She stood and lurched past Samuel, who caught her waist as she began to fall. No words escaped her throat, just a low growl that twisted from her chest, raw with fury. The men froze.

Trace released Ekir, who fell backward into a boneless heap. The woman wiped her mouth with the back of her hand, her eyes bright, her skin less wrinkled. Ten years had been knocked off her life, Maggie thought.

"Run," Trace whispered to the men. "But you remember what happened here. You remember what you owe us, and you stay clean and good. You keep away from people, much as you dare. You know you can."

"No," Maggie began to say, but the men nodded solemnly—if not with some disgust, and fear. They left the bookstore, filing into the night. They did not take the bodies of their brothers. They were perfectly quiet—pale creatures, black hair shining against their backs. Within moments, it was as though they had never been there at all. When Maggie heard the roar of their motorcycles, she ran toward the door. Trace caught her.

"They'll hurt others," Maggie protested. "How can you let them go?"

Trace shook her head. "You can't destroy 'em all. And why would you? There's a balance to these things, Maggie Greene. We took what was our right. The rest would be murder."

Maggie yanked herself away. "Like *they* murdered? There's a room back there full of bodies. Probably more in places where these demons have been."

"And would you kill me?" Trace asked, a touch of hard grim sadness in her eyes.

Maggie stared at her, helpless, and then sank to her knees. Strong, warm arms encircled her shoulders, and Samuel said, "You put too much on her. All of this was too much."

"Now or never," Trace muttered, and settled cross-legged on the floor in front of Maggie. Her eyes were solemn but kind—just like the woman Maggie had always known—but Maggie could not forget the sight of her stealing Ekir's life with a kiss.

Trace glanced at the teeth hanging from the necklace, and then met Maggie's gaze, giving her a long steady look. Maggie waited.

The old woman reached inside her mouth and tugged. Maggie heard a clicking sound, and then—another shock—Trace's teeth came loose in her wrinkled hand. Teeth, set in a neat row, embedded in a ridged plastic shell. A full set, both lower and upper halves. Trace held them in her palm.

"Those didn't come from a shark," she said, pointing at the necklace and showing off her pink gums. "But I got tired of being one way. I got tired of hurting folks for my supper. So I changed. I changed, Maggie Greene, in the same way those men might change one day. That's why I gave 'em a chance. That's why you should, too." Trace bowed her head, and placed her teeth back into her mouth. "Not much difference, you know. Got some of the same blood in your veins."

"How?" Maggie breathed.

"Your momma," Trace said, and hesitated. "My niece."

Maggie caught her breath. She felt woozy. Too much to hear, on top of the two dead men behind her, with more people close by. She swayed, and Samuel was there, bending to scoop her into his arms. He showed no sign of strain, and did not speak to Trace. He carried Maggie from the bookstore, into the cool night.

A great deal of time had passed. The sky was beginning to lighten. Maggie inhaled deeply, and the fresh air helped. Samuel set her down, carefully, on her feet, but she did not let go of him, and his arms remained around her.

"Mister Crow," she murmured.

"I wanted to tell you," he said. "I knew. I knew what Trace was, but I did not know how to share such a thing."

Maggie nodded, numb. "Did she tell you to stay with me?"

"She asked," he said softly. "But only, I think, because she thought it would do us both some good not to be alone."

Tears burned Maggie's eyes. She looked up as Trace exited through the creaking door, and stood there, very still, watching. She looked so human. So human.

Like you, she told herself.

"Did granddaddy know?" Maggie asked, wiping her face. "About you and me? My mother?"

"He was not your granddaddy," Trace said heavily. "He was your uncle."

Maggie stared. "He was an old man."

Trace leaned heavily against the door, and for the first

time, she looked her years. "He didn't start out old. He was young at the end of the Big Death. Not as young as you, but close. He just . . . didn't know what he had on his hands. His sister-in-law didn't mention you had . . . certain gifts."

Maggie pressed her hand over her mouth. "No. No, Trace. I . . . did I hurt him?"

"It was an accident," Trace whispered. "Truth was, I didn't even think you were capable of more than a few tricks. Your mother certainly didn't have much to show for the blood in her veins. But you . . . you were different." She looked deep into Maggie's eyes. "You were so horrified, you shut yourself down. You made yourself forget . . . everything. And I thought . . . I thought it was for the best. So did your . . . your granddaddy."

"My uncle." She breathed, remembering the old man— who had never shown a sign of fear around her, who had loved her as his own. Maggie was certain of that. She knew, in her heart, that much.

Samuel said, "And the demon? How did he find her?"

"Blood calls to blood." Trace crouched in front of Maggie. "He would have felt *something,* the closer he got. I was afraid of that happening one day. When I heard about those men and their motorcycles coming east, raiding Enclaves, I wondered if it might be them. I suspected. Made me worried they could catch your scent. I knew the truth when you described who visited that day, and knocked you flat on your ass. So I took off to find those brother numbnuts. I had words with them. Made a bargain. Irdu had to leave you with free choice, and if . . . if you chose *him,* I wouldn't interfere."

Maggie forced herself to breathe. "Is that why Ekir had your necklace?"

Trace grunted. "I made Ekir think he had a prize. You're not the only one who can see the future. I knew what would make you leave home. Irdu thought it would be him, that you'd be so enamored, you'd think of nothing else. Didn't know my Maggie. Not turned by a pretty head."

Samuel's arms tightened around Maggie. Trace added, "Until now, maybe."

Maggie covered her face. "Why so much interest in me?"

"You would have been strong enough to bear him a child," Trace said bluntly. "Children are rare among our kind. Those we consume don't survive too much, and only if we let 'em. Doesn't happen often."

Chills raced over Maggie's skin. She forced herself to look at Trace and said, "They were scared of you."

A grunt of laughter escaped the old woman's throat. "And now you, Maggie Greene. Now you."

They burned the bodies, including the cape of feathers that had belonged to Samuel's long-dead love. It was easier than trying to dig below the leaves and hit concrete.

Maggie did not stay and watch. At dawn, she walked inside the city, and listened to the birds sing, and watched the sunlight trickle through the green-budding branches. Spring, even here. Among the bones and ruins that in another twenty years might be lost forever in the endless tangled green.

But this place was not dead, she thought. There was life. Maybe not human, but there was life.

Trace had left her mules and wagon hitched somewhere on the northern side of the forest, and she went to fetch them. While she was gone, Maggie found Irdu's and Ekir's motorcycles, parked on the other side of the bookstore. The keys were in the ignition. She had found a gas station nearby.

A crow cawed once, sharply, above her head. Maggie looked up and watched the bird swoop low behind some bushes. Moments later, a human man pushed free, holding his cape of feathers around his waist.

"I think I've seen it all," Maggie said dryly.

A faint flush warmed his cheeks. "Until you return the favor, I think I will attempt some modesty."

She smiled—and marveled that she could. "Thank you. For everything."

Samuel looked away. "I did nothing. You saved yourself." He cleared his throat and looked down at his feet. "I suppose you will be going home. No reason not to."

"I don't know," Maggie said, running her fingers along the motorcycle; no longer quite so in love with the machine, but still in awe. "The world is big. I'm here now. I think . . . I think I might like to see more of it. Other cities. Other kinds of . . . people."

"Your home," Samuel said, moving closer, studying her face. "Your things."

Maggie swayed near him. "Things are just that. And I know where to find more now, if I really need anything." She hesitated, searching his eyes—trying to see the root of him, the corners of his soul. "You want to come with me? I could use a friend."

So simple. A straightforward question, heavier than the air around them, but Maggie had been through too much to care. Too much.

And she was not going to be afraid of her heart.

Wind sifted through Samuel's dark hair and feathers, and a faint, warm smile touched his mouth. "What would we do?"

"Talk, I guess," Maggie said carefully, also beginning to smile. "Same as always. We could find another forest. One without . . . you know, life-stealing demons."

"You're a life-stealing demon."

"But I won't steal *you*."

"Are you sure about that?" But Samuel was laughing now, silently, and when Maggie climbed on the motorcycle, he slid behind her, naked, his large elegant hands curling around her waist. Maggie turned her head and kissed him hard on the mouth. He tasted good.

She started the engine. And they flew away, into the forest.

DOWN IN THE GROUND
WHERE THE DEAD MEN GO

A Tale of Black London

Caitlin Kittredge

Been down with the devil in the Dalling Road
One place I don't want to go

—The Pogues

Edinburgh, 1990

The Crucifixion Club smelled like whiskey, smoke, and piss. The Poor Dead Bastards were on the downside of their second set, and the crowd had thinned to the diehards, the drunks, and the groupies.

Jack Winter leaned on his mike stand, feeling sweat droplets lick their way down his spine. Thank fuck for the groupies. They were the only thing that made some nights worthwhile.

Brown glass from a lager bottle crunched under Jack's boots as he grabbed the mike again, Gavin's drumming, like a heart in fibrillation, signaled the start of "Lockstep," the big finish, the big ending that should have them on their feet in the pit, at one another's throats—punks throwing elbows into skinheads, blood washed out by the janitor's mop at the night's end.

No one in the Crucifixion Club got the message. Jack shot a glance to the right, Rich the guitar player, to the left, Dix on bass. Then he threw the microphone down, into the pit. "You know what? Fuck it. You can piss off, the lot of you kilt-lifting wank-sacks."

A pint glass sailed past his head and shattered on the backdrop, a garish neon Jesus with purple blacklit blood spilling from his wounds. Jesus's eyes rolled up into his head, in a way that made him look like there was a weasel chewing on his privates.

Rich shucked his Fender and hopped down into the pit, retrieving the mike. He covered it with his long, spidery fingers, the calluses on the ends making rough noise against the PA. "Jack, the fuck are you on about?"

Jack wiped sweat off his face with the back of his arm, the salt blurring his eyes, making the shapes and shadows of the Crucifixion Club into a fever dream, just for a moment. "Come on, Rich. Let's get a drink and end the evening with our dignity intact. No one in this piss-miserable city wants to hear us play."

Gavin stopped drumming, the heartbeat bleeding away to flatline as he sensed the ugly black knot between guitarist and vocalist. Dix thumped his thumb on his bass in a discordant rhythm, his tattooed knuckles fluttering under the stage lights.

"Right or not, we have a contract," Rich said, gesturing with his head at the owner of the Crucifixion Club, an intractable Scot with a thatch of white hair and a face like a lorry wreck during rush hour. "Somehow, I don't think the old goat over there is going to be overjoyed if we cut out before finishing two hours." Rich shifted his weight, hid his next words with his back to the pit.

Jack scanned the crowd, more with his magic than his eyes, to make sure no skinhead was taking the golden opportunity to shank his guitar player in the kidney. Rich might be a pain in the arse, but he could make six strings sound like wailing bansidhe or angel tears, you just had to tell him which.

"We need the money, mate," Rich said. "I'm skint, and you know Ella is counting on me to make rent on the flat this month."

"Fine," Jack said. "Do 'Falling Down,' and I swear if another one of these kilt-lifters chucks a bottle at me fucking head, it's curtains."

Dix beat out the baseline, Rich hit the first chord, and Jack sang. He felt the smoke, raw in his throat. Most of all, he felt tired.

The night ended without a bang, without even a whimper. Jack helped Rich pack up his amps while Dix carried equipment back to the van, an arthritic Peugeot that oozed smoke and rust like a pustule on wheels.

"Hey, you. Boyo, with the Billy Idol up top." The Scot jabbed his cigar stub at Jack.

"Yeah?" Jack crossed his arms. He was half the Scot's breadth, but he had a good head on him. The old bastard would be trying to dick around with their payment, and it fell to Jack to deal with him, since they hadn't a manager, not even a proper roadie since Lefty Nottingham got pinched for passing bad checks.

"You got a girl out front." The Scot leered. "Nice gear, too. Real top of the pops."

"Jack." Rich glared warningly. "We have to start the drive back."

Jack went to the rat-eaten curtain and gestured to the Scot. "Point her out to me." Rich was engaged to Ella. He'd never dipped his pen in even when he hadn't been. Dix would go for anything that breathed, and Jack had a fair notion that Gavin was a poof, although it made no difference. Good drummers were worth their weight.

The girl sat alone at a table dead-center in the empty club. She was all black—black bob, black sweater, black pencil skirt that showed of a bit of Snow White leg in black fishnet stockings.

"Yeah?" said the Scot.

Jack stepped out from the curtain. "Yeah."

"Oh, fuck off!" Gavin shouted. "I want to be driving *out*

of bloody Scotland, not sticking around to sample the locals."

Jack flipped him the bird and walked over to the table. Pulled a chair and sat on it backwards. "You wanted to perform sexual favors for me, luv?"

She exhaled from a black cigarette with a gold band, blue smoke. Her face was heart-shaped, like a black-and-white film starlet's. Her severe bob and straight fringe made Jack feel as if he were looking at someone who might have conjured herself off celluloid, too refined for the likes of the Crucifixion Club.

Or Jack Winter himself, if Jack were being honest.

"Meet," she corrected coolly, the low throaty American voice sending gooseflesh over not-unpleasant parts of Jack's skin. "I wanted to meet you, Mr. Winter."

"Fuck," he choked out, losing himself in laughter. "*Mr. Winter* would be me dad, if I had one. Never met the bastard, so you can just call me Jack. What name will I be panting out for you, darlin'?"

"Ava," she said, and killed the ember of her fag in a Jesus-shaped ashtray. Even her name was posh and fantasy. Jack put his chin on his forearms and smiled at her.

"Pleasure's all mine, Ava. Or will be."

"Mr. Winter—Jack—if you'd stop for one moment, you'd discern I'm not interested in you. At all."

Jack felt his hard-on die a quick death underneath his ripped denim. "Ah," he said. "Then why're you wasting me time, exactly, luv?"

"Like I said"—Ava produced a pack of Turkish cigarettes and a silver lighter engraved with the initials DVB—"I wanted to meet you."

"And why's that, if not for a quick roll?" Jack demanded. "Any bloke can see you're not here for the music. If the outfit weren't a tipoff, the fact you've had a bath is. Bloody Scotland."

Ava's lips twitched. Jack consoled his loss of a fine, taut piece of groupie with the fact that she was at least pretty, and he'd at least made her smile.

"My friends in the city told me you were a mage. One who's good at what he does," said Ava. "And when I found out you were playing a gig here in Edinburgh, well . . ." She lit the fag with a hiss and pursed her full lips, full like fruit bursting with juice. "I figured you were just the man for the job."

"Someone's been speaking out of school," Jack said. It was probably Lawrence, that chatty bastard. He was only too happy to brag of his association with Jack fucking Winter to his little sewing circle of white witch mates, who in turn spread hideous rumors all over the fucking isle like they were some magic edition of *Hello!*.

"Don't be angry with your friends," Ava said.

He snorted. "You're assuming I have any."

Ava narrowed her eyes. Jack saw when she turned the lighter that her nails matched her lips, both kissed with false blood. She blew smoke out through her nose. "I can be very persuasive."

Jack looked her up and down obviously, taking in the breasts pushing at the sweater, the rear bumper that some would consider generous, but he considered fully serviceable. "I'll just bet you can, sweetheart."

"Do you ever pull yourself out of the gutter?" she demanded. Her brown gaze flashed daggers at him.

"No," Jack said, helping himself to one of the fags. When he reached for the lighter, Ava's hand shot out like an arrow off a longbow and closed on his wrist before he could touch it. "I rather like my gutter," Jack said softly, meeting those melting eyes. "I know all of the rats that live in it."

"I can give you money," Ava said. "I can give you anything you want. I need someone who won't fuck up, someone who'll do a sensitive task for me."

Jack got up at that. "Sorry, luv. I'm not a hire car."

"Wait," Ava said. "Don't you even want to hear my terms?" She leaned forward, a move that told Jack he very much wanted to hear her terms.

"I'm not an idiot, Ava," he said. "It's going to take more than a smile and a flash of the goods. I'm nobody's rent boy."

Rich came to the curtain and jerked his head, *Aren't we going yet?*

Ava trailed her finger down Jack's arm, past the line of razor cuts, road map to the twin cigarette burns on his wrist. "Been meaning to get a new tattoo," Jack said. He pulled his arm away.

"I'll make you a very good deal," Ava said. "For a very easy job. I promise."

"Demons deal in promises," Jack told her. "I don't like deals. In my experience, somebody always ends up fucked."

Ava stood. She was taller than Jack had imagined, tall enough to look him in the eye. "Funny you should mention demons." Her mouth curled, a little more blue smoke escaping.

"Not much about those buggers that calls forth a laugh," Jack said. Ava grinned at him—sly, and full of secrets, like an old fortune teller.

"Despite that, demons are exactly why I need your help."

Ava took them to a pub, a hole in the ground in a basement suite where water dripped from exposed pipes and you could smell the bog no matter where you sat.

Dix grunted as a droplet of condensation splashed into his pint. "You take us to the nicest places."

Gavin was sitting ramrod-straight, trying to avoid touching anything in the pub, including his glass. Rich was in the van, sulking.

Ava tilted her head. "Not to your liking, Gavin?"

"I'm going to get a disease, I know it," he muttered, and sunk into his army jacket up to the chin.

"Give us some privacy, lads," said Jack. "Won't be a moment to straighten this out."

Dix hit Gavin in the shoulder. "Come on, you great pair of girl's knickers. I fancy a smoke."

They left, and Ava let the door shut against the cool past-midnight air before she spoke. "You haven't tried to exorcise me, so you must have dealt with demon problems before."

"No," Jack said. "Haven't tried because it wouldn't do any bloody good. You're as human as they come, luv. The flesh is weak, through and through."

"You don't know that." Ava didn't have a drink, just a smug grin. Jack was reminded of a fat and well-groomed black moggy.

"You stay around the Black long enough, you learn to tell," Jack said. "Not knowing for sure can mean your skin. Your soul."

It was a pat excuse, a weak one at that, but Jack rubbed his forehead and gave Ava a wan smile. It was better than admitting to possessing the sight. Psychics were freaks, deranged and babbling at you in the entrance to the tube station. Mages, by comparison, were pillars of society.

By comparison.

Ava's aura furled back from her, red shot through with jet, like a solar storm or a sunrise that sailors would abjure. There was something dark riding with her, something curled on her shoulder to be sure, but she didn't make Jack dizzy as a two-day bender just to look at her. Definitely human.

"Fine, maybe I am," she said. "But my . . . problem isn't. I guarantee you she's as demon as they come."

"Name," Jack said, draining his pint to the dregs. He knew

what Lawrence would say—*Fuck off, you crazy bird*. But Lawrence wasn't around, and Ava *was* pretty.

Demons aside, the night could be going in worse directions.

"You think I know the true name of a demon?" Ava snorted. "We flesh-puppets aren't privy to that sort of information."

"You'd be surprised what people cough up when they're dying. Desperate. Pick your D-word." Jack pushed his glass at Ava. "Another, luv, and get me a plate of food, if this place has any that won't land me with botulism. If we're going to talk about demons, I'm going to need something to eat."

Her face glowed. "So you'll do it."

"Did I say I would?" Jack said. "Americans. So quick to jump their little six-guns. Get me another pint and order me a fry-up and we'll discuss it."

Ava narrowed her eyes. "Why? You were going to say no before."

She could read him well. Jack remembered that for the future, when he had the sneaking suspicion it would bite him in the arse. "You interest me." There, frank and open. "Not many humans deal with demons. Fewer call them a 'problem.' Must have a pisser of a story behind that."

Ava pushed back her chair and went up to the bar, passing the bartender a wad of notes. He grumbled, but went in back and turned on the grill.

Jack watched her, pulling a fag out of the air and touching his finger to the end. A moment before sweet, blessed tar filled his lungs. He should say no to Ava. Say no and walk away before he heard anything that would get a demonic boot in his arse, or outright killed in the street. Mages already had a short enough lifespan in the scheme of the Black, the harsh and gleaming world of magic they and a host of nastier creatures inhabited. Mages were forever damned to playing both sides, standing in the Black and the mundane, belonging to neither.

Just say no. Jack snickered at himself. Here he was, as if he were fourteen again, seeing ghosts and scared of the dark, and not a man who survived, who walked in and out of light and shadow like passing under a bridge.

The good: Ava meant money, a change from hours on the road, nights in clubs that smelled like piss and lager, kips in places that smelled worse.

The bad: he could end up in a backstreet with his heart torn out. Death in bloody Scotland.

Jack liked music, liked the life. He liked fronting the Bastards and having time with people who weren't aware of the Black any more than your average housewife.

But he admitted he liked the prospect of meeting Ava's demon even more.

"It's simple, really," Ava said. "I just need you to get me into the demon's city."

They were walking through narrow streets watched over by silent shops and terrace flats. Jack had convinced Rich, Dix, and Gavin to get bunks in a hostel. Rich complained, but Jack paid. Tomorrow they'd go back to England and he'd be here. But if it went sour tonight, Jack liked the idea that he wasn't alone.

He took a forkful of eggs from the takeaway container in his hand and chewed before he answered. "Never simple. Not with demons. Especially the type that have their own cities."

"What's your problem with demons?" Ava's heels made a sharp heartbeat on the pavement.

"What's your romance with them?" Jack said. The fry-up tasted of year-old grease and stale ingredients, but he was starving and Ava'd paid.

"Demons and I go back a long way, and I don't have any illusions about them," Ava said. "They took away someone I cared very much about. Let's leave it at that."

"What sort of deal did you make to get 'em back, then?" Jack glanced at her as he licked bacon grease off his fingers.

Ava rounded on him. "I *didn't* make a deal. My soul is my own."

"Ain't that a fucking bit of poetry," Jack snorted.

Ava took his container away and tossed it into a passing bin, then looped her arm through his.

"Aren't you curious? To know what type of girl I am?"

"I already know," Jack said. "Dangerous. Dangerous to a bloke like me."

"Look. I need to speak with a particular demon at a particular time, and I'm not welcome. I need a guide who knows the Black and has neutral associations with the demon contingent. That's where you begin and end. Sound dangerous? In the least?"

"I didn't say the job was dangerous, luv," Jack said. "Said *you* were dangerous."

Ava stopped him, with a hand on his chest, and pressed two fingers against his lips. "Take the job and you'll see I'm a pussycat."

She was warm, much warmer than the air around them. Jack curled his fingers around hers. "As long as this demon of yours will keep until morning."

"Yes," she agreed. "Morning will be fine."

Her skin was warm, and she smelled like heat and smoke. She tasted like magic burning.

Ava pushed him against the brick wall, the rough mortar scraping Jack's neck. Her fingers closed over the spot and her other hand tugged his belt, heavy with nail heads, free.

Jack pushed under her sweater, the cold of the night and

the heat of her skin combustible. He let her pull his head down, bruise her mouth against his and smiled around them at her gasp as his cold fingers trailed up her back.

Ava jerked his fly free, her hand freeing his cock from the confines of his jeans.

Jack tugged back against the hand on his neck. "You know I would have done the job without the favors, luv."

Ava kissed him again, biting his bottom lip before she let go and slid down his chest to waist level. "Shut up, Jack. That's not why."

Jack decided arguing any further would be pure idiocy. Her lips pressed down on him, and Jack's head snapped back against the brick, fingers knotting in the dark corn silk of her hair.

Her tongue, rough and insistent, stroked and curled around him, and Jack's throat caught, the only sound that escaped a groan as Ava moved.

He watched her head bob fore and back, hair gleaming under the streetlamps, each stroke of her mouth hotter and firmer and harder to resist than the last. Jack rolled his eyes upwards, to the rusted terraces and swaybacked rooflines of the mews.

Ava's tongue trailed along his underside, curled and sucked like she was savoring something sweet, and Jack shut his eyes, breath scraped from his throat. He put a hand on Ava's head, fingers tangling in her hair, trying to beg her to slow down, though he doubted he could actually speak. Ava didn't take his message, more insistent with every stroke, and Jack swore he could feel her grinning.

Her free hand hooked fingers over the waistband of his jeans, pads stroking against his hipbone, and it was that small, oddly intimate gesture that pushed Jack over the edge. He pushed his hips forward, and Ava let out a mewl as she allowed it, sticky lip gloss and spit and her frantic, hungry movement combining so that Jack let out a shout. "Fuck!"

Ava raised her eyes, alight with mischief. She sat back on her heels, tucked her hair behind her ear, and stood. She traced the crescent of her lower lip with her thumb. "Serviceable, I take it?"

Jack started to laugh as he buttoned himself up. "You know exactly what that was, you wicked tease."

Her mouth quirked up. "I do indeed." She slid a hand into his. "Come on, Winter. Let's get you to bed."

When he woke up, in the hostel bed on a mattress that barely deserved the title, the sun was just a possibility, a little ghost-light and shadow beyond the broken window shade.

Ava was gone, her clothes absent the floor and her heat vanished from the pillow next to him. Jack rolled out of the sheets and felt under the bed until he found his trousers and boots, and pulled them on.

The hostel was a Victorian pile, and there was a terrace, too small to really stand on but big enough to smoke a fag. Jack caught the eye of the mirror and ran a hand through his hair to make it stand up.

Just pink around the edges, the sky glowed, that unearthly glow that made normal people stay indoors. Jack lit up and blew smoke toward the heavens. Two drags in, the doorknob turned, creaking like dead bones in the old house.

"That was fast," Jack said. "But you didn't need to freshen up for me, luv. I rather liked you filthy." Hearing no reply, he half-turned. "Ava?"

A great weight hit him from behind—hands, Jack realized, massive hands—and bounced his skull off the door-jamb before taking him to the floor. A voice curled forth, over the ringing in his skull, like a tendril of smoke through the air. "Hold his arms, Barney."

Jack's face pressed into the musty Persian rug, and Barney planted a knee in his kidneys. Jack grunted. "Love you too, darling."

"Shut up," Barney intoned.

"Well," the voice said. Scots, the thick, expansive brogue that made tourists and Americans mistake the city of Edinburgh as friendly. "Jack Winter, is it?"

A toe reached under Jack's chin, lifted his face. The shoe was shiny snakeskin, emerald green dotted with black. The owner of the foot in the shoe reeked of burnt paper, the grand mal scent of demons.

"It's your fucking mum, is what it is," Jack snarled. He had a hangover, too much beer and sex, and too little sleep, and his mood in the mornings was uncharitable on any day.

"Just listen," said the voice of the shoe. Jack rolled his eyes up and saw a young git, angelic fat baby face, blond hair long enough to be fashionable in 1987 but no later, and a loud white suit that screamed *gangster*.

"You want me to listen, have your villain here leave off feeling me up. My gate don't swing that way, son."

Barney bashed Jack's nose into the carpet for his trouble. Bright Lad snapped his fingers. "Barney! That's quite enough. I'm sure Mr. Winter agrees there's no need for violence."

"Mr. Winter is going to shove your blond gob straight up your arse if you don't let him go," Jack grunted.

"Senseless altercations will only hurt you, Mr. Winter. Now, do I have your guarantee as a gentleman that you'll refrain from any antics if I let you up?"

Jack began to laugh, shaking the weight of Barney on his back. "Someone told you I was a fucking gentleman? You should pay him, mate, because that's a hell of a story."

"If you're not going to cooperate," Bright Lad said, "I do have other ways of keeping you compliant."

Jack sighed. "Just let me up. This carpet smells like piss."

Barney retreated, and Jack climbed to his feet, rubbing his forehead in a futile attempt to ease the throbbing. "Now tell me why you broke in here before I get all sorts of cranky fuck and do you in on the spot."

"That would be ill-advised, Mr. Winter," Bright Lad cooed. "Humans against demons tend to end in very small pieces."

"Little 'uns," Barney agreed, like lorries colliding. "Bite-sized."

Opening his sight just a little, Jack took another look at Bright Lad. White hair in a sharp point over his forehead, teeth even sharper, a lipless mouth, and great, screaming black holes for eyes. You could fall into those eyes, be torn apart by the knives in his empty gaze. . . .

Jack shook his head and passed a hand over his eyes. The screaming faded.

"Now that you've ascertained that I am, in fact, what I say I am," said Bright Lad, "I have a simple message for you."

"Hardly seems fair," Jack said. "You seem to know all about me, Tony, and I don't even know your name."

Bright Lad cocked his head. "Tony?"

"Montana. The suit? It's a bit over the top, mate."

The demon pursed his lips. "My name is Nazaraphael, Jack Winter. Now may I state my business?"

Jack picked up his leather coat, the liberty spikes pressing into his palm, reassuringly flesh and blood. He rattled around in the pockets until he found a bottle of rotgut whiskey that still had a mouthful left. He sat on the bed and swallowed it down. "Go right on ahead, Francis."

"Stay away from the woman you call Ava," said Nazaraphael. "Stay away from the underground. Leave Edinburgh today and don't come back. She's bringing more trouble on your head than you could imagine."

"Let me guess." Jack regretfully tossed the bottle at the bin. "If I don't, you'll do unspeakable things to my person and soul?"

"If you don't, you won't need my ministrations to regret your decision," said Nazaraphael. "You have no friends in this city, Mr. Winter. Make the right choice." He snapped his long fingers. "Come along, Barney."

Barney snarled at Jack as he passed. Jack caught a flash of black and red skin, muscle, chains anchored by hooks in weeping flesh. A berserker. He'd have to watch that one. Whatever magic Nazaraphael was using to control his attack dog, it wasn't enough.

Ava came back a few minutes after the demons had left. "What's wrong, lover?" she said, handing him a paper mug from Lavazza. "You look like a man who's just realized he's playing *The Crying Game*. I'm all woman, FYI." Low laughter, like velvet rubbing on skin. "But I think you've found that out."

Jack set the coffee aside. "I just had a visit from a right nasty member of Hell's Fashion Victims and his mate." He narrowed his eyes at Ava and she backed up a step, unconsciously. When the magic was up, Jack could feel the witchfire writhing behind his gaze, giving it a glow. It was a nice trick, for scaring the piss out of someone.

"That doesn't have anything to do with me." She came and straddled Jack's lap, breath warming a spot on his neck. "Maybe you looked at him funny."

Jack pulled back, far as the yoke of her arms would allow. "How about you put aside the femme fatale act, and you tell me the truth?" he said.

Ava licked her lips. "Or what?"

"Or I might take it into my head you're not as friendly as you first appeared, darling. And that might upset me greatly. What's the man say? You wouldn't like me when I'm angry."

Ava rolled her eyes. "I'm not crazy about you right now, either. This inquisitive streak is less than cute."

"You like them dumb, eh?"

"I didn't say that."

Jack ducked out from under her arms, and waited until Ava climbed off his lap. Reluctant as he was to lose the firm weight of her against his fly, the expression in her eyes was frozen over, cold.

"You're not just human, are you?" he said.

She sighed. "You weren't supposed to ask questions. They told me you'd do it for money and a quick roll. No questions."

"*They* were misinformed," Jack said. He watched Ava's aura unfold as she got up and paced. It was almost entirely red now, and there was a hot, hard sort of magic flowing from her that he'd mistaken for lust the previous night.

To be fair, Jack allowed, he probably would have pegged her correctly if he hadn't been drunk off his arse.

"What are you?" he asked softly.

Ava threw his shredded T-shirt at him. "Put your clothes on. It's better to talk in the open."

"Nazaraphael has spies everywhere," Ava explained when they were walking in the Prince Street Gardens, the sleeping bums and early joggers the only company.

"So you've had the displeasure," said Jack. He smoked, and the cloud of blue met the mist of the rising sun and mingled, interchangeable.

"Nazaraphael is the direct competition of Areshko, the demon I'm trying to speak with." Ava hunched her shoulders. "He's bad news, like we say across the pond."

"I sort of figured that bit out, him being a great bloody demon and breaking into me room and all."

"No, he's more than that." Ava rubbed her hands together, her sweater little help against the bite of the air. After a minute, Jack pulled off his coat and gave it to her, pulling the ambient pale green magic of the park around him and warming it so he wouldn't shiver.

"Thanks." She wrapped the battered thing around her,

sinking into it. "There are demons in Edinburgh that don't agree with the way Nazaraphael does things. Areshko is one of them." They stopped at a copse of bushes and Ava looked over her shoulder. There was just a bum wrapped in newspapers, mumbling to himself. Jack saw the silvery flash of a spirit hanging over his shoulder, talking back.

There's your future, Winter. Jack blinked the spirit out of his view. It used to be easy to shut them out. Lately, it was like someone had set an amplifier next to his head and cranked every knob to ten.

"You know, this cryptic bullshit might fly with the bell, book, and candle ponces, but not with me," Jack said. "Still haven't explained what your stake in this is and who you are."

"I'm me," said Ava. "I didn't lie about that. What I am . . ." She chewed on her lip, making it look bruised, kissed.

"If you say 'It's complicated,' I'll fetch you a smack," Jack warned. "Crow help me."

"I'm a demon hunter." Ava stopped and stared at him, daring him to react badly. Jack laughed instead.

"What, like you run about with a sword and a little cross, exorcising for the greater good? Americans have some bloody strange hobbies, don't they?"

"I'm dead serious," Ava said. "Nazaraphael is a bastard, but Areshko is worse. I had a friend, Daniel. She killed him and picked his bones clean."

"You think you're the only one in the whole of the Black had a mate come to a bad end?" Jack snorted smoke from his nose.

"He loved me." Ava's face went hot, blossoms of blood coloring her pale cheeks. "The only way I'm getting close enough to take her out is on the arm of someone like you. I'm murdering the demon who murdered my friend, Jack. Now you've got the whole truth."

"And I'm rapidly walking the other way, luv," Jack said,

turning to do just that. "You think I'm going to lead a fox into a birdhouse and have any sort of life expectancy after you've slung your weight around?" He shook his head. "Mages live because we're useful, because neither side claims us. Once I throw me lot, I might as well throw me person off a car park." He snatched for his leather. "Give the jacket back."

"You don't have a choice." Ava's voice rang over his shoulder, sharper than the cold air, after he'd gone a few yards.

Jack flipped two fingers at her over his shoulder and kept walking.

"*STOP!*"

The spell unfolded and spread its fingers over him, loops and shackles of magic like red-hot iron, and Jack stopped with a gasp as every bit of his body lit up with flame. He couldn't move, could barely breathe, and tasted ash in his mouth.

Ava walked around to his front and shook her head. "That was just my safety, but you're as stubborn as they say."

"What . . ." Jack felt sweat work down his temples, his spine, and the magic was consuming him, reaching down to his core as the spell writhed on his skin. He wanted to grab Ava, push her skirt aside, tear at the lace tops of her stockings, and lose himself in her until he was spent. The desire was wrenching, consuming. "What did you do?" he managed.

"Relax," Ava soothed. "It's a geas."

Jack felt the tendons in his neck twitch, as he fought against the spell that kept him rooted, the desire that clenched at his core. "You didn't cast a geas on me. You didn't do any magic."

"I did," Ava said. Her lips twitched. "Sex magic."

Jack's heart plummeted to the vicinity of his boots. "Fuck off. No one practices that in this age."

Ava trailed her finger from his jaw down his neck and across his chest, skin-on-skin contact through the holes in his shirt. Jack let out an involuntary moan, his cock jumping painfully against his fly.

"Don't they?" Ava purred. "Funny. This little trick usually works pretty well."

"You can't . . ." Jack tried to fight, pushing against the great pulsing loops of the geas with his own talent, but all that he could see was a great red blur of lust and compulsion that made his heart hammer a hole through his chest.

"I just did." Ava snapped her fingers. "Enough."

The geas retreated and Jack collapsed, his muscles aching like he'd come through a fever and gotten seven colors of shit kicked out of him in the bargain.

"Until my business with Areshko is done, consider yourself my employee," Ava said. "And if you cooperate, you won't feel that again. I'd much rather have you on my side than force you there."

"You'd better pray you can run far and fast enough when I slip your leash, you trixy wight," Jack panted. He managed to get up, soaked in sweat and still horny as a sailor on his first hour of leave. "Because if I catch hold of you . . . I'm going to make you sorry you clapped eyes on me."

"Talk, talk, talk," Ava said. "Believe me, Jack, talking is not your strong suit." She leaned and kissed him, and it quenched a little of the ache inside him. Jack felt a sort of filthy miasma slither over the exchange, like something glimpsed down a side alley in a bad neighborhood.

She had her hooks in him. He hadn't seen the knife behind her back, and now he was fucked.

"Come on," Ava said, and the geas tugged him. The worst part was, he didn't entirely want to disobey.

"I figured it out when I was around fourteen." Now that she had him on a tether, Ava was positively chatty. They left the gardens and she hailed a cab. "Train station, please. Thanks." She put her hand on Jack's knee, and he shrugged her off.

"Oh, don't be mad at me." Ava sighed. "Live long enough and you're bound to run into someone smarter than you. It'll happen to me, too. Just remember that it was really incredible, wall-shaking sex that got you into this mess."

"Trust me," Jack said with a grimace. "That's exactly what I'm doing."

"Like I was saying"—Ava leaned her forehead against the window, as the early morning furled by the misted windows of the cab—"I figured it out when this friend of my father's came after me. He did what he did, but afterwards . . ." Her lip curled back. "Afterwards he was all mine. They found him hanging from his balcony."

"Thrilled as I am that you're working out your daddy issues with me," Jack said, "what do you expect me to do, hurl fireballs at whoever you aim me toward?"

Ava snorted. "I'll take care of Areshko. You just stand there and look pretty."

"I don't suppose reiterating that you'll literally be putting a stopwatch on my life expectancy if you make me do this will sway that icy heart, my princess?" Jack shifted, to be as far away from her as he could.

"No." Ava slid over, closed the distance, started nibbling at his neck. "Sorry. I'll try to make it up to you."

He wanted to shove her off, tell her to keep her filthy magic paws off him, but it felt . . . It felt like a hunger that he'd never known he possessed was finally being sated. Jack moaned and leaned into her.

"Train station," said the driver, clearly glad to have the sex-crazed American and her fling out of his cab. Ava paid and took his hand.

"I have to put a few things together before we make this attempt. I suggest you get your affairs in order and tell your band to go home before Nazaraphael decides to use them as leverage." She stepped away from him. "And if you get an idea to break the geas, or run . . . don't. I'll find you. And no matter how cute you are, I won't be pleasant when I do. Clear enough for you, Jack?"

"Crystal," said Jack. He lit a fag and sucked on it. If Ava didn't get him, Nazaraphael would. Might as well poison his lungs while he had lungs to poison.

"Good boy." Ava blew him a kiss. "Meet me right here at noon."

Jack returned her smile with a snakelike grin of his own. "You're not getting out of this free and easy. Don't think you are."

"That sounds like a promise." Ava waggled her fingers at him. "Noon. Don't be late."

Jack found a pub. It was the natural thing to do when you were fucked, and English.

He stared at his pint, the bubbles slowly working their way from bottom to top.

Ava had him over a barrel. Even if Jack could assemble the workings to break a geas in a few hours, he wasn't sure it would work, whether it would snap back and kill him outright. Dying of lust wasn't the worst way to kick it, but it wasn't on his top ten list, either.

Damn the bitch. She'd zeroed in on his weakness and his arrogance, that he was Jack fucking Winter, untouchable, and she'd slipped inside his armor as neatly as a serpent. Now she wanted him to be party to the assassination of a demon.

"Not bloody likely," Jack said to his pint, and drained half of it in a go. Ava wanted his help badly, that much was plain, and equally plain was that she wasn't giving him the whole story, playing the cryptic woman who comes out of the rain into the private dick's office, asking for help, poison on her red lips. Playing it to the hilt.

Jack drank the rest of his pint and didn't taste it, turned over the question some more. Could he afford to believe Ava was simply an arrogant sorcerer with an inflated sense of her own superiority on a half-cocked revenge drive? That she couldn't dent Areshko, this boogeyman demon?

Devious as the bint had shown herself to be, Jack doubted he'd get off that easily.

A fresh pint banged on the wood in front of him. Rich, Gavin, and Dix joined the table, drinks in hand. "Now that you've kept us here far past the freshness date, what're you banging on about staying?" Rich demanded.

"Yeah," said Gavin. "We've got a gig Thursday, mate. Sort of need our lead singer. I can't swap—I already took the personal day." Gavin worked in a chain record store on Oxford Street, the sort that made you wear a colored shirt and a name badge. Jack and Dix gave him endless shit about it.

"That girl in the Crucifixion Club," Jack said. "She's got a gig for me. Just me."

"Fuck off, you're not *that* good. Or handsome." Rich took an irritated sip of his beer.

"Not a Bastards gig, you git. The other sort."

Dix just nodded gravely. Gavin chewed a hangnail, and Rich rolled his eyes. "Not more of your spooks and specters shite, Winter. Those Goths always pay in bent pennies and mournful stares. We need you in London. For *real* work."

"I'm serious as a tombstone," Jack said. "And I'm also staying. You can whinge about it all you want. Get it out of your system. Cry if you have to."

Dix grunted. "Bad idea, this."

Rich pushed back from the table. "He's right. And if you feel that it's a bright one, you can bugger yourself sideways with a lager bottle. I'm going back to London. Shall we audition a new singer tomorrow, or after we cancel our engagement and can't pay the electric or the phone?"

Gavin watched him go, and then sighed. "I can't disagree with him, Jack. I've got my job, and my mum isn't well. . . . This rock star shite doesn't fly in my life as it is."

Jack dropped his fist down. All of the glasses jumped. "Fine. Go skip on back to London in your pinafore, you great girl. Not like I could expect a little backup from my *friends*."

Gavin pursed his lips. "No need to be that way, Jack. . . ."

"You've made yourself clear," Jack said. "Go on, get lost. And tell Rich he can use that lager bottle on himself, if he's so keen."

Dix nudged him before the tiff with Gavin could dissolve into a real John-and-Yoko slugfest. "Ey. That your bird?"

Ava stepped in, pausing to unwind a crimson scarf from her sausage-curled hair. There was a light mist on the gray day, and droplets of moisture gleamed on her skin.

She glided over to the table, sliding into Rich's empty stool and running her fingers down Jack's arm, over the Celtic knot tattooed on his bicep—the triple insignia, done in plain blue ink, by hand, signifying that he'd been trained in magic by the Fiach Dubh. Jack had never met a villain yet on either side of the Black who was impressed by the mark.

"You weren't where I told you to be. Aren't you going to give me a kiss hello?" Ava inquired. Dix raised his eyebrows an inch, the equivalent of shouting, for most. Gavin just rolled his eyes.

"Sorry, luv, but you're not very popular among my mates at the moment," Jack told her. Ava pressed her lips to his cheek. Jack felt the hot wax and wet of her lipstick mark his skin sure as the tattoo.

"Hello," she said. "And hello to you, Jack's mates. What's a girl have to do to get in your graces?"

"Scratch," said Dix. "Or tits."

"A man of few words." Ava smiled, just this side of mockery. "I'm entranced."

"They were just buggering off back to London," Jack said. "I guess I'm at your service, milady."

Ava smiled, all teeth. "You bet your ass you are." She turned to Gavin and Dix. "Nice meeting you. Run along. Drive safely."

"Go fuck yourself, slag," Gavin said sweetly. "Our mate may be fooled by you, but I know cheap damaged goods when I see them."

"My, my," Ava said. "You've got some grit behind that limp wrist, boy."

Jack turned a glare on her. "Leave them out of this or I swear I'll slit me own throat with the cutlery before I go another step with you."

Ava and Gavin traded simmering glares for a moment, before Gavin pushed his chair back with a shriek. "Just don't come crying to me when you get fucked, Winter."

"Don't you worry." Ava's hand slid over the black denim up Jack's thigh and into coastal waters. Jack tightened his jaw and cast her a pained look. "He's in good hands."

Jack briefly saw stars under her ministrations as the sex magic ran fingers and tendrils of sweetly scented power over his face. "Gavin," he ground out, "stop being a nonce. I'm fine."

Dix shrugged. "No, you're not." He scraped back his stool and pulled on his shredded denim jacket. "Happy trails, mate." They left, and Jack squeezed his eyes shut. The Bastards barely tolerated the other half of his existence as it was. And if Jack was honest, he liked the easy time they had making the music come together. Ava had burned all that down with a few words, a touch.

She stopped her hand moving and stood up. She was wearing a black satin pencil skirt now, and a red cardigan with cherries for buttons. Her hair was pinned back in a waterfall of curls. She looked like the pouty-lipped American birds that Jack's uncle Ned had collected on the walls of his locksmith shop in Manchester. Uncle Ned had been a good bloke for the few years that Jack knew him before his liver said *Bugger this* and gave out under an onslaught of off-license vodka.

"Let's go," Ava said. "With friends like those . . ."

"If you had any friends," Jack said, following her as the geas pulled on him like a sharp hook through the flesh of his spirit, "you wouldn't say that."

"Look who's got a mouth on him," Ava said. She gave his arse a squeeze. "Cheer up, Jack. I'm very good company, if you let me be."

"Need the loo," he said. "I won't be a minute, mistress."

Ava's mouth turned down at the sardonic tone. "Jack, I told you this wasn't how I wanted things."

"And yet you don't seem to be shedding any tears over having your very own mage in sexual bondage." Jack stepped away from her, experimentally, and she let him. None of the white-hot need to rip her blouse open and savage her, teach her the wrongness of making a man like him her pet, reared its head.

"Go pee," Ava said, an impatient click of her pump heels on the pub floor. "We don't have all day."

Jack turned his back to her, and she let him walk. He knew the part of himself that responded to her geas. It usually manifested as temper, or as the row of paper-thin white scars on his forearms, rather than a savagery toward a woman.

But Ava was no usual woman, and Jack didn't have perfect control.

He locked himself in the bog and pulled the frayed light chain. Shadows danced and settled into all of the corners. Jack splashed rusty water on his face and dried off on the tail of his shirt.

Even though she'd shown herself to be colder than stone, he could almost fancy Ava. She had balls, and she wasn't afraid, of him or the demon. Not to mention that she was a regular talent in the sack.

Which had gotten him into this, hadn't it?

A snuffling from the corner broke Jack's concentration, on a cracked mirror hung crooked over the basin. Cold ran up and down his neck, like sleet melting on his skin.

"Please . . ." A whisper came from all directions, higher than a dog whistle, and skated across Jack's skull, and he flinched. He didn't want to turn and see. He never truly wanted to see, and never had, but he always looked, eventually.

The ghosts wouldn't allow otherwise.

"Please," the ghost snuffled. He was a sad scrap of spirit, a skin-and-bones teenage boy in life with raggedy hair in his eyes. A crooked star, drawn around the left with eye pencil, scrubbed off as his tears slid down his glitter-pocked cheeks. His silk shirt was open to the waist, and his pants were worn away at the knees. *"Please, don't tell them where I am,"* he begged Jack, worrying a glass vial around his neck.

Jack pressed his thumb between his eyes, the pounding inside his skull threatening to send him to his knees. The sight took everything away, sound and sensation—everything except the sucking, screaming void where spirits lived.

"Fuck off," he told the ghost. "I can't help you."

"Can't help me," the ghost singsonged. *"Can't help your-self."*

"Oi, shut it," Jack warned. "I don't need your second-rate prophesizing."

"They found me." The ghost sighed. *"They kicked me and hit my skull against the sink. They beat my queer face in."*

"And I'm sorry," Jack gritted as warm blood worked its way out of his nose. Ghosts always wanted help. Always wanted to let go and never could. And the harder they fought to be seen, the more it hurt.

"Not sorry," the ghost whispered. *"Not like you will be."* The boy jerked up straight, his coke vial bouncing against his wasted chest, rife with bruises from the beating that had

ended him on the scarred tile floor. *"Turn back, Jack Winter. The demon city waits for you like the open mouth of the beast, and will swallow you."*

Jack smeared the blood away from his face. "That's not a ghost talking."

The boy's eyes shone, white as headlamps in a fog. *"Leave Edinburgh, Jack Winter. Before you go down under the ground. Forever."*

"Bugger off, Nazaraphael," Jack said wearily. He was upright, barely, by grace of clutching the sink basin. "Leave that poor spirit be."

"It's a fair warning, mage, and the last you'll get," the boy-ghost growled, before the glow died from his eyes and he went back to sobbing.

Jack shut his eyes and willed to see only a filthy pub loo when he opened them. The sight burned him up from the inside when it truly took hold, made him sick and dizzy as a lifetime of hangovers. It never slept, never stopped.

But finally, it retreated enough for Jack to stumble back into the pub and take hold of Ava. She blinked at him.

"What's wrong?"

"Nothing," he grumbled. "Let's get the bloody hell out of here."

"You don't look good . . . Are you *bleeding*?" Ava demanded.

Jack squeezed her arm hard enough to feel the bone under the skin. "Sodding walk. I need fresh air."

Ava went silent, and after a time, Jack's vision cleared and his heart stopped hammering and the earth stopped churning under him. Ava smiled, leaning her head against his shoulder.

"Better now?"

Jack swiped greasy sweat from his forehead. "Still a bit sick. No one really wants a demon manifesting to them in the bog."

Ava went on tiptoe and licked his ear. "Believe me, after this is over . . . I'll make you forget *all* about big bad Nazaraphael." She turned and led Jack into the train station, the slow sway of her hips like the passage of a ship.

Jack shoved his hands into his pockets and looked anywhere but her admittedly pristine rear bumper. On the opposite side of the street, shadows moved in concert, as if the sun were setting in cadence with his footsteps.

Trackers. Maybe ghosts, maybe demons. Certainly employed by that white-suited ponce Nazaraphael. Jack flipped two fingers at the shadows and turned into the cavernous innards of the train station, feeling like a man walking the last mile to his death.

Ava stopped on the train platform like a flickering spirit from a movie about love, and loss, and wartime, done up in black and white.

Jack found a fag, lit it with his finger, and wrinkled his nose. "Stinks down here."

Ava cast a nervous look back over her shoulder, and Jack didn't doubt her instincts. This was a good place for an ambush. Not from ghosts or the Fae—too much iron—but demons—or fuck it, humans—could be three feet from him, tucked back in the dark places, and he'd never see it coming.

Jack muttered under his breath, felt the ambient magic of the Black pluck at him, and sent a small tendril outward, searching, feeding back. Ava was a hot spot, her humanity and the spell that bound them, but otherwise the tunnel was blank and cool, devoid of feeling.

Lots of people could keep themselves under wraps against an inelegant finger of mage spellcasting. Every demon could. Cold comfort was better than no comfort.

"We're alone," Ava said, and he coughed.

"No offense, luv, but I already got jumped by a great

bloody demon wanker today and I'm not keen on a repeat. Not to mention that you, yourself, qualify as a hazard to me health."

"Whatever makes you feel better, lover." Ava jerked a thumb at the mouth of the tunnel, ringed with lamp-teeth and wires. "Come on. I'll brief you on my plan on the way down."

"Down where?" Jack asked, but Ava shook her head.

"Good things come to those who wait," she teased.

Jack watched Ava duck under the barrier at the end of the platform and push free a small service door. It tugged at him, that primal urge not to stray from the campfire, but Jack hadn't spent his life being part of the pack. He knew the things that lived outside the circle of light, knew them by name.

Because he knew, knew why ordinary people were afraid of the dark. And rightly so. He flicked his fag away and followed Ava. Nothing nasty leaped out at him, and the geas eased a bit, lessened the shrieking in his brain, if he stayed close. She'd probably planned it that way. Clever little bint.

They walked through a curved service tunnel with yellowed tiles cracked and leaking from the Blitz. Jack saw a little girl in a car coat, clutching a doll to her chest as she crouched against the wall. She flickered, one moment staring at the floor, the next at him. Black pools of eyes. Lips curled back from pointed teeth, hands sprouting claw-nails.

"Can't help you, luv," he said quietly. "No sense in rattling your chains at me, is there?"

Ava looked back when he stopped walking. "Problem?"

"Not in the least," he said. The angry little ghost faded from existence as quickly as her life had been snuffed by the Luftwaffe. Jack brushed off the chill from his neck and walked on.

The tunnel was long, lit with bulbs in steel cages that flickered and fluttered like a spirit trapped under glass.

Ava's hair gleamed like oil under the light. Jack ran his hand over his own peroxided bristles, felt dampness from the aboveground world clinging to his skin.

"How far are we going?" he said.

Ava smiled over her shoulder, teeth bright.

"As far as we need to."

Jack's hand flashed out and wrapped around her arm. "That's not much of an answer, luv."

Ava twisted, like a snake in his grasp, and Jack felt her small hand close at his throat and his head slam into the tile, sending grout and grime loose and clattering to the floor.

"I am being nice, Jack," she whispered. Jack felt her breath, she was so close. "Don't make me be naughty."

"Are we having a lovers' quarrel?" he rasped.

Ava's lips trembled. "I am not screwing this up," she said, her voice like steel. "I have waited too damn long for my shot at Areshko."

"What's your epic love with this Daniel bloke?" Jack said. "Areshko snatch his soul away before you could have the white wedding? He go rushing in to defend your honor? Or was he a stupid git, like all the others a demon kills, and you think you can make it not so by avenging him?"

"You shut your mouth," Ava spat. There was something in her look, in her touch that sent a peculiar heat all through him. Not the heat of her magic, skin-on-skin, sweat and release. This was the kind of heat that warned a bloke that he was about to catch on fire.

"You haven't told me anything close to a whole truth, and I haven't pressed," he said. "But when I can't help you no matter how hard you push or how much you beg, remember you had the chance of help from the goodness of me fucking heart, and you chose to be cryptic."

After an interminable second, her grip eased enough that he could breathe again. "I can't tell you," she whispered. "I can't."

"Fine," Jack said. "You had your chance."

"And you are a bastard if I ever saw one," Ava snapped. "With your lectures and your holier-than-thous."

"Holier? Hardly." Jack snorted. "I never had a problem with a lady taking the lead. It's a bit sexy, really."

Ava brushed her hands over the front of her skirt, like touching his skin had dirtied her, and moved on.

Jack was left to trail again, and wonder what the bloody hell she was lying to him about when she had no reason to keep secrets at all. She had the cards. Every last bloody one.

Ava stopped at a metal fire door, long rusted shut, the warnings that no one except employees of the city of Edinburgh were allowed beyond this point obscured with graffiti endorsing a variety of gangs, ethnic groups, and bands. *PAKIS GO HOME* warred with *SKINHEADS FANCY BLACK COCKS* and the eternal sentiment *FUCK THATCHER*.

"I'll take a pass on that last," Jack said.

Ava pressed on the door and there was a grumbling of wheels and gears from beyond the wall. The door swung back with a great tomb-creak that would have done Count Dracula—the Lugosi version, of course—proud.

Beyond was a flight of stairs, and the dank breath of underground. "Down here," Ava said. "This is the fastest way to Catacomb City."

"Isn't that precious and twee. Catacomb City." Jack let witchfire blossom around his palm, the blue glow lighting the stairway in sharp relief.

"A demon city, in the catacombs," Ava said, her heels clicking on the damp concrete. There was moss, and rot, and water dripping invisibly. No one had come this way in a long while.

Jack itched for a fag as they descended. His wasn't sight tweaking, like it had in the old railway tunnel, but there was something else here, some eidolon waiting in the dark that whispered and clawed at him from the Black.

The curving stairs and the geas made him stick so close to Ava that he was practically in her pocket, and she smiled back at him like they were on a lovers' walk. Jack saw lamps clipped to the pipes overhead, so old they were just rust lace in great spreading patches. A utility tunnel, in its previous life. The ceiling jogged lower and he ducked, the very top of his hair flattening out against the slimy surface.

Ava turned back, her cheeks dimpling. "A little close, isn't it?"

"It's a bloody grave," Jack said, bending over and flexing his palm. The flames of witchfire leaped higher, a wreath of slow-motion flame enclosing his hand, showing all the bones. Just ambient magic burning off in the world of the solid and real, but the effect usually kept people at a distance.

Ava sighed. "Put it back in your pants, Jack. Areshko's buddies won't be pleased if you come in with guns blazing."

"Thought that was why you bloody tricked me into this," Jack said.

"Yes, but we're trying to make love, not war, if you can wrap your mind around that," said Ava. "Until I'm ready, Areshko needs to think I'm one of hers."

"What am I, then?" Jack regretfully let go of the slip of Black that allowed his witchfire to burn, and the light went out. It got colder, and he shivered in his leather.

"Look at that." Ava smirked. "The bad nasty mage is afraid of the dark."

"Anyone with sense is afraid of the dark," Jack told her. He felt for his lighter and found instead a leftover glow stick from a music festival in Brighton––frightful new-wave synth-pop, lots of girls in baggy pants and flannel; all around, a wasted weekend.

Jack cracked the stick and alien green flared, making Ava blue-tinted where she walked beside him. His own flesh just went a little paler, ghost pale, and he could see all of his veins, the road map of the skin.

"So here's how we work it," Ava said, loud enough to carry along the length of the tunnel. The pipes petered out, and it was brick now, the mortar hollowed out and rats skipping in and out of gaps in the stone. A Victorian sewer, with the smell to match. The fetid river trickling through the dip in the floor splashed on Jack's boots and promptly soaked his socks.

"Bloody hell. This Catacomb City better have plumbing, luv."

"Don't worry," Ava said. "Your delicate sensibilities won't be tested for long."

" 'Delicate,' hell. You can *taste* the air down here." Jack's feet squelched and echoed off the tunnel walls.

"I'm going to tell Areshko I want to make a deal with her." Ava slipped her arm through Jack's. "For something or other—I think best on the fly. When she brings me in to her private chamber to seal the bargain, I'm going to kill her."

"Just another day as a demon hunter, yeah?" Jack muttered. "You can't kill a demon, Ava."

"Don't start with me," she said. "I've done it. Believe it or not, Jack, not everyone lives in fear of hellfire. Some of us have learned to fight, and if you cared a little bit more about your fellow mages and a little bit less about yourself—"

"You don't finish that thought, if you know what's good for you," Jack snarled. His heartbeat overshadowed the sound of their steps. "You know *nothing* about me, Ava. Bloody skint."

"And you don't know me, either," Ava said. "Demons don't come out on top with me, Jack."

"Let's hope so," Jack muttered.

Ava's heart was pounding, those extraordinarily statuesque breasts rising and falling fast.

"You were trained by the crow monks," she said. "I saw the ink and I know what it means. *I* was trained by a hunter who knew his shit. You should try a little trust with me, Jack."

"Not a vice I make a habit of, trust," Jack said. "I find it allows treacherous little bitches with sad eyes entirely too close."

Ava rolled her eyes. "I like you, Winter, but this is getting . . ."

Something tickled across the back of Jack's neck before he could snap back, cold and sharp like a scale, or a fingernail. He hushed Ava. "We're not alone."

Ava stiffened, and they both looked down the black mouth of the sewer tunnel. "Kill the light," she said.

Jack shoved the glow stick into his pocket. He tried to burn a hole in the darkness, see through it, but it was only a weak white glow from up ahead.

"Shit," Ava hissed, so quiet as to be just another breath. Jack heard a rustle as she crossed herself, a quick economical motion like cocking a shotgun. His own heart thumped against his bones.

The white glow grew, bobbing through the dense air of the tunnel, and the figure within it floated into view. A woman, or really a girl, her long nightgown stained with blood, black tears coursing down her cheeks, her arms, covered in cuts, outstretched in supplication.

The terrifying thing wasn't the spirit. It was the fact that Ava saw her, too.

"What is it?" Ava asked. Her breath made a puff of cold as the temperature dropped around them. Frost grew on the bricks, feathers and fingers reaching out for Jack's cheek.

"It's a ghost," Ava whispered to herself. "I've never seen a ghost—"

"Ghosts don't bring the cold with them," Jack said. "That isn't a ghost."

The girl locked eyes with him. They were black, like a spirit's, but white flame danced in their depths.

She opened her mouth and let out a moan, and then, she was against Jack, her hands at his throat, freezing, burning with cold.

Jack slipped in the water and found himself flat for the second time that day, the thing howling and scratching at him. He felt it latch on to his magic, the part of him that lived, bright and burning, in his chest.

Sorcerers could leech your magic and Fae could drink it like nectar, but nothing could yank it from him like this, this pain that made him scream and snap his teeth together as a convulsion gripped him.

The girl's hand was in his chest, in his heart. Jack forced his eyes open and looked into her howling face. Only one thing could turn the air cold and drink down human energy.

"Ava . . ." Jack gasped. "Ava, help me . . ."

Ava, her face a flat sheet of white, yanked a knife from her sweater pocket and flipped the blade open. "Get out of the way!" she shouted.

Jack struggled against the creature, feeling ice-chip nails digging into him, his blood freezing as it came in contact with the air.

"Move!" Ava shrieked, and Jack clawed at the thing, his fingers passing through the girl's face, her shrieking mouth.

"I'm bloody trying!"

Ava gritted her teeth, and flipped the knife in her palm to hold it blade first. She cocked it back and threw it. The blade passed through the howling, screeching girl and she wavered, trailing off like blood in water. Jack felt a sharp, short tug in his shoulder, and then pain, as hot as crematory fire, chased away the cold. The knife was in his flesh, and the ghost was shrieking and thrashing, pinned by the iron surely as a butterfly on a tray.

Jack reached into the Black and locked his hand around the ghost's neck in turn. Blue fire blossomed. "That's the end for you, luv," he said, and pushed the girl off him. She was hungry, but Jack was desperate and bloodied, and his raw piece of magic blasted her off him and dissolved her into a thousand black strands of smoke.

Ava leaned down and pressed a hand over the wound. "Hold still. This will hurt." She yanked the blade free without any warning, and Jack let out a yelp several octaves higher than he would have liked. Ava shook her head as she helped him up. "What the fuck," she said, "was that?"

Jack accepted the silk handkerchief she handed him and pressed it over the knife wound, below his collar bone, but it still spread a dull, sick ache all through him, and his vision blurred. "A revenant," he said. "A citizen of the City of the Dead. Bansidhe, black dogs, those sorts of things. Hungry dead things, looking for their next meal."

"Is that . . . *normal*?" Ava picked up the blade from the ground, wiped it carefully on her arm, and folded it back in on itself.

"Iron destroys revenants." Jack felt the bloody scratches on his neck. "Much as it buggers me to say it, you saved my life."

Ava shrugged. "Of course I did. I need you, Jack. And I like you, a little."

Jack popped the kinks out of his back from where he'd hit the brick. His shoulder was bleeding slowly, a steady leak that would do him serious harm if he didn't get it stopped. He wadded the silk up tighter, shoving it under his shirt, hissing as the pressure sent fresh fingers of pain up and down his arm. "I suppose I can stand the sight of you, as well."

"Touching. Let's keep moving," Ava said. "The city is much safer than these tunnels."

"You're wrong," Jack said quietly, after they'd been walking for a time. "Revenants don't just appear. Someone has to let them out of the City."

"So?" Ava said. "Obviously, Nazaraphael has a problem with you being down here, with me."

"So, demons don't need revenants to do their work," he said. "Nazaraphael has Barney, and a hundred others he could have sent if he really wanted us out."

"We're not the only humans down here," Ava said. "Some kid must have been messing with necromancy."

"Undoubtedly," Jack said. His voice dripped ice, just as the revenant had.

"You can rot in Hell, Jack," she said. "I'm not a liar."

"Oh, you are," Jack told her. "We all are, luv. What matters is the reason for the lie, the core of truth. Feel like telling me that much yet?"

Ava sighed. The sewer diverged in two, and she ducked down into a tunnel that was old enough to be of rough stone instead of brick, the floor packed earth. "We're close," she said. "I promise, Jack, this isn't malice. I picked you out of practicality."

"For both our sakes, darling, I hope you were telling me the truth just then."

"Me too," Ava murmured, slipping ahead into the dark.

The tunnels got so low that Jack banged his head unless he bent at the waist. He cursed when he left hair and blood behind. "I'm going to need a new head, we keep this up."

"Might improve things," Ava teased.

"Up yours," Jack muttered, but the mood had softened as they wound deeper into the ground. Jack could be patient. He could wait until Ava slipped, and then he, in turn, would slip the geas and perhaps show her what he was about sans sex magic, when Ava wasn't in control. He had a sneaking suspicion she'd enjoy herself. Crow knew it was better fun than skulking in manky tunnels.

His scratches still hurt, small fingers of flame on his neck and shoulders. The skin would go black in the next few days, the contact with something from the City of the Dead spreading small deaths of its own.

A set of stairs appeared, narrow and slick with moisture. "These aren't any sewers," Jack said.

"No," Ava agreed. "These are the Catacombs. Not the tourist trap, but the real thing, lost to the city but not to the Black. Most people . . . humans, that is . . . don't even know they exist."

"And how, exactly, is it that *you* know?" Jack said.

Ava sniffed. "In my training, we do plenty of research. There are plague pits down here," she said. "When the Black Death was dancing on bones, they walled up hundreds down here. Sealed them up alive."

"Cheery." Jack rubbed the back of his neck, his vision prickling like a thorny collar.

"Don't worry," Ava said. "I won't let the boogeyman get you." She patted the pocket of her sweater, where the knife lived.

"How does someone like you get into something like this?" Jack asked. The stairs were dizzying, never-ending, like an illusion.

"You mean someone like a nice human girl?" Ava laughed lightly.

"You're the last person I'd describe as 'nice,' luv, if I used that word to describe someone at all." Jack's foot skidded on the slime underfoot and he caught his hand against the wall, leaving a wide streak of blood.

"After my family put me out for turning in that guy who came after me—for all the good it did—I was in a bad way. Daniel found me. He was a good man. He taught me how to use this abomination inside me for a purpose. I became an exorcist, like him. I kill demons now."

"File that under touching stories guaranteed to make a tear well up," Jack said.

Ava snapped her gaze on him, like dog teeth. "You think

I'm making this up? Would you rather I went around seducing men and stealing their life force, like a sorceress would use her sex magic?"

"What about me?" Jack said.

Ava tossed her head. "This is a war. You're not a civilian. You don't count."

"Just what a bloke wants to hear from the bird he's shagging." Jack kept silent as the air got thicker and the darkness heavier outside their small circle of green light.

The stairs wound around and around, in spirals that grew tighter and tighter, and then suddenly they ended and Jack was free, standing in the open air before a massive wooden door spiked with iron nails.

"It's a church," he blurted out. The Gothic wheel of window above the door was half-crushed under the rubble that had grown over it like the roots of a tree, but the shape was unmistakable.

"It *was*," Ava corrected him. "Now it's the gateway into Catacomb City."

Jack gave the church door a raised eyebrow, feeling like perhaps he should stand up straight, or worry about his immortal soul.

Ava lifted her hand to the door and placed her palm on it. After a moment, she shook her head. "You do it."

Jack felt a warding hex curl around his hand when he stepped in and touched the door. It wasn't strong, it didn't have teeth, but it felt like the bands of an open trap—one wrong move and the whole mess would snap shut and take off his fingers.

Who goes?

Jack swallowed. "Jack Winter."

Ava gave him a dirty look. He sighed. "And a friend." If they decided they didn't like the look of him, the hex would kill him before he even had time to tell Ava this was all her fault.

There was a painful moment of consideration on behalf of whoever held the hex. *You mean us harm.*

"Not me, mate. Just out for a walk, really."

Something that could have been laughter tickled his mind. *Then be well, and enter, brother of the crow.* The hex curled back, like lace in a flame.

Jack pushed on the door, and it groaned its way open. The hex kissed his skin, a memory of heat as Jack crossed the barrier, and then he looked ahead and stopped, his boots crunching on old masonry and older bones.

They stood in a great sweeping space, roofed like a medieval cathedral. Curling stone beams made up the structure's bones. The arch rose high enough to disappear into the shadows. Along the walls, hollows showed coffins, descending to shrouds, descending to stone sarcophagi carved with illuminations of saints and devils. Ossuaries at the lowest level were packed with skulls.

Catacomb City stretched vastly, lights flickering along upper levels, and ladders and stairs curving at angles that made Jack's neck cramp. The floor was a course of culverts from a Roman sewer system, dotted with mausoleums and dark shapes slinking in and out of light, like a life-size and utterly peculiar rat maze.

"Welcome to Areshko's pride and joy," Ava said. "Impressive, isn't it?"

"*Horrifying* would be more apt," Jack said. "But for the sake of keeping all me limbs attached, we'll use your phrase. How did she build this place without Nazaraphael's notice?"

"The dead are a powerful ward against prying eyes," said Ava. "You of all people should know that." She rubbed her arms in the draft as they looked out from their ledge. "I always wonder what it was like before the demons came."

"I expect when humans trod it it was a graveyard, and then the dirt underneath a graveyard, and then nothing at all," Jack said. "That much, I do know. Demons fill up the spaces that people can't or won't see. They crawl into gaps left by fear and desire and make themselves at home."

"We should pay respects to Areshko," Ava said. "Before she gets suspicious."

"Yes, yes, by all means." Jack flipped a hand. "Lead the way, Jeeves. And once we've doffed our top hats to the demon lady, fetch us a spot of Earl Grey."

"Your posh accent is atrocious," Ava told him. "Stick to what you are, Manc."

Jack's mouth quirked. "Most Yanks can't be bothered to tell the difference."

Ava leaned up and kissed his cheek, feather-light and quick. "I'm not most."

They descended to the level of the floor, winding among the mausoleums. Jack frowned. "People down here seem awfully dead."

"We're in a giant tomb," Ava said. "You're surprised?"

"No . . ." Jack whipped his head around as something moaned from behind the closest stone wall. "I mean 'dead' quite literally." He watched a hunched figure still wearing a few scraps of hair and skin scuttle from one shadow to the next. "I hate to tell you, Ava, but you've got a zombie problem."

She snorted. "Not everyone sees things the way you do, Jack. Areshko uses them for cheap muscle and labor."

Jack rubbed his nose. "Smell a bit. Could be right nasty if they think you're threatening their mistress."

"Zombies are easy," Ava said. "Stab them in the head or light them on fire. One of the first things Daniel taught me."

"How nice for you," Jack said. "I wish I had my own personal Mister Fucking Miyagi."

"Jealous?" Ava's hand skimmed across his arse and gave a light slap.

"Just hoping that when you have Areshko's angry zombie armada on your tail, you're as confident," said Jack,

"Do your part and there won't be any drama like that. Fuck around and I'll make sure I leave you to be a chew toy."

Jack sighed. If she wasn't so bloody attractive, he would have thrown in his lot by now, geas or no. Zombies put a lid on any bloke's libido.

The light grew stronger and the dark spots fewer, as they came to a much older ruin—a pagan place, Jack guessed, something that had sat on the land long before there was an England or a Scotland behind Hadrian's Wall. Candle flames filled the glassless windows, and the tiny graveyard next to the chapel showed its teeth, the stones worn down to nubs amid mummified nettles and vines.

"This is where she holds court," said Ava. "I'm a human. I'm not allowed inside."

"You're about as human as I am," Jack muttered, raising his hand to bang on the scarred oak door.

Ava's face twisted in surprise, like he'd slapped her. "What's that supposed to mean?"

"It means that you can either accept you have a talent for sorcery, or pretend you're not touched by the Black, like that Daniel wanker seems to have trained you to," Jack said. "Trust me, Ava, the first way is easier."

"You have no idea about me," she said. "You have no idea who or what I am."

"Not for lack of trying," Jack reminded her.

The door of the chapel popped open, and a small scavenger demon, a carrion eater of some kind, shoved its pointed head out, its large, lidless eyes rolling over Jack and Ava. "Yeah?" it squalled, a long tongue flicking over its chapped lips.

"Be careful," Ava told Jack. Her face, for the first time, was flat and her posture heavy.

Jack looked down his nose at the scavenger. "Areshko. I need to see her."

"Yeah!" the demon shrieked, and hopped away on bird

feet, its leathery wings fluttering like a curtain at the wrong time to show a multitude of piercings and an unfortunate PVC onesie.

Here were zombies and the things that ate them. It wasn't a city, Jack thought, it was an abattoir. For who, he wasn't sure yet. Hopefully not him, or Ava. She wasn't bad—devious, damaged, perhaps deranged, but she wasn't one of the dark things slipping along the underside of the Black. Just a lost girl, like a hundred others he'd seen.

Jack knew lost when he saw it. Until the Fiach Dubh had found him, he was as lost as Ava still appeared.

She tugged at his jacket. "Tell Areshko who you are. Tell her that you have someone who wishes to be graced by her. Use those words." Ava's whisper sounded like a ghost.

Jack rolled his eyes. "I'm not a virgin at bullshit, Ava." He shoved the door wide open and stepped into the chapel. Rich honeyed light spilled from all directions, from hundreds upon thousands of candles set into every crevice and crack of the stone.

Ava's face, pale and narrow, watched him until the door rumbled shut.

"Who comes?" The voice was cool as the light was sensual, a hint of a foreign land much, much farther than a channel away. It rolled over him, cool and sweet like rain.

"It's Jack Winter." He coughed. "And I've brought someone who wants to be . . . er . . . graced by you." Ceremonial words were as much a part of being a mage as the magic under his skin, but they always struck Jack as faintly antique and ridiculous. He felt awkard in a way he never did just sitting still with the magic.

Areshko sat forward from her seat in the front of the chapel, near the altar. It was a Victorian high-backed chair, the red velvet worn away to the pink of skin, the wood carved with flowers and fancies of nymphs.

The chair wasn't that striking. The demon woman seated

in it was. She had skin pale as a corpse, but covered in blue—blue tattoos that swirled over every inch, eyelids, lips, tongue, the tops of her thin breasts that pushed against a corset made from the ribcage of some poor creature that hadn't been quick enough to avoid having its flesh picked clean.

"Come closer," the demon said. Jack started forward, wishing he had Gavin, Rich, and Dix arrayed in that loose triangle formation that had served him well when he'd lived on the street and had to fight something larger and nastier than himself.

"Just yourself, though. The one who wishes grace will not show her face?" The demon's flat nostrils flared.

Jack bowed his head. "I'm sorry . . . er . . . lady. She thought it would be better if we didn't disturb you."

The carrion demon peeked out from behind the throne and squawked at them in its own language. "Piss off, then," Jack said, "if I upset you so."

Areshko's teeth snapped together. "Mind yourself."

"I apologize if I've offended you." Jack didn't mean a word of it, but he was pragmatic, when the thing across from you could rip out your larynx and pick her teeth with it. "I'll go."

The demon pointed at him. "I know you, Winter man." Her voice dropped to a purr. "They call you the crow-mage. You are the one who sees the dead and the dark."

"Right," Jack murmured, keeping his gaze on hers, like you did with angry dogs. She had pure-white eyes, as those who'd looked too closely at what they oughtn't and come away perfectly blind had. Lawrence's grandmother Winifred, in Jamaica, was blind, but she could smell a storm or a liar for miles. Jack sent her marzipans at Christmas every year.

"Come, Jack Winter," Areshko said. "I don't bite, except in the right places."

Jack stepped closer, not within range of her finely wrought, bone-thin arms, but definitely within range of a hex. Trust in baby steps, if demons had such a concept. "So, my companion . . . she can come in? And let the gracing begin?"

"Of course." Her lips pulled back. Her teeth were blue. Jack saw with a start that the white marks weren't skin— the white marks were the tattoos—burns, rather. The blue of the demon was everything else.

Jack whistled against his teeth. "Ava, luv. The lady of the house says come along in."

Ava stepped through the door and bowed her head low. "My lady Areshko. I am honored."

"Come, child." The demon extended her hand, curled her fingers, long nails clicking. "Do not stand on ceremony if you seek my grace so heartbrokenly."

Ava folded her hands and walked forward, head bowed, like a little girl taking first Communion. Jack had dated a Catholic girl the year after he had left Manchester, liked her enough to sit through a mass or three. The ceremony was comforting. Powerless, but comforting, and comfort counted more for ordinary people.

"My lady Areshko," she repeated, "I've come a very, very long way to receive your blessing. Might I approach?"

"How do I know you are not an agent of the demon of Edinburgh?" Areshko tilted her head, flirting with a smile.

Ava twitched. Her mask didn't slip, but it wasn't perfect. Jack eyed the door, calculated how long it would take one skinny, too-tall punk singer to run for it.

"I'm not working for Nazaraphael," Ava whispered.

Areshko spat a curse when she heard the name. "That snake in a tree, that foul torturer. May the Triumvirate pick over his bones."

Jack held up his hands. "Easy. You know me, yeah? Jack. No one here has any love for that ponce in the suit. You have my word." That, at least, was something he didn't have to lie about.

Areshko took a shuddering breath, and stilled. Her hair was wound in thick braids, at least ten, smoke-colored and wire-thick. "Very well. The word of the crow-mage. Words written in blood."

"Touch me?" Ava said plaintively. "Hold me in your embrace, Lady? Your touch brings wonder. I've heard it all the way across the ocean."

Before Jack could tell her that she was laying it on a little thick, at least to his taste, Ava dropped to her knees at Areshko's feet. Jack saw her knife hand drop as she spread her arms. "Please."

The demon tensed, her long white nails curling against the wood. The chair creaked and Jack thought for a moment she was going to open Ava like a Christmas goose with the force of her gaze. Her long sweeping forehead and curious face, nearly alien with its planes and points, finally relaxed.

"Of course, child," she said at last. Her skirts rustled. They were paper, hundreds of vellum pages sewn together with the same thick thread Jack had seen at funeral homes.

Jack allowed himself a smile thin as a razor blade. "Go ahead, Ava luv. This is what you've been waiting for."

Ava shot him a dirty look. "I accept your grace," she told Areshko. "I accept the stillness of your blessing."

Areshko stretched out her hand, laid it on Ava's forehead. A great shudder ran through Ava, one she played to the hilt, as though the feeling of Areshko was more than the last, longest climax she'd shared with Jack during the night in the hostel. Her hand dipped. It came up. The blade flicked free like a tongue of flame in the candlelight.

"Now accept death, you bitch," Ava hissed. She swung the knife, a smooth and economical movement that Jack recognized. He'd met blokes who could work a knife, gangsters, Russians mostly. Ava put them to shame.

Areshko was still faster.

She opened her mouth and Jack felt a great weight settle on him, a blinding, oppressive echo inside his head, like he'd just stepped out of airlock doors into hard space.

Ava shrieked as Areshko reached down, her mouth gaping impossibly wide. Jack saw white, bright. He saw leaping licks of flame, and he heard himself scream, the sound rip raw from his throat, as his sight locked on Areshko's power.

He saw it all—white cities, white fire. Great white wings made of metal and feather and flame. He knew that his brain was boiling in his skull and his eyes were bleeding, bursting, but he could not look away.

The sight would not allow it.

Areshko opened herself wider still, and then Ava was gone, just blinked out, like she'd never existed. The great sucking void subsided until Jack was on his knees, blood dribbling from his nose. He was crying blood tears. Everything ached, like he'd been battered by a wave of the Black itself.

Ava's scream snuffed out quickly as she vanished. Jack reached for the spot where she'd been, but there was just the heavy air of Catacomb City.

Ava was gone. Jack blinked away the blood, as his eyes stung.

Areshko stood from her throne, no longer a beautiful demon but a hateful thing pregnant with power. "Don't weep for your companion, child. She could come back to you."

Jack shied away from her hand. "I don't deal."

"I am not a demon who deals," Areshko said. "Hell frowns on bargains that are not overseen."

"I know the Triumvirate's law well enough," Jack snapped. "I ought to. I've seen what it's done to a score of mates—to a girl who wanted nothing more than fair play for what you took off her." Ava was gone. The geas no longer sunk claws into him. It left a score of bleeding holes.

"A human gives up a soul willingly," said the demon. "What happened to old friends is not my concern." She reached forward, quicker than a viper, and grabbed Jack by his neck, pulling him down and pressing her other hand over the center of his forehead, the spot where the sight looked outwards. "What concerns me is what I can give you, what you will do, to keep this transgression private."

For just a moment, everything stopped—the wash of the Black in his mind, the whispers of the spirits that clung to the catacombs, the restless stirring of magic that breathed from the air and the dead, and the demon herself.

It was perfectly blank. Jack felt wet on his face, and realized he was crying real tears, silent and cold against the chilly underground air. Ava was gone and he was sane and the demon's embrace was the sweetest thing he could ever imagine.

"You see what I can do?" Areshko said. She released him and everything rushed back with a snap, like opening the window of your silent bedroom to morning traffic—the misery of the city, the ache of the sight, the small cold place that whispered *Ava's dead.*

"I can make your life very pleasant, crow-mage, and all you must do in return for my silence and my favor is stay. Stay here. Stay hidden."

Jack stumbled, feeling drunk, or as if he'd just taken a jackboot to the head. "How . . . How can you . . ." It had been so cool, so calm, so . . . empty. To not see was the greatest peace he could have imagined.

"You have a talent, I have a talent," Areshko said. "And if you spurn it, I will spread the news far and wide that you brought a viper into my house."

"I can't stay here," Jack whispered. "I don't belong with the dead. . . ."

"Ah, and there is the dilemma," Areshko whispered.

"Die above, or live below? How to escape the trap? That is your talent, mage. Escaping traps. But not this trap, I fear."

Jack suddenly wanted Ava very, very badly. She and he could have done something, gotten away now that everything was wrong. But he was alone.

Figure it out, Winter.

"Do you accept my terms? Your continued presence for your sight?" Areshko's blue tongue flicked out.

Ava was devious, but Jack considered himself more of a talented liar. "You got yourself a bargain," he said, taking a step toward the chapel door.

Areshko smiled. It was terrifying, nearly slitting her face in half and revealing an extra row of teeth. "Then your secret is mine as my blessing is yours, Jack Winter."

She held out her hand. "Come here."

"Yeah," Jack said. "That's likely." He stepped back again, and then spun and broke for the door, bones crunching under his boots. He clawed at the chapel door, bloodying his fingers. The fucking thing weighed a thousand pounds. . . .

"I am Areshko." The demon inclined her head. "Now, what made you think that such a base deception would be effective?"

Jack spread himself against the door, panting. "Hopes and dreams, mostly."

Areshko rose. He could hear her skirt moving. She moved in the space between them, until her fingers were on the back of his neck. When she touched him, everything around Jack went dead. He was alone, as a normal person would be, except for the hot breath of the demon on his neck.

Her nails tore at his shirt. "Traitor." Areshko lapped up the blood she'd drawn. "Deceiver." Jack screamed as she lashed him with her nails again. "Liar." Areshko shoved him against the door hard enough for Jack to see stars.

"You thought you were clever," Areshko said. "But you're human, and I am demon. You stand no chance."

Areshko kept touching him, whispering to him, tasting his blood. Jack stopped screaming after a time, went still as the corpses around him, and waited for it to be over.

When Jack came back to himself, he was looking up at a stone ceiling, in a snug, warm space, on something soft.

He hurt. Like he'd hurt only a few times before, as when he'd met a skinhead with a pipe, alone. That had been two days in hospital and a few permanent markings. This felt worse. His shoulder was stitched, rudely, and his deeper cuts smeared with iodine, but the pain still coursed all through him.

Jack coughed, his tongue thick and his lips cracked. "Anyone there? Anyone who doesn't want to kill me?"

The door swung open and the candles guttered. Jack sensed he wasn't alone in the mausoleum—smelled it, really, a fresh and dense scent rather than desiccated and dry like everything else in the catacomb.

He tried to pull something to him, magic or anything, but all that responded was a weak trickle of power.

"Relax," said a girl standing in the shadow of the door. Where Ava was robust, she was skinny, and where Ava was sultry, she was pale and thin as parchment. "I'm not here to hurt you," she said.

"Drawn by my good looks and charm?" Jack tried to smile, found it split his head in new and agonizing ways. "You aren't the first, darling, and I doubt you'll be the last."

She didn't crack a smile, just set down a metal lockbox and popped it open, pulling out plasters and syringes and a bottle of antiseptic. She moved like she was used to it, her heroin-thin arms and hands moving like moths in the light. Glowing white skin showed through her cut-up shirt—

something Jack himself would have worn ten years ago, when he was still shaving half of his head and putting fags out on his arm for kicks.

"I know who you are, Jack, and I know why you came and what Areshko told me to do with you." She slashed a thumb across her throat.

"You're me executioner?" Jack wished for a fag. "Guess I could be looking at worse things when I kick."

"I'm not under Areshko's thumb," the girl countered. "We have a business partnership." She tapped a menthol out of her pack and stuck it between Jack's lips, lit it with a cheap disposable lighter. Then she picked up one of her syringes. "Nicotine and painkillers," she murmured, and then laughed to herself.

Jack pulled his arm away and blew smoke out his nose. "I don't fancy needles, luv."

"Don't be a bloody baby," she said, and jabbed him with it. A moment later Jack was under a warm morphine ocean, and everything seemed softer and far more pleasant.

"So, you're in bed with Areshko," he murmured, trailing a hand lazily over the scratches that had appeared everywhere, shallow wounds that felt like briars in his skin. "Is that literally and figuratively?"

The girl didn't flinch. Her eyes were burning from under her black fringe, accented by makeup that was both angrily and inexpertly applied. "It's neither. She ordered me to murder you if you woke up."

"So?" Jack cocked his eyebrow. "Going to smother me, or euthanize me? You've got enough in those sharps for an OD."

"I'm not going to fucking kill you, Jack," she snapped in irritation. "Subtlety's not your strong suit, is it?"

Jack exhaled. The smoke was ghost blue in the dense air. "I don't make a habit of it, no."

The girl jutted out her chin like a small, defiant cat. "I'm no demon's prozzie. I have a talent and I get paid for it, but I draw the line at assassination. I'm not some chav with a shank and a hard-on for blood."

"What's your name?" Jack said. "You know mine. It's an unfair exchange this side of the Black if I don't have yours."

"Nina," she said, "My name's Nina, and I think it's time that you and I got out of here, Jack Winter." She finished his bandages, laid the rest of the fags by his bed, and slipped from his room like the shadow of a crow's wing passing across the sun.

Nina came back as more and more candlelight blossomed through the catacombs, patches and glades and gardens of gold amid the bony fingers of the broken tombs and the hollow eyes of the ossuary walls. Jack watched it from the small arrow-slit in the wall of his prison—the door was locked and no amount of fussing on his part could budge the ancient tumblers.

Not that his hands were too steady—bloodied, ragged, and drugged as they were.

"There's a celebration tonight," she said. "On account of you being Areshko's new chew toy, I imagine." She handed Jack a tray with a suspicious bowl of stew and a cup of water. Jack ate it anyway, his stomach pitching against the morphine.

Nina sat on the edge of his bed. "Areshko has strong hexes on all of her boundaries, so making a run for it is out of the question. Got any bright ideas in that area? You're supposed to be clever."

"Sure, I'll just wave my wand, twitch my robe, and do a lap on me broomstick while I'm at it." Jack leaned back against the stone of the mausoleum. His head throbbed in time with his heartbeat.

Nina leaned forward and put her wrist against his forehead. Her fingers ruffled his hair. Jack felt a chill down his spine. "No fever," she said. "You're healing up. Tough bastard, aren't you?"

"Worse things to be," Jack said.

Nina's mouth quirked. "It's almost fate, you know. If I believed in a stupid thing like that. I've been down here for a long time."

"You're not more than twenty-two if you're a day," Jack said. "How long can it have been?"

"Long enough for me to turn pale as Princess Diana." Nina tossed her head. "My dad's from Pakistan. I'm not supposed to be Snow bloody White." She got up and stood in the doorway, watching. "Areshko told me it would be one job."

"And she tackled you and jammed her nails into your flesh when you tried to go topside?" Jack guessed.

Nina nodded. "She'll keep me here until I die. It's what she does. She is the Hunger. She consumes."

"I saw," Jack muttered, sitting up. Between the drugs and the food, he felt like the tail end of a drunk, rather than the beginning of death. "Ava's gone," he said.

Nina cocked her eyebrow. "That demon-hunter bird who dragged you in here? She's not dead."

"I'm pretty sure that when a demon vaporizes you with the sheer force of her rage, you're dead." Jack passed a hand over his face. He needed a bath, and a shave.

"Areshko . . ." Nina sighed. "Look. We both want something, yeah? I want out of here and you want your girlfriend back."

"I suppose, yeah," Jack muttered. Ava had tricked him, nearly gotten him killed, but she hadn't bored him.

"I saw your look." Nina smiled. "You cared for her."

"She was . . . a bit of a crazy bint, really," Jack said. "But innocent, in a way. Too many innocent people burn in the Black."

"You'll have her back," said Nina. "Areshko didn't kill her."

"How can you be so sure?" Jack said.

"Because the last demon hunter come down here, she kept alive for a good long time. Until he was sorry he'd ever been born."

Jack flinched. "That's a demon for you."

"We can get her back," Nina said. "But we have to get to the surface first." She leaned in, and put her hands on his shoulders. "Can I trust you, Winter?"

"Probably best if you don't," Jack said.

Nina laughed. "Sleep. We'll leave after the festivities start." She picked up Jack's empty tray and left. Jack let himself drift for a time before he fell into an orange-tinged morphine sleep, dreaming of twisting black spirits bending over his bed, cooling his fever, silencing his dreams.

Jack woke with a raging hangover and a crick in his neck, to Nina shaking him.

"It's started." Through the stone wall, Jack could hear music, wild and keening, bansidhe song or goblin band.

"What kind of security does Areshko keep about?" he said. Nina pulled his boots from under the bed and thrust them at him.

"Scavengers, mostly. A few of her human groupies who get a bit too involved with the whole 'child of the dark' bit."

Jack pulled on his leather and followed her to the door. He felt like he might wobble off keel at a breeze, never mind having to cut through a swath of border guards.

"You're a mage, yeah?"

Jack nodded, focusing on putting his foot down on stone instead of air. Nina chewed on her lip.

"Ever met a demon like Areshko?"

"No." Jack's foot slipped and Nina grabbed his sleeve. A zombie grumbled and swerved to avoid them. It still wore a tattered corset, mostly whalebones, and one shoe from its burial.

"Not like her," Jack said. "She's a fright, that one."

"You've really never dealt with demons before?" Nina cocked her head. "You seem like the type who wouldn't blink."

"Me, never," Jack said shortly. "Friends, yes. Too many friends. I've seen what demons do, and it's never worth what they take from your hide. Demons are for people who have a weakness in them, a fragility."

Nina's eyes froze over. "You really do have a narrow mind inside that pretty head, don't you?"

"I just know what I've seen," he returned.

"Some people have no choice." Nina snapped. "Some people have a choice between a demon and something much worse. Don't act like you know the mind of the entire world, Jack."

Jack raised a hand. "Hit a nerve, did I?"

Nina just rolled her eyes. "Mages. Sanctimonious bastards, the lot."

"Where do you get off?" Jack caught her wrist when she turned to walk away. "You came down here on your own. No one forced you."

"My dad, the one I mentioned?" Nina said. "He's ill. Needs to go to America and get experimental treatment NHS won't pay for. I'm supposed to let my da die?" She disengaged his hand from her cool skin and walked away.

"Oi." Jack followed her, both of them sticking to shadows and avoiding the zombies drifting aimlessly up and down the length of the steps. "I'm sorry," he hissed. "I'm not bloody telepathic, am I?" *That would be worlds better than the sight*, he thought.

Nina sighed. "You're a wanker. But I'll let it go for now."

"Guess I'm lucky," Jack said.

"Not what I'd call it." She flipped her spiky black head and led him down the steps to the lowest point in the catacombs. They skirted a gentle bowl with a fire pit at the center, a mass of demons and dead gathered around the blaze.

Areshko stood at the edge of the stone depression, her hands folded over her swollen stomach. Jack tugged Nina in the opposite direction, and she stuck close to his back, small and warm.

He'd lost sight of the avenue that Ava had brought him down when they came, but he ducked into one of the tunnels leading out of the catacombs and stepped carefully, like he would through a back alley in a bad part of London.

"Cold down here," Nina said. She pulled a flat silver flask from the pocket of her painted-on jeans and swigged, then wiped her mouth with the back of her hand, left the sheen of bruised lips. "Never realized how cold."

"It's all of the spirits," Jack said. "The dead steal all the warmth out of a room."

There was a sound in the tunnel ahead of them, coughing and scraping, like a bum spending his last hours on a steam vent. Nina's breath hitched. "Can you see what's up there?"

"I'm not a television psychic," Jack said. "I can't do tricks like that."

Nina sneered. "Might have known. Typical mage wanking."

Jack knew he'd regret it, but he reached out a hand and clapped it on Nina's shoulder. Her bones were lighter than a bird's. She felt fragile, under all the black and posture.

Her magic slammed into his sight with all the force of a waterfall. It was deep, and dark, like sinking into a pool, at night, with just moonshine to guide the way. Fronds of it brushed his face, his skin, feathery and decayed as a dead man's hand reaching aboveground.

Jack had felt that cold, dry power only once before, and he recoiled as visions of bones and flesh and skin wound together flashed in front of his eyes. "'Strewth," he said.

"You're a . . . you're the necromancer. No bloody wonder all of your zombies gave us a berth."

"You don't have to look so disappointed in me," Nina said. "Reminds me of my da."

They shuffled to the curve of the tunnel and peered around. Jack saw the carrion demon who'd been hanging around Areshko.

"I'm not disappointed," he said.

"Shocked?" Nina whispered.

"A bit," Jack agreed. "You're much more attractive than the last skin dealer I ran into."

"So, Mister Big Mage, what are we going to do about him?" Nina asked.

"I look like a thug, do I? I don't bloody know," Jack said.

The demon flapped and scratched itself between the legs. Nina wrinkled her nose.

"Well, I'm not a ninja, Jack. My tricks mostly work on stuff that's already dead."

Jack narrowed his eyes. "That gives me an idea."

The carrion demon picked bugs off the wall, weevils and maggots crawling over a new body stuffed on top of the old in the crevice of the tunnel. It slurped them with a smacking of lips and tongue. Jack flinched as it ripped a finger off the fresh body and sucked the bone and marrow like it was a chicken leg.

Jack stopped a fair distance away, but close enough to surprise it. " 'Ey. Ugly."

The demon spun around, wobbling on its clawed feet. "Yeah!" it shrieked.

"I can't figure out what's worse," Jack said. "That you look like a bat smashed arse-first into a donkey, or that your mum actually fucked something like that to get you."

The demon stripped its lips back from its teeth and let out an angry squawk. "What!"

"You heard me." Jack spread his arms. "You're ugly, you're stringy, and you've got nothing between those legs to even scratch at."

The demon snarled, a long black tongue unfurling, its eyes bugging out.

Jack grinned. "What are you gonna do about it, Arseface? Wank me off with those little T rex arms?"

He sidestepped as the demon sprang, its claws catching him across the abdomen. They fell in a heap of wings and limbs, the demon snapping at Jack's neck. Jack punched it, and skinned his knuckles on the thing's teeth.

Nina's shadow fell across them. "Any old time now, luv," Jack grunted, as the thing kicked at him, coming dangerously close to the goods.

She hooked her upper teeth over her bottom lip, and cocked her head to one side. The fingers of her left hand twitched, and the carrion demon jerked, twisting to and fro like there were hooks in its skin.

"No!" it screamed, and then its skin bubbled, swollen, and the great boiling mass of dead flesh the demon had ingested burst through its stomach.

The carrion demon screamed again, twitched, and died.

Nina ran her hand through her hair. "Good idea."

Jack felt warmth and wet on his face, and Nina's eyes widened. "You've got a bit on you. Just there." She brushed her fingers over her cheek.

"Help a bloke up?" Jack extended his hand. "Not as young as I used to be."

Nina pulled him to his feet. Behind them, voices rose and fell, and footsteps followed.

"We're not alone, luv," said Jack. He swiped a hand over his face to get rid of the blood and bile and pulled Nina along with him.

"What grand plan have you?" Nina said, as they ran along the catacomb tunnel. "If we make it topside, I mean."

"Tell you if we make it," Jack said. All of his cuts and aches were starting again, and he could feel the press of more demons behind them, along with a few bright, malignant human minds that unfurled darkness across his sight.

"There!" someone shouted.

Jack saw a broken brick wall and an old sewer line beyond. He jerked Nina hard left, pulling them into the dank blackness.

They ran until Jack was completely out of breath, starbursts exploding in front of his eyes, and his ribs stabbing him every time he sucked in the moist air.

Nina pulled back, tugging his arm. "We have to stop. There's something here."

Jack bared his teeth. "Exactly. Care to speculate what, Nina?"

"She slipped out, all right?" Nina growled. "Going to crucify me for a little slip?"

"If I get some sort of undead virus from those neck scratches and start craving the brains of humans, it'll be your fault," Jack said. He stopped joking when Areshko's minions came around the corner.

The two men who closed in on them weren't anything remarkable—young, skinny, the sort of street kids you could find in any city, in any country, starved and starving for connection. Their eyes, however, burned with the fire that Jack usually saw only in cultists.

Having been touched by Areshko, he knew she'd have no trouble inspiring such devotion.

"Don't worry, Nina," he said. "Just back up slowly." A chill kissed the scratches on his neck.

" 'Don't worry'?" she demanded. "One of them has a knife!"

"I've got a knife, too," Jack said.

"Areshko told us about you." The one with the knife

smiled, his eyes bright. "She told us what she did to you. She said we'd taste your blood."

Jack shivered, taking another measured step back. "When I say get down, curl up in a ball. Don't move."

Nina cut a look at him, back at the two advancing men. "You'd better not get me killed, mage."

Jack's sight blossomed, tendrils of silver curling like fog around his face, and he folded at the knees. "Down, Nina!"

She dropped, pulling her knees up to her chest, and Jack felt the revenant pass over them, her feet trailing through his back, the chilling shock of this making his heart skip.

The revenant fell on the two men in the tunnel, hungry and moaning, her hands spreading frost over their skin.

Nina's eyes widened. "That really was a mistake, you know."

"Likely. Never let a mistake steal any sleep from me yet." Jack extended his hand. "I need fresh air, and a pint. What do you say?"

"I say you're an odd sort," said Nina. "But all right."

Jack squinted in the sun as they emerged from a utility hatch. He hadn't expected it to be morning, the world looking as usual as it ever had.

Nina jerked her chin across the small cobble street. "Pub."

Jack followed her. "Hallelujah. The gods *are* kind."

"Not particularly," said Nina. Jack snorted.

"Woman after my own heart."

He ordered a whiskey instead of a pint, drained the tongue of liquid fire down his throat, and ordered another.

"You want your Ava back, yeah?" said Nina. "You're going to have to challenge Areshko to do it."

Jack shook his head. "Not something I fancy." Ava's face, just before she vanished, wasn't leaving his eyes, even as he got a third glass of whiskey.

Nina snorted. "Yeah. I'd worry about you a bit, if you did." She sucked on the straw in her tonic water. "The things some blokes do for love."

Jack raised an eyebrow. "What makes you say love?"

She snorted. "Please. I saw her tits. It's love."

"Barely know her," said Jack. "But I did like her, and I don't like demons. Not at all."

"So, demon killer"—Nina grinned at him over her drink—"how will you slay the dragon this time?"

"I'm thinking that there's another bloke in this city who doesn't have any love for Areshko," Jack said. "And that he might be interested in what I've got to tell him."

Nina drained her drink. "Do I know this person?"

Jack tossed back the last of his whiskey and gave her the rakish grin it inspired. "I don't think so, nice little girl like you."

"I may be little," Nina retorted, "but I'm no little girl."

Jack thought of the gray, grasping sorcery that she commanded, the sort of power that could pull a spirit back from beyond the Bleak Gates, out of the City and into its own dead flesh. "I suppose not," he agreed. Lighting a fag, he ran a hand over his hair. It was hopeless, a rat's nest of lopsided spikes. "Poor choice of words. You with me, or going to slap my face and storm off?"

Nina sighed. "Depends. Are you always so arrogant?"

"On me good days. And on days when a demon kills a friend and I nearly get chewed to death by Hell's mistakes." He gave Nina a grin, from the wicked spot inside his heart. "You fancy shagging me cheerful again? Might work." Dimly, he realized he was drunk and exhausted, which was the only reason to be such a chav, but he didn't stop.

Nina slapped his hand away. "I have a dirty talent but I'm a nice girl. Fuck you, Jack Winter."

Jack pulled out his sharpest razor of charm—his smile. "That's the general idea."

Nina shook her head. "Just because I helped you, just because I owe you something for helping me get out of Catacomb City, doesn't mean you can be a wanker and put your hands anywhere you bloody please!"

"Could just be a hummer round back," Jack muttered, feeling the venom on his tongue. Or maybe that was just stale whiskey. "That's how the last one got me, you know." He was being exactly the kind of cunt he despised when he was in clubs or out drinking, and he cursed the whiskey that he could feel rising in his throat.

"You're drunk," Nina said. "And you did get me shut of Areshko, so I'm going to forgive you." Her eyes darkened. "Speak to me like this again, and I'll slit your throat and raise you to carry my purse about while I'm out at the shops."

She jerked him up elbow. "Come on. You want to get your Ava back, you need to be sober. And not a twat."

Jack sneered as they left the pub, but he leaned against Nina's small frame and stayed close. He owed her that much. He was a twat, no argument.

Nina was nowhere to be found when Jack woke up. He heard a telly from another room, saw a water-stained ceiling and a patch of wall, and smelled a curry cooking.

He winced when Nina came back into the room. "Me head."

"Serves you right," she said, handing him a paper cup of tea and a sandwich, transparent with grease. "Breakfast of champions. Eat up, drunkard."

"Wicked woman," Jack moaned, downing the tea and burning his tongue.

"I am," Nina said. "You don't care to know how wicked."

"Not until my head stops vibrating." Jack forced himself to bite into the egg and bacon butty. Noise rose from the telly, like a night bus in the fog.

"Manchester's playing," Nina said. "Think you can make it into the front room?"

The room didn't swim much when Jack sat up, so he nodded. "Where are we?"

"My mum's flat," said Nina. "I still had a key."

"Your mum in?"

Nina shook her head. "She and I haven't spoken since my da took sick. We'll have to light out before her shift at Sainsbury's ends."

Jack settled himself on the sofa and watched Man U's red jerseys dart up and down the field against Chelsea for a few silent moments. "You know, Nina," he said finally, massaging the center of his forehead, "you don't have to be involved any further. Going up against something like Areshko . . . well . . . you're just a necromancer."

Nina sighed. "I'm going to pretend I didn't hear that, boyo. Drink up your tea and tell me your grand scheme."

Jack followed Nina up a flight of stairs that had nearly collapsed back to the floor below, and down a narrow hallway where the air was drunk with the scent of herbs and magic. Nina waved a hand in front of her nose. "Never could stomach that smell."

"That's funny, coming from a girl who digs up corpses," said Jack.

"Not that," Nina said. "That sulfur smell." She gestured at the open flames lighting their way through the condemned flats.

"Tar," Jack said. "Makes the torches burn longer."

"It's foul," said Nina. "Just like Catacomb City. Foul and rotten, through and through."

"No argument here," Jack said.

Nina kicked against the last door in the hallway. After a pause it swung open, letting out a puff of rancid air. Inside,

Jack saw candles, a bed, and a threadbare velvet chair, no doubt nicked from some nice old pensioner's flat.

"You sure this is the place?" he asked Nina.

"Said you needed supplies for a summoning," Nina said. "And I didn't ask precisely why you would want to summon *another* demon after what we just went through, so take me at my word, yeah?"

A cat prowled from under a sofa and hissed at Jack. He hissed back and stepped into the flat. "Hello?"

One whole wall of the flat was comprised of apothecary shelves, the kind any good magic shop had by the score.

"It's self-serve," Nina said. "You leave the money in the cashbox at the door when you walk out."

"Or?" Jack said, as he started pulling down herbs, salt, and charcoal.

"Or you don't walk out." Nina fetched a paper bag and snapped it open, holding it while Jack dumped his supplies into it. "So, you know I'm going to ask," she said, as Jack pulled a crumpled wad of fives and tenners from his back pocket and shoved them through the slot in the rosewood cashbox.

"Ask what, luv?" he said.

"What demon you think can possibly help you get Ava back?"

They descended the stairs, the wood shuddering under Jack's feet.

"Promise you won't be mad?" he said.

"No," Nina said.

Jack stopped on the landing and pressed his thumb and forefinger between his eyes. "Nazaraphael."

"You're mad, you know that?" Nina shoved a hand through her hair. It stood up like a porcupine. "Summoning the demon of the city."

Jack felt in his pockets and came up empty. "Got any chalk? Forgot it when we stopped off at Magic Tesco."

Nina pursed her lips, but passed him a nub. She sat on the steps of a crypt, watching him. "A graveyard's a bit theatrical, don't you think?"

"Graveyards are repositories," said Jack. Every good sorcerer knew that for a quick fix, burial ground offered the best high you could stomach. The Black curled, radiant and radiating, among the tombstones and frozen grass and silvery moonlight, tendrils of it passing over his mind like fingers through his hair. The air was thick, cold, puffing from his mouth in waves.

If he hoped to bind a demon of the city, a graveyard was the only place that would do it. And he had only one chance at Nazaraphael, before the grinning demon tore him limb from limb.

The symbols he needed were easy enough, since he didn't know what stripe of demon Nazaraphael was, besides a resident of Hell and a walking fashion disaster.

He should be doing this with a copper circle, properly, safely. Jack sucked in air through his teeth, trying to banish Lawrence's voice and his own doubts from his mind. He sketched a circle, closed himself in, scooped up a hand of graveyard dirt, and made the circle again. Double, and tight as he could make it.

Nina offered him her flick-knife, and Jack accepted. She chewed on her lip. "Please be careful. I've grown rather fond of you, Jack."

Jack grinned. "I have that effect on women, darling."

"On second thought, I hope Nazaraphael picks his teeth with your bones," Nina said sweetly.

Jack chuckled and held up the flick-knife. He paused before he sunk the blade into the pad of his thumb. Summoning demons wasn't something a man did if he had a desire to keep breathing. Summoning demons was for the desperate, the pathetic, or the plain bloody stupid.

He was at least one of those, Jack thought. He wasn't certain which.

The blade bit into his skin and blood welled, warm against the air. Jack turned his hand over and squeezed three droplets into the center of the circle. The graveyard ground sucked it up, drinking down his life force and his talent.

"I call upon the power of the ancient circle," Jack said. "On the wings of the crow, I call the true name of Nazaraphael, demon of the city of Edinburgh."

For a moment, nothing happened at all, not even a negative, not even his circle breaking and his own talent throwing him to the ground as Nazaraphael shook off his summons.

Then Jack felt a tingling start on the backs of his palms and his sight flared, a bright pinpoint of light growing in front of him, flooding into the chalk lines that bound the earth.

"Stay back, Nina," Jack said, and stepped out of the circle just before it snapped with power, and a shape began to grow in the center of it.

Nazaraphael fought, and fought hard. Jack felt claws raking his mind, felt the tug of the circle against him, knew that if Nazaraphael overwhelmed him, the magic it commanded would rip out his heart and show it to him.

"How dare you?" Nazaraphael shouted. "You are filth, Jack Winter! You think a circle of graveyard dirt can hold me?"

Jack felt the summoning begin to fray as Nazaraphael struggled. "Not forever," he said. "But long enough."

"I'm going to strip your flesh off and fry your fat," Nazaraphael snarled.

"Not yet, you're not." Jack wagged his finger. "I told you I didn't like it when you burst in and kicked me around, Nazzie. Now you're going to listen to me, and you're going to be polite about it."

Nazaraphael's eyes gleamed. He wasn't like any demon Jack had seen—he looked alarmingly close to human, with his fine-line nose and full lips. The eyes were the giveaway, as they were with all things of the Black—the windows to the soul.

Nazaraphael's were empty.

"Make it fast, boyo," he said. "Because when I break this circle, you're not going to have time to scream."

Jack took his time pulling out a fag. He offered one to Nina, who accepted, keeping her eyes on the demon. "See, luv?" Jack said, as he touched his finger to the tip and was rewarded by an orange ember. "They're not so spooky, when you see them in the open."

"Damn you, Winter," Nazaraphael shouted. "I am the demon of the city and I deserve that respect!"

"All right, all right." Jack exhaled. "You and Areshko, yeah? You want her gone, I want her to give back a bird she's holding and torturing."

Nazaraphael's nostrils flared, but his eyes lit with interest. "So?"

"So," Jack said, "I'll show you where she's hiding, and you'll convince her to give me back my good friend Ava." He flicked his fag end away. "You can help me, Nazzie, or I can bind you and make you. You're a demon, but I'm through fucking about. So what do you say?"

Nazaraphael stood very still. "I get Areshko? You don't have some silly human vendetta against her?"

"I want the bitch gone as much as you do," said Jack. "Will you help, Nazzie?"

The demon considered for only a moment. "You've got yourself a deal."

Jack grinned at him. "I very much hope not."

The return to Catacomb City was slower and even more unpleasant than the first time, with Ava. Nazaraphael hummed to himself, and when they reached the two bodies, now frozen and with gaping sockets where the revenant had taken their eyes, he chuckled.

"The follies of mortals. They'll follow anyone."

"Look," Jack said. "Not really keen on hearing you talk, mate, so why don't we all take a vow of silence until we get back to the city?"

"Do I frighten you, mage?"

Jack looked Nazaraphael up and down, from the top of his blond ponytail to his white-on-white wingtips. "Yes. I am completely terrified."

Nazaraphael actually let out a chuckle. "I don't hate humans. I do what I do because what I am compels me to. I can show mercy, Jack. Even if you did threaten me."

Nina snorted. "Because your kind are so famous for mercy."

Nazaraphael whipped his head around like a snake. "Be careful of what you're insinuating, little skin trader. I can lose my good humor very quickly."

Nina flared her fingers. "Shaking in my boots."

Jack ducked under the arch at the city entrance and nearly smacked into Areshko. She stood, hands folded, a serene smile revealing the tips of her pointed teeth.

"I knew you'd return to me, Jack Winter."

"Good for you," he said. "And look, I've brought company."

Nazaraphael tipped his head. "Lady Areshko. How very long have I been looking for you! I've lost count of the years."

Areshko hissed and swiped at Jack with her claws. "You think this changes anything? I'll never give her up."

Nazaraphael stepped forward. "You will, and you will do it now, if you wish me to spare your city." He reached out and laid hand on her cheek, and Areshko shuddered. "You will perish, but Catacomb City can live on."

Jack didn't have to see Nazaraphael's eyes to know that he was lying, but he was a demon. It was hardly surprising. What *was* surprising was that Areshko softened under his touch, her eyes welling with blue tears that stained the white brands curling across her cheeks.

"I didn't harm her," she whispered. "I just kept her close."

"I know," Nazaraphael said kindly. "And now it's time to return her to Jack."

Areshko bowed her head. "So be it." She bent down, her mouth unhinging and opening wide, as wide as Jack's hip bones. Areshko's body rippled and convulsed, her spine flexing like a lizard's, and then she screamed.

Areshko expelled a cloud of magic and Ava shimmered back into being, naked and covered with blue bile. She choked, and then her eyes flew open. "Jack?"

"I'm here, luv." Jack stripped off his leather and wrapped it around her.

Nazaraphael knelt on Ava's other side.

"She's beautiful, Winter. I see why you'd come back down into this hole for her."

Ava threw her arms around Jack and pressed her cheek against his. "It was awful," she whispered. "She did things . . . But I knew you'd come back for me."

"You did?" Jack stroked her sopping hair. "You actually had faith in me, darling? I'm bloody touched."

"Not faith," said Ava. "Not in you."

Jack pulled away from her. "Ava, are you all right?"

"Nazaraphael," she said, "we brought you. We brought you to Areshko. . . ." Her hand darted out, and Jack saw the bile-covered knife a second before it embedded itself in his chest.

He let out a cough and swatted at the knife. "What the bloody fuck . . . *iron*?" Cold fingers wrapped his heart and pain seized him. "Iron . . ." Jack fell on his side, his cheek digging into the stones.

Ava pulled her knees to her chest. "I'm sorry, Jack."

Nazaraphael stood and brushed off his knees. He lifted Ava up by the hand, as if she weighed nothing. Jack's leather slipped off her, as crumpled as he was.

Nina's face obscured Jack's swimming view of the pair. "He's not dead," she said in a hollow voice. "But he's bleeding. . . . Why did you do it? He *helped* you."

Areshko swiveled her head from Nazaraphael to lock Jack's gaze, as his life unspooled at a terrifying rate.

"Nina," Jack said. "Nina, get away from me!" He felt it again, the sickening sensation of Areshko's magic, the great sucking void, and then he was moving, dragged across the ground toward the demon's sphere. He wrapped his hands around Nina's thin shoulders, trying to hold on, but he was left with a shred of her T-shirt, as she vanished into the void of Areshko's magic.

Jack wanted to scream, but he hadn't the breath or blood left. Beside him, Ava shrieked as Areshko's influence scrabbled at her, nails cutting lines in her cheek and Nazaraphael's shoulder when he shielded the demon huntress from harm.

Areshko swayed, shuddered, and smiled. Her terrible magic quieted, sated. "So sweet." She sighed. "To taste the blood of the seraphim. It burns."

Jack blinked at her, levering himself onto his arms. He felt nothing, floating as from an opiate high on the cold, fathomless water of shock. "Hold on just a bloody minute. What?"

Ava gave him that sad gaze. "Nazaraphael, Jack."

Jack felt his mouth work. "He's a . . ."

"I am not a demon," Nazaraphael said. "I am Fallen. I reside in Hell but I am not a denizen."

Ava swayed unsteadily, shivers wracking her naked skin. "I'm sorry, Jack, really I am. But he's promised me. He promised me if I delivered Areshko, he'd . . ."—she swiped bile from her eyes—"he'd bring Daniel home to me."

Areshko let out a moan, and Jack grabbed his head.

Feedback reverberated through his sight, and he watched as Areshko's stomach swelled and her mouth opened, a great sucking void through which he could hear screams and a harsh, hot wind.

"Ava," he whispered, "you know there's no such thing as angels."

"You hate demons as much as I do," she said. "They make deals, and they steal souls. Daniel . . . *She* tortured him, and in the end he made a deal to end it." She stood, wavering. "But now I have Nazaraphael. One of the Fallen, for the Triumvirate. And I have the means to go before them and bring his soul out of Hell." She pointed to Areshko. "Take me. I want to go." Ava took a wavering step toward Areshko, who held out her hand.

Jack reached up and grabbed Ava's wrist. "I can't let you do this, Ava. If you let her kill you and send you down, you'll die in Hell. Nazzie here can't deliver a soul any more than a mail boy can."

"No," she flared. "He is an angel. They'll have to give Daniel back to me."

"Daniel is dead!" Jack shouted. "And before he died, he made a deal to save his own arse! That's not a man worth dying for, Ava."

She jerked away from him and fell toward Areshko. "Take me! I want to die! The Fallen will resurrect me!"

Jack watched Areshko as her belly swelled even more, with the possibility of another meal. "We can't stay here," he said. "Ava. There are no angels. There are no Fallen. Demons lie."

Ava pulled free of him and ran to Areshko, kneeling before the demon woman and spreading her arms wide. "Kill me. You want me. I was Daniel's favorite."

Areshko leaned down and caressed Ava's cheek, then she bared her teeth and slapped Ava aside. Her mouth opened, and her magic swelled. Jack clutched his head, the blood chilling on the front of his shirt, as the air in the catacombs frosted with malice.

Nazaraphael threw up his hands, but Areshko was too much for him. The demon of the city withered, skin ashing and skeleton disintegrating, before he disappeared like dust in a wind.

Jack managed to get to his feet, one hand over the wound, which felt as wide and deep as a river. "Ava. Come with me. Come now."

Areshko laughed at him. "Oh," she said in a new, legion voice. "I don't think we're going anywhere."

Jack tugged Ava, only to find his way blocked by a crowd of zombies drawn by the ambient magic. "Why did he have to be the bloody demon of the city?"

Ava looked to Jack helplessly. "He said he was an angel. . . ."

Jack watched the zombies ebb around Areshko. "I know," he said. "I know. But what do *you* know about Areshko?"

"She killed Daniel," Ava moaned. "Killed him in spirit. She is the Hunger. She hunts."

"And when she eats—what then?" Jack drew back his fist and popped the nearest zombie in the jaw. It staggered away from him, and Jack bore Ava on toward the exit.

Another zombie lunged and caught her across the stomach. Blood made its lazy way down her abdomen. "Areshko . . . she'll consume Nazaraphael, his talent and his power," she said.

Below them, Areshko opened her mouth as wide as a sewer grate and bit down on a zombie's neck. There was no blood in the dried-out thing, but Jack saw the vile cloud of magic escape all the same, grayish green like a punctured bladder of gas. Areshko drank it down, her blue skin taking on the glow of an oil slick, the white brands hissing as they heated. She ate like she was the Horseman of Famine, hungry moans issuing forth.

"Bollocks to that," Jack said. "We can't let her have that sort of power. . . ."

"Jack," Ava said, as he dropped her hand, "I'm so sorry."

"I don't care," he said plainly. "You aren't the first a demon's lied to."

"But I need you to know," Ava said.

Jack shook his head. "Save it for when we're out of the ground, yeah?"

"Can't stop her," said Ava. "Need a sanctuary, to wait for the end."

Jack tossed her a look. "Sacred ground won't stop zombies and demons. You think any necromancer or Hell fiend gives a bollocks what a priest said over a patch of dirt?"

"A warded house, then," Ava said. "A bunker, a fucking tank. *Something.*"

Jack scratched the back of his neck. He felt like sleeping—sleeping for a hundred years, like some old tale. He was halfway to passing out, and bits of ghost and magic fluttered at the edges of his eyes, the sight waiting to pull him under.

Areshko would keep growing her hunger until it consumed enough of the Black to spill over into the world of the living.

"No," he said. "No, we're not leaving her to finish what she started."

After a moment, Ava nodded. "We can't."

Jack stopped, still clinging to her, and swung himself around.

"You wish to petition me for mercy?" Areshko growled when Jack turned back.

"Fuck off," he said. "Let the Fallen ponce go and just fuck off, back to Hell or wherever you came from."

Areshko bared her teeth at him. "And if I do not?"

"Then, luv, I'm going to exorcise you," Jack said. "And I'm going to enjoy it."

The toe of his boot nudged Ava's iron knife and he scooped it up.

"Die, mage," Areshko hissed. "Meet the Triumvirate head-on."

Jack spread his arms, even though the pain lanced him like hot iron. "I'm right here, darling. Come and take me."

Areshko sprang, and Jack took her swipe full on, letting her hands grip him and pull him close.

He turned the iron knife in his hand and threw it to Ava.

She gripped it and said the banishing words. "Return to the place called home. Return to the darkness. Return to the void. Areshko, you are welcome no longer. Begone."

Areshko latched her lips on to his, blue pointed tongue and white pointed teeth slicking and cutting his lips. Jack's senses deadened, and just for a moment the agonizing scream of Areshko's power ceased inside his mind. "I could give you this, mage," she whispered against his mouth. "I could take it all away from you."

Jack's stomach twisted. No more nightmares, no more visions. No more feeling his mind fraying with every hour that passed.

All he had to do was turn around and stop Ava, and allow Areshko to consume Nazaraphael. All he had to do was nothing, as she grew fat on her Hunger.

"The flesh is weak," Areshko said. "Too weak to see what you see. It will be your end, mage, slow and rotting from inside to out."

"I have no doubt." Jack sighed. He met her blazing eyes. "But I don't deal with demons." He spun Areshko like a lover into Ava's path as she swept the knife up and buried the blade in the soft portion of Areshko's back, between the ribs, blue blood spilling on white brands.

"Return to Hell, your mother," Ava rasped. "Bound by iron, begone."

Areshko screamed, and Nazaraphael shimmered back

into existence on the ground. Areshko twitched and twisted against the banishing iron, wielded by an exorcist, and then she began to fade—first her skin and then her bones and finally the brands, hints of ghostly white, before she evaporated completely.

Ava held out the knife to Jack, her hand quivering. "Take it. I don't need it anymore."

Jack took the knife and flipped it, crouching so that he held the point against Nazaraphael's neck. Jack's wound hurt again, but at least he wasn't slipping away toward the Bleak Gates.

"Now," he said, "you're going to tell this poor girl how you lied."

Nazaraphael's lip curled. "I am full-blood Fallen."

"You're full of shite, is what you are," Jack snarled. "*Say* it. Tell Ava what you did."

Nazaraphael looked into him, with his dead eyes. "Your soul will dance on the coals for this, Winter."

"Tell me news, wanker." Jack pushed the knife in, drawing a bead of blood, and Nazaraphael hissed.

"I am demon." He gritted his teeth, trying to crawl away from Jack's ministrations.

Ava let out a cry. "Daniel . . ."

"He burns. And he will forever." Nazaraphael grinned. "I wanted Areshko. I said what was necessary."

Jack stood up, swaying. "Go back to Hell and pray I never set eyes on you again."

Nazaraphael faded in a swell of smoke, and the only sound echoing throughout Catacomb City was Ava's sobbing.

When Ava was fit to move, Jack took her to Nina's mum's flat. The lock wasn't anything special, and he let them in and left Ava to wash herself off and find clothes.

Jack waited in the sitting room, looking at Nina's family pictures.

"She had a nice family." Ava was wearing a jumper and jeans. Her face was scrubbed, her hair tangled and damp.

"She seemed like a nice girl," Jack said. "For a necromancer." He fished in his pocket for the last of his gig money, a hundred quid, and laid it on the mantle next to the picture of Nina and her dad grinning outside the O2 dome in London. He knew it was meaningless, considering what had been lost, but it was the only thing he had to give.

"I shouldn't have lied to you," Ava murmured, "about Nazaraphael and I bargaining. I met Daniel when I was so young. He loved me, and I loved him, and when he died—"

"Ava." Jack shook his head. "Ava, Ava. Enough with that. I know what you are. You're a liar and a sinner, just like me."

Her mouth curved up. "We had fun though, didn't we, Jack?" She leaned up on her tiptoes and kissed him softly.

Jack returned it, and then regretfully stepped away. "I could get used to you, Ava. Even if you are insane."

"Mmm. You could come to New York." She tugged on his waistband. "Help me hunt. Might be fun."

Jack chuckled. "I do like you, Ava. If I never meet another one of you, it will be too soon." He opened Nina's door. "Take care of yourself, luv."

"Jack." Her eyes filled up. "Don't leave. We could do so much good together. . . ."

"Ava"—Jack shook his head—"I'm not a good man. You should know by now."

"I suppose," she sighed, "that's why I picked you."

"We've both got our shadows," said Jack. "Don't let them drown you, Ava."

Jack left the flat and stepped out under an iron gray sky, walking away from Ava and waiting for the rain to fall.

SIN SLAYER

Jenna Maclaine

ONE

Paris, 1889

I leaned forward in my seat, resting my hands on the railing of our private box at the Paris Opera, and watched my friend Justine take the stage. As the music washed over me, I smiled, remembering the night when Henri Meilhac, Bizet's librettist, had first seen her perform, and had announced that she had been born to play the role of Carmen. It was fortunate that Devlin, Justine's consort, had turned her into a vampire, or she would have missed the opportunity by about two hundred years.

The door behind me softly opened and closed a moment before Michael slid silently into the seat next to me. Glancing at him, I admired how handsome he looked in his black evening clothes. I turned to scold him for missing the opening, but the expression on his face halted my words.

"What is it?" I whispered.

"I was delayed by a warden who insists on speaking with you immediately," Michael replied.

I glanced across the theater to the box where Antoine, the vampire Regent of Paris, sat surrounded by his lieutenants and ladies.

"Why the devil does one of Antoine's wardens need to talk to me?" I asked impatiently.

Michael shook his head. "He's not Antoine's, love. He's English."

"Oh, bugger," I muttered and sank into my chair.

Devlin, Justine, Michael, and I were The Righteous.

We were in essence the police force of the vampire world, answerable only to the High King of the Vampires. It was our job to deal with anything that a Regent or his wardens couldn't handle. Mostly this consisted of executing rogue vampires who broke the laws set down by the High King. Sometimes, however, we were called in to deal with more delicate matters, such as deposing a ruler who had gone mad, or refereeing a local power struggle. The names of The Righteous were spoken in fearful whispers throughout the vampire nation and no Regent would ask for our help lightly. If a warden had come all the way to Paris from England to find us, it could only mean that our brief holiday, and Justine's run as Carmen, was about to come to an abrupt end.

I leaned over and whispered to Devlin, "Duty calls. We'll be back as soon as we can."

Devlin nodded. "Let me know if you need me," he said, never taking his eyes off the stage.

I smiled at the look of intense pride and raw lust on his face as he watched his consort below.

"You enjoy the performance," I said. "We'll handle this."

I turned back to Michael and he stood, offering me his arm. Curling my fingers into the fabric of his coat, I felt the hard muscles underneath leap in response. He glanced down at me as we exited the box and gave me a wicked smile.

"Ah, my whiskey-eyed lass, have I told you yet tonight how much I love you and how beautiful you are?" he asked.

I paused and turned to him, sighing inwardly as I brushed his hair away from his sparkling blue eyes. Michael's dark blond hair, which he always wore longer than was fashionable, never failed to look as though I'd been running my fingers through it. Probably because I had. After nearly three quarters of a century together, I still couldn't keep my hands off my dashing husband.

"You've told me at least twice," I replied softly, "but a woman can never hear it too many times."

I thought my new burgundy evening gown, with its black lace and jet beads, was particularly lovely. Hoop skirts had thankfully gone out of style years ago, and the use of bustles was in decline. I sincerely hoped such good sense would soon herald a return to the more uncomplicated fashions of my youth. My new dress was the first one in years that I truly adored. My blood-red hair was done up in artful curls, and Michael reached out to tuck an errant strand behind my ear.

A discreet cough came from somewhere behind me. All thoughts of my handsome husband were suspended as I turned to see a rather grim-looking dark-haired young man waiting in the hall. I closed the distance between us and silently regarded him. He'd been young when he was turned, perhaps only eighteen or nineteen years old. He didn't look as one would expect a warden to look, but I'd learned long ago never to judge a vampire in such terms. Michael was a prime example of that. He didn't have Devlin's great height, or his massive build, but he was a brawler, and infinitely the more dangerous of the two. I would reserve judgment on this young man until I'd seen him in action.

"Miss Craven," the warden said, executing a respectful bow. "My name is Grady and I am a warden for the Regent of London."

It was rare for vampires to use surnames. Though Michael and I had been married for well over half a century, there was no tradition among our kind of a wife taking her husband's last name, as there was in the human world. I had not abandoned the use of my family name after I was turned, therefore I would forever be "Miss Craven" to those showing respect. To those who spoke my name in fearful whispers, I was Cin Craven, the Red Witch of the Righteous, or simply the Devil's Witch.

"Warden," I said coolly. "You've traveled a long way. What is so important that it couldn't wait until the conclusion of the opera?"

"I was instructed by the Regent to come here with all haste and speak to you immediately," he said, glancing nervously at Michael. "And privately."

"You may speak freely in front of my husband, Warden," I assured him. "We keep no secrets from each other."

The warden shifted his weight uncomfortably. "My instructions were very clear, ma'am, and I dare not disobey the Regent. I am to speak to you, and only you."

Well, that certainly isn't going to happen, I thought. Already I could feel the tension in Michael's body at the warden's strange request.

I cocked my head to one side. "I don't recall Charles being such an ogre," I said.

"Charles is no longer Regent," the warden replied. "He was challenged and defeated last year. The new Regent is young, but he's strong and ruthless.

"Who is he?" I asked out of curiosity. Whoever he was, he had already begun to annoy me.

"His name is Sebastian," the warden replied.

I stilled, my stomach clenching. "Sebastian Montford?" I asked.

Grady nodded. "I believe that was his human name, yes."

At that confirmation Michael shot forward, his hand curling around the warden's throat.

Grady's eyes widened in fear, as well they should have. Once, when we'd both been human, Lord Sebastian Montford had wanted to marry me, though I had not returned his affections. Perhaps my polite but firm rejection of his offer had hardened his heart to me, or perhaps it had only turned his love into some dark and twisted thing. Whatever the case, when Sebastian had been made a vampire, he and his master had come for me. Sebastian had wanted me in his power, and they'd both wanted control of my magic. Fortunately, though, The Righteous had come to my aid. In order to save me, Michael had turned me into a vampire. I had become his lover, and later his wife. I don't think Sebastian would ever forgive either one of us for that.

"What game are you playing at, boy?" Michael growled.

There was a soft gasp from the hallway behind me, and I turned to see a white-haired dowager flutter her fan and duck back through the door to her private box.

"Michael," I said calmly, laying my hand on his shoulder. "You're going to make a scene."

"It's not a game," the warden said. "I was sent to bring the Devil's Witch back to London."

Michael laughed harshly. "Does Sebastian Montford not recall that I promised to kill him if I ever saw him again?"

"I am supposed to bring her, and her alone," Warden Grady said.

Michael pulled the warden closer. "You go back to your Regent," he said in a voice that sent shivers up my spine, "and you tell him that if he ever again tries to get to Cin, I will hunt him down and set him on fire."

Michael released the warden with a shove and Grady staggered back. Righting himself, he straightened the collar of his shirt and tugged at his coat.

"So you won't help me?" he asked.

"Help you?" Michael replied incredulously. "Help you put the woman I love in the hands of a man who tried to enslave her when she was human? I think not."

Warden Grady clenched his jaw and a very firm look of resolve settled on his face. "I don't know what history you have with the Regent," he said, "and I don't bloody well care."

Michael raised his eyebrows and started to say something, but I laid my hand on his sleeve to still his invective.

When he realized that Michael wasn't likely to grab him by the throat again, the warden stood taller, and continued. "I assure you that the threat to our city is very real. We've lost ten percent of the vampire population in just over three months. I did not travel all this way to reignite whatever feud you have with the regent. If that had been Sebastian's intention, he would have sent someone else. I am not one of his lackeys. I am a deputy warden of the city of London, and the policing and security of our vampires is my responsibility. In point of fact, I have argued long and hard to call you to help with this problem, and I believe it proves just how reluctant Sebastian was to have you in his city that he waited this long to allow me to do so. If it had been entirely up to me, I would have tracked you down two months ago."

"What's happening in London?" I asked with concern. Ravenworth, my home when I'd been human, was only thirty miles from the city. As a human and a vampire, London had been like a second home to me.

Warden Grady looked at me grimly, and asked, "Have you heard of Jack the Ripper?"

TWO

Michael scoffed. "What does a human killer have to do with us?"

"The Ripper is not a human," Grady replied. "He's a demon."

Cold dread washed over me at his words. "I hope you're speaking metaphorically," I said.

The warden shook his head. "I wish I were. We paid little attention to him when he was killing humans. As you said, a human murderer is none of our business. But eventually he tired of slaughtering humans and moved on to vampires. I can only assume it's because we're harder to kill."

"Better sport," Michael said grimly.

"Exactly," Grady agreed. "The wardens have tracked him down on several occasions, but we've been unable to kill the bastard. We assumed that he was a vampire, but we once managed to stake him through the heart, and that only angered him. The last time we went up against him, the Chief Warden managed to take the Ripper's head."

"That certainly should have done it," I said.

Supernatural creatures (vampires, werewolves, faeries) are susceptible to different things (sunlight, silver, cold iron), but beheading will kill anything. Correction: beheading *should* kill anything.

"That's when we realized what we were up against. You see, at first we thought we were tracking a whole group of rogue vampires. It made sense because the human police have had such varying descriptions of the Ripper." Grady paused, as if trying to collect his thoughts, and a faraway look crept into his eyes. When he continued, his voice was soft and gently laced with fear. "There were four of us that night. We had him surrounded and we all rushed him at once. Even so, I didn't think we were going to be able to take him down. His strength was incredible. Then James got in a lucky blow and sliced the Ripper's head right off his body. The body fell and . . . and an eerie blue light rose up out of it. The light, it rushed over James, surrounding him, and then it disappeared. We all stood still for several moments, unsure of what had just happened. And then James looked at us and his eyes were glowing red. He turned on us then. The only way I can describe it is that the Chief was no longer in control of his body. The demon was."

"So the demon now inhabits the body of your Chief Warden?" I asked.

Grady shook his head. "We found James two weeks later, wandering the streets. Physically, he was unharmed, but he doesn't remember anything that happened to him from the time he cut off the Ripper's head until he woke in an alley in Whitechapel. I have no idea whose form the demon has taken now, but it seems to only be able to occupy dead bodies—those of humans who are already deceased, or vampires."

I blew out a breath, trying to reconcile what I knew of demons with what the warden had just told us.

Finding a true demon is rare, Devlin had once told me. *For one to exist in this reality, it has to take a shape that is natural to our world*, he'd said. *Demons find the human body too limiting. You could live five hundred years and never see one.*

Wouldn't that have been nice? I thought.

"Warden," I said, "go back to your Regent and tell him that I will come to London, but I will not come alone, and I will not grant him the courtesy of an audience. In fact, considering that Michael swore to kill Sebastian if he ever saw him again, I think it might be a wise idea for you to keep him inside his townhouse while we're in the city."

"Thank you, Miss Craven," Grady said, smiling. "You are our last hope."

I smiled back, putting a great deal more confidence into the gesture than I felt. "We will find a way to slay this demon, but I give you fair warning—if I discover that Sebastian had anything to do with summoning it into our world, he will answer for it with his life."

The warden nodded gravely. "I've seen firsthand what the Ripper has done to my vampires, Miss Craven. The young ones, they don't turn to dust like the old ones do. I know what tortures they endured before he put them out of their misery. I'm sure the Regent wouldn't do anything to bring harm to our vampires. But if evidence should come to light that he has any connection with this monster, I will gladly stand by your side against him."

THREE

I hate winter. You'd think that, as a vampire, it would be my favorite season. After all, the days are shorter and the nights are longer, which is undeniably helpful if you're a prisoner to the sun. To me, however, winter is such an ugly time of year. I would gladly trade shorter nights for leaves on the trees and flowers in bloom, for the smell of green grass under my bare feet. Looking out the carriage window at the streets of London—thick with the soupy gray sludge of dirty, melting snow—I longed for spring.

"What has you so pensive, *mo ghraidh*?" Michael asked, his Scottish accent barely discernable anymore, unless he was speaking Gaelic.

I turned my attention from the world outside to the man who sat next to me. Devlin was driving the carriage and Justine had elected to ride up top with him, so it was just Michael and me inside. Devlin didn't care much for sea travel and, after being confined all day to his cabin on the ship, he was fairly itching for some fresh air. Our poor driver had been somewhat confused to be sent home in a hack.

"I was just thinking how long it's been since we were last in London," I replied. "Can it really have been three years ago this spring?"

"I believe it was," he replied. "If I'd thought we would be so long between visits, I might have objected to you buying that house. Not that it would have done me any good."

I smiled. "I don't see any sense in all that money just lying about."

"It isn't lying about," Michael groused. "It's earning interest."

"And plenty enough to allow me to keep one small house in London and still be a wealthy woman."

Michael arched a brow at me and, the way the moonlight cast his cheekbones in sharp relief, he looked more like a devil than the archangel he was named for. "One small house in London, and a rather large house in Spain. Then there's the villa in Italy, and the plantation in America."

I ran my fingers lazily down his chest, toying with the buttons on his vest. "Are any of them likely to bankrupt me?" I asked.

He snorted, as if I'd asked a ridiculous question. Which I had. If there was one thing I didn't worry about in this world, it was money. Michael, with his Scots frugality, was a genius with finances. Over the years, he had managed to multiply my substantial inheritance almost beyond imagining.

"Then don't complain about the houses," I said. "You know how much I dislike living out of hotels."

He gave me a look. "Aye, every time we're in one place longer than two weeks, I'm afraid you'll buy an estate."

"But, darling," I purred, slowly popping the buttons of his vest open one by one. "Won't it be nice to be in our own house and not some noisy hotel?"

He growled and pulled me onto his lap so that my legs were straddling him. "Only if Ginny's got a fire blazing in the hearth and fresh sheets on the bed."

"Sleepy?" I asked, calling up a little practical magic. With a thought and a flick of my wrist the curtains of the carriage snapped shut. Being a witch often has its advantages.

"Not remotely," Michael replied, pushing my skirts up until his hands gained access to my bare thighs. "Why, you wicked girl. You're not wearing any drawers."

I bit my lip and smiled. "Are you shocked?"

"Scandalized," he murmured, just before his fingers found me.

By the gods, I was hot and wet and so ready for him. Furiously I tried to calculate if we had time to finish what we'd started. Then all reasonable thought went out of my head as his hand snaked up to wrap around the back of my neck and pull my lips to his. His tongue entered my mouth as one long finger entered my body, and I arched against him, swaying with the rhythm of the carriage.

"Please, don't stop," I begged as he withdrew from me.

He ran his fingers gently over my womanhood, spreading the slick moisture across me.

"Such a greedy lass," he whispered huskily. "Do you want more?"

I looked down at him, at the look of masculine triumph in his blue eyes. Michael was the sort of man who enjoyed foreplay. He often made a game of seeing how many times he could make me come before he joined me. I would have been happy to free the buttons on his trousers and take him right there, but I knew that watching me find my own release was almost as pleasurable to him as achieving his own.

"Yes," I said on a ragged breath. "Give me more."

He growled and plunged two fingers into me, stretching me. I quivered and threw back my head. His lips traced the tops of my breasts, his tongue running just under the edge of my bodice. My nipples tightened, wishing they were free to feel the heat of his mouth. I dug my fingernails into his shoulders, reveling in the feel of the deep, hard strokes of his fingers. I was almost there, so close . . . and then the carriage came to a halt in front of my townhouse.

With a sigh of regret, Michael stopped.

"No!" I cried, collapsing against him.

Stroking his fingers one last time across me, Michael modestly pulled down my skirts, put his hands around my waist, and gently set me on the seat next to him. When Devlin opened the carriage door, the muscles in my legs were shaking so violently, I wasn't sure I could walk. I turned and looked at Michael.

"You're such a tease," I scolded.

"I never promise what I can't deliver," he assured me. "If you don't spend all night talking to Ginny, we can go upstairs and finish this."

I looked down the length of him, imagining that lithe but solidly muscled body naked beneath me.

"I'll give her five minutes," I said, "and then you're mine."

"Are you two coming?" Devlin asked impatiently from the sidewalk.

"Not at the moment," I said with regret and great meaning. "But soon."

FOUR

Ginny McCready was the eldest daughter of the manager of my island plantation off the coast of Savannah. Shortly after I'd bought the London house eight years ago, I'd received a letter from Ginny, then an unmarried woman of twenty-seven, expressing an interest in leaving Georgia and seeing more of the world. I'd immediately hired her to come to London and run the house in Mayfair and any other estates I might eventually purchase in England. Standing in the open doorway with her round, pink cheeks and her golden hair piled up in braids, she was a welcome sight.

The tall, lanky young footman who had brought our carriage to the docks rushed past her to tend the horses. He nodded respectfully to me as we passed and I glanced back, watching him eagerly take instructions from Devlin regarding our plans for the conveyance this evening. I shook my head. Skinny young men with red hair and freckled faces weren't what the upper class traditionally looked for in a footman, which is probably why Ginny had hired him. She'd always had a soft spot for strays.

Ginny glanced up at the thick, gray storm clouds that hung low in the dark sky and pulled her shawl more tightly around her shoulders.

"Y'all had better get inside," she called out, and then laughed. "I almost said 'before you catch your death'!"

I chuckled. Ginny had known about vampires since she was eight years old, when Michael and I had bought the plantation where her family lived, on what the locals called Devil's Island. I gave her a quick hug as she shooed us all inside and closed the door against the chill night.

Justine was humming softly as she removed her hat and gloves. She was tall, long-legged and gorgeous, with her silvery blonde hair done up in the latest style. She was also the closest thing I'd ever had to a sister. We'd lived, played, and fought by each other's sides since I'd become a vampire.

As Ginny gathered up our cloaks, chattering away in her delightful southern accent, Justine reached out and tugged at the crooked neckline of my gown.

"*Merde*," she muttered in her native French. "You two find yourselves alone in a carriage and the clothes, they come off."

I cocked a brow at her. "Need I remind you of the last time Michael and I drove? I opened the carriage door to find you with your skirts up over your head and Devlin crouched—"

She slapped her hand over my mouth. "Point taken," she said hastily, glancing at Ginny.

"Right in front of the Paris Opera, no less," I whispered defiantly.

Justine glanced at Devlin with her coquette's smile, and I knew she and I had very similar plans for our first evening in London.

"The men from the ship came this morning to tell me of your imminent arrival," Ginny was saying. "They delivered your trunks, and everything is all unpacked in your rooms."

"I'm sorry for showing up on such short notice, Ginny," I said. "I hope you haven't gone to any trouble."

We had come in on the morning tide but naturally had

not been able to leave the ship until dark. One of the benefits of sailing on the vampire-owned Blood Cross line was that there was no need to explain such behavior to the crew. The human sailors who manned the ships had worked for the line for generations, and could be depended upon to be helpful and discreet.

"Why, Cin," Ginny scoffed, "it's no trouble at all. You pay me very well to be ready for just such an occasion, though I must say it would be nice to see y'all more often. I went to the market and stocked up on your favorite whiskey. Also, champagne for mademoiselle," she said with a nod to Justine. "The piano has been tuned, there are fresh paints for Michael in the studio upstairs, and all the correspondence that I had yet to forward to you is on your desk in the study."

I shook my head. "Ginny McCready, you are a wonder. I wish I had five more just like you."

"Well, you might get your wish soon enough," Ginny said, barely able to contain the enormous smile that bloomed on her face. "I have a beau."

"You do not!" I gasped.

I couldn't have been more shocked if she'd hit me in the head. From the time I'd met her when she was eight years old, Ginny McCready had consistently and vociferously vowed never to marry.

"I most certainly do," she assured me. "And he's simply lovely."

"I'm so happy for you," I said. "You'll have to tell me all about him."

Michael cleared his throat. The only problem with Ginny was that she was a true southern belle. She was as much a master of the art of conversation as Michael was at the art of swordsmanship. And that is saying quite a lot. Often a simple exchange with her turned into a chat that lasted for hours. Ginny had never met a stranger—she could draw anyone, be they countess or chimney sweep, into a conversation—

and often people found themselves telling her things they normally wouldn't share. Perhaps it was her innocent, farm girl appearance, or perhaps it was that delectable southern accent, but Ginny had an uncanny ability to know absolutely every bit of scandal there was to know in London society. I'd often wondered if there was a patron goddess of gossip, and if Ginny McCready had erected an altar to her in her bedroom.

"Perhaps in a few hours, after we've all rested a bit," I said, glancing back at Michael with a wink.

"Yes," Devlin agreed, slipping his arm around Justine's waist and pulling her back against his massive chest. "I think we could all use a bit of relaxation. The crossing was so choppy. I didn't sleep a bit."

I was fairly certain that the Channel wasn't what had kept Devlin awake, but I didn't say so.

"Well, that's to be expected this time of year," Ginny said. Suddenly her hands flew to her mouth. "Oh, dear Lord! I entirely forgot about your guest!"

My eyes widened. "We have a guest?"

"Yes, I told him y'all weren't here yet, but he said he'd wait. I put him in the parlor an hour ago. You vampires are so fiendishly quiet I forgot he was there."

"Did he give you a name?" Michael asked.

Ginny bobbed her head. "Warden Grady."

All four of us groaned. I think we were all looking forward to one evening of quiet to get settled before we started demon hunting.

"Well, we mustn't keep the warden waiting," I muttered.

"Would you like me to fetch y'all some tea?" Ginny asked.

Before I could answer, Michael said, "Miss McCready, I think you'd better break out the whiskey."

My husband knew me so very well.

FIVE

As promised, Warden Grady was waiting patiently in my parlor. He had helped himself to a glass of cognac and was stretched out in one of the wing chairs in front of the fire.

"Warden," I greeted him as we entered the room, "I trust we didn't keep you waiting long."

"Not at all," he replied, rising swiftly to take my hand and execute a courtly bow. He then greeted Michael, Devlin, and Justine. As we all took a seat he continued, "I apologize for showing up on your doorstep before you've even had a chance to settle in, but I appreciate you coming so quickly. I just arrived back in town myself yesterday."

Devlin leaned forward. "I take it there has been some new development," he said, his gravelly voice sounding surly, even to me. "Or surely tomorrow night would have been soon enough to call."

Grady looked at him nervously. Devlin was the oldest of us, the leader of The Righteous. That, coupled with the fact that he was nearly six and a half feet tall and built like a brick wall, was enough to inspire respect, and perhaps a bit of fear, in any sane vampire.

"Another vampire disappeared last night," Grady said.

"Something must be done before the Ripper decimates the entire population of the city."

"What Devlin is trying to say," I explained gently, "is that since we've literally just walked in the door, I haven't yet had the time I need to look through my spell books, which I keep in the library here."

Grady looked disappointed, as if he had assumed that because I was a witch I should somehow instinctively know how to vanquish demons.

"But you do have something that will stop him?"

"I know that there is part of a spell in one of my books. I need to acquire the ingredients that fuel the magic, though. Ginny, is there still an apothecary shop on Panton Street called Little and Sons?"

Grady glanced at Ginny as she filled our glasses. "There is," she replied hesitantly.

Ginny glanced around the room at everyone's expectant looks, and leaned down to whisper, "As a matter of fact, you know how I said I have a new beau? His name is Warren Little and he happens to own that particular shop."

She needn't have whispered. With our keen vampire hearing, everyone in the room knew what she'd said.

I blinked up at her. "Oh. My. Well, that is fortuitous. We shall pay him a visit tonight and that will bring us one step closer to tracking down this monster."

"And until we slay him, though," Devlin said to the warden grimly, "keep your vampires off the streets. Tell them not to go out to feed unless they absolutely have to. And if the blood will come to them, so much the better."

Grady nodded. "The Regent hasn't left his mansion in weeks," he replied. "The blood whores are brought in to feed the court."

A blood whore was exactly what it sounded like, a human who sold his or her blood, and often their bodies as well, to vampires. It was a very lucrative and tightly regulated business, but blood whores were considered a delicacy, and only those in the upper echelons of vampire society were able to afford to drink from them on a regular basis. As a result, there were nowhere near enough blood whores in London to feed the entire vampire population. Unless we caught this bastard soon, the vamps would eventually have to go out to feed. And the Ripper would be there, waiting.

SIX

Our carriage pulled to a stop in front of the apothecary shop on Panton Street. Michael leapt from the box and opened the door with a flourish, interrupting Ginny's discourse on the hiring of Will, my redheaded footman, and his young bride Amy, who was apparently my chambermaid. Thankfully, they had their own lodgings and did not live in my house. It would be hard enough to explain why all the windows were shuttered during the day without having them underfoot all night as well.

Ginny and I descended from the carriage. Devlin and Justine had stayed behind to look through the books that were in my library. I'm not an accomplished spellcaster—my magic tends to be a bit more active—but I have acquired quite an abundance of books on spellcraft and the arcane over the years.

As Ginny rang the bell, I paused in the shadow of the carriage. Pulling Michael's head to mine, I kissed him quickly but thoroughly.

"What was that for, lass?" he asked.

"Just to remind you that I haven't forgotten what's been promised to me," I said, trailing my fingers across his chest, then lower, smiling contentedly when the muscles of his stomach leapt to my touch.

The jingle of the shop's bell drew my attention as Warren Little opened the door. A bachelor, he lived in the small apartment above his shop. It was apparent that he'd already settled in for the night. His dark hair was rather a mess and the buttons of his shirt were slightly askew, as if he'd dressed in a hurry.

"Miss Virginia!" he exclaimed, and then softer, "Ginny."

I winked at Michael. "We'll be back shortly," I said, leaving him to mind the horses.

"Warren," Ginny said, "this is my employer, Cin Craven."

Warren looked startled, and why wouldn't he be? Two women showing up on a bachelor's doorstep in the middle of the night was highly improper, but time was of the essence. I couldn't go out in the daylight and I knew what I was looking for. Coming to the shop tonight was the most efficient use of our time.

Warren finally regained his composure and bowed to me.

"Mrs. Craven," he said, "won't you both come in?"

I wasn't prepared for the memories that assaulted me when I entered the shop. So much had changed in the world over the last century, but this shop was exactly the same. I closed my eyes and inhaled. It even smelled the same. I had played here when I was a little girl, my mother having also been a witch and a regular customer of this establishment. I knew there was a private room in the back of the store that sold anything a witch could want. I stared at the counter and the jar of peppermints that still sat there, the bright red and white candies beckoning me. Silently, I crossed the room and ran my fingers over the glass. Warren's grandfather, Archie, had always given me one or two when Mother and I had come to shop. I looked up at the ceiling. Somewhere upstairs was the bedroom where I had woken the night I'd become a vampire. It was also the same room I'd sat in as I'd watched Archie Little take his last breath in this world.

"Is she all right?" Warren whispered to Ginny.

"She's fine," Ginny whispered back. Louder, she said, "Cin, may I introduce Mr. Warren Little?"

I reached up and brushed a tear from my cheek before turning back to them. Warren was the very image of his father and a more handsome version of his grandfather. He was a big man with dark hair and dark eyes. And, like his father and his grandfather before him, not the sort of man you'd expect to find behind the counter in an apothecary shop.

"Hello, Warren," I said softly.

His eyes grew round and he backed up quickly, nearly upsetting a display of bath salts in the process. It occurred to me that, while I could see perfectly well outside at night, this was the first look he'd had of me in the light.

"I remember you," he whispered.

I nodded. "I thought you might. You were just a boy the last time I was here. You were what? Ten years old?"

"I was eleven," he said hollowly. "It was the night my grandfather died. You and a blonde woman came to see him."

Warren walked slowly to me, staring as if he was seeing a ghost. His gaze flew over my face and the Craven Cross that hung from its gold chain around my neck. It was a large Celtic cross studded with rubies and diamonds, and not something that one would forget. When he was standing not a foot from me, he reached his hand out, but it wasn't the cross he touched. It was the long lock of blood-red hair that fell over my shoulder. I stood very still as he ran his thumb and forefinger over that curl. Then he raised his dark eyes to mine.

"I'll never forget the color of your hair. Grandfather used

to tell us stories of vampires and demons, but I thought they were just tales meant to entertain a young boy," he said.

I closed my eyes and pushed away my memories of Archie Little. One of the prices you pay for living forever is that the humans you love die all too quickly. I looked at Ginny, trying not to think of the day when I would lose her, too. It never gets easier, and yet I can't seem to help but make those bonds.

"Mrs. Craven," Warren said, snapping me out of my dark thoughts. "Why have you come?"

"I need some supplies for a spell, Warren," I said. "I'm hoping that Little and Sons still sells the type of items I require?"

Warren smiled. "That we do. Just tell me what you need and I'll be happy to get it for you."

I felt slightly uncomfortable as I gave him a list of the ingredients I needed. This combination of herbs was innocent enough, but when I found the rest of the spell . . . well, what I intended to do with them was not exactly white magic. My mother definitely would not have approved. In fact, when I'd been a young witch, arrogant and unwilling to use any sort of magic that might be tainted with darkness, I had once balked at using this very binding spell. But many years ago I had been infected with black magic. It was a part of me and had been for almost as long as I'd been a vampire. I had made my peace with it and I was not so squeamish now about such things.

The front door burst open, causing the three of us to jump in surprise, and Michael rushed into the shop.

"Cin!" Michael yelled. "I saw him!"

"Who is that?" Warren asked as I rushed past him.

"Her husband," I heard Ginny respond.

"Who?" I asked. "Who did you see?"

"The Ripper," Michael replied.

"Jack the Ripper's dead," Warren announced. "Or so they say. There hasn't been a Ripper murder in months."

"That's because he's been killing vampires," I informed him. "Michael, we don't even know what he looks like now. How do you know it was him?"

"A man in a deerstalker hat stopped at the end of the block and stared at me for quite a long time," he said.

"That doesn't mean anything," I pointed out. People often stared at Michael, though usually it was women. He was just so damned beautiful. "It was undoubtedly just someone out for an evening stroll."

"With glowing red eyes?" Michael asked smugly.

"Oh. Well, probably not."

"Exactly," he said, turning back to the door. "Let's go."

I rushed to catch up with him, grabbing his arm as he reached the door.

"And do what?" I asked. "Get ourselves killed? Let it go tonight, Michael. We'll be much better prepared tomorrow."

Michael glowered at me. I loved him more than anything in this world, but by the gods, he was hotheaded. He and Justine were like two peas in a pod that way and, more often than not, Devlin and I were the voices of reason that kept them alive.

"Cin?" Ginny called out, her voice thick with worry. "What's happening?"

I turned back to her. "Absolutely nothing. Everything is fine."

When I turned back around, Michael was striding out the door.

"Michael," I yelled. "Michael, don't!"

But he didn't stop.

"Oh, bugger," I cursed. I had no weapons other than my magic and I wasn't dressed for fighting. I looked back at Warren and Ginny. "Warren, take her upstairs and don't open that door until I come back. A vampire can enter this shop without an invitation, but not your apartment."

He nodded to me and I gritted my teeth and strode from the shop. I paused as I closed the door, thinking about how the demon could take over any dead body it chose. Sticking my head back inside, I amended my order. "Actually, don't come back down until morning."

Both of their eyes grew wide at the implication, but I didn't have time to worry about Ginny's virtue. I rushed off after my husband, cursing with every step. The slushy snow was soaking into my cloak and the hem of my dress, and the dragging weight was an annoyance I did not need at the moment. Not to mention, my beautiful new slippers were undoubtedly ruined, and it was a good thing I wasn't susceptible to frostbite. By the gods, I hate winter.

SEVEN

I caught up with Michael fairly quickly, which surprised me, considering he didn't have sodden skirts and petticoats hampering his movement.

"What the devil do you think you're doing?" I hissed as I came up alongside him.

Michael reached out and took my hand, his warm skin enveloping my cold fingers. Still, he didn't take his eyes off the man walking down the sidewalk in the distance, and he didn't slow his pace.

"Don't worry," he replied. "I'm not going to engage him. But it might be helpful to track him, don't you think? He must call someplace home, and knowing his daytime resting place could undoubtedly be useful."

I couldn't argue with his logic. "All right," I agreed. "We'll follow him, but not for long. What if he waits until dawn to go home? I don't fancy burning to ashes on the streets of London, thank you very much."

"Let's just see where he's headed and then we'll turn back. He's not wandering, he's walking with purpose. Wherever he's going, it can't be far or he would have taken a hack."

I looked at the figure ahead of us. From the back he looked like any other well-dressed gentleman, but if Michael said his eyes had glowed red, I believed him. We trailed him for quite some time until he entered St. James's Park. We were following at such a distance that by the time we entered the park, he had vanished into the shadows of the trees. Michael stopped, and I was grateful for it.

"Something isn't right," I said, a sense of unease gripping me.

"We're not tracking him," Michael said softly. "He's baiting us."

"Can we go back now?" I asked.

"Yes," Michael replied. "And quickly."

We turned to go, but it was too late. The Ripper was behind us, leaning negligently against one of the barren oaks, his features obscured by the shadows.

"How kind of you to come," he said.

Michael opened his coat and pulled his sword. The Ripper smiled.

"I have one of those too," he informed us, and his eyes flashed red as he drew his own blade. "This might be amusing."

I almost laughed. Demon or not, he was still limited by the confines of his human body. Or perhaps this body had once been a vampire. It didn't matter. There was a reason they called Michael the Devil's Archangel. He was merciless in battle and no one, except perhaps the High King of the Vampires, could match his skill with a blade. The Ripper would lose. But what then?

"Cin, run," Michael said, as if he had already thought through the answer to my unspoken question.

"I won't leave you," I argued.

Almost painfully he grabbed my arm, never taking his eyes from the demon slowly advancing toward us. "I was a fool to allow you to come with me. If he takes your body, we're all doomed."

The Ripper paused and looked at me. Now that he was

out from under the cover of the trees, I could see his face clearly. Whoever's body he was wearing, the man had been handsome. Nothing out of the ordinary, but he had pleasant enough features, with thick brown hair and green eyes. It was his eyes that caught my attention. There was nothing behind them. Despite his words, there was no sense of anticipation to be found there. No excitement. No fear. Nothing. He cocked his head in my direction, and for the briefest moment I thought I saw curiosity in his eyes. His gaze raked over me in an impersonal, almost scientific, assessment of my worth, and then that eerie blankness fell back in place and he turned his attention back to Michael.

"Run," Michael said again, "and don't stop until you get home." He shoved me away as the Ripper raised his sword and the battle began.

I stumbled backward, but I didn't run. Michael was right, of course. Were the demon to invade my body and take control of my magic, nothing would stop him. I knew well the terrifying extent of my powers, the things that I *could* do, but would not. I should run. I was endangering hundreds, if not millions, of lives by staying. Yet I could not leave Michael.

What I did do was move to the far edge of the field, so that my continued presence wouldn't distract Michael, and watch as they circled each other, blades clashing. Michael was by far the better swordsman, but the demon was so strong, stronger even than a vampire. Every time their swords collided I could see the force of it reverberate through Michael's body. How long could he take that punishment before he ended it and took the Ripper's head? And when that happened, would the Ripper take my husband's body as he had taken the Chief Warden's?

Frantically, I tried to think of some sort of magic that would incapacitate him long enough for us to get away, but not kill him outright. Without knowing whose body he was in, it was a dicey decision. Fire would kill a human slowly enough for us to run, but vampires were much more combustible. It was too risky. But perhaps I could freeze him, make him immobile just long enough for Michael and me to get to safety.

I made an effort to clear my head and concentrate on what I wished to accomplish. Calling up my magic, I let it build within me, like bringing a pot to boiling. I waited far longer than I normally did to set it free, hoping the magic would be that much stronger. When it felt as though I could no longer hold all that power within my own skin, I raised my hands and focused on the demon.

Freeze, I thought. *Be still.*

The Ripper stumbled and turned his head to me. Michael took advantage of that moment of distraction and shoved his sword into the demon's chest. That got his attention. His sword came up, slicing at Michael's head. Michael moved just quickly enough to avoid most of the arc, the tip of the blade slicing along one cheek. Michael didn't flinch. He spun away from the sword and came up directly in front of the Ripper. Blocking the demon's sword arm with his left hand, Michael pulled his sword from the Ripper's chest and swiftly stepped out of range.

Meanwhile, I stood well back from the fray, completely dumbfounded. What had just happened? Other than my magic not working, obviously. It was inconceivable. The clash of steel once again broke the stillness of the night and I shook my head, unable to dwell on the matter any longer. Somehow he was immune to my magic, but I was certain the bastard wasn't immune to fire.

Holding my hand out, I conjured a ball of fire a few inches above my palm. It was a frightening bit of magic and one that I'd only done a couple times. Fire is not a vampire's friend, after all.

"Michael, get as far away from him as you can!" I shouted.

Having fought by my side for so many decades, Michael instinctively moved away from both the demon and the sound of my voice. It only takes getting in the crossfire of my magic and its intended target once to learn that lesson.

I pulled my hand out from under the ball of fire and, focusing on the Ripper's dark form, I used my power to hurl it in his direction. Like a comet streaking through the night sky, it flew from me and hit the demon with enough force to knock him to the ground.

"Come on, Michael!" I called to him, holding out my hand. "Now!"

Without looking back, he ran to me. As I waited for him to cross the field I watched the demon burn. I'd seen vampires burn before. There was always thrashing and screaming, but the demon did neither. He lay there for a moment and then he slowly got to his feet. Like a straw man burned in effigy, he simply stood there, ablaze and unmoving. And then it happened.

Just as Grady had described, the demon broke loose from the body it had stolen. The creature that emerged from the burning corpse pulsed with an eerie blue light. It was essentially human in form, though its long limbs and body were shapeless and genderless. It had to find a new body, and quickly. It couldn't survive in this realm without one. Its red eyes glowed like burning coals . . . and they were looking directly at me. Seeing the panic on my face, Michael turned to look behind him. He was between me and the demon, but it didn't want him. It came directly at me.

With a roar of denial, Michael threw himself into the demon's path. The two of them collided, and screaming, Michael sank to his hands and knees as the blue light absorbed into his body.

"Michael! No!" I shouted and ran forward.

Just as I reached him, he raised his head and looked at me. I skidded to a halt. His blue eyes were now demon-red.

"Michael?" I whispered.

He looked down at himself, at the sword he still held in his hand, then his gaze moved back to me. I stood, unable to move, as he came toward me with that graceful predator's stride I knew so well. My head was telling me to run, that the demon now had control of my husband's body, but my heart could not accept it.

"Witch," Michael said. "He told me you would come."

Before I could ask what he meant, the man I loved raised his sword and plunged it into my chest. I staggered back, falling to the ground. Gripping the sword, I blinked up at him in disbelief. He knelt before me, balancing on the balls of his feet.

"The sword does not hurt that much," he said, as if he were impartially observing the outcome of some experiment. "Yet there is such pain in your eyes. How interesting."

Whatever reply I might have come up with was forestalled by the sound of running footsteps. Michael, or rather the demon who now occupied his body, and I turned to see Warren Little dashing across the field toward us.

"Warren," I gasped, pain radiating through my chest, as he came to kneel by my side. "Get out of here."

"Mrs. Craven," he said aghast, ignoring me. "You've been stabbed." Turning to Michael he snapped, "What have you done?"

The demon stood and I looked up at him. His eyes were now Michael's own blue but briefly they flashed red in anger. Actually, I wasn't sure if he could even register such an emotion as anger or annoyance, or if he'd done it just because he could. Whatever the case, it had the desired effect. Warren finally understood that something had gone terribly wrong.

"I've grown weary of killing humans," the demon said. "But I will make an exception for you."

Warren, with a presence of mind that both impressed

and astounded me, grabbed the Craven Cross and jerked it off my neck. Brandishing it before him, he placed himself between me and the demon.

"Be gone, demon!" he shouted.

Michael hissed and staggered backward. I wasn't sure if it was the vampire or the demon that objected to the cross. A cross, or just about any religious object, will repel a vampire if it's wielded by a true believer and the vampire means the human harm. I wasn't certain about demons, but it seemed likely such methods would work on them as well. Otherwise, what was the point of exorcisms?

"I will have you, witch," the demon said. "But first I must fulfill the terms of my bargain. I promised him I would bring you unimaginable pain." He held out his arms and glanced down at his body before smiling at me. "I think this will do."

Tears sprang to my eyes as I watched him turn and walk away. Warren was talking to me, but I didn't hear what he was saying. The demon stopped at the smoldering corpse and kicked it, rolling it over and over until the flames were extinguished. He reached down into what was once the man's chest and gingerly pulled out a gold chain. A round pendant with some sort of stone set in its center hung from the chain, glittering in the moonlight. Slipping the artifact into his pocket, he calmly disappeared into the shadows.

"Cin!" Warren said snapping my attention back to him. "We followed you in your carriage. We waited, thinking you might need a ride home."

I blinked at him barely understanding his words. "Pull the sword out, Warren," I said numbly. "And help me home."

EIGHT

My cloak managed to hide the gaping hole and the blood stains on my dress as I walked into the house on Upper Brook Street. Ginny followed behind me, and Warren had graciously offered to see to the carriage and the horses, since we'd sent Will the footman home hours ago. Devlin and Justine emerged from one of the parlors, and it occurred to me then, for the first time, that I would have to tell them what had happened.

Devlin inhaled sharply, his vampire senses easily detecting the scent of blood. His gaze roamed over my face and then dropped to my hands. I tried to hide the red stains in the folds of my cloak, but Devlin crossed the room and took my hands in his.

"Cin," he said softly. "Where is Michael?"

I looked up into his dark eyes and I realized I didn't have to be strong anymore. I'd had to hold myself together in front of the demon, and then with Warren and Ginny so that they could remove the sword and get me home. But now that I was here with Devlin and Justine . . . the tears started falling and, with a wrenching sob, my knees buckled. I would have hit the floor if Devlin hadn't caught me and swung me into his arms.

I'd lost him. Michael had thrown himself in front of a

demon, knowing it would take over his body, in order to save me. And I had been powerless to stop it. I clutched Devlin's shirt in my fists and cried so hard I thought I might break. I should have run when he'd told me to.

"*Mon amour*," I heard Justine say, "take her up to her room. I will clean her up, but you must find blood for her."

Cradled against Devlin's massive chest, I felt like a child being carried to bed by her father. He set me down on the mattress and then vanished as Justine and Ginny fussed over me. I let them do as they willed, the whole time thinking over and over of what I could have done differently to save him.

My cloak came off first, followed by my gown and underthings. In a daze I stood, I sat, I lifted my arms when they told me to, but I wasn't really there. My body was in the house, but my mind was still out on that field. Justine cleaned the blood off my face, hands, and chest before sliding my nightgown on over my head. Sitting down beside me, she grasped my shoulders and gave me a little shake. Woodenly, I turned to her.

"Cin, *chérie*, tell me what happened," she said.

I shook my head, the words coming out in a broken whisper I barely recognized. "He saw the Ripper. I told him not to follow him, but he wouldn't listen. It was a trap. My magic didn't work against him. I panicked. I set the demon on fire. I thought we'd have enough time to get away, but we didn't. Michael . . . forced the demon to take him instead of me."

"How did you get wounded?" she asked.

I looked up into her brilliant blue eyes. "Michael did it," I said.

"You mean the Ripper?"

"Yes," I answered, forcing myself to remember that. "And please don't call him the Ripper anymore, not when he's wearing Michael's body."

"Of course, *chérie*," she whispered. "What did he say to you?"

"That he knew I'd come. That he wanted to hurt me," I replied.

Remembering Michael's face, his voice saying those things to me, made the tears start again.

"Justine," Devlin said softly from the doorway. "Leave her be for now. Let her rest. I'll go find someone to feed her. Fresh blood will help the wound heal."

"She can take my blood," Ginny said.

I shook my head. I'd almost forgotten she was there. She sat down next to me and pushed my hair back over my shoulder.

"It's all right," she said. "I remember my mother feeding you once when you needed blood. I'm not afraid."

She held her wrist out to me and I looked up at her, too weak and weary to argue. She nodded to me.

"Go ahead," she said. "Take it."

My eyes locked on hers and it took every bit of energy I had left to bespell her so that she wouldn't feel the pain. When I knew she was under, I raised her wrist to my lips and bit. Her sweet, coppery blood washed down my throat and the pain in my chest lessened as it filled me. Before I was ready to stop, Justine intervened and pulled Ginny's wrist from my mouth.

"That's enough for now," she said and ushered Ginny toward Devlin. He put one arm around her and guided her from the room.

As Justine tucked me into bed, I grabbed her hand.

"Will you stay with me?" I asked. "Just for a little while."

"Of course, *mon amie*," she replied.

She walked around the bed and pulled back the covers. I turned on my side and she slid her body against mine, wrapping her arms around me.

"Do not fret," she whispered. "We will get him back."

Softly, she sang to me until I fell asleep. Thankfully, I didn't dream.

NINE

I slept until noon, when the chiming of a clock somewhere in the house woke me. Rolling over, I expected to see Michael's pale, perfect body stretched out beside me. But the bed was empty, and my heart clenched in pain as I remembered why. *We will get him back,* Justine had said. Yes, by the gods, we would.

I threw back the covers and stalked from the room. Vaguely, I remembered the books Devlin and Justine had gathered together in the library last night. I carried them into the parlor and shut the door behind me. The room was cold and dark, all the windows in the house having been shuttered and the curtains drawn so that we could move about freely in the daytime. There were logs in the fireplace, though, and I held my hand out toward them. A moment later a fire erupted, roaring nicely in the grate and allowing enough light and warmth for me to spread the books out on the rug in front of it.

For hours I flipped through page after page until, in the last book, I found what I was looking for. "Binding" the script at the top of the page read. And the rest of it looked like a blurry watercolor. Most of these books had traveled with me for many years before I'd bought this house and, at some point in all that time, this grimoire had sustained significant water damage. I remembered the invocation and part of the herbs needed, but the rest of it was lost.

"Damn it!" I cursed, snapping the book closed and hurling it against the wall.

"Cin?" Justine asked, sticking her head in the door. "May I come in?"

"Of course," I said with a sigh.

Dressed in a soft pink morning gown, with her long blonde hair pulled back in a neat chignon, Justine looked lovely. I felt rather bedraggled sitting there on the floor in my nightgown, with my hair uncombed. She picked up the book I had tossed, closed it, and handed it back to me before sitting down in one of the chairs flanking the fireplace.

"I take it the news is not good?" she asked.

I shook my head. "The writing is too obscured by water damage. I can't make anything out."

"So we have nothing?" she asked.

"No, we have part of the spell which is basically useless without knowing what the other half of the ingredients are."

"Hmm," Justine murmured and sat back in her chair. I watched her face and could almost see the ideas running through her head. "You don't usually use spells and potions."

"No," I agreed. "My magic bends to my will."

"Then why must you use this spell to bind the demon?"

I blinked at her. "Because I don't believe my magic is strong enough."

"Perhaps it is worth a try," she suggested. "You say this spell is gray magic. Is that not what you have? Both the light and the darkness inside you?"

I thought about it for a moment. Could I do it? Bind a demon with nothing more than the magic I could call? As I was considering this, Devlin and Ginny entered the room. Justine explained our progress to them and they all waited while I thought through the obstacles and implications of what Justine had suggested. Finally I nodded.

"I think I could do it. For Michael, I will be strong enough to do it. But as I see it, we have three problems."

Devlin arched one dark brow. "Only three?"

I continued on, ignoring his sarcasm. "The least of our problems is figuring out a way to get the demon to vacate Michael's body without physically harming . . . well . . . Michael's body. I think I have an idea, but none of you are going to like it, and I haven't exactly worked out all the details, so for now I'm going to keep that to myself. The second problem is what to do with the demon after we get him out of Michael's body. The Ripper is not going to make it easy. Once he leaves Michael's body, I'm going to have to force him into some other vessel that he can't escape from, before he can infect a new body."

"Or you," Justine pointed out.

I nodded. "Or me."

We all fell silent, thinking.

"Oh!" Ginny exclaimed, making me jump. She pointed to the bookshelves that lined the wall next to the fireplace. "Will that work?"

I followed the direction of her finger and if my heart had been beating it surely would have stopped at what I saw.

"Ginny," I said slowly, "Is that what I think it is?"

"After y'all left Devil's Island, I kept it in my room as sort of a keepsake to remind me of . . . everything. When I came to London I brought it with me. I thought it should be here."

Sitting there on the shelf (serving as a bookend no less!) was a large Grecian urn. I rose to my feet and slowly walked over to it. Reaching out I traced my fingers over the lid and down the sides, making sure it was still intact. And why wouldn't it be? It was said to have been forged by Hephaestus himself.

I turned back to my friends and smiled. "An unbreakable

jar that once held a god of war trapped for millennia. That will do."

"Before we get ahead of ourselves," Devlin said, always the voice of reason, "what is the third problem?"

My excitement waned. "The demon is apparently immune to my magic."

"How can that be?" Devlin asked, stunned.

"I have no idea," I replied. "But I'll think it through today and maybe something will come to me. The minute the sun sets, though, we need to find Grady. Until I can figure out why my magic won't work and how to remedy the problem, we can't fight this demon. In the meantime, I want to make it very clear to Grady that no one is to harm the Ripper while he's in my husband's body."

TEN

As twilight settled over London, I went from room to room in the house, checking the locks on all the windows and doors. If the demon decided to pay us a visit, I wanted to be sure he had to break down something solid to get in. At least we would have that as a warning. Ginny had flatly refused to leave the house at night, even though I had offered to put her up in a fine hotel, or turn a blind eye if she wished to stay with Warren. She was certain that I might need her, though, as I had the night before. Since I had taken her blood, I could use vampire magic to bend her to my will, but I wouldn't do it. Instead I had sent the footman to Warren's shop with a request that he come talk some sense into her as soon as he closed for the day.

That task had taken all of five minutes and the previous argument with Ginny had been short-lived. The other hours of daylight I'd spent poring over every book I owned, trying to stay busy so that I wouldn't go mad with worry. Amy, the housemaid, had come in several times to ask if I needed anything. I had politely declined both lunch and tea, refilling my whiskey glass at a rate that would have been alarming in a human. None of it had kept my mind from wandering to Michael, though. To what the demon might be doing, at this very moment, in his body. For the thousandth time since I'd woken alone in our bed, I pushed the thought aside.

Entering my bedroom, I pulled my coat from the wardrobe and tossed it on the bed. Tonight I wouldn't be tramping through the slush in skirts and slippers. This time I would be ready for whatever came my way. I was wearing black leather breeches tucked into a pair of thigh-high boots. A black leather vest topped the ensemble. I rarely wore the vest alone, with no shirt underneath. A full-sleeved shirt helped to hide the knives strapped to my forearms, but tonight I would do without it. I wanted to look as dangerous as possible.

I slid Michael's claymore into the scabbard at my hip, feeling closer to him because I was wearing his blade. It wasn't the great claymore that he called Ophelia, but one he'd had made as a scaled-down version of his favorite weapon. Wearing a sword in public will get you arrested in most places, and it's difficult to conceal a blade nearly four and a half feet long. The sword he carried now looked like the claymore but was substantially smaller and easier to hide under a cloak or long coat. Ignoring the fact that the last time I'd seen Michael he'd shoved this blade into my heart, I opened the trunk that held our weapons and pulled out a long, flat box.

As a rule, vampires, especially the older ones, don't like guns. They seem to view them as cheating. If you can't win a fight by your own physical strength and skill with a sword, then you deserve to lose. However, last year I'd won a Smith & Wesson .38 from an American in a game of poker and, as it turns out, I'm an excellent shot. Of course, it's nearly impossible to kill a vampire with a bullet, but it will get their attention. Sometimes that's all you need. I loaded the gun, tucked it into the waistband of my breeches at the small of my back, and shrugged into my coat.

Michael called this my general's coat. It was long and black with burgundy silk braiding that decorated the turned-back cuffs and ran along the edge of its stand-up collar. A smart row of oriental frog buttons in the same burgundy silk marched from the collar to just above my waist. The rest of the coat was open, allowing me swift access to the weapon at my hip or the knives strapped to my thighs, hidden by my tall boots. The coat belled out just enough to hide the fact that I was a woman wearing very scandalous and masculine attire. That is, if you didn't look too closely.

As I reached the top buttons I touched my bare neck, wondering if Warren still had my cross necklace or if he'd dropped it in the park. It seemed a trifling thing to worry about, considering everything else that had happened. Still, it was one more thing that I'd had yesterday that I didn't have today.

As I was tying my hair back at my nape with a thick black satin ribbon, I heard Devlin and Justine leave their room, murmuring to each other as they walked down the hall. I closed my eyes and imagined Michael standing behind me, his arms wrapped around my waist, his lips kissing my neck. It was what he always did before we went out. This evening I wrapped my arms around myself instead.

"I will get you back," I said to the empty room. "I swear I will."

Warren had just arrived, and in fact was still standing in the foyer arguing with Ginny, when I came downstairs. He looked up at me and his mouth fell open. While I was walking down the stairs the coat did little to hide my boots, breeches, or the sword I was wearing, but I was certain that my clothing wasn't entirely responsible for the expression on his face. Ginny, however, conspicuously cleared her throat and Warren swiftly regained his composure.

"I can't believe it," he said. "Last night I saw you with a

sword sticking out of your chest and now you look completely healed."

I shrugged. "Already being dead sometimes has its advantages."

"I suppose so," he murmured.

"Have you had any luck talking this hardheaded girl into leaving the house for the night?" I asked.

Ginny glared at me, but I ignored her.

"I'm afraid not," he said, holding up a large canvas sack. "But I brought crosses. I'll stay with her until you return."

Ginny rolled her eyes and I tried not to laugh, for he was so earnest.

"If I don't check the pot boiling on the stove," Ginny said, "I'm liable to burn the whole house down, and then we won't have to worry about it. Warren, make yourself at home in the parlor. I'll return shortly when supper is ready." She turned to me. "And you be careful with yourself."

"Yes, ma'am," I said in my best imitation of her southern drawl.

As Ginny headed toward the kitchen I leaned over and whispered to Warren. "Of course, you realize that this means you're going to have to marry that girl, don't you?"

He smiled. "Oh yes," he said happily. "But she hasn't realized that yet."

Hearing my voice, Devlin and Justine emerged from the parlor and the three of us headed for the door.

"Mrs. Craven!" Warren called out. "I almost forgot."

I turned to see him reach into his coat pocket and pull out my necklace.

"I sent it to a friend of mine who's a jeweler this morning and had the clasp fixed for you. It's good as new now."

Seeing him pull the chain and pendant from his pocket triggered a memory from the previous night. The demon had taken something off the dead body, hadn't he? I had been in so much shock, I'd entirely forgotten about it until this moment.

"Warren," I said, "did you see Michael take a gold amulet on a chain from the dead body last night? Or was that a hallucination?"

Warren thought for a moment. "No, I remember. I couldn't see it clearly, but he did remove something from the body that shined in the moonlight. It could have been an amulet."

That was why my magic hadn't worked. I closed my eyes as I felt the anger rise inside me. The Ripper had a charm to protect him against magic. The last time I'd seen such a thing, I'd taken it off Sebastian's neck.

"Damn that man to everlasting hell!" I shrieked.

"You don't believe in hell," Justine said dryly.

I glared at her. "That's hardly the point."

Living in such close quarters for so many years, it was easy to pick up each other's phrases. It also meant that we knew each other well enough that when I turned and strode purposefully to the front door, they followed me without question. I jerked the door open just as Warden Grady raised his hand to knock. His eyes widened in surprise. Then he caught sight of the look on my face and took a hasty step back.

"Just the man I wanted to see," I said, reaching out and grabbing him by the collar of his coat.

"What's going on?" he asked as I dragged him back to his carriage.

"You're going to take me to see the Regent," I replied as I opened the carriage door.

Grady stopped and shrugged one shoulder, dislodging my grip on his coat.

"Wait just a minute now," he said indignantly. "I'm not taking you anywhere until I know what's happening. You said very specifically in Paris that you had absolutely no wish to see the Regent."

I felt Devlin's looming presence at my back. "The lady's changed her mind, mate," he said in that low, gravelly voice that could, on occasions such as this, be utterly terrifying. "Get in the carriage."

For a moment, I thought Grady might challenge him, but wisely he gave in and nodded to the driver.

"Take us to the Regent's estate," he said, and we all climbed in.

The carriage lurched forward and we rode in silence until Justine leaned over and said softly, "I trust your judgment, Cin, but you are going to tell us at some point, are you not?"

I glanced sideways at her and then looked across the carriage at Devlin and Grady, who were regarding me expectantly.

"I have the answer to problem number three," I said. "My magic didn't work against the Ripper because he was wearing a talisman to protect him. A gold disc with what I'm sure we will find to be a ruby stone set in its center."

Looks of comprehension dawned on Devlin and Justine, but Grady was at a loss.

"I still don't understand," he said, glancing at each of us in turn. "You saw the Ripper? Do you have this talisman? And where is Michael?"

"Do not," Justine said, putting her hand up, "go any further with that line of questioning."

For a few moments Grady looked even more confused, but when the expressions of disbelief and sympathy crossed his face, I knew he'd finally figured out what had happened. I was thankful for that because I truly didn't want to have to say those words again.

"We have to figure out a way to get that amulet out of his possession," I said.

"If we do that," Grady asked, "then what?"

"Then I end this," I replied.

Relief washed over him. "If that's our objective, then why are we going to see the Regent?" he asked.

"Because Sebastian is responsible for this," I said. "I've known it in my heart from the beginning."

"You believe this because of the amulet?"

"First of all, that demon is in possession of a talisman that once belonged to Sebastian. Secondly, the Ripper said, and I quote, 'Witch. He said you would come.' "

"Everyone knew you were coming," Grady argued. "Any vampire he crossed paths with could have told him that."

"Cin," Devlin interrupted, "the warden does have a point. Perhaps we should allow you to cool down a bit before we proceed with this."

"I won't kill Sebastian. Not yet," I said flatly. "But I know what he's done. And he knows what he's done." I turned back to them and let them see the determination on my face. "And whether any of you like it or not, he and I are going to have a reckoning."

Devlin's eyes locked with mine, and we stared at each other for a long time. Finally, he nodded. "All right."

ELEVEN

When the Ripper had started killing vampires, Sebastian and his court had moved from their London townhouse to a small estate just outside the city. The carriage ride was reasonably short, but infinitely longer than I would have liked. When we arrived, the drive to the manor house was lined with carriages, making it appear as though a society ball was in progress. I looked questioningly at Grady.

"It's the blood whores, come to feed the court," he said in response to my silent inquiry.

I opened the window and leaned out, counting the carriages between ours and the front door. There had to be at least ten. Flinging open the door, I bounded out and began to walk. I passed carriage after carriage filled with giggling girls and handsome young men, eager for the money and the pleasures that awaited them.

Two vampires, almost as tall and broad as Devlin, attempted to stop me at the door. Before I could even voice an objection, one of them noticed Grady, who had followed swiftly at my heels with Devlin and Justine.

"Good evening, Warden," the vampire said respectfully.

"Good evening to you, Ben. These are my guests," Grady announced.

"Of course, sir," Ben replied and opened the doors.

I entered a house filled with more vampires and humans than one generally saw together. There were people lounging about in every open room, but the blood whores who had arrived before me were being escorted up the grand staircase, so I followed them. Wherever the blood was going, that's where I would find Sebastian.

"I hope you know what you're doing," Grady hissed in my ear. If all of this ends badly it will be my head, quite literally, that rolls for it."

I paused at the top of the stairs and turned to him. "And if it goes as I plan, you could end up as Regent."

I smiled at his shocked expression and proceeded through the doors of the second-floor ballroom. I had expected a pit of debauchery, but that's not what I found. There was an orchestra playing, and people were laughing and dancing, like so many balls I had gone to in my youth, when I was human. I don't know why I was surprised. Sebastian was a son of the aristocracy. Here, he would be in his element.

"Your name, miss?" a well-dressed man at my elbow asked.

For a moment I stared at him, not comprehending why he was asking. Then I realized that he was one of the Regent's servants and it was his duty to announce the arrivals. Good lord, had it really been that many years since I'd been to a proper ball?

Then again, as I looked out over the crowd I realized that it wasn't an exact imitation of a society ball. The dresses were quite risqué, and there didn't seem to be a gentleman in the room who hadn't lost several buttons on his shirt. The humans were easy to identify by the smudges of dried blood at their necks, or breasts, or wrists. It was like some sort of macabre Cyprians' ball. I turned to the gentleman waiting for my name and almost laughed at the incongruity of it all. It was exactly the sort of thing I would expect of Sebastian.

"Cin Craven," I finally replied.

He nodded, and turned to make the announcement.

"Cin Craven," his voice rang out.

A hush fell over the ballroom as all eyes turned to me. Slowly and disjointedly, the orchestra ground to a halt. I took a step into the room as the servant called out Devlin and Justine's names, and the throng of vampires and humans parted like the Red Sea. In a few brief moments I found myself standing not fifty feet from the man responsible for taking my lover from me.

Sebastian sat on a raised dais surrounded by a group of women. Though he had probably begun the evening impeccably dressed, his coat had been discarded and his vest and shirt were open to the waist. He looked much as he had the last time I'd seen him, though his curly black hair was longer, and he now sported a neatly trimmed beard. The beard detracted somewhat from his handsome, aristocratic features, but it lent him a slightly dangerous look. His brown eyes glittered when he saw me and he sat up straighter, watching me expectantly.

Four of Sebastian's lieutenants stepped up on the dais, forming a semicircle around his throne-like chair. The women instinctively retreated, all save one. My eyes flicked over the men, dismissing them each in turn. They were bodyguards or lackeys, nothing more. It was the woman who intrigued me.

She was a vampire, and her position at his right hand declared her to be someone of importance, though I didn't understand why. She had long, dark-blonde hair that hung in a messy tangle of curls down her back. Her face was so thickly painted with cosmetics that it almost looked like a mask. Never taking his eyes off me, Sebastian motioned to her and she leaned down as he whispered something. Glancing up at me, she pushed her mass of unkempt hair from her small, dark eyes. There was something in that look—excitement, perhaps—that I didn't like.

She had been a lot older than most when she'd been turned. Her human years showed in the lines around her eyes and the creases at the corners of her wide, full lips. I wondered what value she had to Sebastian. I didn't believe she was his consort. The Sebastian I knew was entirely too vain to tie himself to someone who looked like nothing more than a cheap prostitute.

At that moment, though, all thoughts of her fled as Sebastian's gaze flicked over me, then Devlin, then Justine. With the three of us together, Michael's absence was glaringly obvious. And Sebastian smiled victoriously. He knew . . . and my temper snapped. I crossed the expanse of the ballroom with a menacing stride, my eyes locked on Sebastian's. As I reached the bottom step of the dais, the sliding metal sound of a sword being unsheathed snapped my attention to one of Sebastian's lieutenants. I paused.

"Cin, how nice to see you again," Sebastian said, his voice dripping with honeyed sweetness. "You are even more beautiful than I remembered."

I glared at him. "And you're still an evil son of a bitch."

The lieutenant with the sword took a step forward, but Devlin and Justine pulled their own blades and flanked me.

"You might want to watch your tone," Sebastian replied smugly. "Jonas has sworn his fealty to me and he is quite the best swordsman in the country."

Devlin snorted in derision.

Sebastian glanced at him and then inclined his head to me. "With the exception of your husband, of course," he said in a gracious tone. "But he doesn't seem to be here, does he?"

Justine growled and started toward the dais, but I reached out and grabbed her sword arm, stopping her. I didn't want this to degenerate into a brawl. Jonas moved to stand between Sebastian and me, his sword at the ready.

"My Regent has done nothing to warrant retribution by The Righteous," Jonas said loudly, so that all the court could hear. "Unless you come bearing proof, you have no grounds on which to offer him violence." His gaze flicked over Justine and me dismissively, perhaps because we were women, and settled on Devlin. "And if you intend him harm, you're going to have to come through me."

Devlin laughed. "Step up then, boy, if you think you can take me."

Jonas was a well-built young man with auburn hair and eager green eyes. Whether or not he could back up Sebastian's boast, he certainly looked prepared to try. Proving him wrong would take time I didn't want to waste. I reached inside my coat and the other three lieutenants drew their swords, assuming that I was going for mine. Instead, I pulled the Smith & Wesson from the waistband of my breeches and in one smooth motion leveled it at Jonas and put a bullet through his heart.

He dropped like a stone, clutching his chest and screaming. Sebastian rose belligerently to his feet, his harlot shrank back against the wall, and his lieutenants stood dumbfounded just long enough for Devlin and Justine to advance on them and push them back. I leapt onto the dais, landing just in front of Sebastian and forcing him to fall backward into his chair. Bracing my hands on the arms of the throne, I leaned over until my face was mere inches from his.

"I am not the inexperienced girl I was when we last met, Sebastian," I said softly, menacingly. "You have no idea the power I have. The stories you've heard about me—they're all true. I could kill you with a thought. And when I do come for you, no one will be able to stop me."

Sebastian glanced down at where Jonas was still lying on

the floor, writhing and moaning. He'd live, but it would hurt like hell for a long time.

Louder, so that the court could hear me, I said, "I know what you've done, Sebastian."

"You can't prove anything," he said, and there was fear in his voice.

I cocked my head to one side. "Now, see, an innocent man would ask what I was accusing him of. But you know, don't you? You conspired with some witch or wizard to summon a demon to kill me. Or perhaps it's still my power you want. Whatever your intentions were, Sebastian, I don't believe even you would turn something like that loose on your own people. You've lost control of it and now it's slaughtering your vampires. And it's infected my husband. I will stop it and I will get the proof I need to satisfy the High King's law. And when I do, I'll be back . . . and you'll pay for what you've done with your life."

"There was a time when I wanted you," he whispered. "But now I just want you to suffer."

"Your wants haven't interested me in nearly a hundred years, Sebastian," I said simply, and with one last, contemptuous look, I turned and strode back through the ballroom.

Hushed whispers from the court followed me and I smiled. Whether or not I could prove Sebastian's guilt, I had just placed the seeds of doubt in the heads of his vampires. He'd be lucky if he lived long enough for me to kill him.

When I reached the doors to the ballroom I glanced back, one last time. Sebastian was whispering furiously into the blonde woman's ear, and from the way she was nodding in response it appeared that he was giving her orders. He was a cunning bastard, I'd give him that. I was certain he enjoyed being Regent, and he couldn't afford for there to be any proof of his direct involvement in this. No, he would have gone through intermediaries. And I was practically positive that his harlot would lead me straight to the demon.

Grady was waiting by the door and I pulled him aside.

"The woman with Sebastian," I said. "Who is she?"

He glanced across the room. "Barbara? She's a ruthless bitch, one of the Regent's lackeys."

I nodded, thinking. She's the one who does the things he won't sully his hands to do.

"I need something that belongs to her. A piece of jewelry would work best, something personal. Can you get it for me?"

Grady nodded. "I think so."

"Good. We'll meet you at the end of the drive."

He disappeared into the crowd just as Justine reached my side. She linked her arm with mine as we descended the stairs.

"You should have let us fight them, *mon amie*," she complained. Much like Michael, she loved a good brawl.

I shrugged. "It was beneath us. Besides, we have a much bigger fight ahead of us."

TWELVE

When we returned to the house on Upper Brook Street, Ginny met us at the door, her face ashen. Warren stood behind her, looking grim.

"He was here," Ginny said.

I grasped her by the shoulders. "Michael? Are you hurt? What happened?"

She shook her head. "No, we're both fine. I never even saw him but . . . well, you'd better come look."

We followed her up the stairs to the door of my bedroom. She paused with her hand on the knob.

"After dinner we went through the house, just like you said to, and checked the doors and windows again. When I looked in your room, the window was open. And—"

She swung the door open. The window was closed now and all of my things were just as I'd left them. The writing on the wall, however, was new. Painted in blood above my bed were the words "I love thee not, chaos is come again." It was part of a line from Shakespeare. And it was in Michael's handwriting.

"What does it mean?" Ginny asked.

"It doesn't mean anything," I said numbly.

"It must mean something," Grady said. "Else why would he have done it?"

Just to torment me, I thought, imagining the man I loved writing such words to me.

"It's from *Othello*," Devlin added, saying what I already knew.

Justine walked into the room and ran one finger over the letters. The blood was still fresh enough to come away on her skin.

"It's human," she said.

"Didn't Othello kill his wife?" Warren asked softly from the doorway.

Everyone fell silent, uncomfortably waiting for my response.

"Ginny," I finally said, "could you please clean that up as best you can? If it's stained the wall, Devlin and Justine can rearrange the furniture for you. Put the wardrobe over it. I don't want Michael to see it when I bring him home."

I turned to go, but Devlin caught my arm. "Where are you off to?" he asked, his dark eyes filled with concern.

I held up the silver ring that Grady had stolen from Barbara's room. "I'm going to the library to cast a location spell."

He looked at me like he didn't believe me, but he let me go. In a daze I walked down the stairs and entered the library. Shutting the door behind me, I leaned against it and closed my eyes. All I could see was Michael scrawling those words above our bed. *I love thee not. I love thee not. I love thee not.*

"Stop it," I said to myself. "It's not Michael. It's the demon. Michael loves me. He always has and he always will. I am the other half of his soul and he is the other half of mine."

It was something he said to me often. I had to remember that.

Crossing the room, I cleared the scattered books off the

big table and retrieved a map of London from the bookshelf. I unrolled it and used four silver candlesticks to hold down the corners. The map was old, but it would do. I didn't even bother to take my coat off. This shouldn't take long.

I placed the ring on its side at the edge of the map, and then I laid my palms flat on the oak table and took a deep breath. Spellcasting wasn't easy for me, but location spells were fairly simple. Clearing my head as well as I was able, I thought of what I wanted. The ring would tell me where Barbara was. If Sebastian had anything to do with summoning this demon, she was part of it too. I centered myself and called up my magic.

"Nowhere to run, nowhere to hide, that I won't find where you abide," I called out.

The ring began to move, rolling across the map to the north. It stopped just inside the city but it didn't fall, which meant that she was still moving. I pulled up a chair and waited. After what seemed like hours, the ring finally tipped on its side and lay still, coming to rest on the other side of Whitechapel, near Shadwell. That made sense in regard to the human murders. He would want to hunt in an area near his base, yet not in his own backyard.

I slipped the ring into my pocket and exited the library just as Grady was coming down the stairs, carrying a bucket of pinkish water.

"Grady, is your carriage still out front?" I asked.

"It should be," he replied. "Jensen knows to take the horses around the block if they get restless, but I told him to wait for me."

"Good, come with me," I said and started for the door.

He set the bucket on the floor and looked uncertainly over his shoulder. "Don't you think we should tell the others?"

Justine would happily go with me, but Devlin would never approve of what I was about to do. Somewhere in the back of my mind that thought set off warning bells. I was going to do something that was probably foolish. If it had been anyone else's idea, I would have been the first to object. But that demon had been in control of Michael's body for nearly twenty-four hours and I had to know that he was all right. I wasn't ready to fight him yet, but I had to see his face.

I opened the front door and turned back to Grady. "It's easier to beg forgiveness than ask permission," I said.

"But not necessarily wiser," Grady mumbled.

THIRTEEN

The area of London where the ring led me was filled with brothels, pubs, and opium dens. It was dark, dirty, and dangerous. No respectable person would ever walk these streets. It was exactly the sort of place I would expect to find a woman like Barbara. I reached up and knocked on the roof of the carriage, and it rolled to a stop.

"Do you know which building?" Grady asked as we got out.

"No," I replied. "But it will be somewhere in this block."

We walked in silence for a while, until I caught sight of a man crossing the street at the end of the block. I grabbed Grady's arm and pushed him back against the building. Flattening my back to the wall, I watched. The man wore a long coat and a hat pulled down low over his eyes, but it was definitely Michael. I knew it by the way he walked, the way he moved. Even at a distance I would know him anywhere.

He didn't seem to sense our presence, so Grady and I slowly followed. At the corner, I stopped and peered around the edge of the building. The road was long and narrow, cramped with shops and tenements, and littered with refuse. Barbara stood outside the door to one of the shops, feeding on a human. She held the man with his arms pulled behind his back as her teeth pierced his throat. I knew she hadn't bothered to bespell him because he was struggling to pull free of her.

I heard Michael's voice say something to her, but I couldn't hear what it was. She looked up, blood staining her full lips, and smiled. Then, with such practiced ease that I jerked back in surprise, she snapped the neck of the man she had been feeding from. It wasn't often that someone committed an executable offense right in front of me. When you were the executioner they tended not to do that.

Michael entered the building and Barbara followed him, dragging the body of her victim behind her. Slowly I walked down the street, Grady following me. When I reached the solid, windowless metal door they had used, I paused and placed my hand on it, listening. I could hear muffled human voices from within, but no sound of Barbara or Michael.

As quietly as possible, I pushed the door open. When I didn't sense any vampires in the immediate area, I walked inside. The large, dimly lit room was crammed with rows of cots, nearly all of which were occupied by a human man or woman. Insensible, they lay there, either unconscious or muttering words that had no meaning except in their clouded minds. I wrinkled my nose. Barbara's victim had been dumped unceremoniously just inside the door, and the entire place reeked of unwashed bodies and opium.

"What is this place?" I asked Grady.

"It's an opium nest," he replied. "Vampires purchase the opium and the humans come here for the drug."

"And then the vampires feed from them," I said.

He shrugged. "Human blood laced with opium is quite a sensation, they say. The High King has declared opium nests to be illegal, but it's hard to put a stop to them. You close one down and they just reopen another elsewhere."

I looked around, noting a door at the opposite end of the room. "I'll be back shortly. You stay here in case any vampires decide to drop by for dinner. I'm sure, as a known warden, you won't have any problem deterring them from coming in. I don't want to worry about the possibility that one of these opium-laced vamps might be loyal to Barbara or that demon and alert them to my presence."

"Cin?" Grady asked. "Are you sure you know what you're doing?"

Not remotely, I thought. All I knew was that the man I loved was in this building. The demon might be in possession of his body, but Michael was somewhere inside, trapped. It was reckless and irresponsible, I realized that, but I was drawn to him like a moth to the flame. I just needed to know that his body, at least, was unharmed.

There was a dark hallway beyond the door. Empty rooms opened off either side of the hall, but it was the big metal door at the end that beckoned me. Cautiously I crept up to it and listened.

"I have not fulfilled the terms of my summoning," Michael's voice said, and I stifled a sigh of relief that he was all right.

I should have left then, but Barbara's next words stopped me.

"He doesn't care about that," Barbara insisted. "All he wants is her dead. He says you're to kill her tonight."

Michael sighed. "I grow weary of this conversation."

There was a rustling of fabric and then Barbara said, low and throaty, "Then perhaps there are other ways I can convince you. I do love the feel of this body."

Before I was even aware of what I was doing I'd thrown open the steel door and strode into the room. Barbara was standing with her thin body pressed against my husband's. She turned her head in surprise and then smiled.

"My, isn't this convenient?" she said.

Michael was wearing the same clothes he'd had on the night before, but his shirt was open and the talisman gleamed against his skin. Barbara's hands moved inside his shirt, boldly caressing the rigid muscles of his chest. I wanted to grab her by the hair and slam her face into the wall. I did neither of those things, though. I just stood there, realizing too late what a stupid thing I'd just done. Michael cocked his head to one side.

"The females of your species seem to be unusually attracted to this form," he said.

That was an understatement. Michael had the face of an angel and a body many women would walk through hell to possess. And Barbara was about to get the opportunity to put that to the test if she didn't get her hands off of him. Unfortunately for her, she was as stupid as she looked. Instead of stepping away, she turned and pulled his head down to hers for a kiss.

Michael's eyes watched me as she ground her lips against his before her tongue slid inside. I felt the tears well up in my eyes and my stomach rolled in revulsion. Michael pulled away from her, still watching my face.

"Oh, look," Barbara said. "She's jealous."

He inhaled deeply, as if he could scent what I was feeling. "No," he said. "That isn't jealousy. That is raw hatred."

Barbara's eyes went from him to me. I caught her gaze and let her see every bit of the white-hot anger that was boiling inside me.

"You will die for that," I said, barely recognizing my own voice, it was laced with so much violence. "And for killing the human. But mostly for that."

Under the weight of my icy glare, she backed away from Michael.

Michael took a step toward me, a curious expression on his face. "The thought of this body lying with another female brings you pain. It's almost too bad I have no interest in fornication. I should like to see exactly how much that might torture you."

I breathed a sigh of relief. Some demons, such as incubi and succubi, gained their power through sex. This one fed off of pain and death. It didn't seem to be a better trade, but at the moment I was grateful for it.

"Kill her!" Barbara screeched. "Kill her now!"

Michael turned sharply and hissed at her. "I told you, I have not fulfilled the terms of my summoning. I agreed to cause the Red Witch unimaginable pain and then to take her body. I cannot do the second until I've done the first."

"Sebastian releases you from your oath," Barbara said. "Kill her!"

Michael shook his head. "I do not know this man, Sebastian. My agreement was with the wizard who summoned me, and only he can renegotiate the terms. But he is dead now, the first of my kills."

"The wizard was your master and Sebastian was his," she insisted. "You were brought here to steal her power for him. Sebastian paid the price of your summoning."

"Vampire," Michael scolded. "I have no master. The wizard was a conduit, nothing more. I agreed to take her power. I did not agree to share it with anyone."

"Of course you did!" Barbara shouted, her frustration evident. "Why the bloody hell else would we summon you?"

"I do not know," the demon said, simply. "Perhaps you should have been clearer about the terms of our agreement."

As interesting as the conversation was, I decided to take advantage of the fact that they both seemed to have forgotten I was there and started slowly backing toward the door. I had just cleared the threshold when Barbara realized my intention.

"You're not going anywhere," she said. "I'll kill you myself if I have to."

She ran at me but I stood perfectly still and waited. When she was within reach I grabbed a handful of her tangled mass of hair and pulled her out into the hallway. With one foot I kicked the door closed behind us.

"Lock," I shouted, pushing my magic into the door. It was made to keep vampires out of the Ripper's sanctuary. I was hoping it was strong enough to keep him in, at least until we could get back to the carriage.

Barbara was fighting me, scratching and clawing, teeth snapping within inches of my face. I got a firm grip on her hair and slammed her head into the wall hard enough to daze her.

"Cin!" Grady called out, interrupting the brief moment of pleasure I had taken in knocking the harlot senseless.

The first loud bang came from the other side of the metal door, and I dragged Barbara down the hall and hurled her at Grady.

"Get her out of here," I said urgently. "And make sure she's locked up where she can't escape. We'll need her later."

"What about you?" he asked.

"I'm right behind you," I assured him. "Now, go!"

He grabbed Barbara by the wrist and pulled her after him. I turned and watched the steel door bend under the strain of Michael's hammering. My magic wouldn't hold the door once the hinges gave way. Whirling around, I ran after Grady. One more loud crack and the steel door hit the ground. I had just wound my way around the humans littering the outer room and reached the front door when a strong arm snaked around my waist.

Michael pulled me back against his body and for a moment I relaxed, craving the feel of him against me.

"I'm not finished with you yet," he whispered and my body shuddered in response, even though my mind was screaming that this was not the man I loved.

I cried out in frustration as he dragged me back down the hall. So many weapons at my disposal, and yet I couldn't bring myself to hurt him. When we were once again inside his sanctuary, he threw me violently across the room. I collapsed onto the cot, narrowly missing the wall with my head.

"Humans," he said. "Vampires. There is little sport in either. I thought you would be a challenge. They said you had great power. The power of a god, they promised me. But I see no power here. This form," he said, gesturing to himself, "it makes you weak."

"No," I replied. "It makes me strong. His love is what makes life worthwhile."

"And I have taken that from you. Does it hurt?"

"You can take his body, but you can't take his love. The bond Michael and I share is eternal and nothing you can do will ever change that."

"Are you so certain?" he asked. Reaching down, he pulled one of Michael's daggers from the inside of his boot. Holding it up, he looked at it. And then he looked at me. "How badly would I have to hurt you, I wonder, before you stopped looking at this body with tenderness? Why don't we find out."

He crossed the room and I scooted back against the wall. My magic was useless against him as long as he wore the talisman, and I seriously doubted my ability to physically fight him and win.

"Michael, I love you," I cried. "I love you."

When he had nearly reached me he stumbled and fell to his knees in front of me. The knife dropped from his fingers and he raised his head. Strain was etched into his face, making his cheekbones stand out in sharp relief. His eyes, which had been so blank and emotionless since the demon had infected him, were filled with pain.

"Run," he said.

"Michael?" I asked, unable to believe he was really here, in front of me.

"I don't want to hurt you," he said, his voice ragged with

the strain of fighting the demon for control. "If you love me, run."

"I'm sorry," I said, my voice harsh with unshed tears. I kissed him swiftly. "I promise I'll save you."

He threw his head back and screamed, the muscles in his neck straining with the effort to hold the demon at bay. I grasped the gold talisman and jerked it off his neck.

And then I ran.

FOURTEEN

Devlin and Justine were furious with me when we got back to the house, but there was no time to waste with recriminations and apologies. Dawn was still hours away and I had a feeling the demon would come for me tonight. He fed on pain and suffering, and Michael and I had denied him a meal. I did not believe that slight would go unpunished. I fingered the amulet in my coat pocket. I hoped he would come. I was ready now.

Barbara was screaming and cursing, but we all ignored her. I shoved her toward Devlin and said, "Take her upstairs to Michael's studio. Clear everything out of the room that you can. I need a large, empty space to do this. And arm yourselves. He'll come and he may not be alone."

Barbara protested, but Devlin took one arm and Justine the other and they simply lifted her off her feet and carried her up the stairs. I felt pity for the human she'd killed, but in reality it had been quite a stroke of luck. The instant she'd snapped his neck she'd signed her own death warrant. She would be the bait on my hook and I would carry no guilt over it.

"What can we do?" Ginny asked, her innocent face lit up in eagerness.

"I want you and Warren to go back to his shop and don't

come home until morning," I said. "And for the love of Danu, stop and tell Will and Amy not to come to work tomorrow. There's no telling what state this house is going to be in by the time we're finished tonight."

"But I can help, Cin," she protested. "Tell me what you need."

I took her hands in mine. "There will be no arguing about it this time. You will go. What I need is for you to be somewhere else so that I can do what I must and not worry about your safety. I can't afford the distraction, Ginny."

"She's right," Warren said. "This is something best left to them to handle."

"Grady will see you safely to the shop," I said, looking over Ginny's shoulder to the warden.

He nodded his assent. "Do you wish me to return after I've delivered them?" he asked.

"I think that might be wise," I said. "And perhaps you should bring the other wardens with you when you come. If you should find us all dead—" I paused, considering what advice I should give him. "To be honest with you, Grady, if we fail I don't know what to tell you to do."

"Then you mustn't fail," he said. "I wish you luck."

I hugged Ginny and Warren goodbye, then made a quick list in my head of the things I would need. I found the cabinet where Ginny stored the candles and shoved as many as I could fit into an empty canvas bag. Then I rushed into the parlor and snatched the urn off the shelf, tucking it under my arm. On my way to the third floor where Michael's painting studio was, I made a quick stop at my bedroom.

I was happy to see that the wall had been scrubbed and the furniture rearranged. Depositing the urn and the candles on the bed, I took the amulet out of my coat pocket. Everything that was about to happen hinged on my being able to work my magic against the demon. Thank the gods that Michael had been strong enough to give me that one moment to take the necklace. It was indeed the same one I had taken off Sebastian all those years ago. In some dark corner of my soul I was pleased that he was so afraid of me that he'd kept the talisman for nearly a century. I placed it in my jewelry box for safekeeping and noticed that Ginny had returned the Craven Cross in my absence. I fastened the heavy piece around my neck, feeling a sense of comfort that it was back in my possession. Then I removed my coat and put my pistol back in the weapons chest. Gathering up the urn and the bag of candles, I sprinted up to the third floor.

Devlin and Justine were just carrying the last of Michael's things from the studio and storing them in my study.

"Where is Barbara?" I asked, concerned that they'd left her alone.

Devlin rolled his eyes and pointed to the far corner of the studio. They'd bound her hands and feet and gagged her. I raised an eyebrow but didn't comment.

"She has a foul mouth on her, that one," Justine complained.

"As long as she's there when I need her, I don't care what you do to her," I said.

I handed Devlin the urn and dumped the bag of candles onto the floor. Justine and I worked quickly to lay them out in a perfect circle. I then pulled one of the knives from the sheaths on my forearms and drew it down my wrist. Blood welled up and I walked the circle again, holding my arm out so that the blood fell to the floor just inside the ring of candles. It was a slapdash way to set a circle of protection, but it was quick and powerful. When I was finished I placed the urn in the center of the circle.

"What do we do now?" Justine asked.

"We hope he shows up," I replied. "I'll go downstairs. You two keep an eye on her. If he comes alone, be as unobtrusive as possible and stay out of the way. If he brings reinforcements with him—" I shrugged. "Do what you do best."

FIFTEEN

I sat at the foot of the stairs, waiting, preparing myself. The role of the helpless victim was one I didn't enjoy playing, especially now that I was confident in my ability to use my power against the demon. But he liked my fear and I would do whatever it took to get him where I wanted him.

I hadn't been waiting long when the front door burst open and Michael strode in with six men at his back. One of the downsides of being a vampire is that other vampires don't need an invitation to enter your house. I wondered briefly if he had recruited these vampires from the opium nest. As with humans, there never seemed to be a shortage of idle men willing and eager to follow a strong leader into the thrill of battle. They would not enjoy the experience. For the moment, though, I leapt to my feet and pasted a look of panic on my face.

"Witch," Michael said, in a tone I hoped never to hear directed at me again.

I turned and ran up the stairs, glancing behind me as I reached the landing to make sure he was following me. With slow, determined strides he climbed the stairs, obviously confident in his ability to win this fight. And why wouldn't he be? He'd held the upper hand . . . until now.

"Six at his back," I said as I rushed into the room.

Devlin and Justine were standing on either side of the door, their bodies pressed against the wall. I didn't worry whether or not they could handle the situation. My entire focus was now on Barbara. Her eyes widened when she saw the look on my face as I crossed the room. Perhaps, if she was sensitive enough, she even felt the power beginning to build within me. I thought of her hands on Michael's bare chest, of her lips pressed to his, her tongue invading his mouth. My anger fed the dark side of my magic and that's exactly what I needed right now to tempt a demon. I bent down and picked her up, slinging her over my shoulder. Carrying her into the center of the circle of candles, I dropped her on the floor.

I could hear booted footsteps striding down the hall, and I closed my eyes and called on the darkness inside me. It rolled through me, welling up until it filled every inch of me. There was a time when I would have fought it, been afraid of it, but those days were gone. It was a part of me and with that acceptance I had gained control of it. Now I ruled the darkness; it did not rule me. I opened my eyes, and I knew from Devlin and Justine's worried expressions that my normally whiskey-brown eyes had turned black with the magic I had called.

Michael walked through the door with his sword drawn, moving with that catlike grace I loved so well. The moment he crossed the threshold, Devlin and Justine spun into the doorway, knocking back the six vampires who'd attempted to enter behind him. With my magic I forced the door to close and lock, drowning out the sounds of the fight that had begun in the hall. I didn't worry for Devlin and Justine—there were only six of them, after all. Michael cocked his head to one side in curiosity.

"Do you feel it?" I asked.

He walked forward. "Power," he said, and there was hunger in his voice.

"I want you to leave my husband's body," I demanded.

"No," he replied. "I have grown fond of it. Besides, if I leave his body I must enter another. I have no interest in hers," he said, pointing to Barbara, "and that only leaves yours."

I ignored the last comment. "She is not for you," I said. "She sealed her fate when she broke the law of the High King and killed a human. I saw her do it and she must pay for it with her life."

Barbara tried to struggle to her feet, but I grabbed her by the back of the neck and forced her to be still.

"These vampires," the demon said, "you sit in judgment on them. You weigh their sins and extract retribution from them."

"Yes," I replied.

"You are a god," he stated.

"No. I am The Righteous."

With that I set the darkness free. I stepped away from Barbara as black light poured from my body and surrounded her. The black magic liked blood and death, and isn't that what a vampire was? I threw my head back as I felt the pull of it feeding on whatever magic it was that animated a vampire's body. I didn't have to look to know that she was shriveling, disintegrating, as the darkness consumed her from the inside out. I didn't have to look to know that there would be nothing left but ashes when the black magic returned to me. I had seen it all before.

I pulled the darkness back inside me, my skin tingling with the rush of power it brought with it. Opening my eyes, I looked at the evil bastard wearing my husband's skin.

"What are you?" he asked.

I spread my arms wide. "I am everything they said I was, and more. Leave Michael's body and come and take me if you can."

His eyes flashed red a moment before his long, unnatural blue form slid through Michael's skin. Michael fell to the floor and the demon entered my circle. Power vibrated through me and the candles surrounding us flared to life, black flames rising from the white wax. I felt the pop of the magic that set the circle. I had trapped him inside with me, and only one of us would walk out.

I stepped backward, never taking my eyes off the demon as I leaned down and removed the lid from the urn. Moving to the opposite edge of the circle, I positioned the urn between me and the demon.

"What is this?" the demon asked, his voice harsh like the sound of breaking glass.

I spoke the words I had learned so long ago. "By blood I bind you! By the power of this circle I bind you! By the power of my will I bind you!"

He rushed forward and I put my hands out in front of me, pushing against him with all the power I could call, praying it would be enough. The demon pushed back and I felt his power beating against me, hammering at me until I thought every bone in my body would break from the force of it. And then I felt him stumble.

Like a slip of the foot, something shifted, faltered. The darkness inside me surged forward anew, a hungry predator that had scented weakness in its prey. The demon screamed and I thought my ears might bleed from the sound of it. His form lost what little definition it had once possessed and before my eyes he turned to vapor. Like a genie being sucked back into its bottle, the demon was drawn into the urn. I slammed the lid down on it and stood there, shaking, unable to believe that it had actually worked. The black magic, sated with the life it had taken and the victory it had won, settled back into whatever corner of my soul it resided in, content to stay there quietly until I needed it again.

"Cin?" Michael's voice came to me on a whisper.

He was sitting up on his knees, staring at me like he didn't know what was happening. I staggered out of the circle and collapsed in front of him. His hands reached out to cup my face, brushing back the tears.

"*M'anam*," he said softly. *My soul*.

I threw my arms around him and leaned into the hard wall of his chest, burying my face in the side of his neck. He held me tightly and I thought that I'd never been happier to be anywhere than I was to be right here, with him.

"You left me," I cried brokenly.

"Never, *mo chridhe*," he said, gently rocking me back and forth. "I will never leave you. I promise, I will never leave you."

It was the last thing I heard before my body shut down from utter exhaustion.

SIXTEEN

I woke to find myself in my bed with Michael's arms wrapped around me. I could have wept with the pleasure of it. Feeling as though I had slept for a night and a day—and perhaps I had—I stretched lazily, reveling in the feel of Michael's body against my bare skin. I might have been content to just lie there, blissfully enjoying the moment, if he hadn't woken at my stirring.

I sighed at the feel of his lips against my skin, and when he gently bit me at the juncture of my shoulder and neck, my body shuddered in response. It seemed it had been weeks since I'd last had him, not days, and my body cried out for us to finish what we had begun in the carriage. I turned in his arms and pushed him back until I could crawl over him, straddling his hips.

"Welcome back," I said, staring down into his beautiful face.

"Cin—" he began, but I swallowed his words with a kiss. There would be time enough to talk about what had happened later. At the moment I just wanted to *feel*.

I moved against him, back and forth along his shaft, feeling the moisture build with each stroke. Normally I enjoyed letting him be the dominant one. Nothing excited me more than giving myself over to him and having him take me as he willed. Tonight though, after all that had happened, I wanted to be in control. I felt the driving need to possess him, to reassure myself that he was here, and that he was mine. I wanted to put my mark on him.

Ever so slowly I moved to take him inside me. Teasingly I slid down an inch, then two, and then out again, over and over until the muscles in his chest quivered from the torment. His fingers bit into my thighs as he tried to make me take all of him, but I wouldn't allow it.

"Cin," he said raggedly.

"Such a greedy man," I replied, mimicking the words he had said to me in the carriage. "Do you want more?"

"Please," he growled.

I sank down on him, burying him to the hilt inside me, and we both cried out with pleasure. My body quivered in ecstasy at the feel of him stretching me, filling me. I laid my hands on his chest and my hair fell over us like a scarlet curtain as I rode him at a punishing pace. We came together quickly, violently, and as my body ebbed with sated bliss, I collapsed onto his chest, spent.

"Do you have any idea how lucky I am to be loved by a woman like you?" he asked.

I paused from licking the blood from the crescent-shaped wounds my fingernails had left on his chest.

"Almost as lucky as I am to be loved by you," I replied. "Will you love me forever, Michael?"

"Cin, my heart, my soul," he said earnestly. "The moon will fall from the sky and vampires will walk in the sun before the day comes that I ever love thee not."

EPILOGUE

News traveled quickly throughout the vampire population that I had slain the demon. Sebastian fled the city the following night. Legally, I probably couldn't have executed him for his involvement in the Ripper murders. We had no concrete evidence, and I had, after all, incinerated our only corroborating witness. But Sebastian had apparently decided to save his own skin on the chance that someone who didn't care so much for solid proof would assassinate him—either that or my infamous temper would finally get the better of me and I'd kill him out of spite. Michael had been furious when Grady told us the Regent had disappeared, but I wasn't surprised. Sebastian was a sneaky bastard and he was a survivor. I was fairly certain our paths would cross again one day. Hopefully in a dark alley where no one would be the wiser if I allowed Michael to carve him up like a Christmas goose.

Since it rarely happened that a regency was vacated without a challenge and a resulting victorious party, the London vampires were left in a bit of a quandary over who would take control of the city. In a surge of democratic fervor, wholly uncharacteristic of vampires, the court decided to put it to a vote. Grady suggested that his Chief Warden should be elected Regent, by virtue of court seniority, since all of Sebastian's lieutenants were now being looked upon with suspicion. Warden James declined the nomination, and in the end it was Grady who was elected Regent, mostly because of his help in toppling a corrupt ruler and vanquishing a demon, but having The Righteous endorse his nomination certainly helped. I thought he would make a fine Regent.

We stayed in London long enough to see Grady elected and to attend Ginny and Warren's wedding. Warren moved into the house, but insisted on keeping the apothecary shop open. It was, after all, a family tradition . . . along with consorting with vampires. Ginny was looking particularly radiant when they saw us off at the docks and, as I waved goodbye from the deck of the *Peregrine*, I wondered how long it would be before they gave me another generation of humans to love, and lose.

As for the demon, Michael and I had taken the urn and dropped it into a large rectangular form filled with concrete. When that had dried we'd loaded it into a specially made steel box with four-inch-thick sides. And then we padlocked it. Somewhere in the middle of the Atlantic Ocean I planned on taking a break from making love to my husband to drop it over the edge of the ship.

And where was that ship bound? We decided to take a holiday and see America again. Perhaps New York this time.